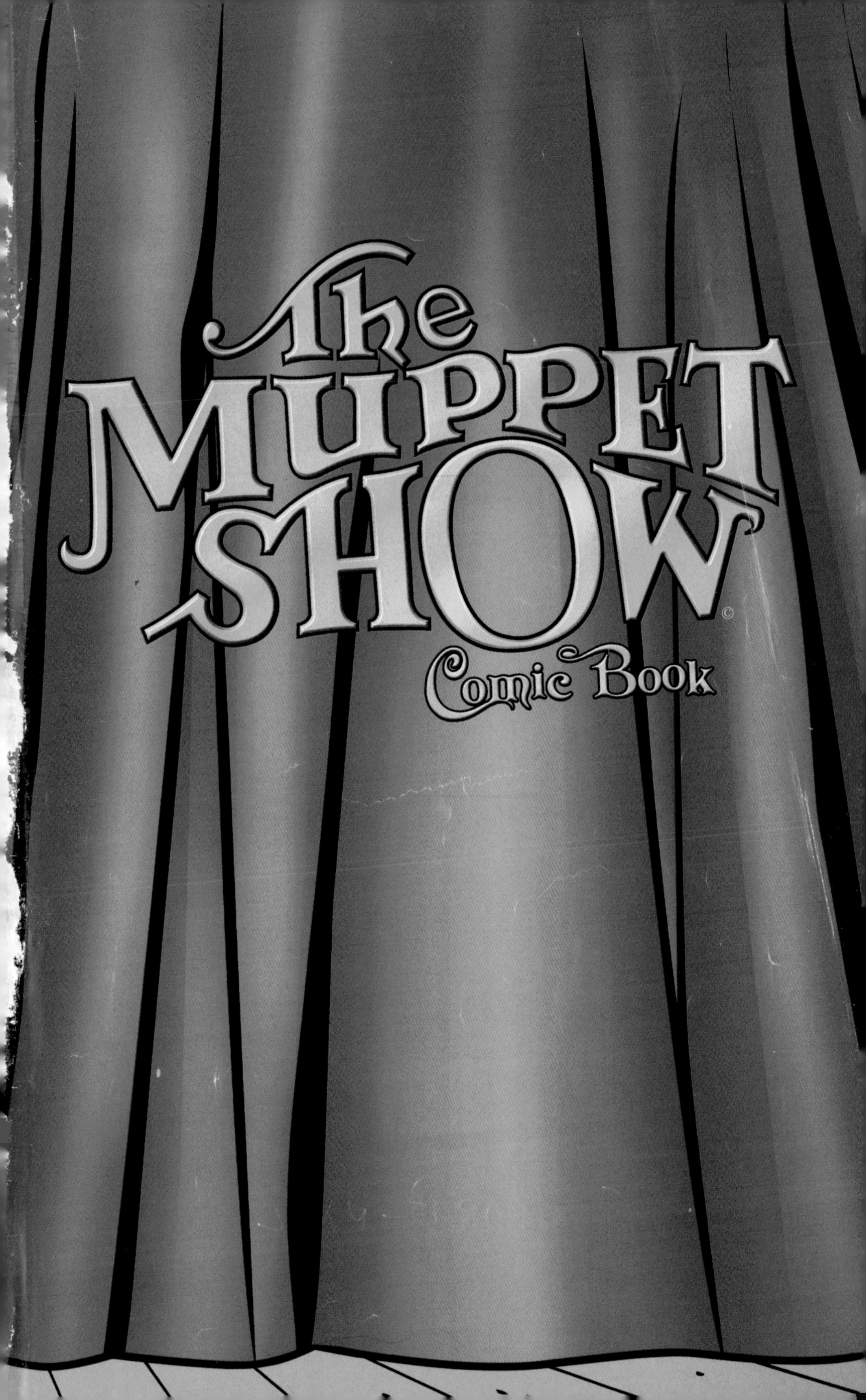
The MUPPET SHOW©
Comic Book

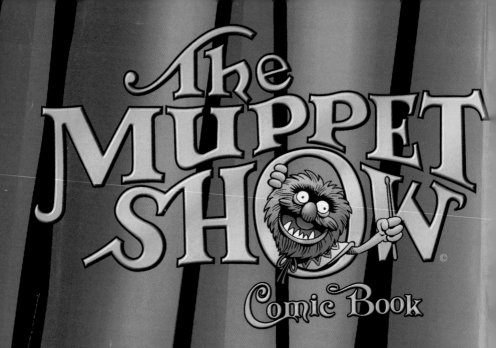

The MUPPET SHOW
Comic Book

SPECIAL THANKS: TISHANA
WILLIAMS, IVONNE FELICIANO,
AND THE MUPPETS STUDIO

AND A VERY HEARTY ROUND
OF APPLAUSE FOR DAVE
SHELTON!

THE MUPPET SHOW – July 2009 published by BOOM! KIDS, a division of Boom Entertainment, Inc. All contents ©
2009 The Muppets Studio, LLC. BOOM! KIDS and the BOOM! KIDS logo are trademarks of Boom Entertainment,
nc., registered in various countries and categories. All rights reserved. Office of publication: 6310 San Vicente

MEET THE MUPPETS

WRITTEN AND DRAWN BY **Roger Langridge**

COLORS **Digikore Studios**

LETTERS **Deron Bennett**

EDITOR **Paul Morrissey**

COVERS **Roger Langridge**

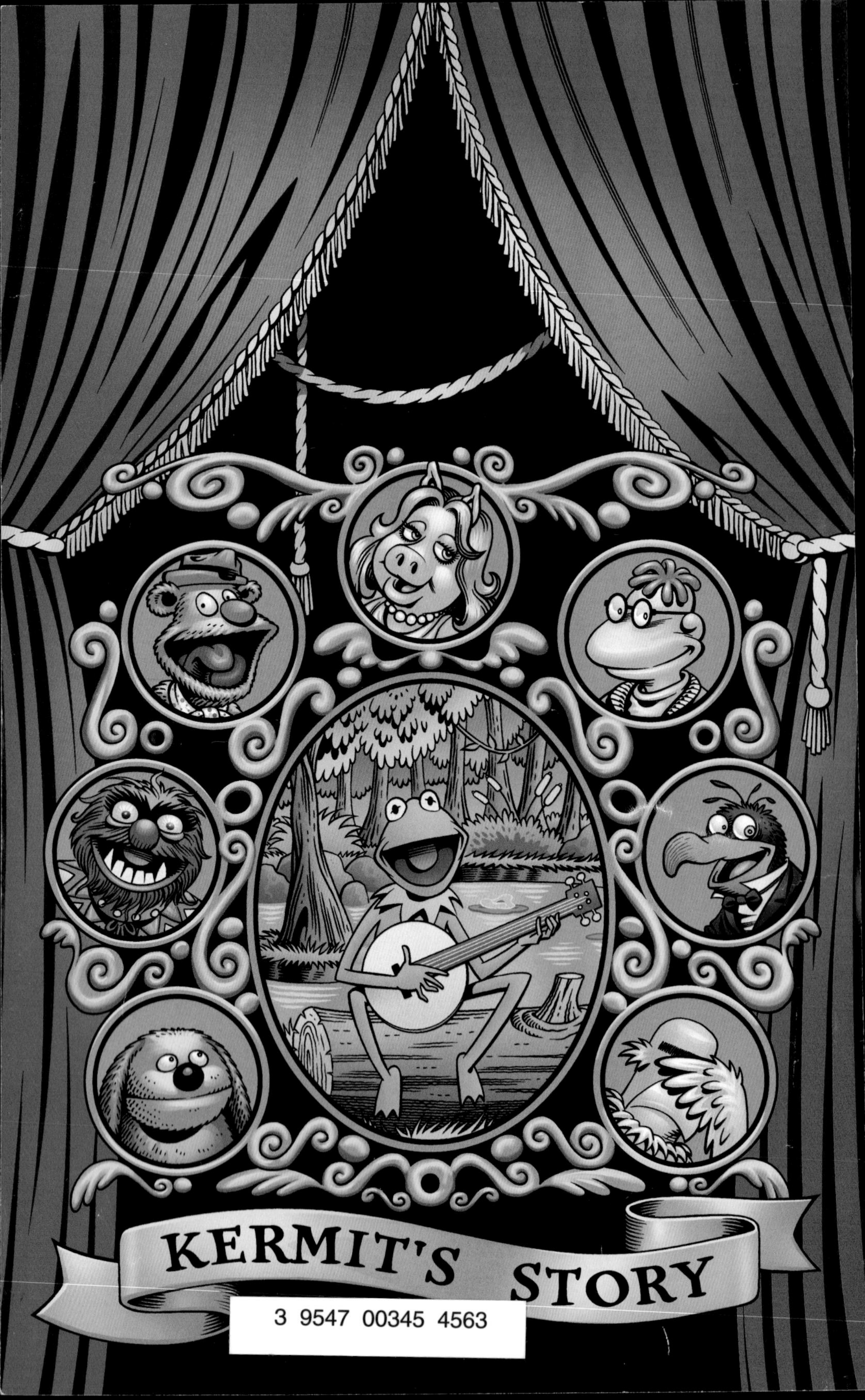
KERMIT'S STORY

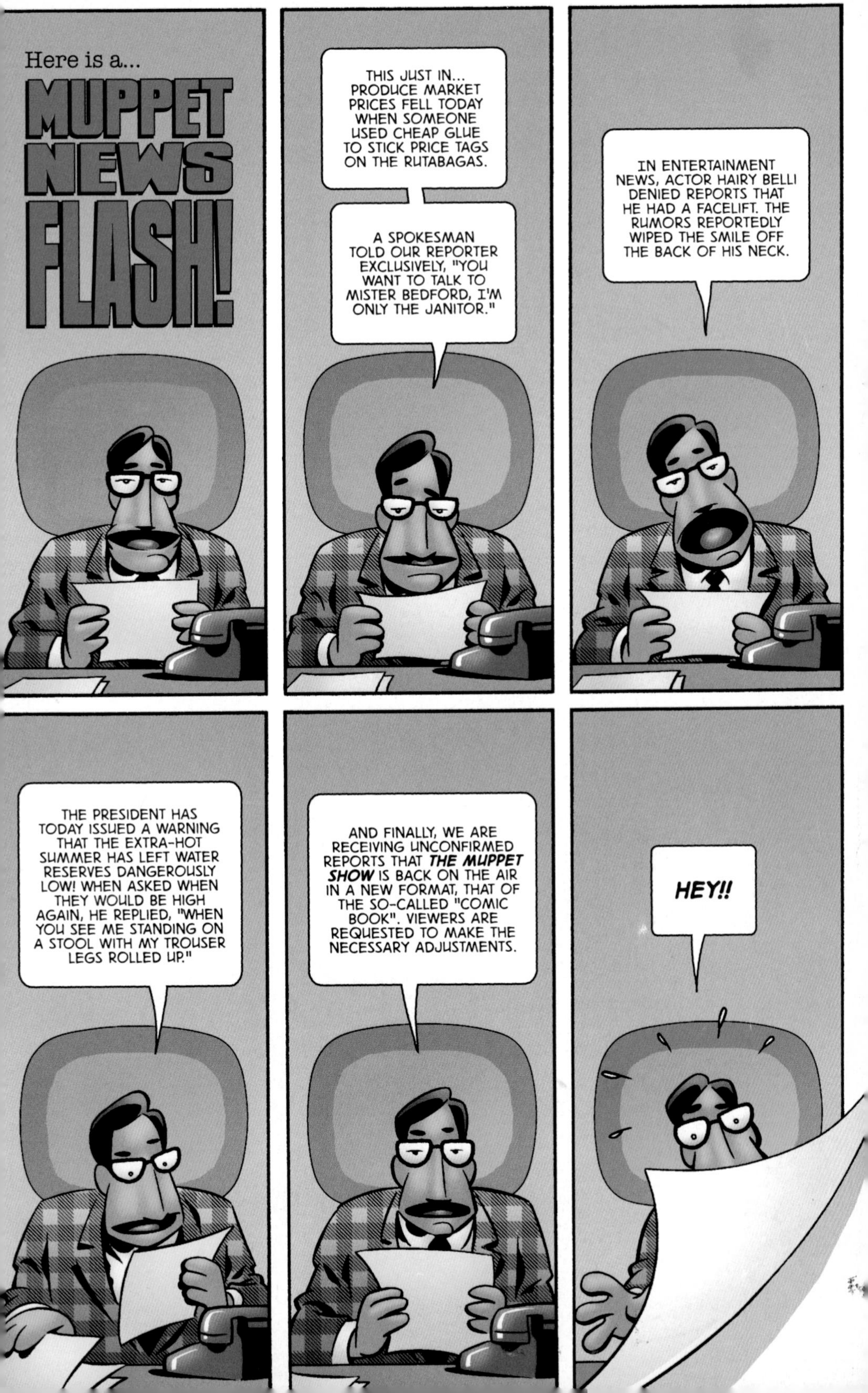
Here is a...
MUPPET NEWS FLASH!
THIS JUST IN... PRODUCE MARKET PRICES FELL TODAY WHEN SOMEONE USED CHEAP GLUE TO STICK PRICE TAGS ON THE RUTABAGAS.
A SPOKESMAN TOLD OUR REPORTER EXCLUSIVELY, "YOU WANT TO TALK TO MISTER BEDFORD, I'M ONLY THE JANITOR."
IN ENTERTAINMENT NEWS, ACTOR HAIRY BELLI DENIED REPORTS THAT HE HAD A FACELIFT. THE RUMORS REPORTEDLY WIPED THE SMILE OFF THE BACK OF HIS NECK.
THE PRESIDENT HAS TODAY ISSUED A WARNING THAT THE EXTRA-HOT SUMMER HAS LEFT WATER RESERVES DANGEROUSLY LOW! WHEN ASKED WHEN THEY WOULD BE HIGH AGAIN, HE REPLIED, "WHEN YOU SEE ME STANDING ON A STOOL WITH MY TROUSER LEGS ROLLED UP."
AND FINALLY, WE ARE RECEIVING UNCONFIRMED REPORTS THAT *THE MUPPET SHOW* IS BACK ON THE AIR IN A NEW FORMAT, THAT OF THE SO-CALLED "COMIC BOOK". VIEWERS ARE REQUESTED TO MAKE THE NECESSARY ADJUSTMENTS.
HEY!!

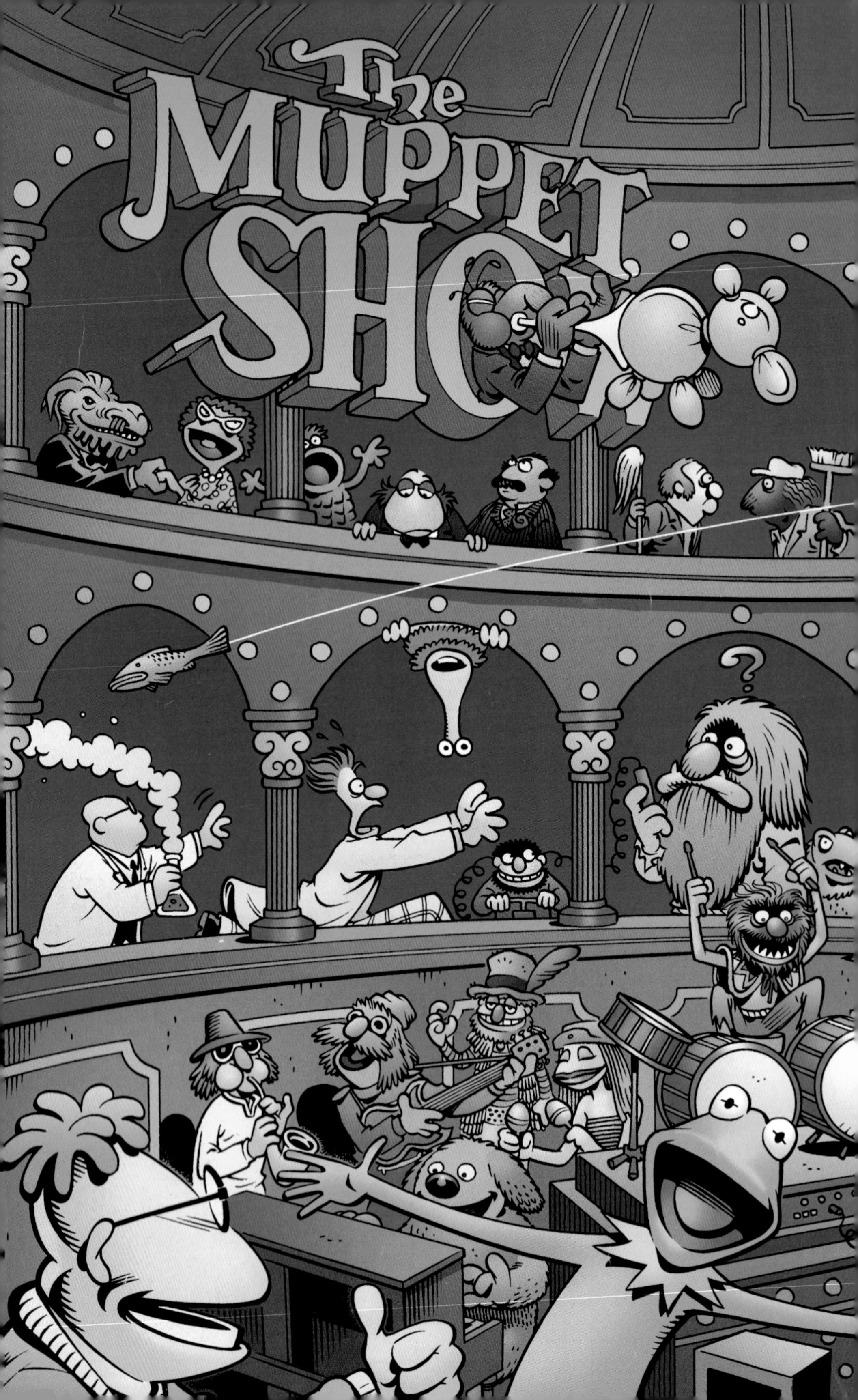
The
MUPPET
SHO
?

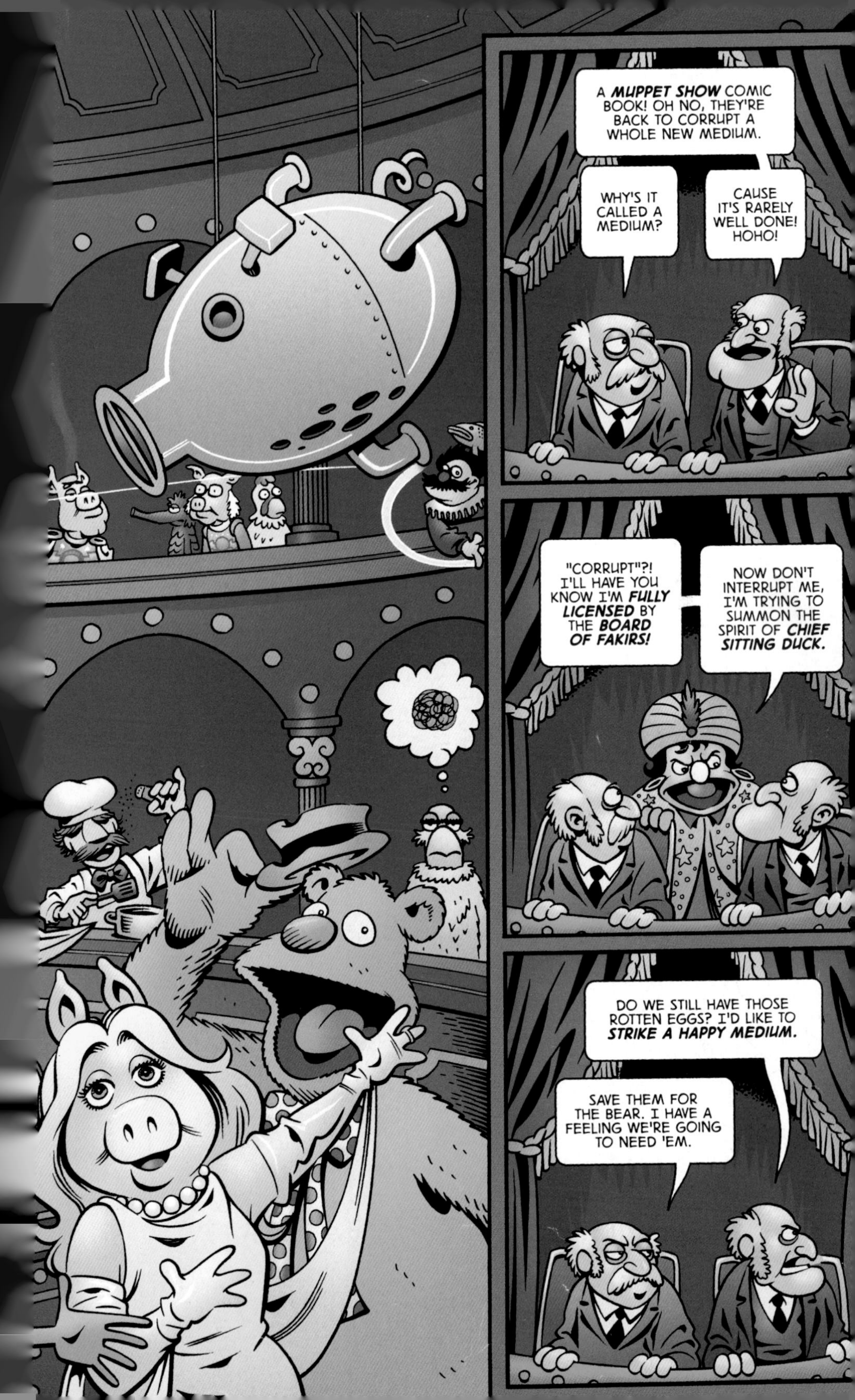
A **MUPPET SHOW** COMIC BOOK! OH NO, THEY'RE BACK TO CORRUPT A WHOLE NEW MEDIUM.
WHY'S IT CALLED A MEDIUM?
CAUSE IT'S RARELY WELL DONE! HOHO!
"CORRUPT"?! I'LL HAVE YOU KNOW I'M **FULLY LICENSED** BY THE **BOARD OF FAKIRS!**
NOW DON'T INTERRUPT ME, I'M TRYING TO SUMMON THE SPIRIT OF **CHIEF SITTING DUCK.**
DO WE STILL HAVE THOSE ROTTEN EGGS? I'D LIKE TO **STRIKE A HAPPY MEDIUM.**
SAVE THEM FOR THE BEAR. I HAVE A FEELING WE'RE GOING TO NEED 'EM.

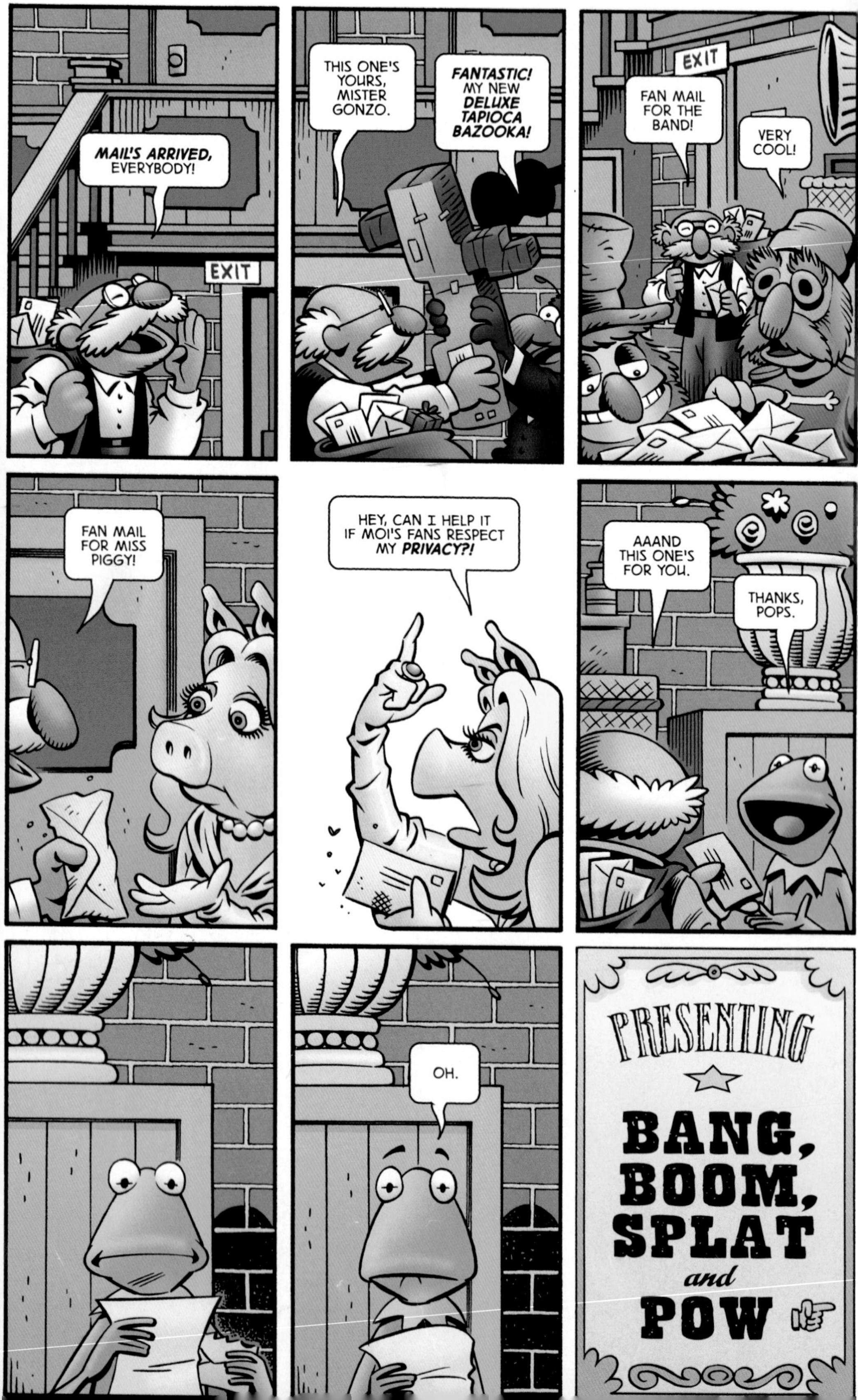
MAIL'S ARRIVED, EVERYBODY!
EXIT
THIS ONE'S YOURS, MISTER GONZO.
FANTASTIC! MY NEW DELUXE TAPIOCA BAZOOKA!
EXIT
FAN MAIL FOR THE BAND!
VERY COOL!
FAN MAIL FOR MISS PIGGY!
HEY, CAN I HELP IT IF MOI'S FANS RESPECT MY PRIVACY?!
AAAND THIS ONE'S FOR YOU.
THANKS, POPS.
OH.
PRESENTING
BANG, BOOM, SPLAT and POW

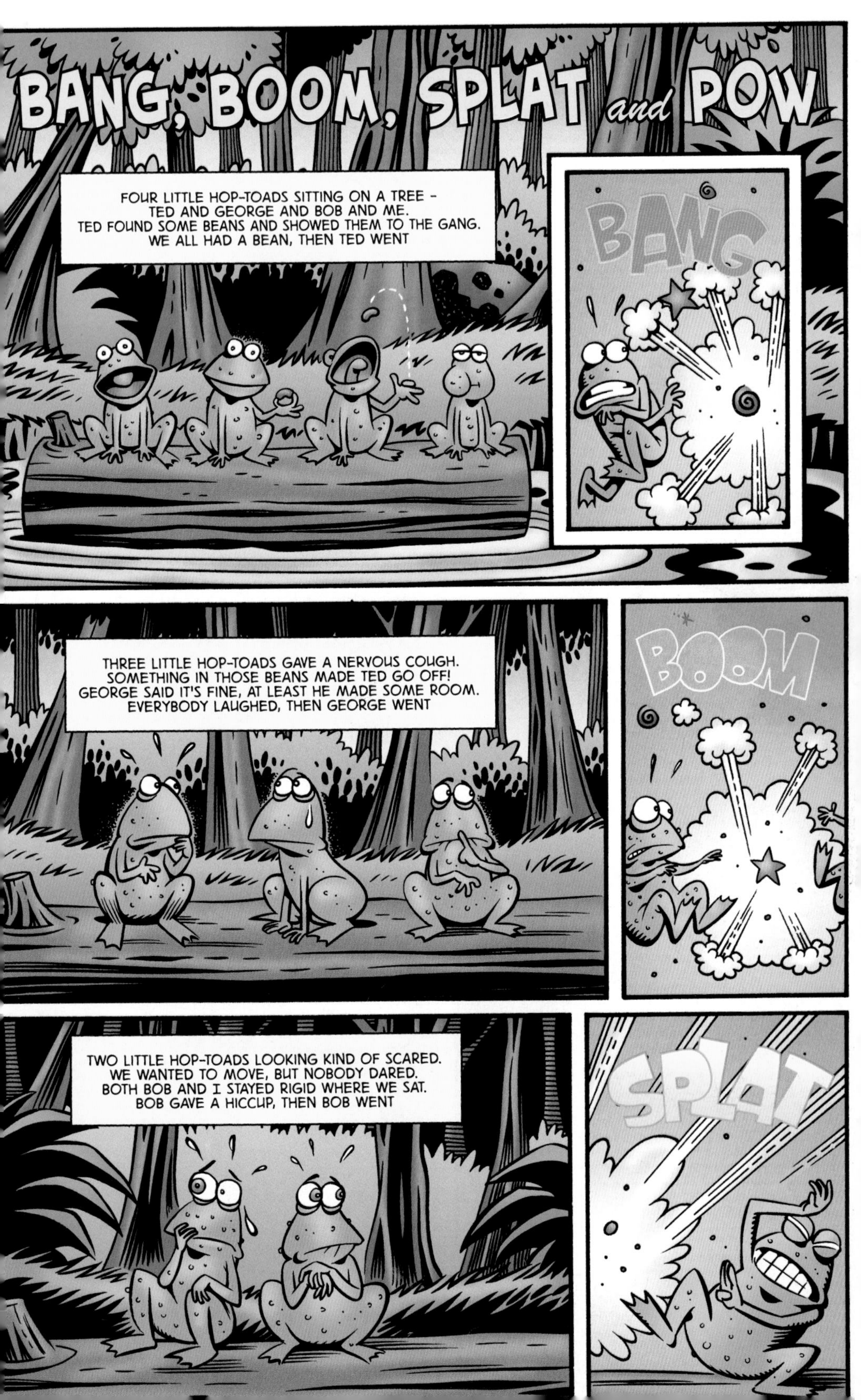
BANG, BOOM, SPLAT and POW
FOUR LITTLE HOP-TOADS SITTING ON A TREE - TED AND GEORGE AND BOB AND ME. TED FOUND SOME BEANS AND SHOWED THEM TO THE GANG. WE ALL HAD A BEAN, THEN TED WENT
BANG
THREE LITTLE HOP-TOADS GAVE A NERVOUS COUGH. SOMETHING IN THOSE BEANS MADE TED GO OFF! GEORGE SAID IT'S FINE, AT LEAST HE MADE SOME ROOM. EVERYBODY LAUGHED, THEN GEORGE WENT
BOOM
TWO LITTLE HOP-TOADS LOOKING KIND OF SCARED. WE WANTED TO MOVE, BUT NOBODY DARED. BOTH BOB AND I STAYED RIGID WHERE WE SAT. BOB GAVE A HICCUP, THEN BOB WENT
SPLAT

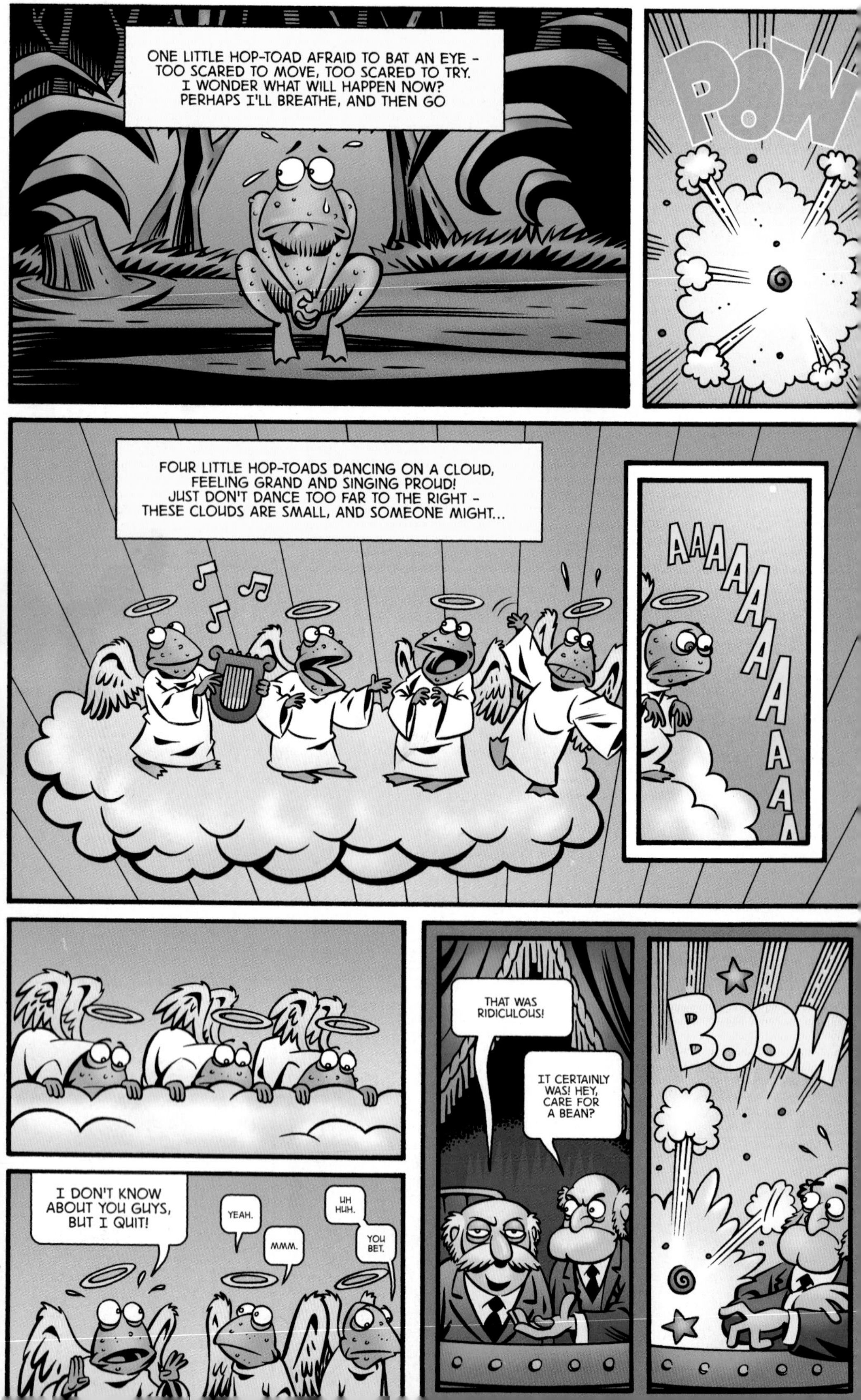
ONE LITTLE HOP-TOAD AFRAID TO BAT AN EYE - TOO SCARED TO MOVE, TOO SCARED TO TRY. I WONDER WHAT WILL HAPPEN NOW? PERHAPS I'LL BREATHE, AND THEN GO
POW
FOUR LITTLE HOP-TOADS DANCING ON A CLOUD, FEELING GRAND AND SINGING PROUD! JUST DON'T DANCE TOO FAR TO THE RIGHT - THESE CLOUDS ARE SMALL, AND SOMEONE MIGHT...
AAAAAAAAAAAAA
I DON'T KNOW ABOUT YOU GUYS, BUT I QUIT!
YEAH.
MMM.
UH HUH.
YOU BET.
THAT WAS RIDICULOUS!
IT CERTAINLY WAS! HEY, CARE FOR A BEAN?
BOOM

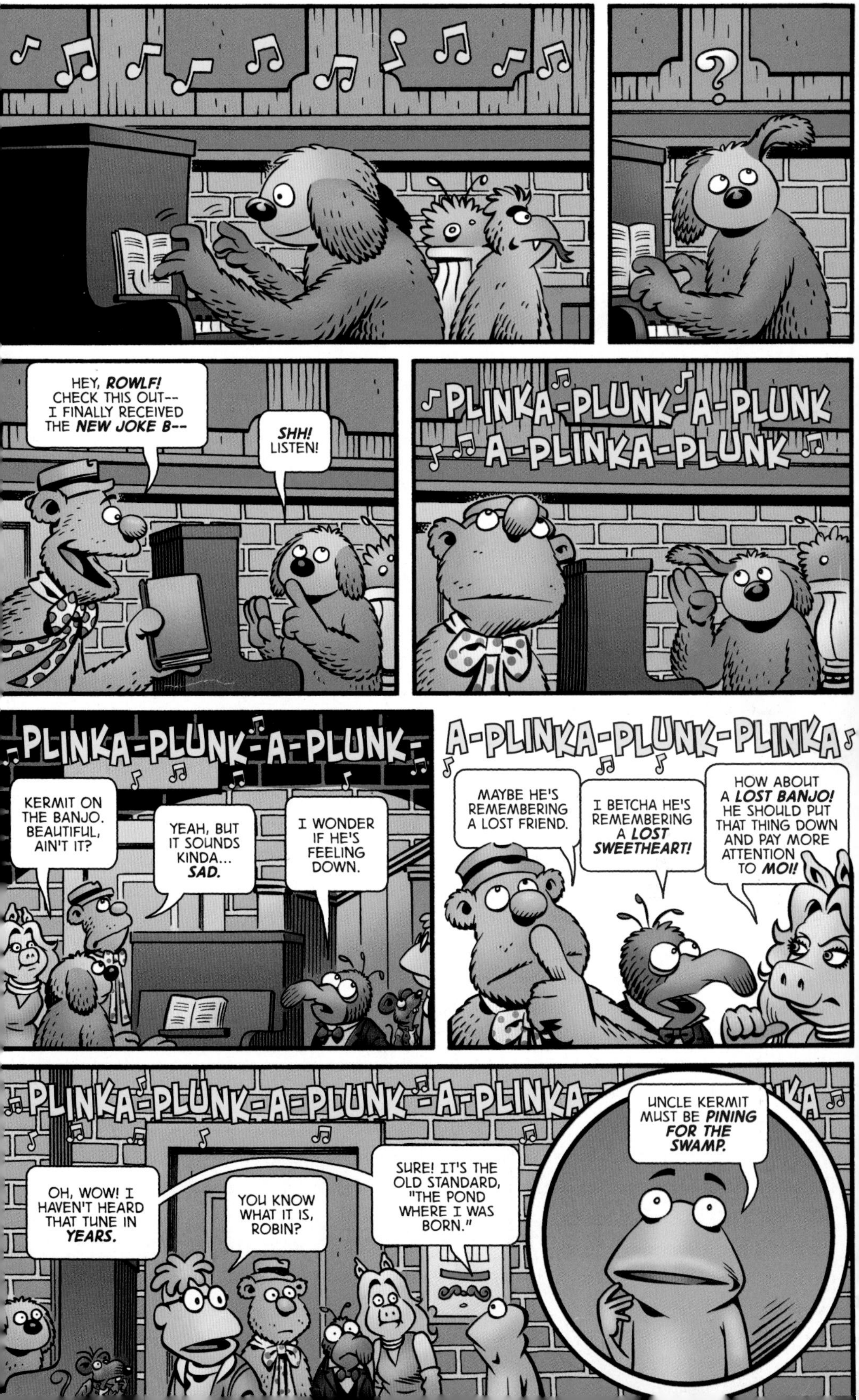

?
HEY, ROWLF! CHECK THIS OUT-- I FINALLY RECEIVED THE NEW JOKE B--
SHH! LISTEN!
PLINKA-PLUNK-A-PLUNK A-PLINKA-PLUNK
PLINKA-PLUNK-A-PLUNK
KERMIT ON THE BANJO. BEAUTIFUL, AIN'T IT?
YEAH, BUT IT SOUNDS KINDA... SAD.
I WONDER IF HE'S FEELING DOWN.
A-PLINKA-PLUNK-PLINKA
MAYBE HE'S REMEMBERING A LOST FRIEND.
I BETCHA HE'S REMEMBERING A LOST SWEETHEART!
HOW ABOUT A LOST BANJO! HE SHOULD PUT THAT THING DOWN AND PAY MORE ATTENTION TO MOI!
PLINKA-PLUNK-A-PLUNK-A-PLINKA
UNCLE KERMIT MUST BE PINING FOR THE SWAMP.
OH, WOW! I HAVEN'T HEARD THAT TUNE IN YEARS.
YOU KNOW WHAT IT IS, ROBIN?
SURE! IT'S THE OLD STANDARD, "THE POND WHERE I WAS BORN."

SO HE'S HOMESICK?
I GUESS THAT WOULD EXPLAIN IT. WE'VE ALL BEEN THERE.
NOT MOI! I COULDN'T WAIT TO LEAVE HOME AND FIND AN ADORING AUDIENCE!
AN AUDIENCE! THAT'S IT! IF WE CAN GET HIM PERFORMING, HE'LL SNAP OUT OF IT IN NO TIME!
EXIT
THAT ALWAYS WORKS FOR ME!
OF COURSE, IN MY CASE, A BROKEN BONE OR TWO REALLY HELPS FOCUS MY MIND ON WHAT'S REALLY IMPORTANT...LIKE TRACTION AND HEALTH INSURANCE!
'EVENIN'.
'EY, SCOO'AH! WE'RE THE ZIMMER TWINS! WHEN ARE WE ON?
SORRY, BOYS--WE'RE GONNA HAVE TO CANCEL YOUR NUMBER. KERMIT'S PUBLIC AWAITS!
LISTEN, MOOSH--IF YOU FINK WE COME ALL THIS WAY TO TURN AROUND AND GO BACK TO THE 'OME, YOU'RE OFF YOUR BLEEDIN' ROCKER! LEIF'S BEEN LOOKING FORWARD TO THIS ALL WEEK AND HE'S VERY EASILY BEWILDERED.
WELL, UH... M-MAYBE WE CAN FIND SOME SMALL PART IN KERMIT'S SKETCH FOR YOU?
I SHOULD FINK SO. LEAST YOU CAN DO, QUITE FRANKLY.
SETTING THAT UP RIGHT NOW, MISTER ZIMMER SIR.
RICK. 'EY, RICK.
PSST.
RICK.
I FINK THE NURSES MUST'VE REDECORATED WHILE WE WERE 'AVING OUR NAP.
AND NOW ...
KOOZEBANE

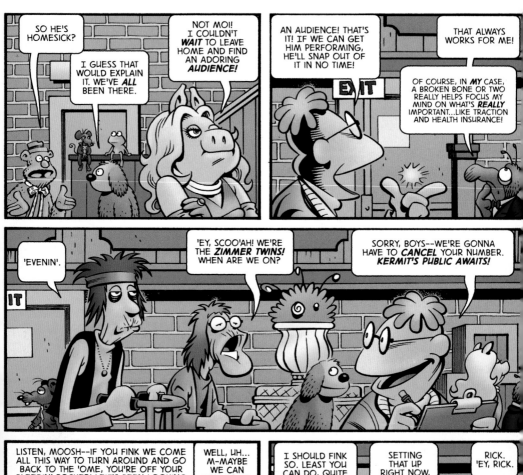

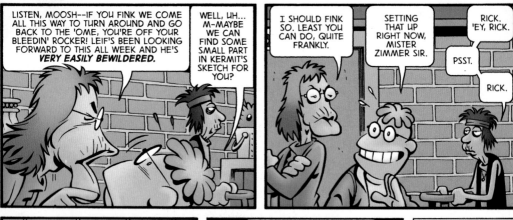

CLOSE ENCOUNTERS *of the* WORST KIND

THE POOBS ARE A FAMOUSLY PEACEFUL RACE OF BEINGS, AND THE KOOZEBANIANS HAVE BEEN AWAITING THIS HISTORIC MEETING FOR GENERATIONS! AS YOU CAN SEE, THEY ARE VERY EXCITED ABOUT THE PROSPECT.

WELL, AH, YES. HERE WE ARE ON THE PLANET KOOZEBANE, AND IT'S A VERY EXCITING MOMENT, BECAUSE WE ARE ABOUT TO WITNESS THE FIRST CONTACT BETWEEN THE NATIVE KOOZEBANIANS AND THEIR CLOSEST GALACTIC NEIGHBORS, THE POOBS.

APPARENTLY, KOOZEBANE ORIGINALLY MADE CONTACT WITH THE POOBS BY INTERCEPTING THEIR RADIO BROADCASTS! EACH RADIO WAVE HAS TAKEN ELEVEN YEARS TO REACH HERE, AND EACH REPLY HAS TAKEN ANOTHER ELEVEN YEARS TO RETURN TO THE PLANET POOBATRON.

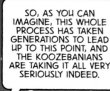

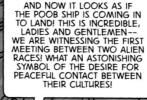

SO, AS YOU CAN IMAGINE, THIS WHOLE PROCESS HAS TAKEN GENERATIONS TO LEAD UP TO THIS POINT, AND THE KOOZEBANIANS ARE TAKING IT ALL VERY SERIOUSLY INDEED.

AND NOW IT LOOKS AS IF THE POOB SHIP IS COMING IN TO LAND! THIS IS INCREDIBLE, LADIES AND GENTLEMEN-- WE ARE WITNESSING THE FIRST MEETING BETWEEN TWO ALIEN RACES! WHAT AN ASTONISHING SYMBOL OF THE DESIRE FOR PEACEFUL CONTACT BETWEEN THEIR CULTURES!

SPLAT

ER, AH... WELL, HERE ON KOOZEBANE THINGS AREN'T QUITE WORKING OUT AS WE'D HOPED. JOIN ME HERE AGAIN SOON, WHERE I'LL ALMOST CERTAINLY BE ACTING AS OFFICIAL WAR CORRESPONDENT.

IN ABOUT A WEEK, BY THE LOOK OF THINGS.

ARE WE ON?

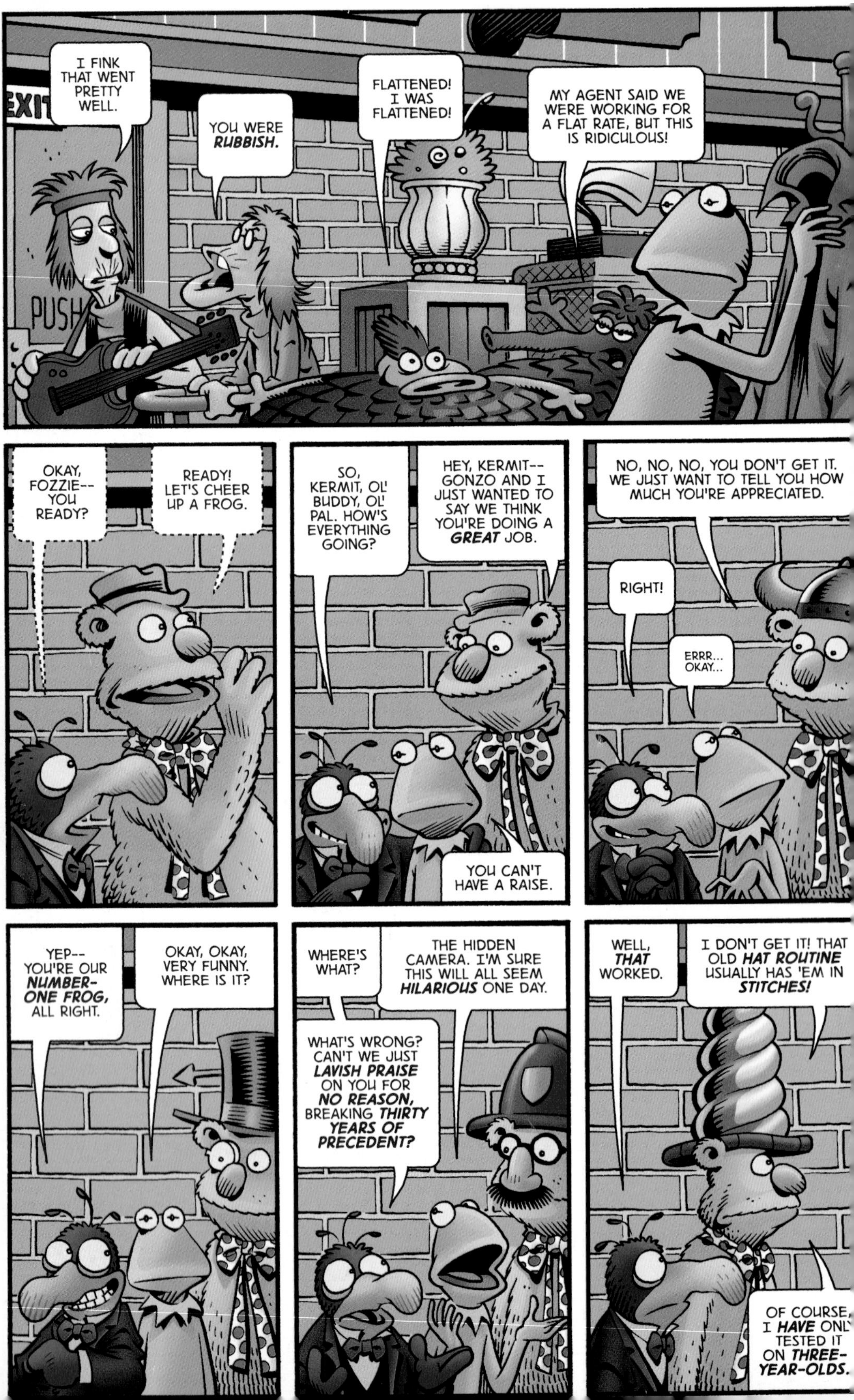
EXIT
PUSH
I FINK THAT WENT PRETTY WELL.
YOU WERE **RUBBISH.**
FLATTENED! I WAS FLATTENED!
MY AGENT SAID WE WERE WORKING FOR A FLAT RATE, BUT THIS IS RIDICULOUS!
OKAY, FOZZIE-- YOU READY?
READY! LET'S CHEER UP A FROG.
SO, KERMIT, OL' BUDDY, OL' PAL. HOW'S EVERYTHING GOING?
HEY, KERMIT-- GONZO AND I JUST WANTED TO SAY WE THINK YOU'RE DOING A **GREAT** JOB.
YOU CAN'T HAVE A RAISE.
NO, NO, NO, YOU DON'T GET IT. WE JUST WANT TO TELL YOU HOW MUCH YOU'RE APPRECIATED.
RIGHT!
ERRR... OKAY...
YEP-- YOU'RE OUR **NUMBER-ONE FROG,** ALL RIGHT.
OKAY, OKAY, VERY FUNNY. WHERE IS IT?
WHERE'S WHAT?
THE HIDDEN CAMERA. I'M SURE THIS WILL ALL SEEM **HILARIOUS** ONE DAY.
WHAT'S WRONG? CAN'T WE JUST **LAVISH PRAISE** ON YOU FOR **NO REASON,** BREAKING **THIRTY YEARS OF PRECEDENT?**
WELL, **THAT** WORKED.
I DON'T GET IT! THAT OLD **HAT ROUTINE** USUALLY HAS 'EM IN **STITCHES!**
OF COURSE, I **HAVE** ONLY TESTED IT ON **THREE-YEAR-OLDS.**

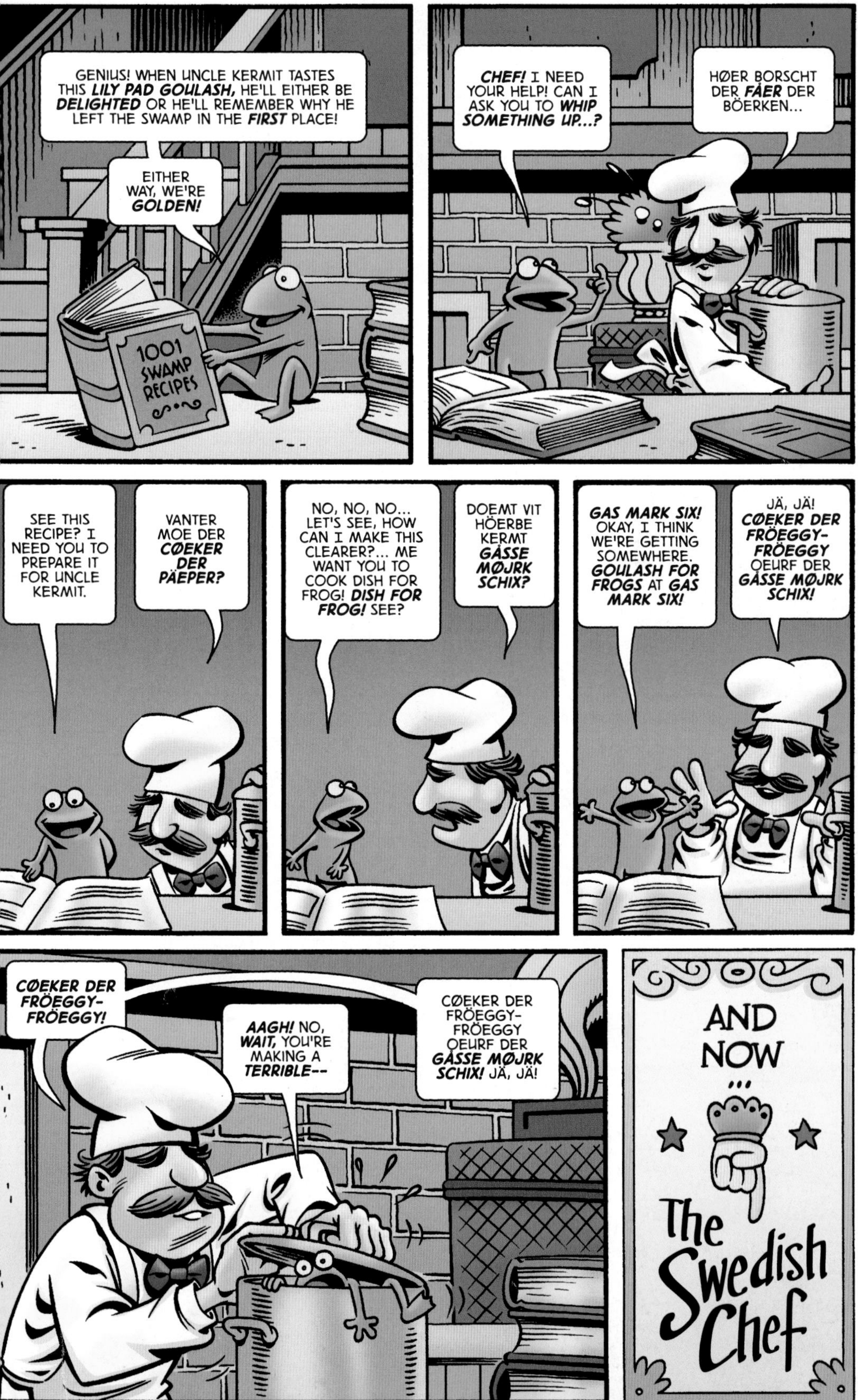
GENIUS! WHEN UNCLE KERMIT TASTES THIS LILY PAD GOULASH, HE'LL EITHER BE DELIGHTED OR HE'LL REMEMBER WHY HE LEFT THE SWAMP IN THE FIRST PLACE!
EITHER WAY, WE'RE GOLDEN!
1001 SWAMP RECIPES
CHEF! I NEED YOUR HELP! CAN I ASK YOU TO WHIP SOMETHING UP...?
HØER BORSCHT DER FÅER DER BÖERKEN...
SEE THIS RECIPE? I NEED YOU TO PREPARE IT FOR UNCLE KERMIT.
VANTER MOE DER CØEKER DER PÄEPER?
NO, NO, NO... LET'S SEE, HOW CAN I MAKE THIS CLEARER?... ME WANT YOU TO COOK DISH FOR FROG! DISH FOR FROG! SEE?
DOEMT VIT HÖERBE KERMT GÄSSE MØJRK SCHIX?
GAS MARK SIX! OKAY, I THINK WE'RE GETTING SOMEWHERE. GOULASH FOR FROGS AT GAS MARK SIX!
JÄ, JÄ! CØEKER DER FRÖEGGY-FRÖEGGY OEURF DER GÄSSE MØJRK SCHIX!
CØEKER DER FRÖEGGY-FRÖEGGY!
AAGH! NO, WAIT, YOU'RE MAKING A TERRIBLE--
CØEKER DER FRÖEGGY-FRÖEGGY OEURF DER GÄSSE MØJRK SCHIX! JÄ, JÄ!
AND NOW ...
The Swedish Chef

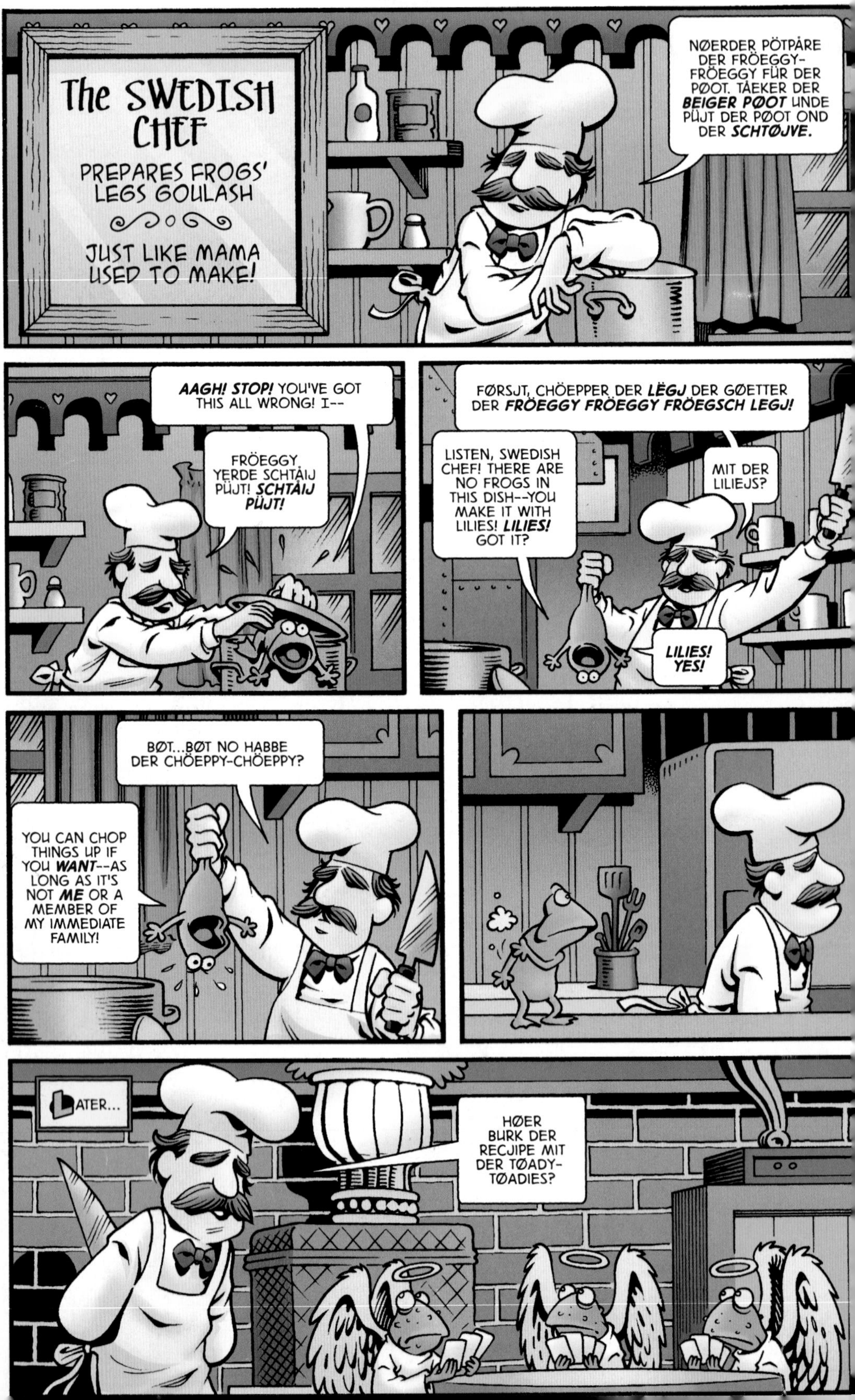

The SWEDISH CHEF
PREPARES FROGS' LEGS GOULASH
JUST LIKE MAMA USED TO MAKE!
NØERDER PÖTPÅRE DER FRÖEGGY-FRÖEGGY FÜR DER PØOT. TÅEKER DER **BEIGER PØOT** UNDE PÜJT DER PØOT OND DER **SCHTØJVE.**
AAGH! STOP! YOU'VE GOT THIS ALL WRONG! I--
FRÖEGGY YERDE SCHTÅIJ PÜJT! **SCHTÅIJ PÜJT!**
FØRSJT, CHÖEPPER DER **LËGJ** DER GØETTER DER **FRÖEGGY FRÖEGGY FRÖEGSCH LEGJ!**
LISTEN, SWEDISH CHEF! THERE ARE NO FROGS IN THIS DISH--YOU MAKE IT WITH LILIES! **LILIES!** GOT IT?
MIT DER LILIEJS?
LILIES! YES!
BØT...BØT NO HABBE DER CHÖEPPY-CHÖEPPY?
YOU CAN CHOP THINGS UP IF YOU **WANT**--AS LONG AS IT'S NOT **ME** OR A MEMBER OF MY IMMEDIATE FAMILY!
LATER...
HØER BURK DER RECJIPE MIT DER TØADY-TØADIES?

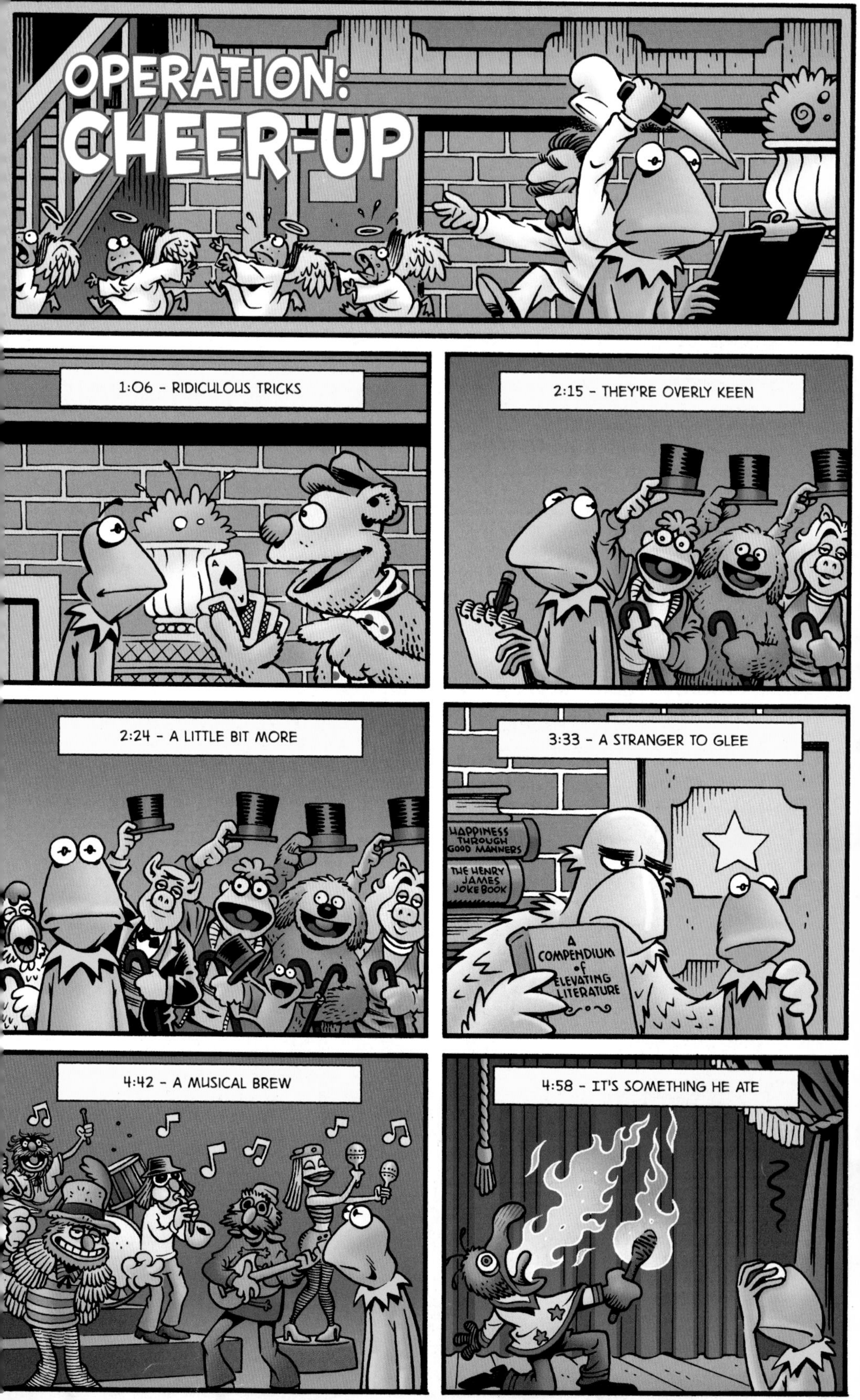
OPERATION: CHEER-UP
1:06 - RIDICULOUS TRICKS
2:15 - THEY'RE OVERLY KEEN
2:24 - A LITTLE BIT MORE
3:33 - A STRANGER TO GLEE
HAPPINESS THROUGH GOOD MANNERS
THE HENRY JAMES JOKE BOOK
A COMPENDIUM of ELEVATING LITERATURE
4:42 - A MUSICAL BREW
4:58 - IT'S SOMETHING HE ATE

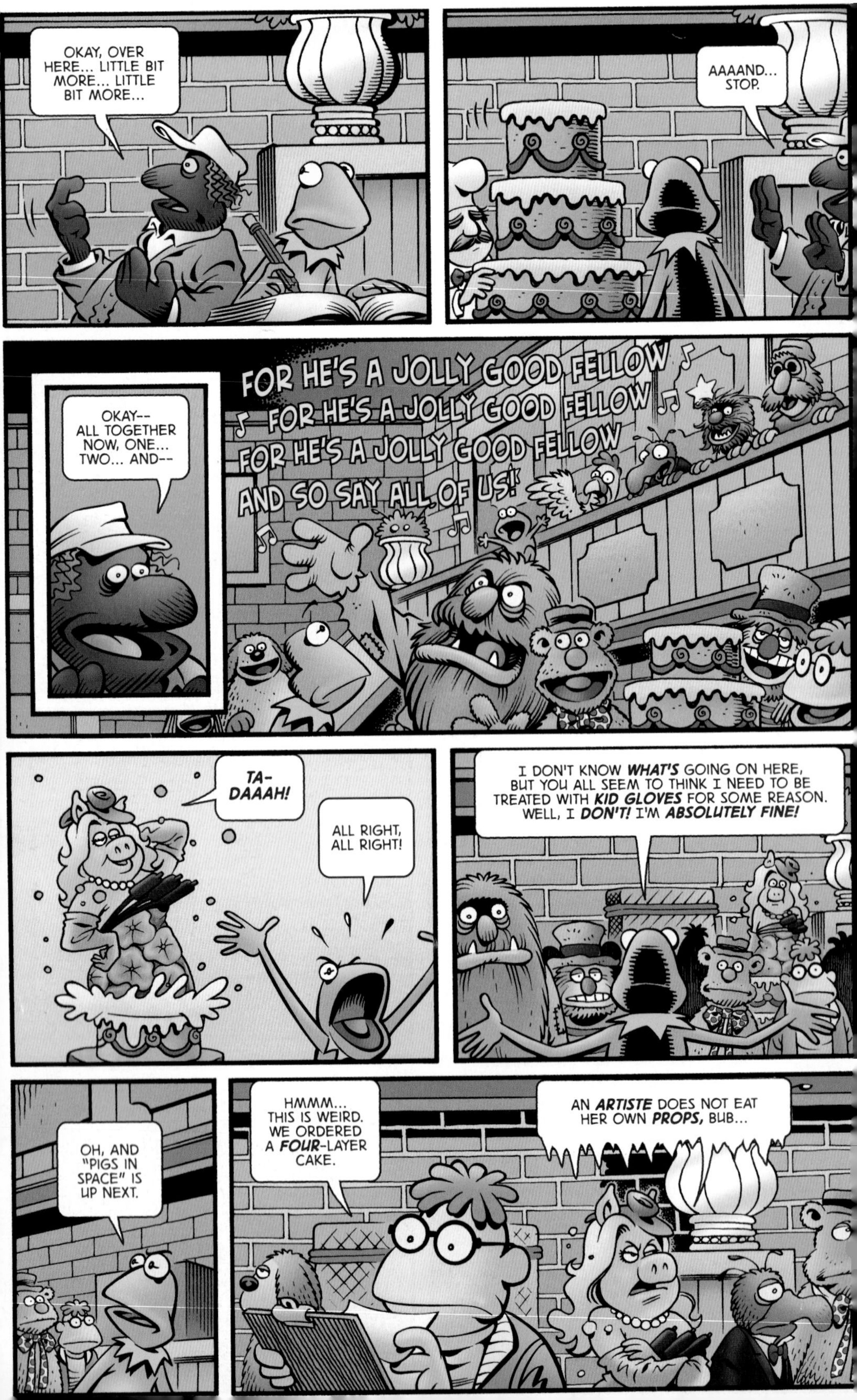
OKAY, OVER HERE... LITTLE BIT MORE... LITTLE BIT MORE...
AAAAND... STOP.
OKAY-- ALL TOGETHER NOW, ONE... TWO... AND--
FOR HE'S A JOLLY GOOD FELLOW
FOR HE'S A JOLLY GOOD FELLOW
FOR HE'S A JOLLY GOOD FELLOW
AND SO SAY ALL OF US!
TA-DAAAH!
ALL RIGHT, ALL RIGHT!
I DON'T KNOW WHAT'S GOING ON HERE, BUT YOU ALL SEEM TO THINK I NEED TO BE TREATED WITH KID GLOVES FOR SOME REASON. WELL, I DON'T! I'M ABSOLUTELY FINE!
OH, AND "PIGS IN SPACE" IS UP NEXT.
HMMM... THIS IS WEIRD. WE ORDERED A FOUR-LAYER CAKE.
AN ARTISTE DOES NOT EAT HER OWN PROPS, BUB...

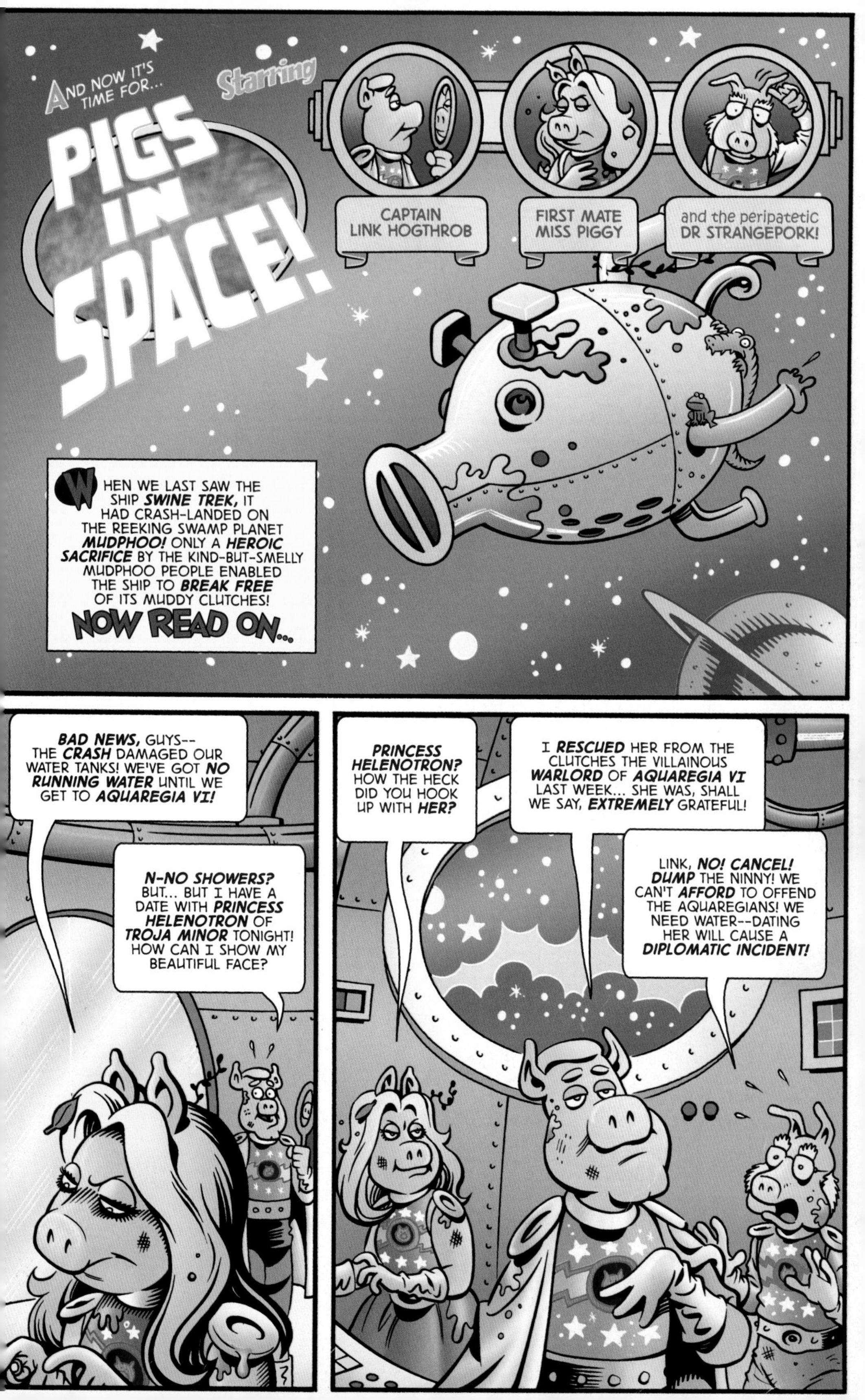

AND NOW IT'S TIME FOR...
Starring
PIGS IN SPACE!
CAPTAIN LINK HOGTHROB
FIRST MATE MISS PIGGY
and the peripatetic DR STRANGEPORK!
WHEN WE LAST SAW THE SHIP SWINE TREK, IT HAD CRASH-LANDED ON THE REEKING SWAMP PLANET MUDPHOO! ONLY A HEROIC SACRIFICE BY THE KIND-BUT-SMELLY MUDPHOO PEOPLE ENABLED THE SHIP TO BREAK FREE OF ITS MUDDY CLUTCHES!
NOW READ ON...
BAD NEWS, GUYS-- THE CRASH DAMAGED OUR WATER TANKS! WE'VE GOT NO RUNNING WATER UNTIL WE GET TO AQUAREGIA VI!
N-NO SHOWERS? BUT... BUT I HAVE A DATE WITH PRINCESS HELENOTRON OF TROJA MINOR TONIGHT! HOW CAN I SHOW MY BEAUTIFUL FACE?
PRINCESS HELENOTRON? HOW THE HECK DID YOU HOOK UP WITH HER?
I RESCUED HER FROM THE CLUTCHES THE VILLAINOUS WARLORD OF AQUAREGIA VI LAST WEEK... SHE WAS, SHALL WE SAY, EXTREMELY GRATEFUL!
LINK, NO! CANCEL! DUMP THE NINNY! WE CAN'T AFFORD TO OFFEND THE AQUAREGIANS! WE NEED WATER--DATING HER WILL CAUSE A DIPLOMATIC INCIDENT!

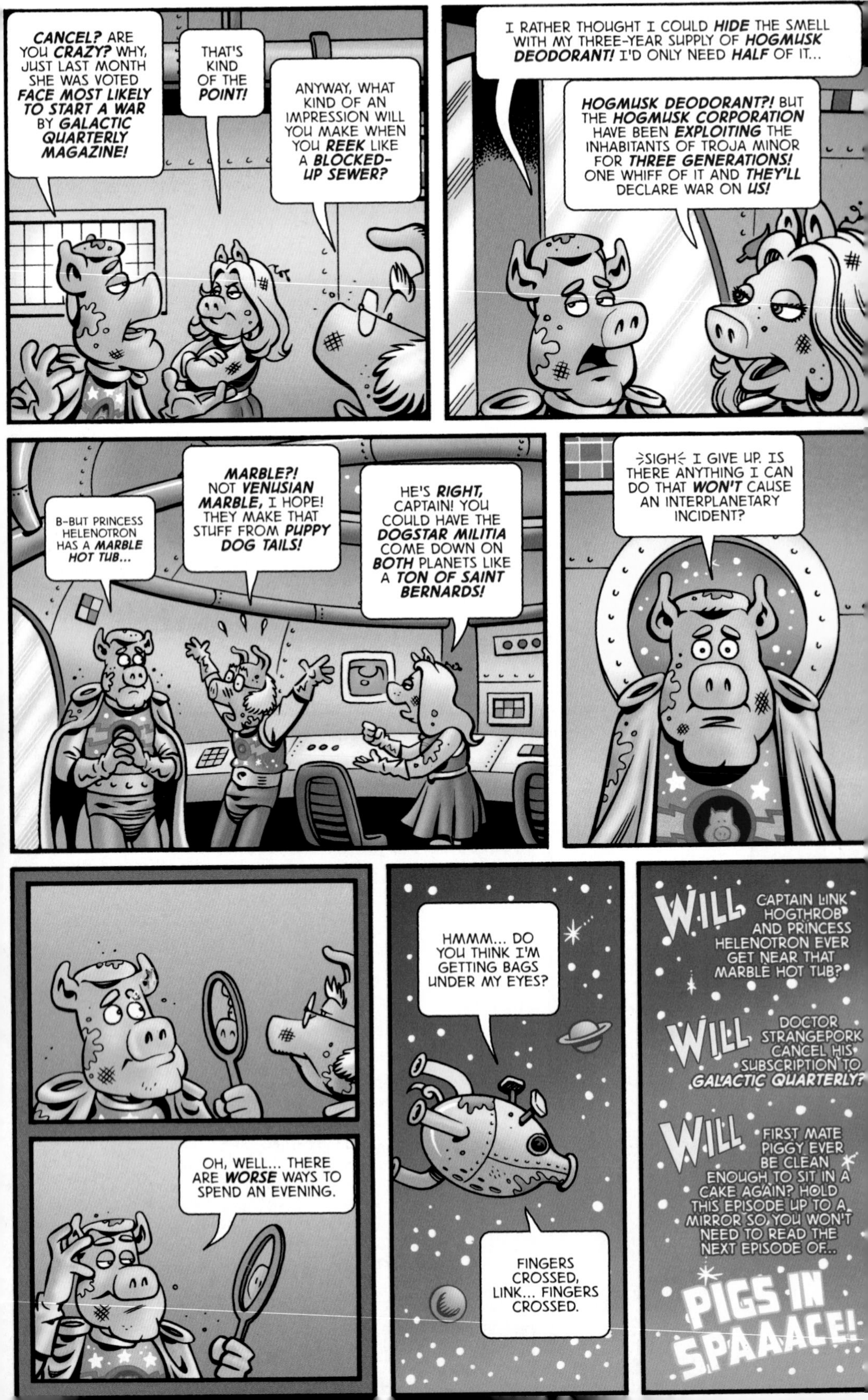
CANCEL? ARE YOU CRAZY? WHY, JUST LAST MONTH SHE WAS VOTED FACE MOST LIKELY TO START A WAR BY GALACTIC QUARTERLY MAGAZINE!
THAT'S KIND OF THE POINT!
ANYWAY, WHAT KIND OF AN IMPRESSION WILL YOU MAKE WHEN YOU REEK LIKE A BLOCKED-UP SEWER?
I RATHER THOUGHT I COULD HIDE THE SMELL WITH MY THREE-YEAR SUPPLY OF HOGMUSK DEODORANT! I'D ONLY NEED HALF OF IT...
HOGMUSK DEODORANT?! BUT THE HOGMUSK CORPORATION HAVE BEEN EXPLOITING THE INHABITANTS OF TROJA MINOR FOR THREE GENERATIONS! ONE WHIFF OF IT AND THEY'LL DECLARE WAR ON US!
B-BUT PRINCESS HELENOTRON HAS A MARBLE HOT TUB...
MARBLE?! NOT VENUSIAN MARBLE, I HOPE! THEY MAKE THAT STUFF FROM PUPPY DOG TAILS!
HE'S RIGHT, CAPTAIN! YOU COULD HAVE THE DOGSTAR MILITIA COME DOWN ON BOTH PLANETS LIKE A TON OF SAINT BERNARDS!
⸗SIGH⸗ I GIVE UP. IS THERE ANYTHING I CAN DO THAT WON'T CAUSE AN INTERPLANETARY INCIDENT?
OH, WELL... THERE ARE WORSE WAYS TO SPEND AN EVENING.
HMMM... DO YOU THINK I'M GETTING BAGS UNDER MY EYES?
FINGERS CROSSED, LINK... FINGERS CROSSED.
WILL CAPTAIN LINK HOGTHROB AND PRINCESS HELENOTRON EVER GET NEAR THAT MARBLE HOT TUB?
WILL DOCTOR STRANGEPORK CANCEL HIS SUBSCRIPTION TO GALACTIC QUARTERLY?
WILL FIRST MATE PIGGY EVER BE CLEAN ENOUGH TO SIT IN A CAKE AGAIN? HOLD THIS EPISODE UP TO A MIRROR SO YOU WON'T NEED TO READ THE NEXT EPISODE OF...
PIGS IN SPAAACE!

... NOTHING WRONG WITH ME, ROBIN!
EXIT
THERE IS TOO, UNCLE KERMIT! YOU CAN FOOL THE OTHERS, BUT YOU CAN'T FOOL ME!
I DON'T KNOW WHY EVERYBODY HAS THIS KOOKY IDEA THAT I NEED HELP, BUT--
I HEARD THE SONG, UNCLE KERMIT.
WHAT?
I HEARD THE SONG. "THE POND WHERE I WAS BORN", WASN'T IT?
YOU HEARD THAT?
WE ALL HEARD IT.
AH.
THE THING IS, UNCLE KERMIT... I REMEMBER HOW THAT SONG GOES. AND I REMEMBER HOW IT ENDS. AND SO FAR YOU HAVEN'T SUNG IT ALL THE WAY TO THE END.
WHAT ARE YOU TRYING TO SAY, ROBIN?
WELL... I THINK YOU NEED TO GET OUT ON THAT STAGE! I THINK YOU NEED TO PICK UP THAT BANJO AND SING THAT SONG WITH ALL YOUR HEART! BECAUSE IF YOU NEVER SING THE END OF IT YOU'LL NEVER REMEMBER WHAT IT'S REALLY ABOUT AND YOU'LL KEEP ON FEELING SORRY FOR YOURSELF!
EXIT
OUCH.
I'M... I'M SORRY, UNCLE KERMIT.
NO, NO... YOU'RE RIGHT. THAT'S EXACTLY WHAT I'VE BEEN DOING. I SEE THAT NOW. AND YOUR IDEA IS SO CRAZY...
EXIT
...IT MIGHT JUST WORK.

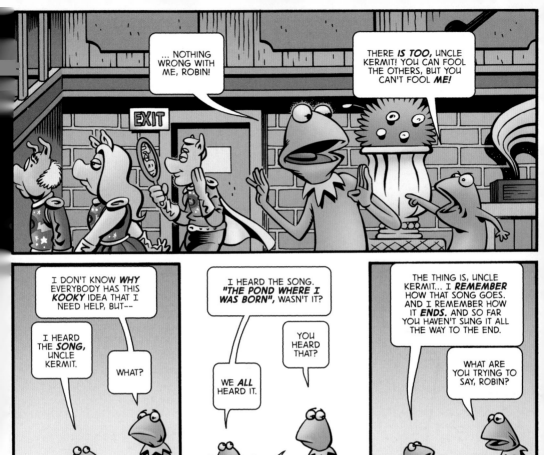

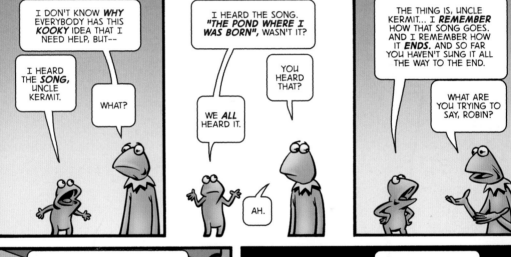

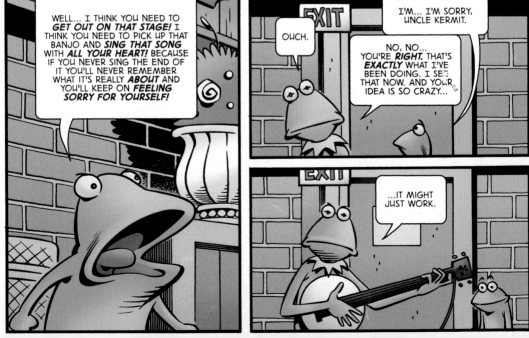

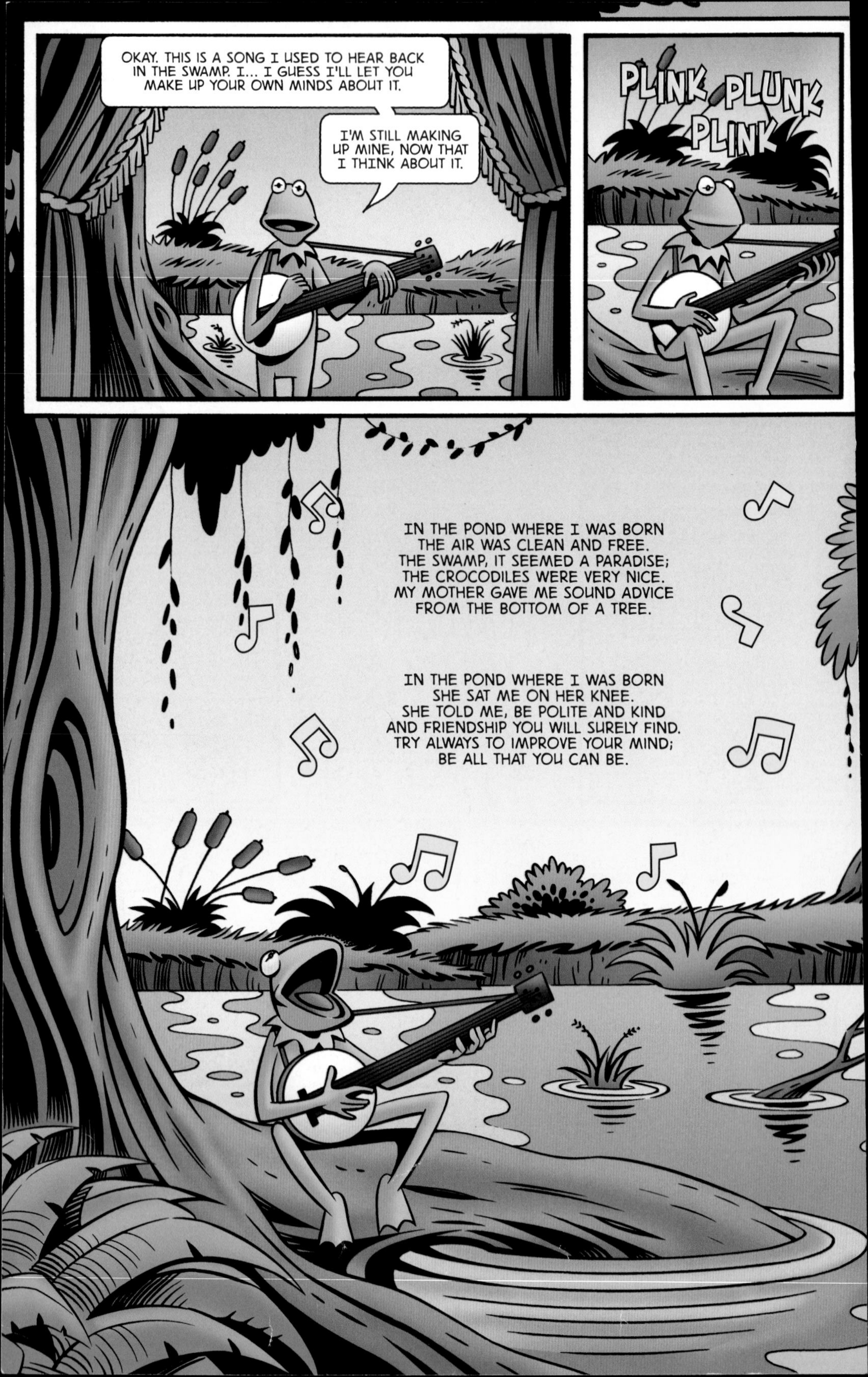
OKAY. THIS IS A SONG I USED TO HEAR BACK IN THE SWAMP. I... I GUESS I'LL LET YOU MAKE UP YOUR OWN MINDS ABOUT IT.
I'M STILL MAKING UP MINE, NOW THAT I THINK ABOUT IT.
PLINK PLUNK PLINK
IN THE POND WHERE I WAS BORN
THE AIR WAS CLEAN AND FREE.
THE SWAMP, IT SEEMED A PARADISE;
THE CROCODILES WERE VERY NICE.
MY MOTHER GAVE ME SOUND ADVICE
FROM THE BOTTOM OF A TREE.
IN THE POND WHERE I WAS BORN
SHE SAT ME ON HER KNEE.
SHE TOLD ME, BE POLITE AND KIND
AND FRIENDSHIP YOU WILL SURELY FIND.
TRY ALWAYS TO IMPROVE YOUR MIND;
BE ALL THAT YOU CAN BE.

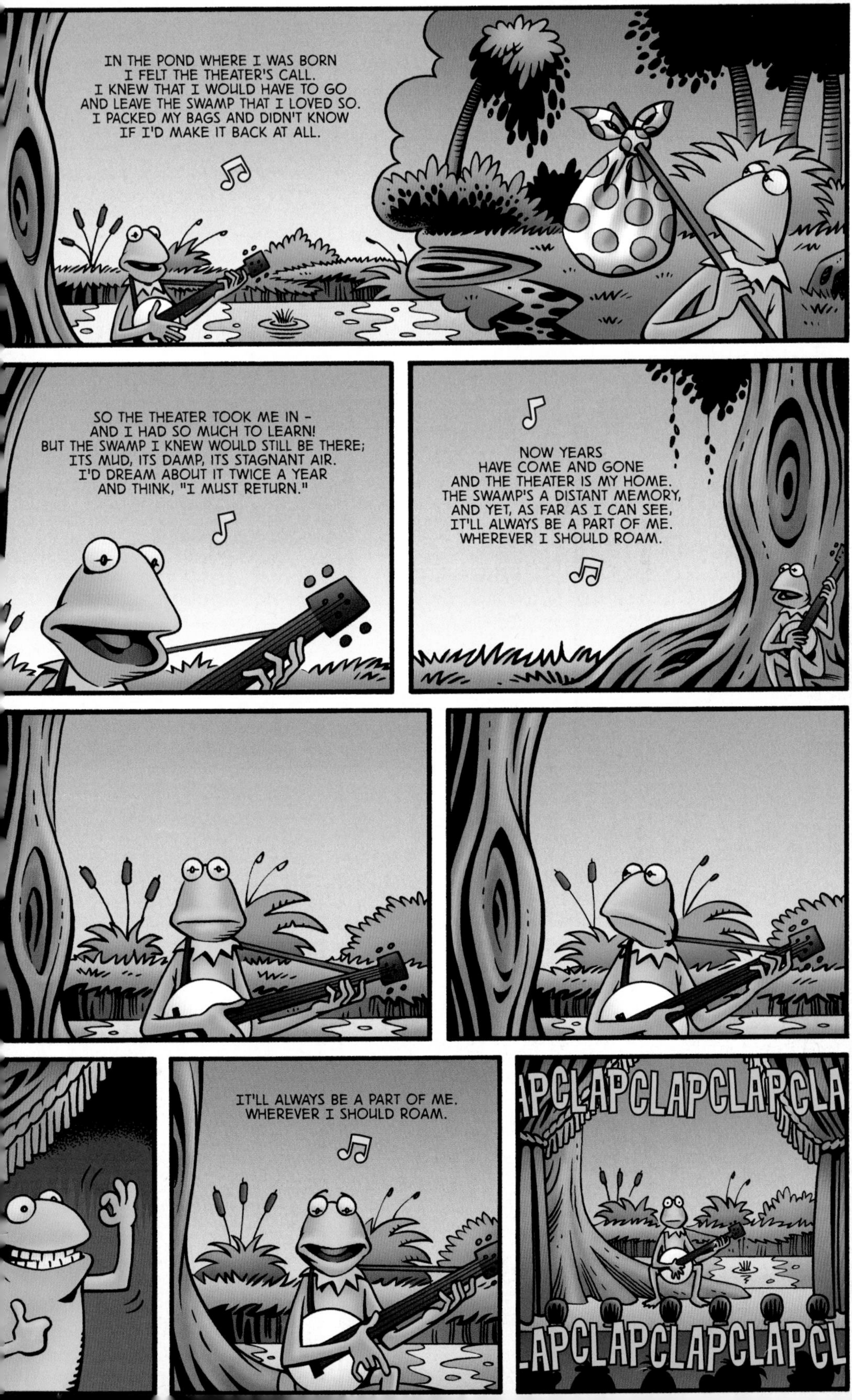
IN THE POND WHERE I WAS BORN
I FELT THE THEATER'S CALL.
I KNEW THAT I WOULD HAVE TO GO
AND LEAVE THE SWAMP THAT I LOVED SO.
I PACKED MY BAGS AND DIDN'T KNOW
IF I'D MAKE IT BACK AT ALL.
SO THE THEATER TOOK ME IN -
AND I HAD SO MUCH TO LEARN!
BUT THE SWAMP I KNEW WOULD STILL BE THERE;
ITS MUD, ITS DAMP, ITS STAGNANT AIR.
I'D DREAM ABOUT IT TWICE A YEAR
AND THINK, "I MUST RETURN."
NOW YEARS
HAVE COME AND GONE
AND THE THEATER IS MY HOME.
THE SWAMP'S A DISTANT MEMORY,
AND YET, AS FAR AS I CAN SEE,
IT'LL ALWAYS BE A PART OF ME.
WHEREVER I SHOULD ROAM.
IT'LL ALWAYS BE A PART OF ME.
WHEREVER I SHOULD ROAM.
APCLAPCLAPCLAPCLA
LAPCLAPCLAPCLAPCL

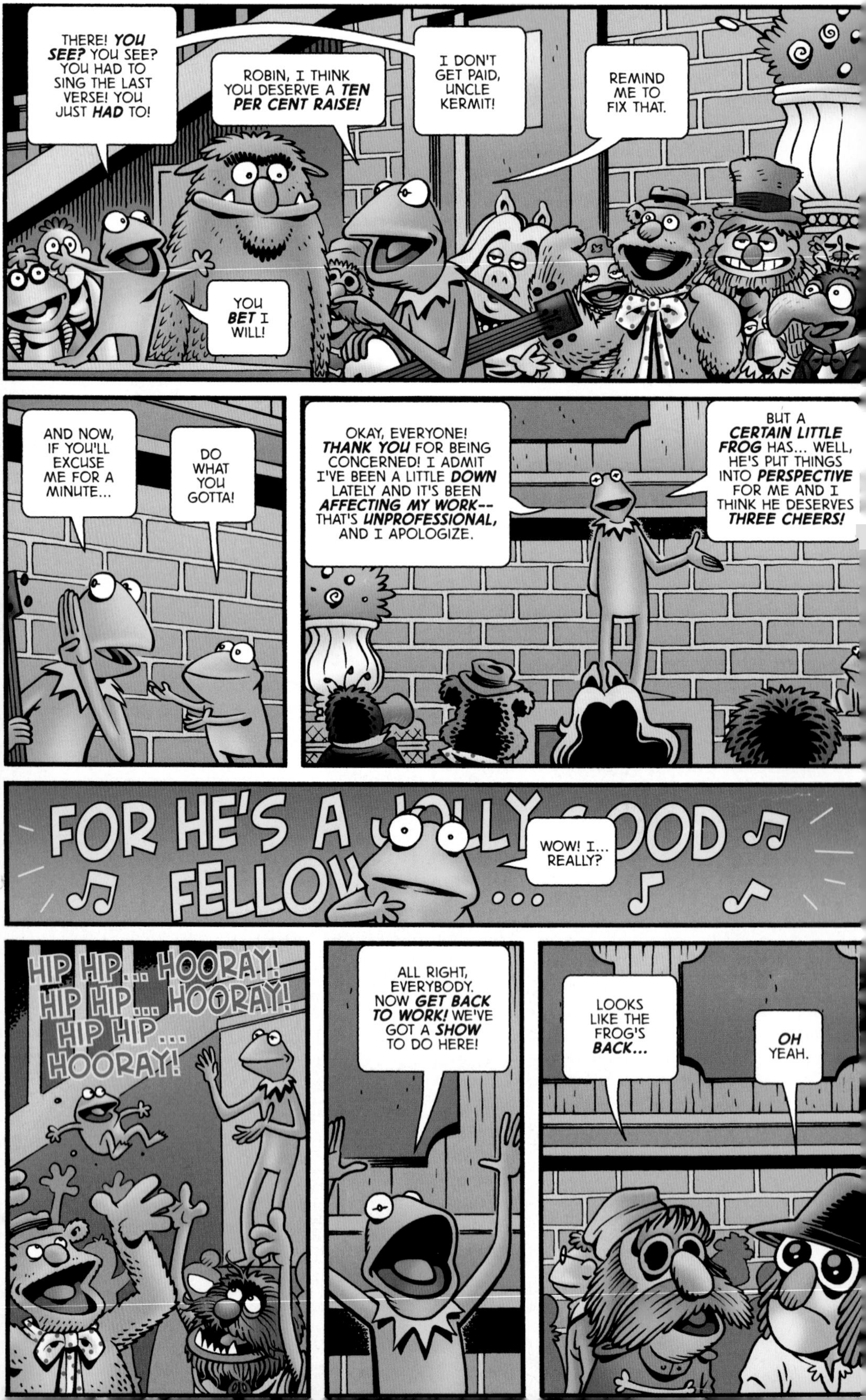
THERE! YOU SEE? YOU SEE? YOU HAD TO SING THE LAST VERSE! YOU JUST HAD TO!
ROBIN, I THINK YOU DESERVE A TEN PER CENT RAISE!
I DON'T GET PAID, UNCLE KERMIT!
REMIND ME TO FIX THAT.
YOU BET I WILL!
AND NOW, IF YOU'LL EXCUSE ME FOR A MINUTE...
DO WHAT YOU GOTTA!
OKAY, EVERYONE! THANK YOU FOR BEING CONCERNED! I ADMIT I'VE BEEN A LITTLE DOWN LATELY AND IT'S BEEN AFFECTING MY WORK-- THAT'S UNPROFESSIONAL, AND I APOLOGIZE.
BUT A CERTAIN LITTLE FROG HAS... WELL, HE'S PUT THINGS INTO PERSPECTIVE FOR ME AND I THINK HE DESERVES THREE CHEERS!
FOR HE'S A JOLLY GOOD FELLOW...
WOW! I... REALLY?
HIP HIP... HOORAY! HIP HIP... HOORAY! HIP HIP... HOORAY!
ALL RIGHT, EVERYBODY. NOW GET BACK TO WORK! WE'VE GOT A SHOW TO DO HERE!
LOOKS LIKE THE FROG'S BACK...
OH YEAH.

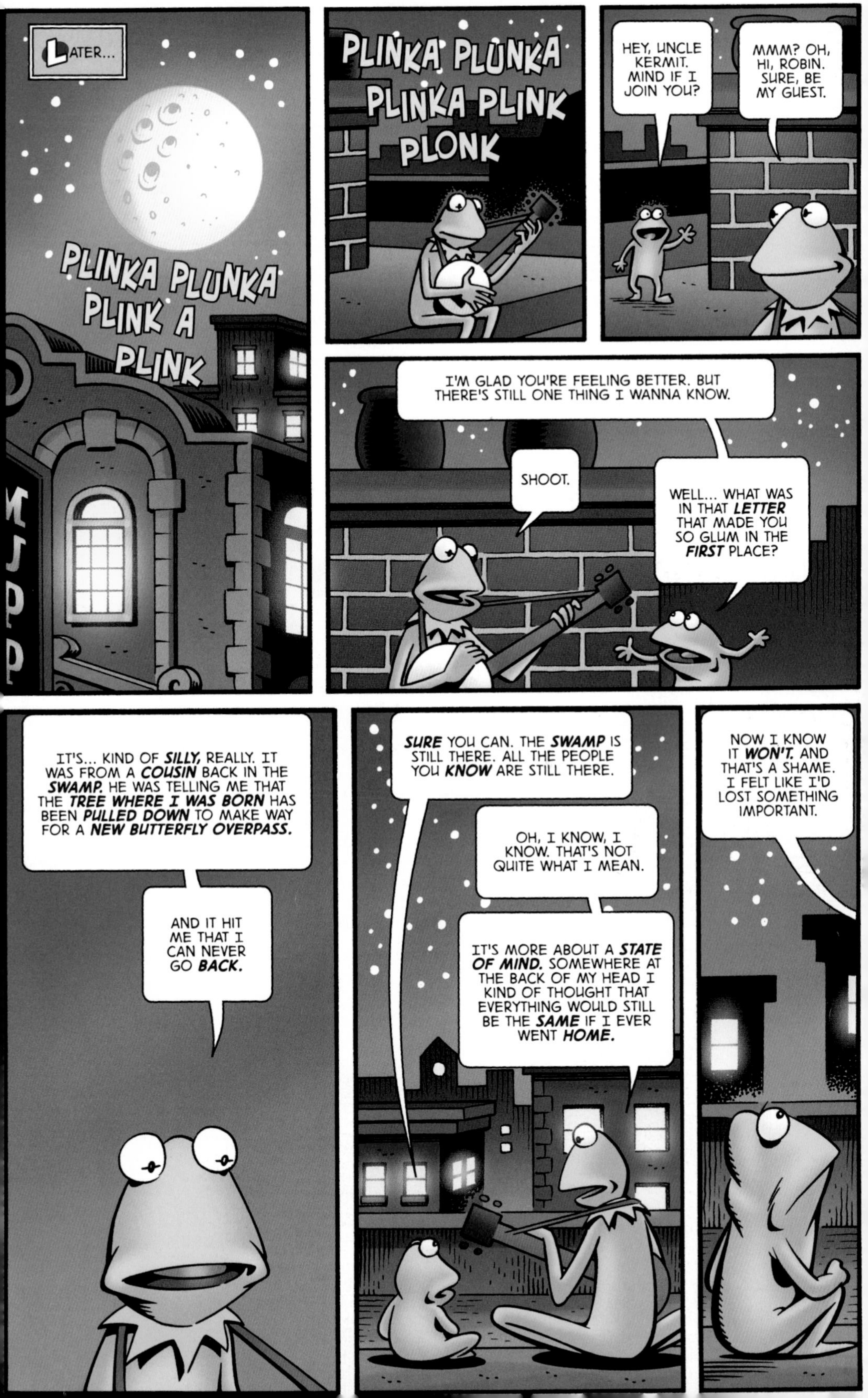
LATER...
PLINKA PLUNKA PLINK A PLINK
PLINKA PLUNKA PLINKA PLINK PLONK
HEY, UNCLE KERMIT. MIND IF I JOIN YOU?
MMM? OH, HI, ROBIN. SURE, BE MY GUEST.
I'M GLAD YOU'RE FEELING BETTER. BUT THERE'S STILL ONE THING I WANNA KNOW.
SHOOT.
WELL... WHAT WAS IN THAT LETTER THAT MADE YOU SO GLUM IN THE FIRST PLACE?
IT'S... KIND OF SILLY, REALLY. IT WAS FROM A COUSIN BACK IN THE SWAMP. HE WAS TELLING ME THAT THE TREE WHERE I WAS BORN HAS BEEN PULLED DOWN TO MAKE WAY FOR A NEW BUTTERFLY OVERPASS.
AND IT HIT ME THAT I CAN NEVER GO BACK.
SURE YOU CAN. THE SWAMP IS STILL THERE. ALL THE PEOPLE YOU KNOW ARE STILL THERE.
OH, I KNOW, I KNOW. THAT'S NOT QUITE WHAT I MEAN.
IT'S MORE ABOUT A STATE OF MIND. SOMEWHERE AT THE BACK OF MY HEAD I KIND OF THOUGHT THAT EVERYTHING WOULD STILL BE THE SAME IF I EVER WENT HOME.
NOW I KNOW IT WON'T. AND THAT'S A SHAME. I FELT LIKE I'D LOST SOMETHING IMPORTANT.

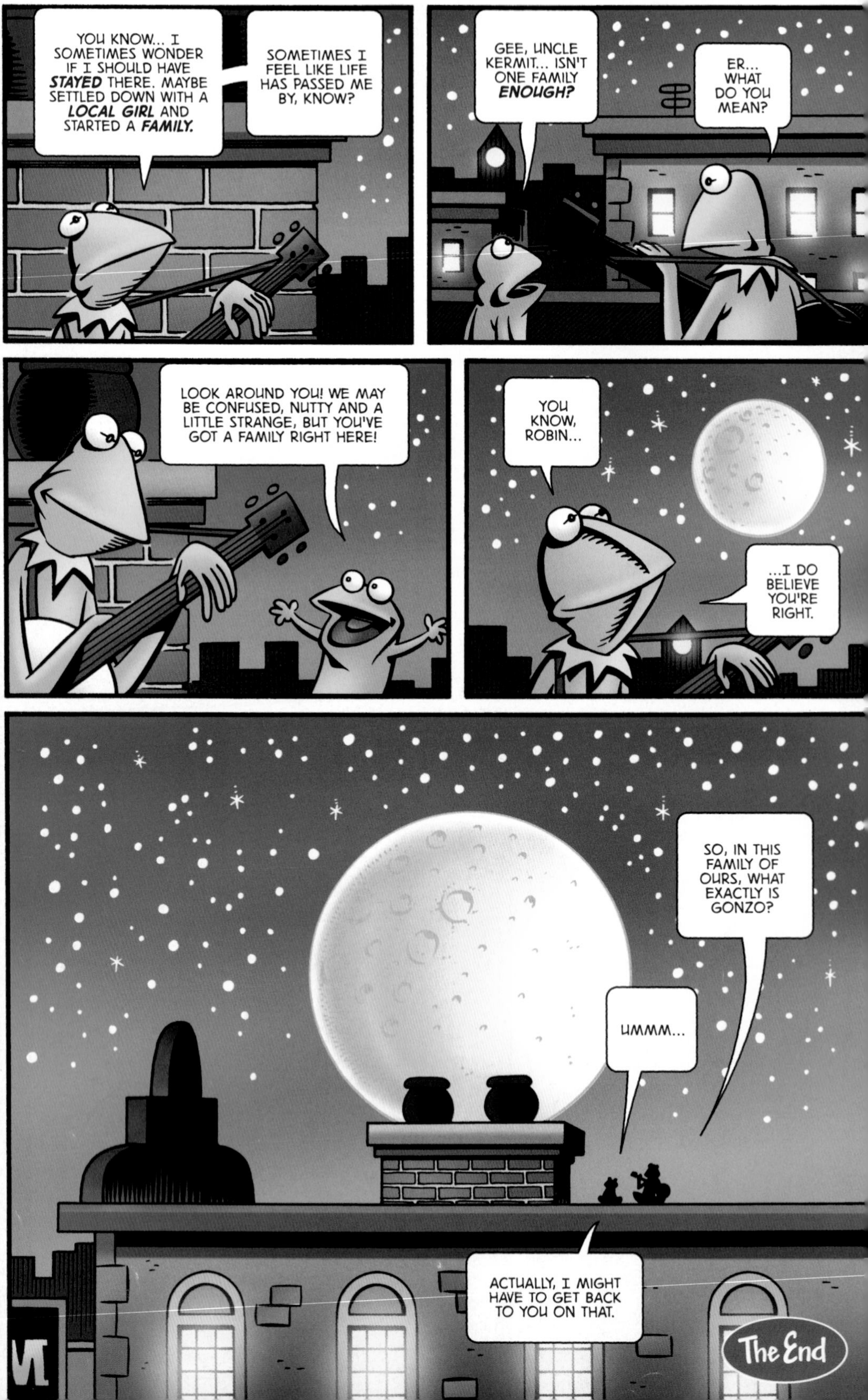
YOU KNOW... I SOMETIMES WONDER IF I SHOULD HAVE **STAYED** THERE. MAYBE SETTLED DOWN WITH A **LOCAL GIRL** AND STARTED A **FAMILY.**
SOMETIMES I FEEL LIKE LIFE HAS PASSED ME BY, KNOW?
GEE, UNCLE KERMIT... ISN'T ONE FAMILY **ENOUGH?**
ER... WHAT DO YOU MEAN?
LOOK AROUND YOU! WE MAY BE CONFUSED, NUTTY AND A LITTLE STRANGE, BUT YOU'VE GOT A FAMILY RIGHT HERE!
YOU KNOW, ROBIN...
...I DO BELIEVE YOU'RE RIGHT.
SO, IN THIS FAMILY OF OURS, WHAT EXACTLY IS GONZO?
UMMM...
ACTUALLY, I MIGHT HAVE TO GET BACK TO YOU ON THAT.
The End

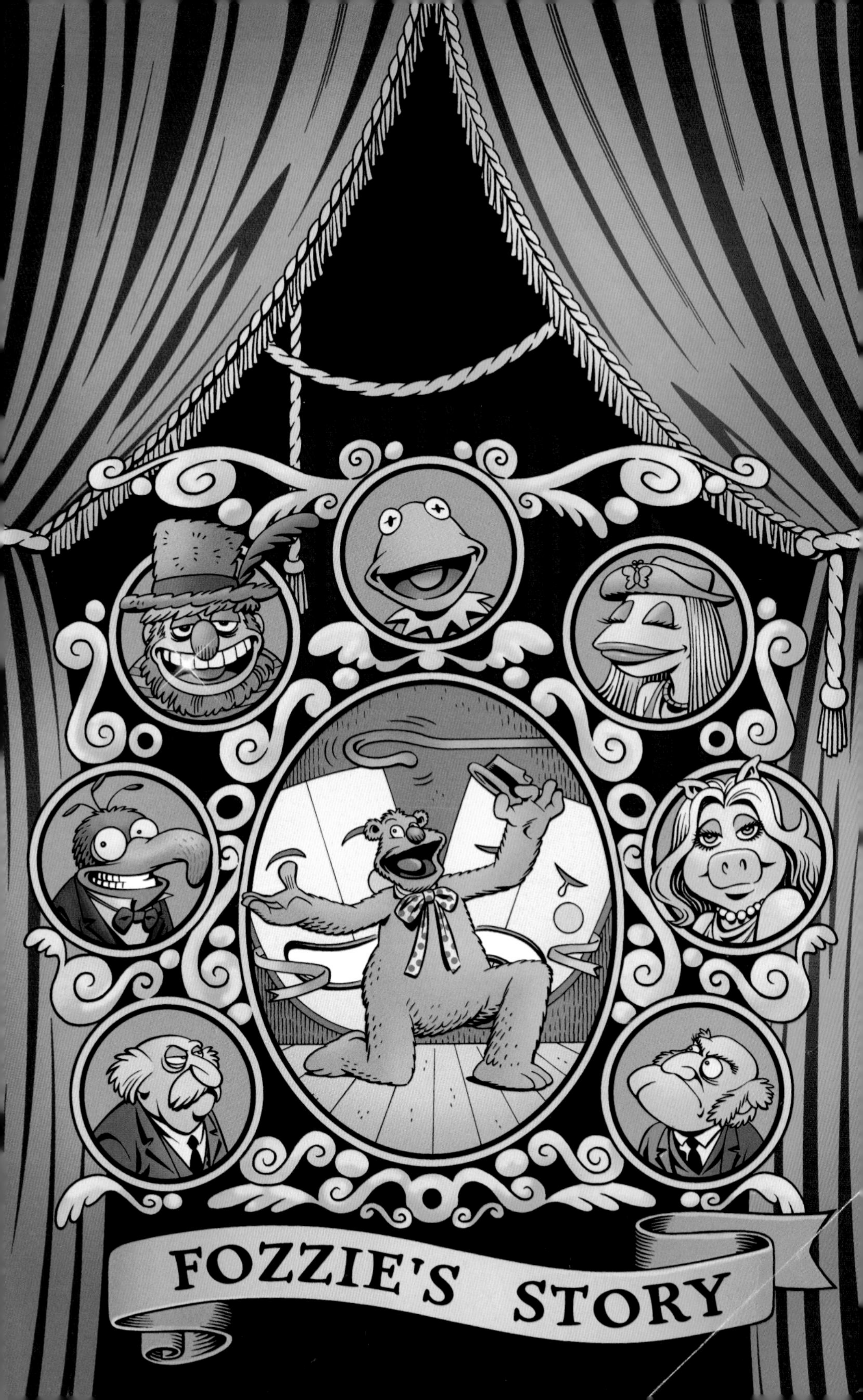
FOZZIE'S STORY

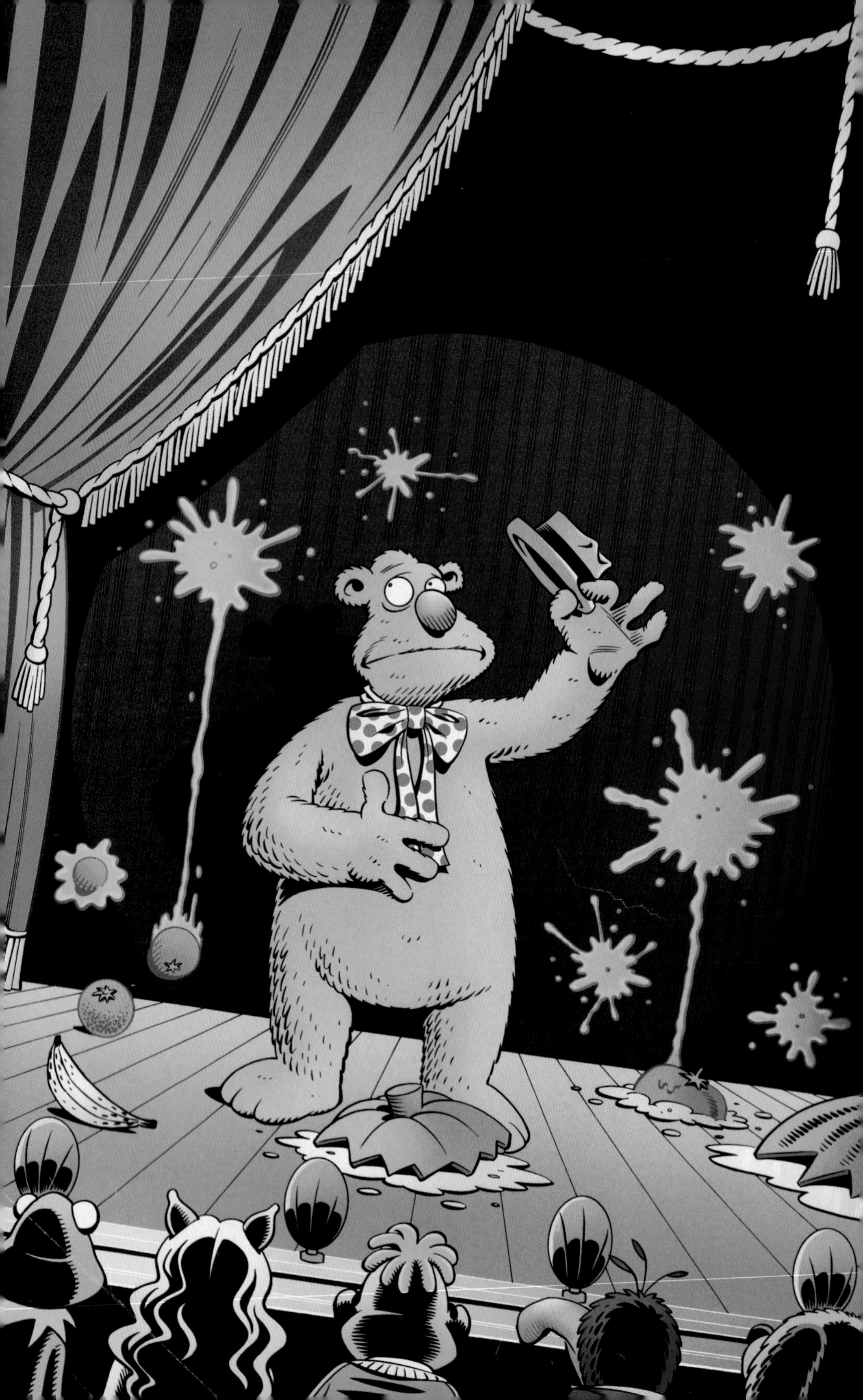

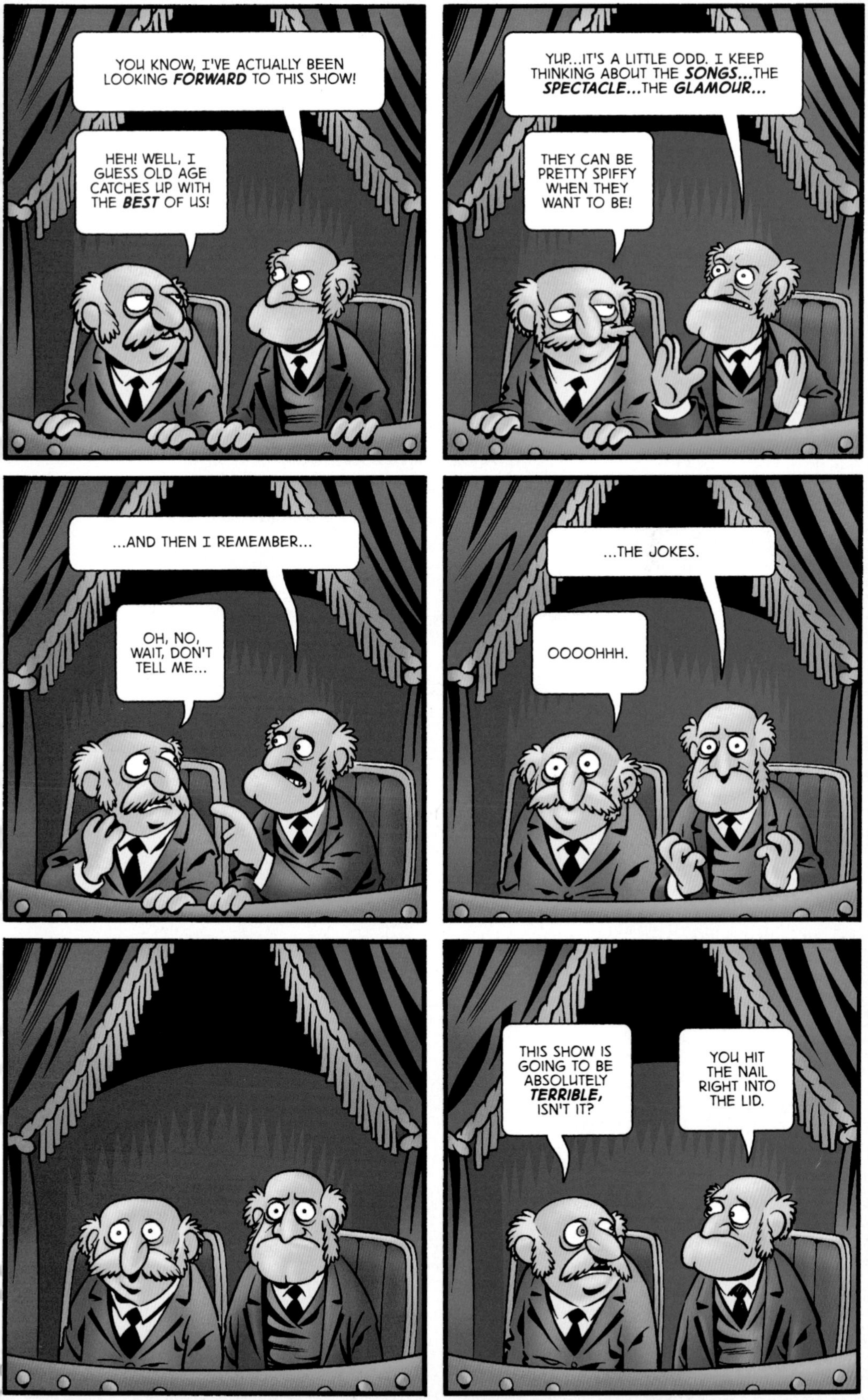
YOU KNOW, I'VE ACTUALLY BEEN LOOKING **FORWARD** TO THIS SHOW!
HEH! WELL, I GUESS OLD AGE CATCHES UP WITH THE **BEST** OF US!
YUP...IT'S A LITTLE ODD. I KEEP THINKING ABOUT THE **SONGS...**THE **SPECTACLE...**THE **GLAMOUR...**
THEY CAN BE PRETTY SPIFFY WHEN THEY WANT TO BE!
...AND THEN I REMEMBER...
OH, NO, WAIT, DON'T TELL ME...
...THE JOKES.
OOOOHHH.
THIS SHOW IS GOING TO BE ABSOLUTELY **TERRIBLE,** ISN'T IT?
YOU HIT THE NAIL RIGHT INTO THE LID.

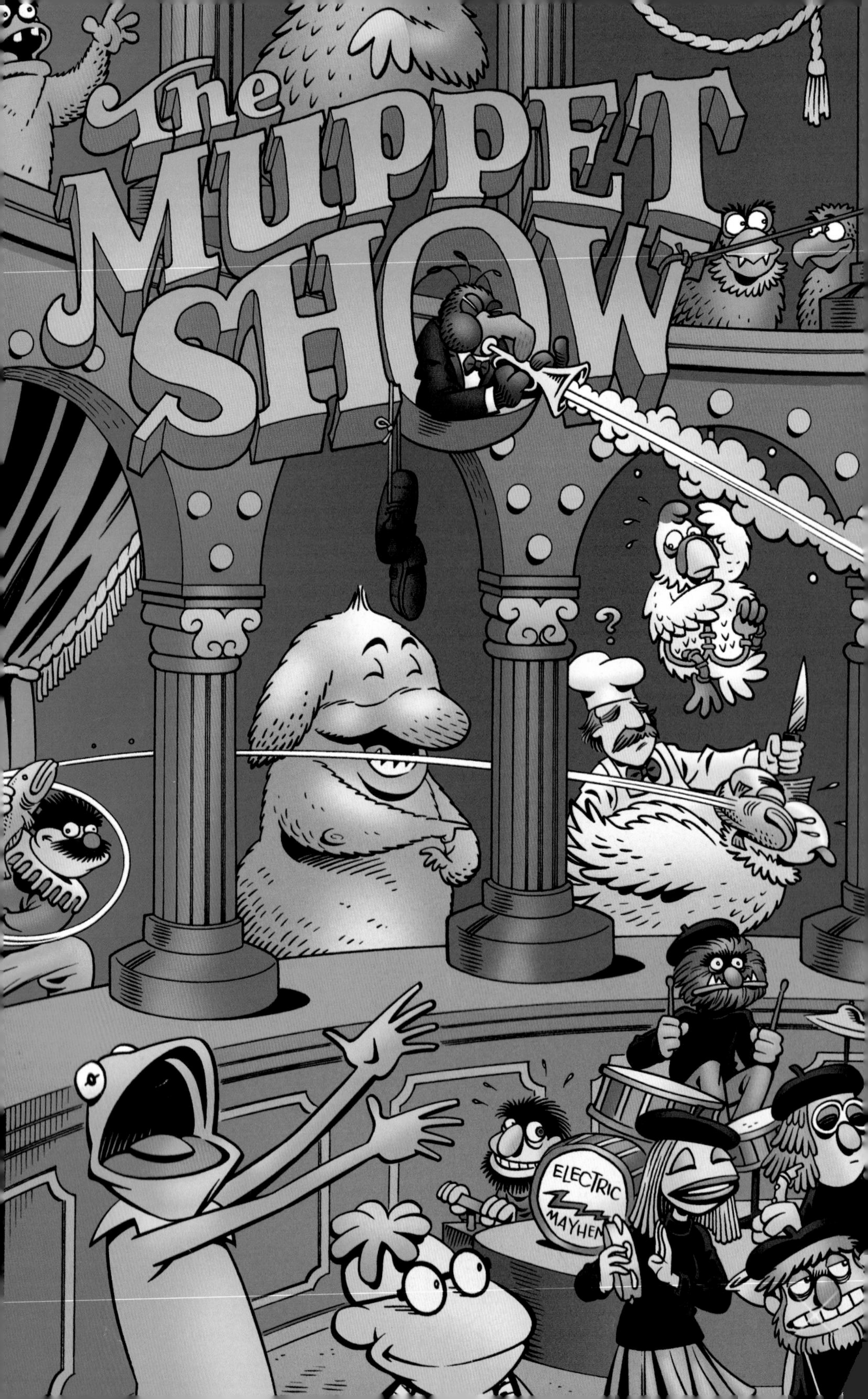
The
MUPPET
SHOW
ELECTRIC
MAYHEM

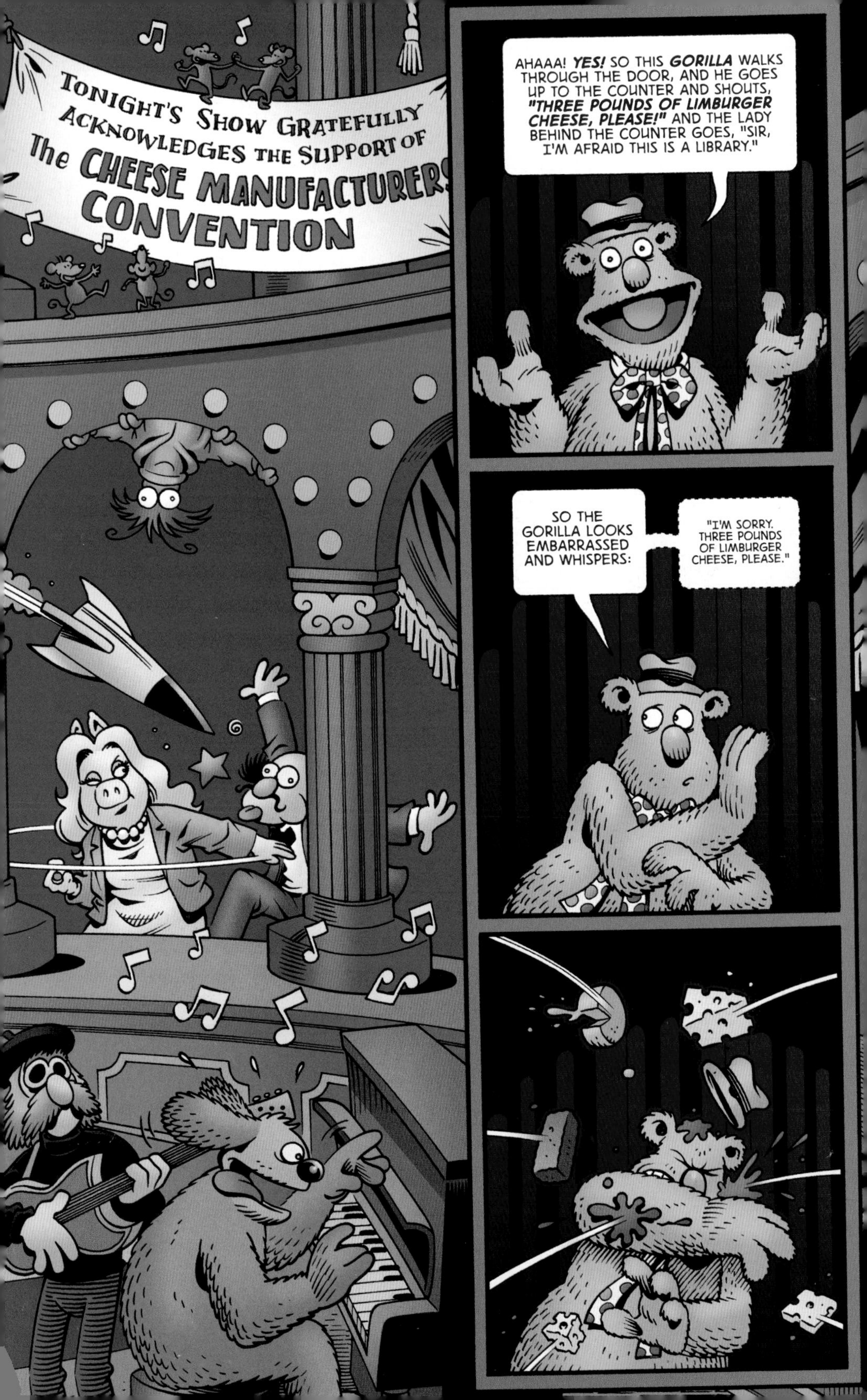
TONIGHT'S SHOW GRATEFULLY ACKNOWLEDGES THE SUPPORT OF The CHEESE MANUFACTURERS CONVENTION
AHAAA! YES! SO THIS GORILLA WALKS THROUGH THE DOOR, AND HE GOES UP TO THE COUNTER AND SHOUTS, "THREE POUNDS OF LIMBURGER CHEESE, PLEASE!" AND THE LADY BEHIND THE COUNTER GOES, "SIR, I'M AFRAID THIS IS A LIBRARY."
SO THE GORILLA LOOKS EMBARRASSED AND WHISPERS:
"I'M SORRY. THREE POUNDS OF LIMBURGER CHEESE, PLEASE."

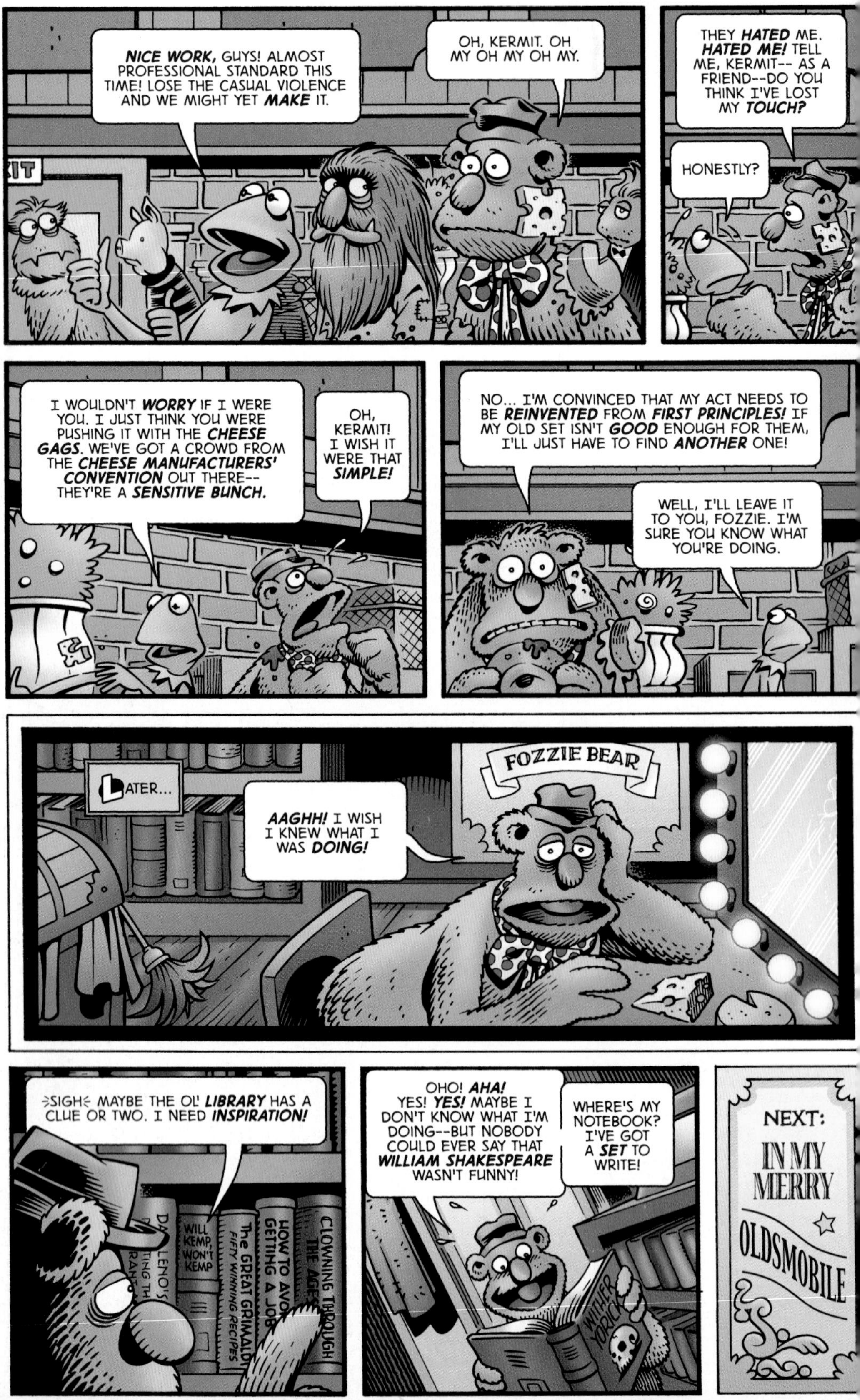
NICE WORK, GUYS! ALMOST PROFESSIONAL STANDARD THIS TIME! LOSE THE CASUAL VIOLENCE AND WE MIGHT YET MAKE IT.
OH, KERMIT. OH MY OH MY OH MY.
THEY HATED ME. HATED ME! TELL ME, KERMIT-- AS A FRIEND--DO YOU THINK I'VE LOST MY TOUCH?
HONESTLY?
I WOULDN'T WORRY IF I WERE YOU. I JUST THINK YOU WERE PUSHING IT WITH THE CHEESE GAGS. WE'VE GOT A CROWD FROM THE CHEESE MANUFACTURERS' CONVENTION OUT THERE-- THEY'RE A SENSITIVE BUNCH.
OH, KERMIT! I WISH IT WERE THAT SIMPLE!
NO... I'M CONVINCED THAT MY ACT NEEDS TO BE REINVENTED FROM FIRST PRINCIPLES! IF MY OLD SET ISN'T GOOD ENOUGH FOR THEM, I'LL JUST HAVE TO FIND ANOTHER ONE!
WELL, I'LL LEAVE IT TO YOU, FOZZIE. I'M SURE YOU KNOW WHAT YOU'RE DOING.
LATER...
FOZZIE BEAR
AAGHH! I WISH I KNEW WHAT I WAS DOING!
≥SIGH≤ MAYBE THE OL' LIBRARY HAS A CLUE OR TWO. I NEED INSPIRATION!
WILL KEMP, WON'T KEMP
The GREAT GRIMALDI
FIFTY WINNING RECIPES
CLOWNING THROUGH THE AGES
OHO! AHA! YES! YES! MAYBE I DON'T KNOW WHAT I'M DOING--BUT NOBODY COULD EVER SAY THAT WILLIAM SHAKESPEARE WASN'T FUNNY!
WHERE'S MY NOTEBOOK? I'VE GOT A SET TO WRITE!
NEXT:
IN MY MERRY OLDSMOBILE

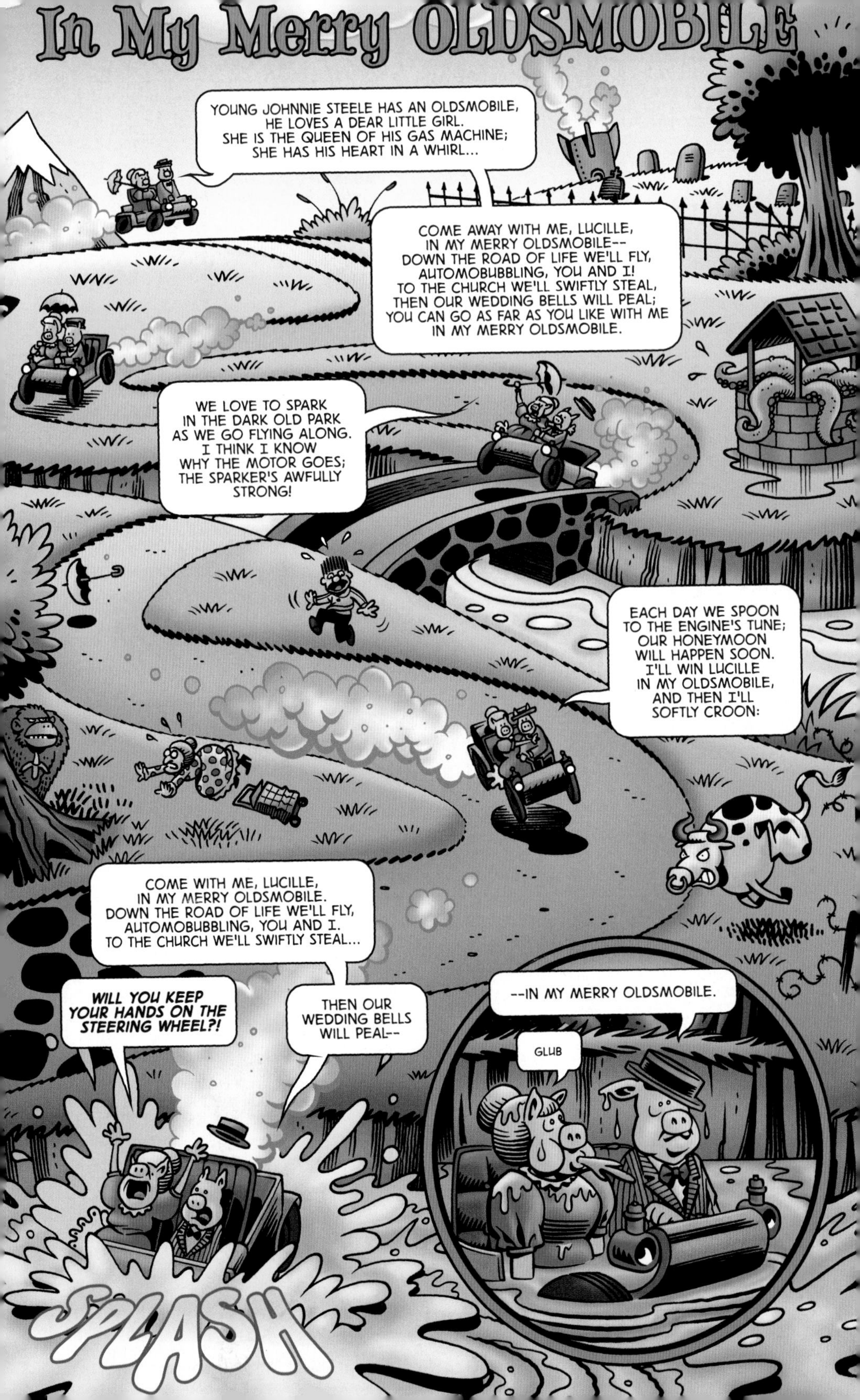
In My Merry OLDSMOBILE
YOUNG JOHNNIE STEELE HAS AN OLDSMOBILE, HE LOVES A DEAR LITTLE GIRL. SHE IS THE QUEEN OF HIS GAS MACHINE; SHE HAS HIS HEART IN A WHIRL...
COME AWAY WITH ME, LUCILLE, IN MY MERRY OLDSMOBILE-- DOWN THE ROAD OF LIFE WE'LL FLY, AUTOMOBUBBLING, YOU AND I! TO THE CHURCH WE'LL SWIFTLY STEAL, THEN OUR WEDDING BELLS WILL PEAL; YOU CAN GO AS FAR AS YOU LIKE WITH ME IN MY MERRY OLDSMOBILE.
WE LOVE TO SPARK IN THE DARK OLD PARK AS WE GO FLYING ALONG. I THINK I KNOW WHY THE MOTOR GOES; THE SPARKER'S AWFULLY STRONG!
EACH DAY WE SPOON TO THE ENGINE'S TUNE; OUR HONEYMOON WILL HAPPEN SOON. I'LL WIN LUCILLE IN MY OLDSMOBILE, AND THEN I'LL SOFTLY CROON:
COME WITH ME, LUCILLE, IN MY MERRY OLDSMOBILE. DOWN THE ROAD OF LIFE WE'LL FLY, AUTOMOBUBBLING, YOU AND I. TO THE CHURCH WE'LL SWIFTLY STEAL...
WILL YOU KEEP YOUR HANDS ON THE STEERING WHEEL?!
THEN OUR WEDDING BELLS WILL PEAL--
SPLASH
--IN MY MERRY OLDSMOBILE.
GLUB

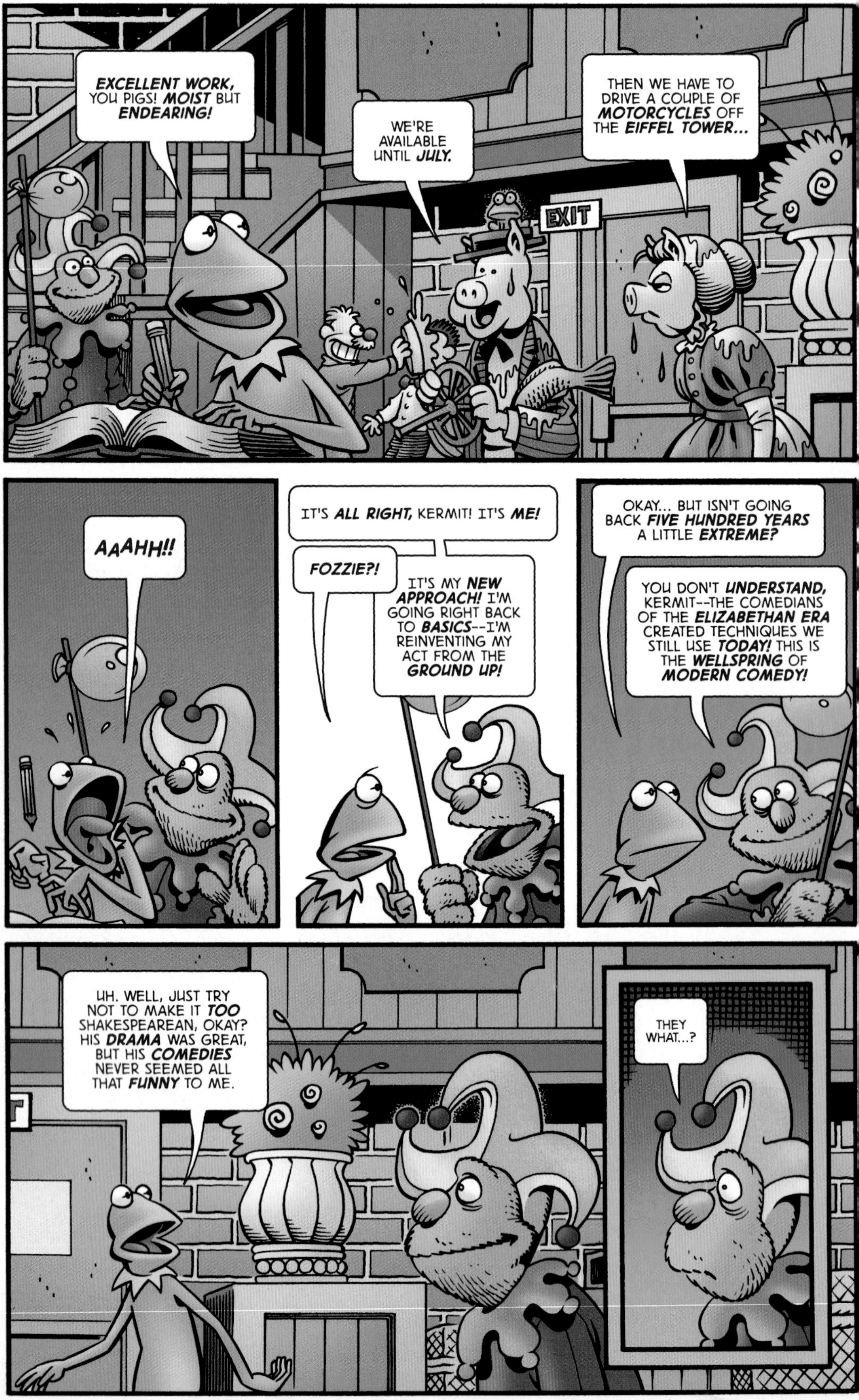

EXCELLENT WORK, YOU PIGS! MOIST BUT ENDEARING!
WE'RE AVAILABLE UNTIL JULY.
THEN WE HAVE TO DRIVE A COUPLE OF MOTORCYCLES OFF THE EIFFEL TOWER...
EXIT
AAAHH!!
IT'S ALL RIGHT, KERMIT! IT'S ME!
FOZZIE?!
IT'S MY NEW APPROACH! I'M GOING RIGHT BACK TO BASICS--I'M REINVENTING MY ACT FROM THE GROUND UP!
OKAY... BUT ISN'T GOING BACK FIVE HUNDRED YEARS A LITTLE EXTREME?
YOU DON'T UNDERSTAND, KERMIT--THE COMEDIANS OF THE ELIZABETHAN ERA CREATED TECHNIQUES WE STILL USE TODAY! THIS IS THE WELLSPRING OF MODERN COMEDY!
UH. WELL, JUST TRY NOT TO MAKE IT TOO SHAKESPEAREAN, OKAY? HIS DRAMA WAS GREAT, BUT HIS COMEDIES NEVER SEEMED ALL THAT FUNNY TO ME.
THEY WHAT...?

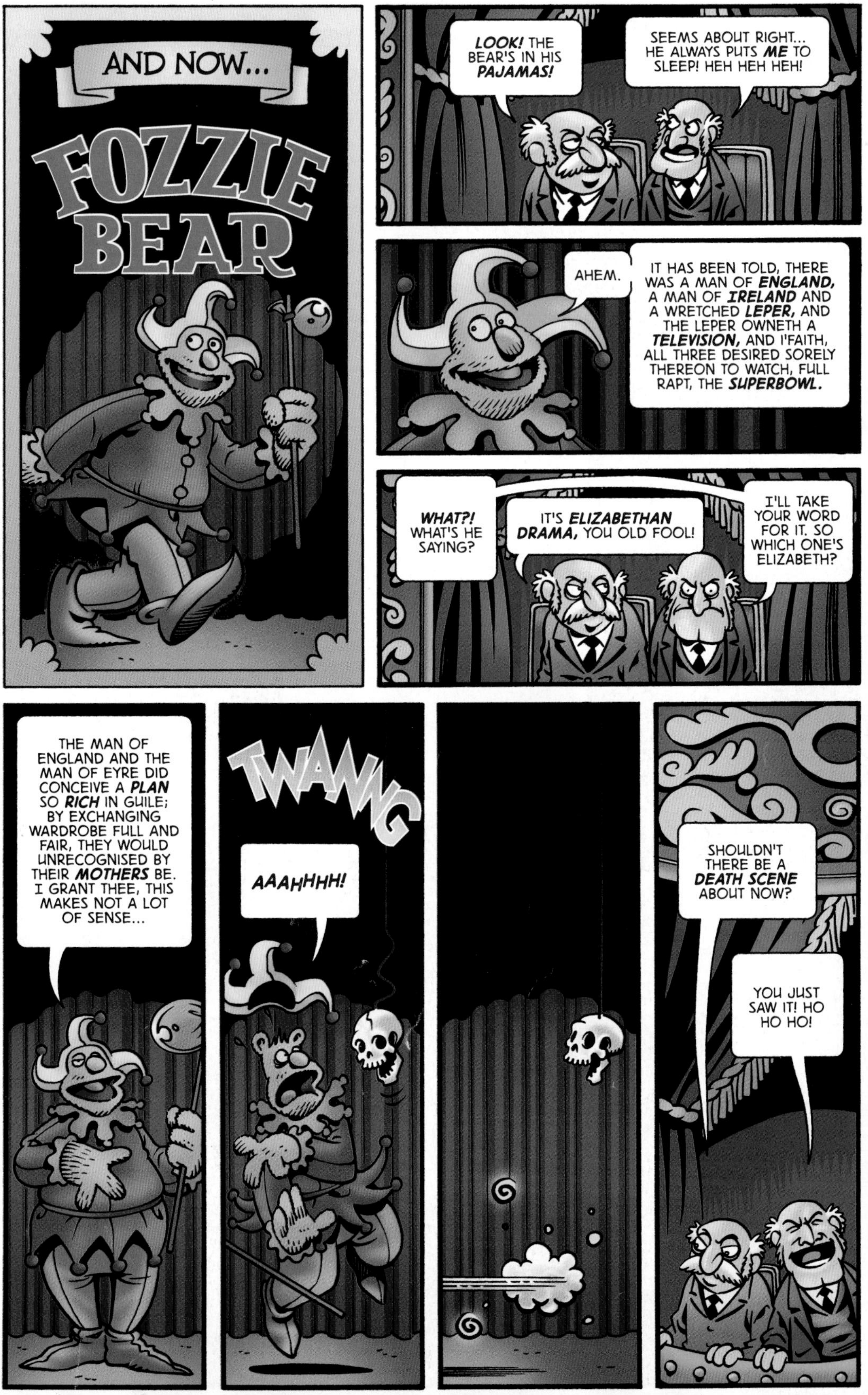
AND NOW...
FOZZIE BEAR
LOOK! THE BEAR'S IN HIS PAJAMAS!
SEEMS ABOUT RIGHT... HE ALWAYS PUTS ME TO SLEEP! HEH HEH HEH!
AHEM.
IT HAS BEEN TOLD, THERE WAS A MAN OF ENGLAND, A MAN OF IRELAND AND A WRETCHED LEPER, AND THE LEPER OWNETH A TELEVISION, AND I'FAITH, ALL THREE DESIRED SORELY THEREON TO WATCH, FULL RAPT, THE SUPERBOWL.
WHAT?! WHAT'S HE SAYING?
IT'S ELIZABETHAN DRAMA, YOU OLD FOOL!
I'LL TAKE YOUR WORD FOR IT. SO WHICH ONE'S ELIZABETH?
THE MAN OF ENGLAND AND THE MAN OF EYRE DID CONCEIVE A PLAN SO RICH IN GUILE; BY EXCHANGING WARDROBE FULL AND FAIR, THEY WOULD UNRECOGNISED BY THEIR MOTHERS BE. I GRANT THEE, THIS MAKES NOT A LOT OF SENSE...
TWANNG
AAAHHHH!
SHOULDN'T THERE BE A DEATH SCENE ABOUT NOW?
YOU JUST SAW IT! HO HO HO!

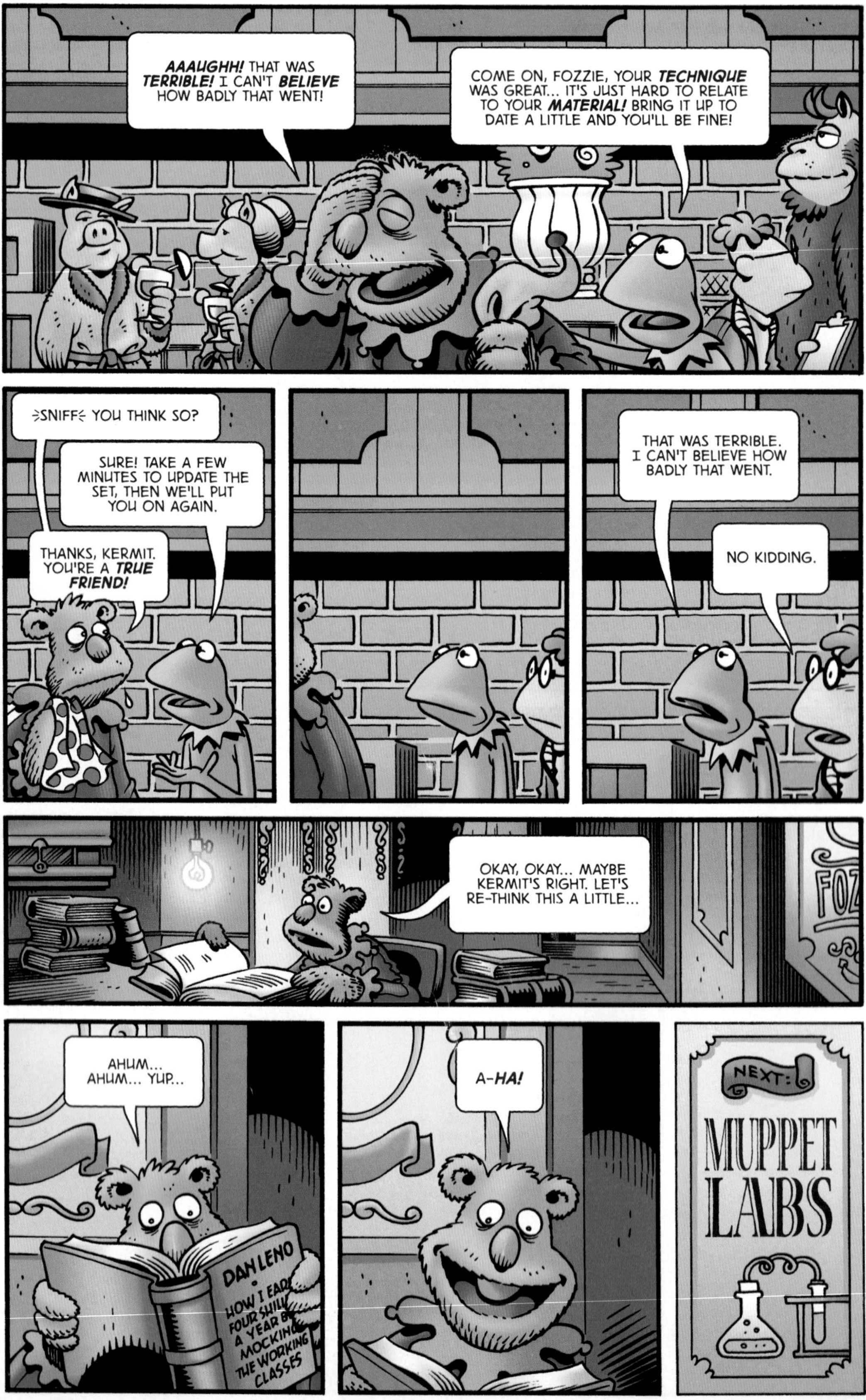
AAAUGHH! THAT WAS TERRIBLE! I CAN'T BELIEVE HOW BADLY THAT WENT!
COME ON, FOZZIE, YOUR TECHNIQUE WAS GREAT... IT'S JUST HARD TO RELATE TO YOUR MATERIAL! BRING IT UP TO DATE A LITTLE AND YOU'LL BE FINE!
SNIFF YOU THINK SO?
SURE! TAKE A FEW MINUTES TO UPDATE THE SET, THEN WE'LL PUT YOU ON AGAIN.
THANKS, KERMIT. YOU'RE A TRUE FRIEND!
THAT WAS TERRIBLE. I CAN'T BELIEVE HOW BADLY THAT WENT.
NO KIDDING.
OKAY, OKAY... MAYBE KERMIT'S RIGHT. LET'S RE-THINK THIS A LITTLE...
AHUM... AHUM... YUP...
DAN LENO
A-HA!
NEXT:
MUPPET LABS

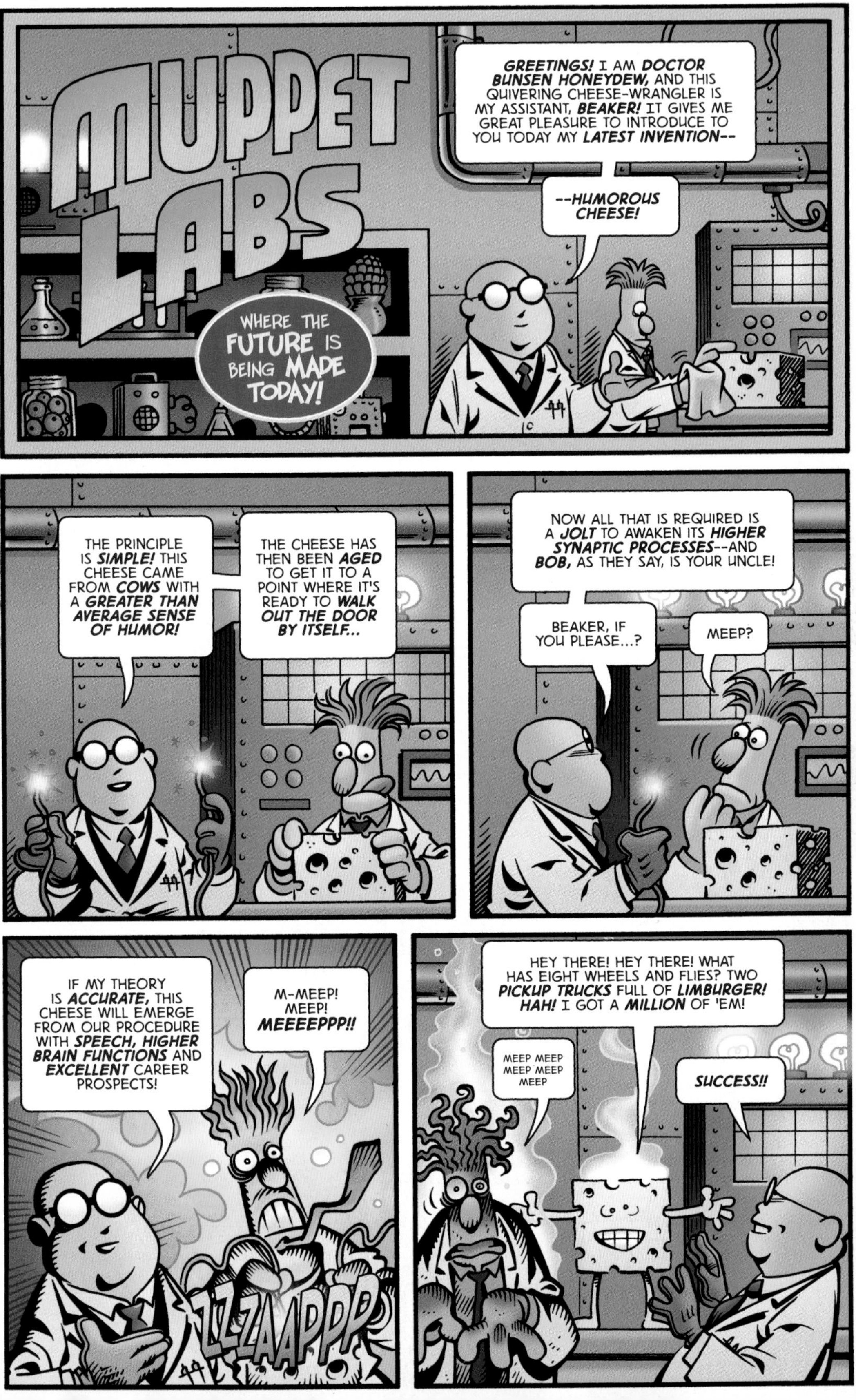
MUPPET LABS
WHERE THE FUTURE IS BEING MADE TODAY!
GREETINGS! I AM DOCTOR BUNSEN HONEYDEW, AND THIS QUIVERING CHEESE-WRANGLER IS MY ASSISTANT, BEAKER! IT GIVES ME GREAT PLEASURE TO INTRODUCE TO YOU TODAY MY LATEST INVENTION--
--HUMOROUS CHEESE!
THE PRINCIPLE IS SIMPLE! THIS CHEESE CAME FROM COWS WITH A GREATER THAN AVERAGE SENSE OF HUMOR!
THE CHEESE HAS THEN BEEN AGED TO GET IT TO A POINT WHERE IT'S READY TO WALK OUT THE DOOR BY ITSELF...
NOW ALL THAT IS REQUIRED IS A JOLT TO AWAKEN ITS HIGHER SYNAPTIC PROCESSES--AND BOB, AS THEY SAY, IS YOUR UNCLE!
BEAKER, IF YOU PLEASE...?
MEEP?
IF MY THEORY IS ACCURATE, THIS CHEESE WILL EMERGE FROM OUR PROCEDURE WITH SPEECH, HIGHER BRAIN FUNCTIONS AND EXCELLENT CAREER PROSPECTS!
M-MEEP! MEEP! MEEEEPPP!!
ZZZAAPPP
HEY THERE! HEY THERE! WHAT HAS EIGHT WHEELS AND FLIES? TWO PICKUP TRUCKS FULL OF LIMBURGER! HAH! I GOT A MILLION OF 'EM!
MEEP MEEP MEEP MEEP MEEP
SUCCESS!!

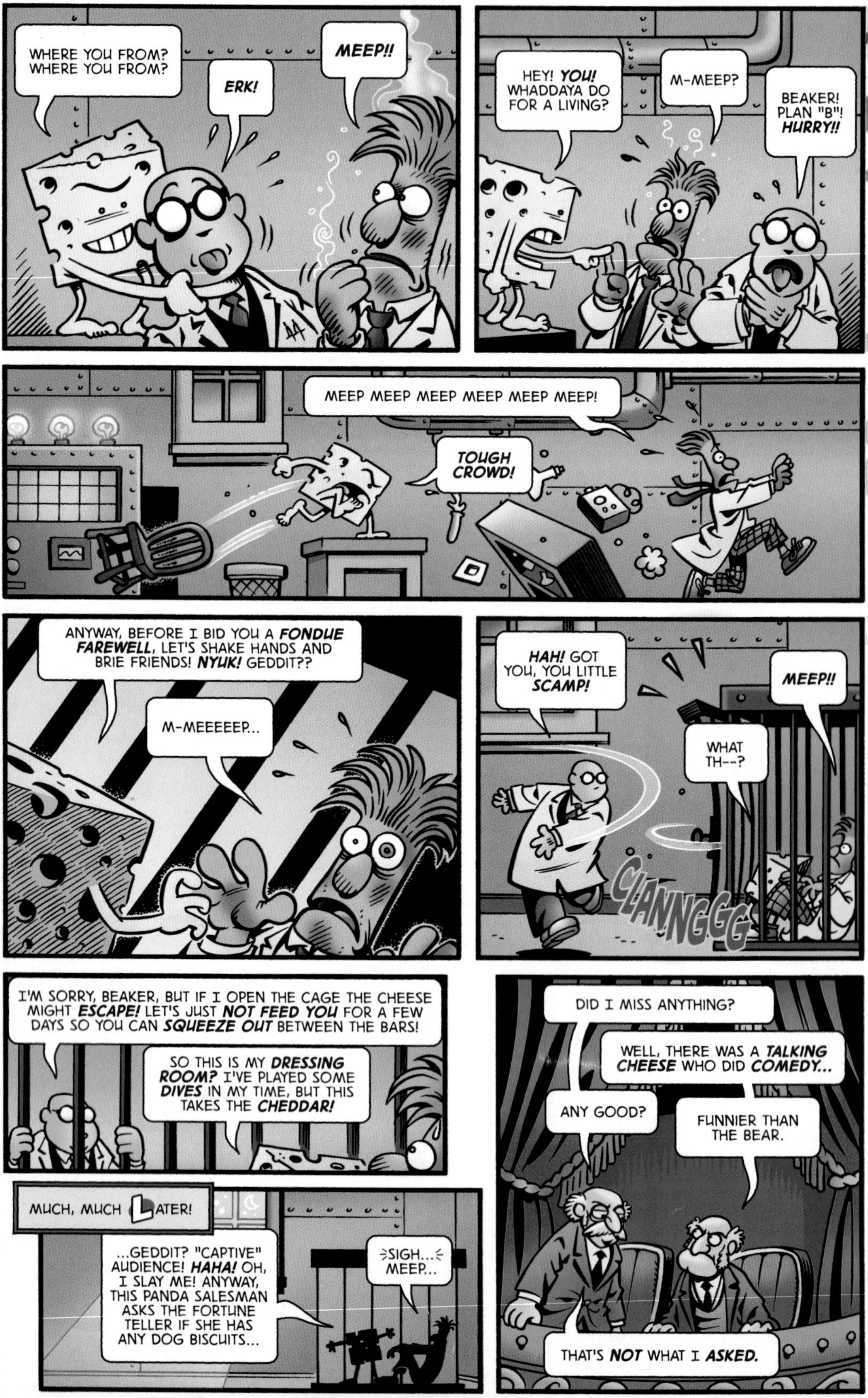

WHERE YOU FROM? WHERE YOU FROM?
ERK!
MEEP!!
HEY! YOU! WHADDAYA DO FOR A LIVING?
M-MEEP?
BEAKER! PLAN "B"! HURRY!!
MEEP MEEP MEEP MEEP MEEP MEEP!
TOUGH CROWD!
ANYWAY, BEFORE I BID YOU A FONDUE FAREWELL, LET'S SHAKE HANDS AND BRIE FRIENDS! NYUK! GEDDIT??
M-MEEEEEP...
HAH! GOT YOU, YOU LITTLE SCAMP!
MEEP!!
WHAT TH--?
CLANNGGG
I'M SORRY, BEAKER, BUT IF I OPEN THE CAGE THE CHEESE MIGHT ESCAPE! LET'S JUST NOT FEED YOU FOR A FEW DAYS SO YOU CAN SQUEEZE OUT BETWEEN THE BARS!
SO THIS IS MY DRESSING ROOM? I'VE PLAYED SOME DIVES IN MY TIME, BUT THIS TAKES THE CHEDDAR!
MUCH, MUCH LATER!
...GEDDIT? "CAPTIVE" AUDIENCE! HAHA! OH, I SLAY ME! ANYWAY, THIS PANDA SALESMAN ASKS THE FORTUNE TELLER IF SHE HAS ANY DOG BISCUITS...
SIGH... MEEP...
DID I MISS ANYTHING?
WELL, THERE WAS A TALKING CHEESE WHO DID COMEDY...
ANY GOOD?
FUNNIER THAN THE BEAR.
THAT'S NOT WHAT I ASKED.

OH, YORICK...I KNOW YOU'RE NOT THE FINE FIGURE YOU USED TO BE, BUT SOMEHOW I JUST DON'T CARE. YOU CAN STILL TURN HEADS, AND DON'T LET ANYBODY TELL YOU OTHERWISE!
HEY! WAS IT SOMETHING I SAID?
TWANG
HEY! FROG!!
UH-OH.
MY "SUFFRAGETTE, CRÊPE SUZETTE" NUMBER CANCELLED?! AND HERE I WAS THINKING YOU'D GONE OFF HOSPITAL FOOD!
IT-IT'S FOR FOZZIE, PIGGY...HE NEEDS TO DO AN EXTRA BIT TONIGHT! HE THINKS HE'S LOST HIS TOUCH!
THE BEAR CAN'T LOSE WHAT HE NEVER HAD. WHERE IS HE, ANYHOW? I THINK MY POWERS OF PERSUASION ARE UP TO THE CHALLENGE...
TOO LATE--HE'S GOING ONSTAGE RIGHT NOW! HE'S BEEN REWRITING HIS MATERIAL IN A 1913 MUSIC-HALL STYLE...
PERFECT! HE'LL BE ABLE TO PASS OFF HIS BRUISES AS CHIMNEY SOOT!
I SHOULD PROBABLY DO SOMETHING ABOUT THAT... BUT SOMETIMES THE KIDS JUST NEED TO WORK THINGS OUT FOR THEMSELVES.

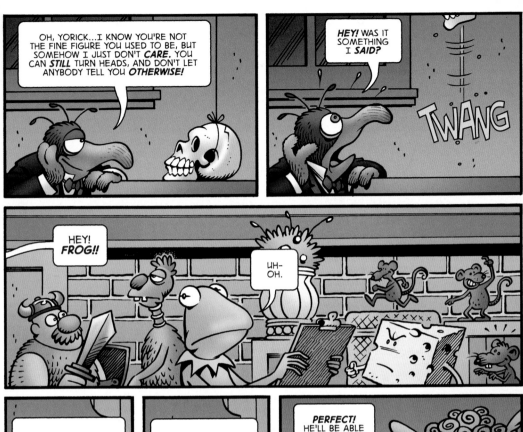

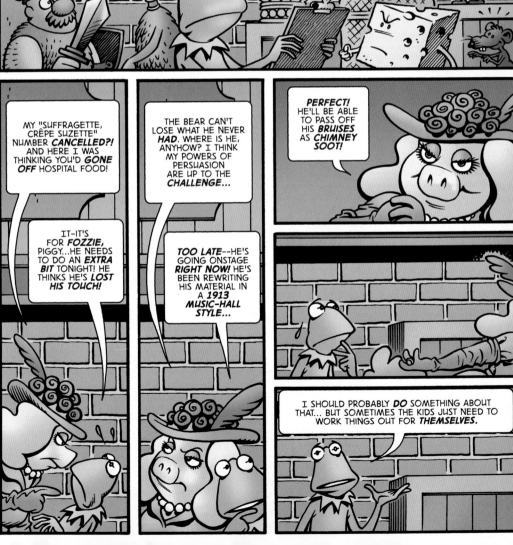

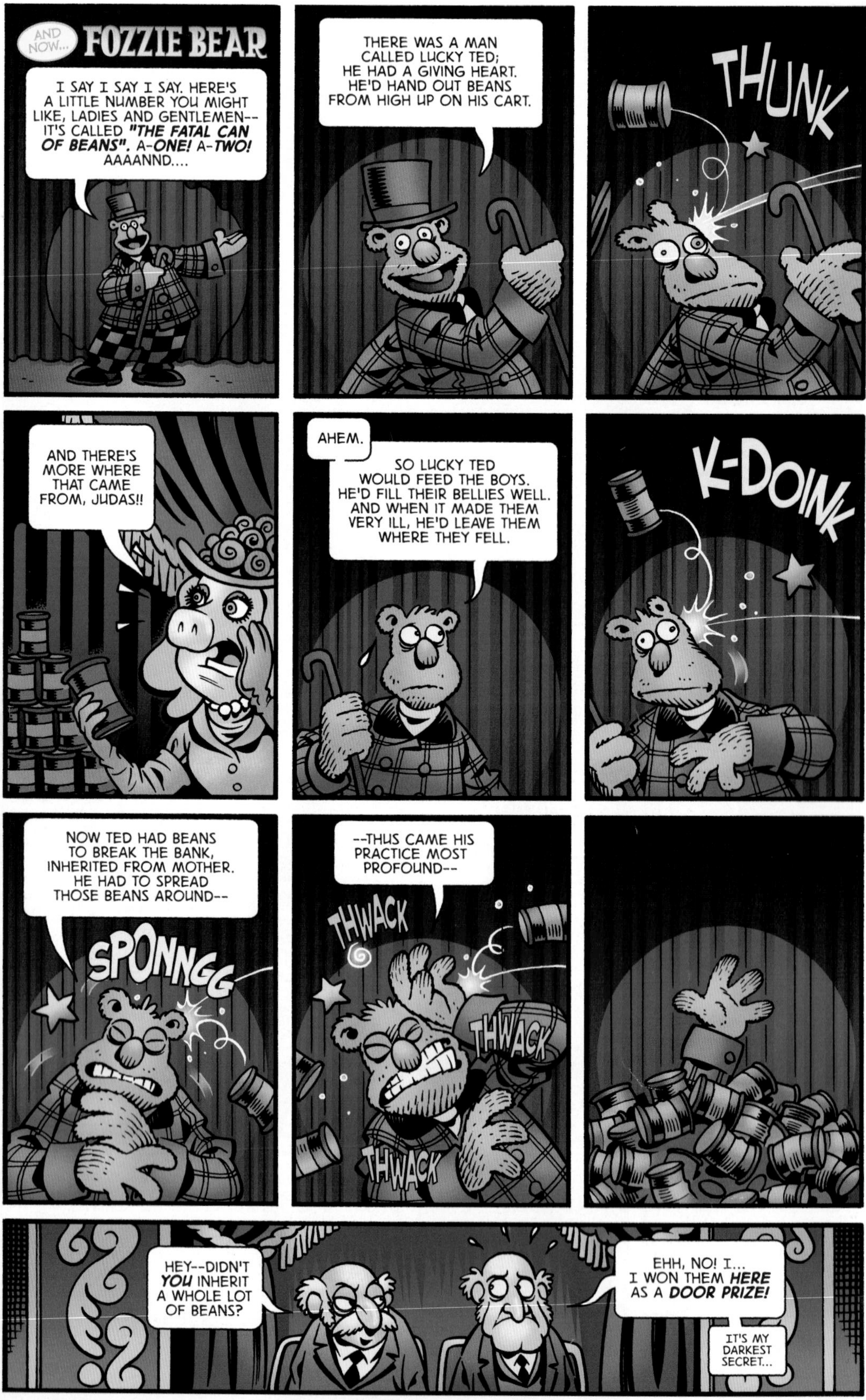
AND NOW... FOZZIE BEAR
I SAY I SAY I SAY. HERE'S A LITTLE NUMBER YOU MIGHT LIKE, LADIES AND GENTLEMEN-- IT'S CALLED "THE FATAL CAN OF BEANS". A-ONE! A-TWO! AAAANND....
THERE WAS A MAN CALLED LUCKY TED; HE HAD A GIVING HEART. HE'D HAND OUT BEANS FROM HIGH UP ON HIS CART.
THUNK
AND THERE'S MORE WHERE THAT CAME FROM, JUDAS!!
AHEM.
SO LUCKY TED WOULD FEED THE BOYS. HE'D FILL THEIR BELLIES WELL. AND WHEN IT MADE THEM VERY ILL, HE'D LEAVE THEM WHERE THEY FELL.
K-DOINK
NOW TED HAD BEANS TO BREAK THE BANK, INHERITED FROM MOTHER. HE HAD TO SPREAD THOSE BEANS AROUND--
SPONNGG
--THUS CAME HIS PRACTICE MOST PROFOUND--
THWACK
THWACK
THWACK
HEY--DIDN'T YOU INHERIT A WHOLE LOT OF BEANS?
EHH, NO! I... I WON THEM HERE AS A DOOR PRIZE!
IT'S MY DARKEST SECRET...

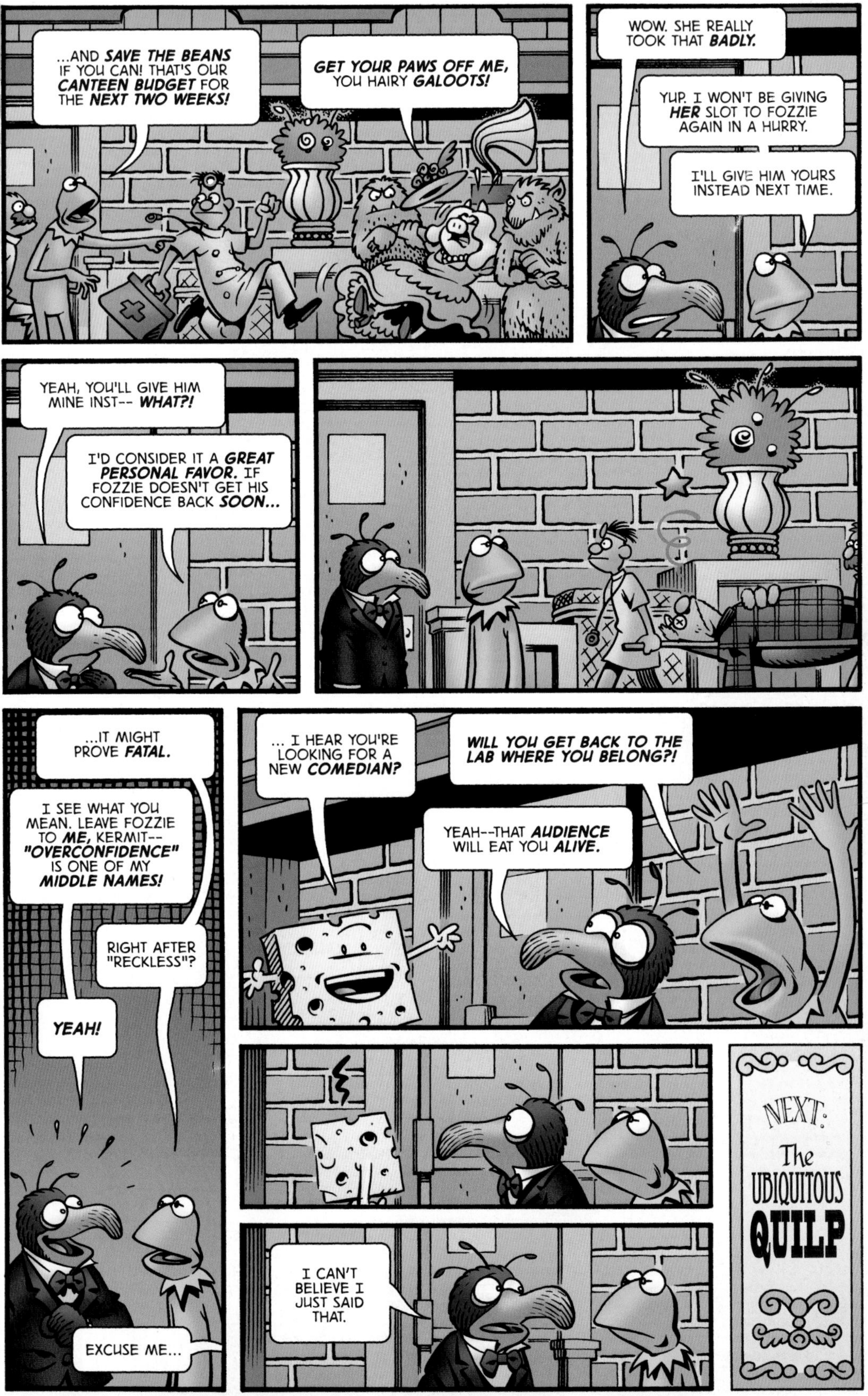
...AND **SAVE THE BEANS** IF YOU CAN! THAT'S OUR **CANTEEN BUDGET** FOR THE **NEXT TWO WEEKS!**
GET YOUR PAWS OFF ME, YOU HAIRY **GALOOTS!**
WOW. SHE REALLY TOOK THAT **BADLY.**
YUP. I WON'T BE GIVING **HER** SLOT TO FOZZIE AGAIN IN A HURRY.
I'LL GIVE HIM YOURS INSTEAD NEXT TIME.
YEAH, YOU'LL GIVE HIM MINE INST-- **WHAT?!**
I'D CONSIDER IT A **GREAT PERSONAL FAVOR.** IF FOZZIE DOESN'T GET HIS CONFIDENCE BACK **SOON...**
...IT MIGHT PROVE **FATAL.**
I SEE WHAT YOU MEAN. LEAVE FOZZIE TO **ME,** KERMIT-- **"OVERCONFIDENCE"** IS ONE OF MY **MIDDLE NAMES!**
RIGHT AFTER "RECKLESS"?
YEAH!
EXCUSE ME...
... I HEAR YOU'RE LOOKING FOR A NEW **COMEDIAN?**
WILL YOU GET BACK TO THE LAB WHERE YOU BELONG?!
YEAH--THAT **AUDIENCE** WILL EAT YOU **ALIVE.**
I CAN'T BELIEVE I JUST SAID THAT.
NEXT:
The UBIQUITOUS QUILP

The UBIQUITOUS QUILP

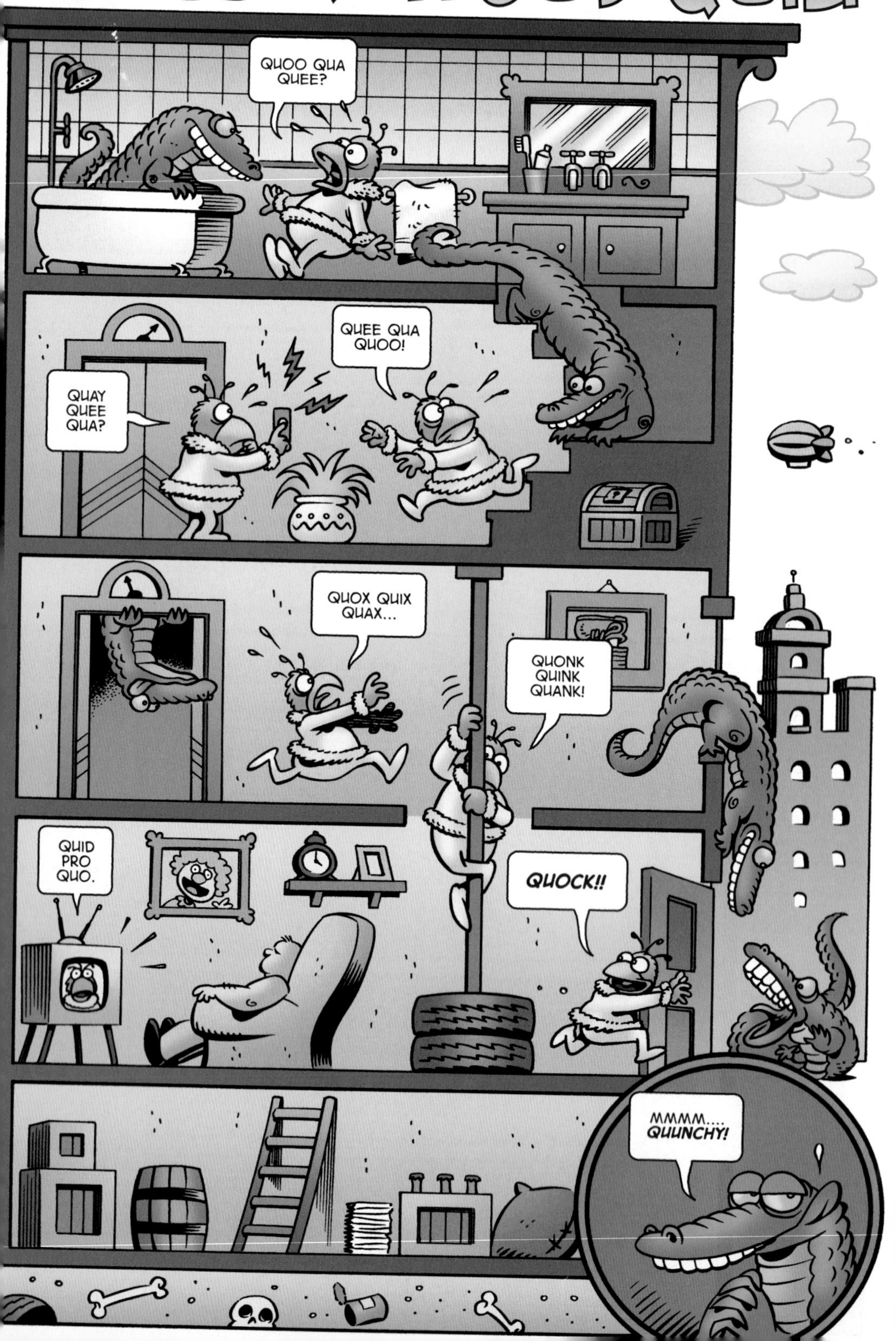
QUOO QUA QUEE?
QUEE QUA QUOO!
QUAY QUEE QUA?
QUOX QUIX QUAX...
QUONK QUINK QUANK!
QUID PRO QUO.
QUOCK!!
MMMM.... QUUNCHY!

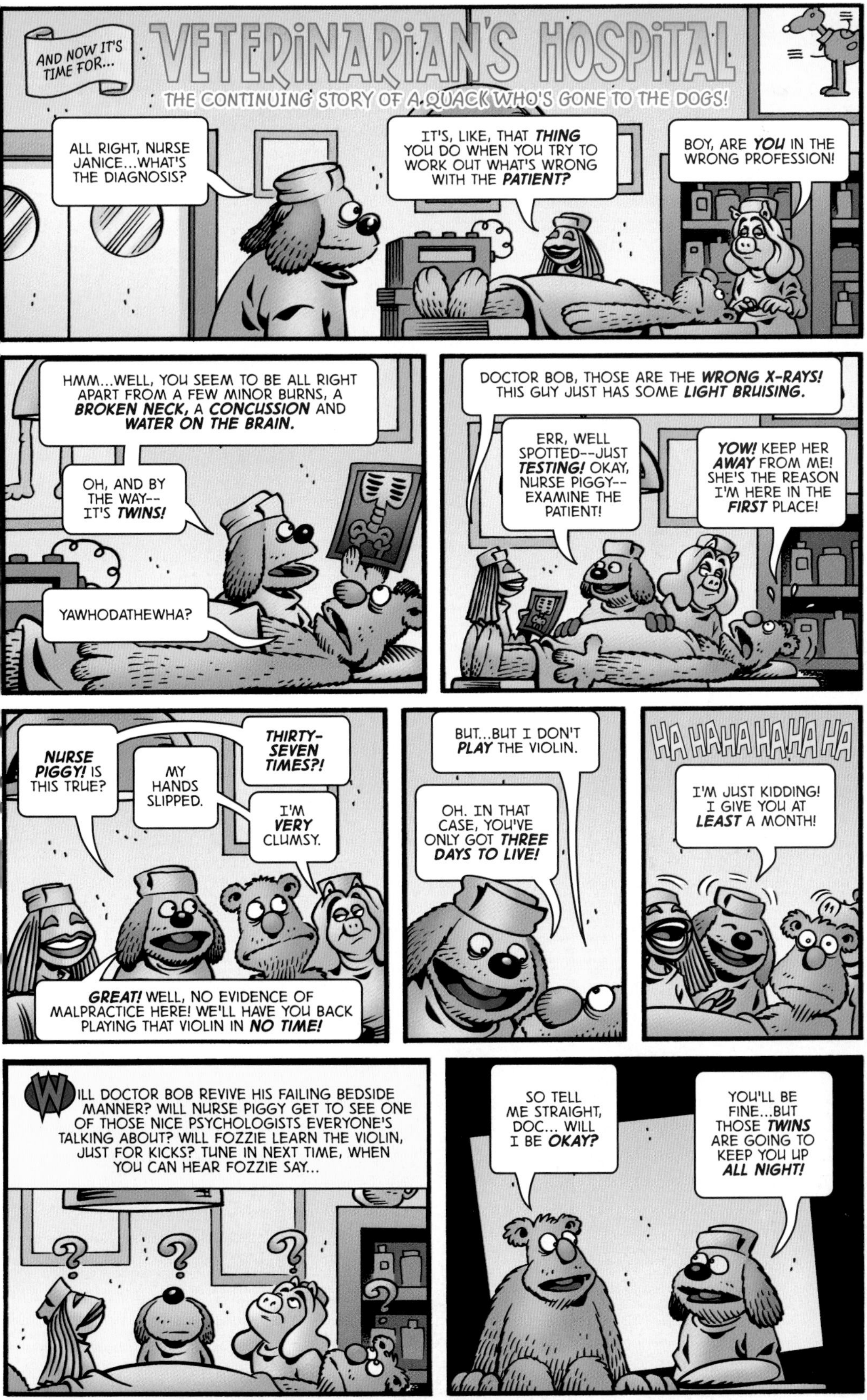
AND NOW IT'S TIME FOR...
VETERINARIAN'S HOSPITAL
THE CONTINUING STORY OF A QUACK WHO'S GONE TO THE DOGS!
ALL RIGHT, NURSE JANICE...WHAT'S THE DIAGNOSIS?
IT'S, LIKE, THAT THING YOU DO WHEN YOU TRY TO WORK OUT WHAT'S WRONG WITH THE PATIENT?
BOY, ARE YOU IN THE WRONG PROFESSION!
HMM...WELL, YOU SEEM TO BE ALL RIGHT APART FROM A FEW MINOR BURNS, A BROKEN NECK, A CONCUSSION AND WATER ON THE BRAIN.
OH, AND BY THE WAY-- IT'S TWINS!
YAWHODATHEWHA?
DOCTOR BOB, THOSE ARE THE WRONG X-RAYS! THIS GUY JUST HAS SOME LIGHT BRUISING.
ERR, WELL SPOTTED--JUST TESTING! OKAY, NURSE PIGGY-- EXAMINE THE PATIENT!
YOW! KEEP HER AWAY FROM ME! SHE'S THE REASON I'M HERE IN THE FIRST PLACE!
NURSE PIGGY! IS THIS TRUE?
MY HANDS SLIPPED.
THIRTY-SEVEN TIMES?!
I'M VERY CLUMSY.
GREAT! WELL, NO EVIDENCE OF MALPRACTICE HERE! WE'LL HAVE YOU BACK PLAYING THAT VIOLIN IN NO TIME!
BUT...BUT I DON'T PLAY THE VIOLIN.
OH. IN THAT CASE, YOU'VE ONLY GOT THREE DAYS TO LIVE!
HA HAHA HAHAHA HA
I'M JUST KIDDING! I GIVE YOU AT LEAST A MONTH!
WILL DOCTOR BOB REVIVE HIS FAILING BEDSIDE MANNER? WILL NURSE PIGGY GET TO SEE ONE OF THOSE NICE PSYCHOLOGISTS EVERYONE'S TALKING ABOUT? WILL FOZZIE LEARN THE VIOLIN, JUST FOR KICKS? TUNE IN NEXT TIME, WHEN YOU CAN HEAR FOZZIE SAY...
SO TELL ME STRAIGHT, DOC... WILL I BE OKAY?
YOU'LL BE FINE...BUT THOSE TWINS ARE GOING TO KEEP YOU UP ALL NIGHT!

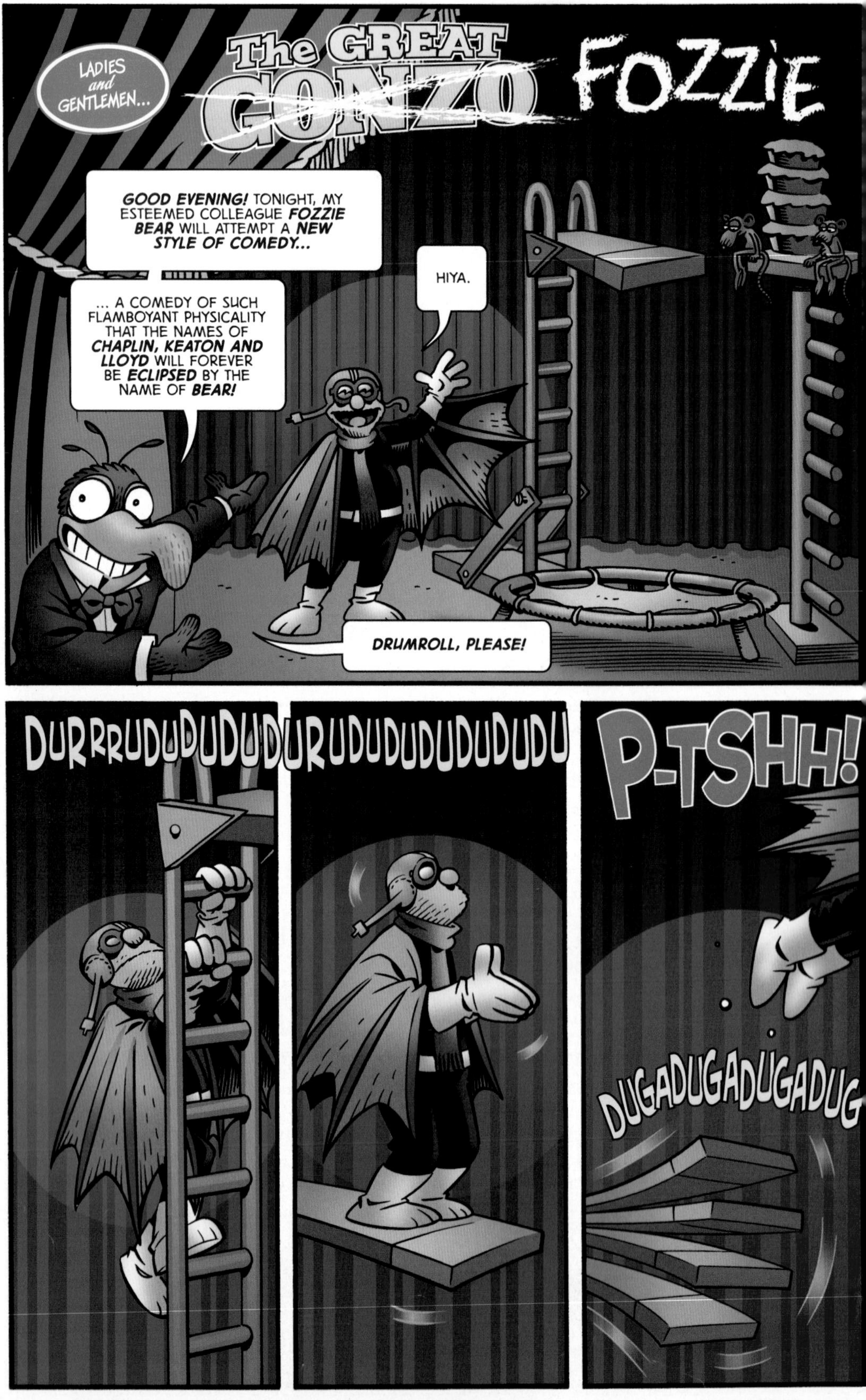
LADIES and GENTLEMEN...
The GREAT GONZO
FOZZIE
GOOD EVENING! TONIGHT, MY ESTEEMED COLLEAGUE FOZZIE BEAR WILL ATTEMPT A NEW STYLE OF COMEDY...
... A COMEDY OF SUCH FLAMBOYANT PHYSICALITY THAT THE NAMES OF CHAPLIN, KEATON AND LLOYD WILL FOREVER BE ECLIPSED BY THE NAME OF BEAR!
HIYA.
DRUMROLL, PLEASE!
DURRRUDUDUDUDURUDUDUDUDUDUDU
P-TSHH!
DUGADUGADUGADUG

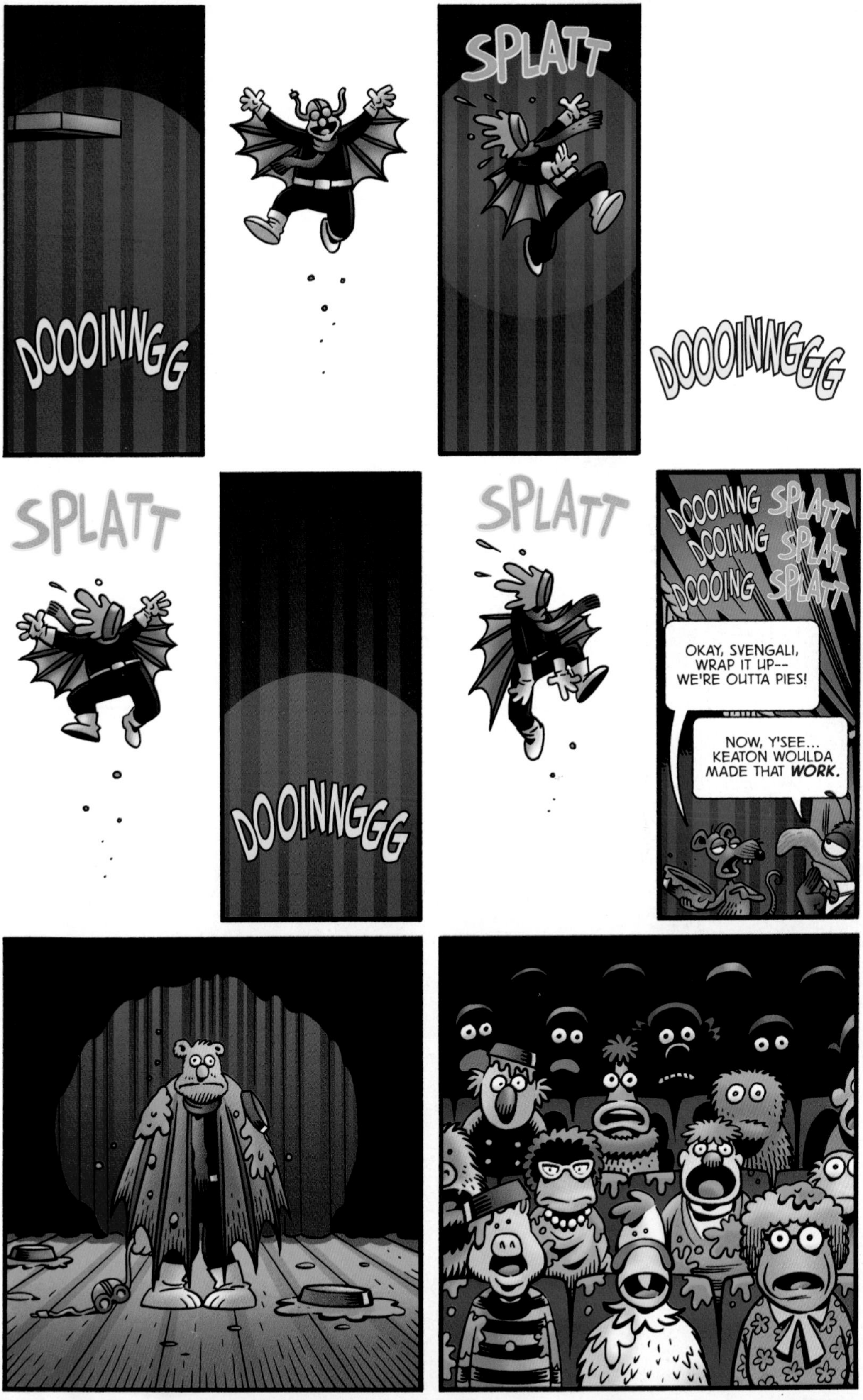
DOOOINNGG
SPLATT
DOOOINNGGG
SPLATT
DOOINNGGG
SPLATT
DOOOINNG SPLATT
DOOINNG SPLAT
DOOOING SPLATT
OKAY, SVENGALI, WRAP IT UP-- WE'RE OUTTA PIES!
NOW, Y'SEE... KEATON WOULDA MADE THAT **WORK.**

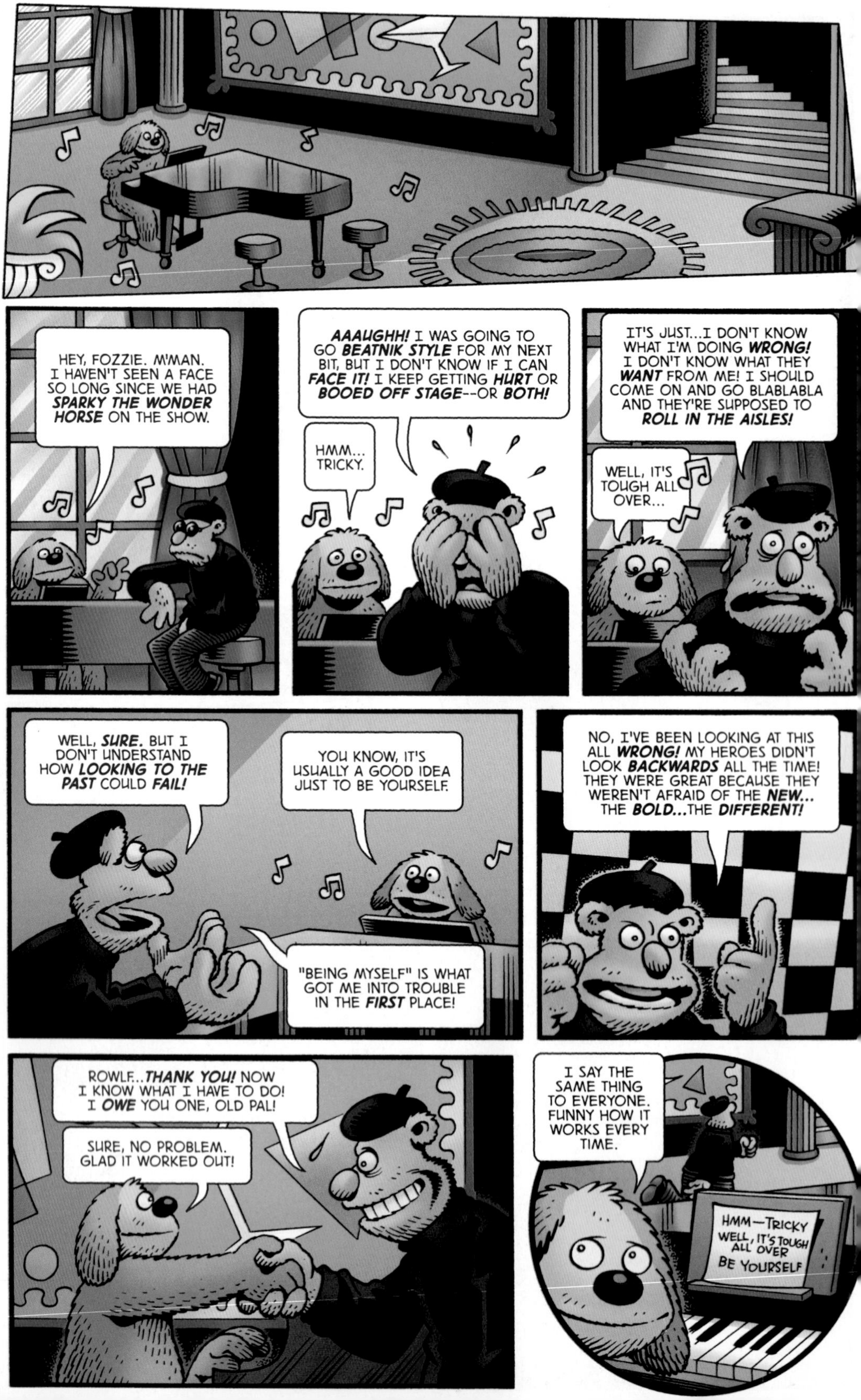
HEY, FOZZIE. M'MAN. I HAVEN'T SEEN A FACE SO LONG SINCE WE HAD SPARKY THE WONDER HORSE ON THE SHOW.
AAAUGHH! I WAS GOING TO GO BEATNIK STYLE FOR MY NEXT BIT, BUT I DON'T KNOW IF I CAN FACE IT! I KEEP GETTING HURT OR BOOED OFF STAGE--OR BOTH!
HMM... TRICKY.
IT'S JUST...I DON'T KNOW WHAT I'M DOING WRONG! I DON'T KNOW WHAT THEY WANT FROM ME! I SHOULD COME ON AND GO BLABLABLA AND THEY'RE SUPPOSED TO ROLL IN THE AISLES!
WELL, IT'S TOUGH ALL OVER...
WELL, SURE. BUT I DON'T UNDERSTAND HOW LOOKING TO THE PAST COULD FAIL!
YOU KNOW, IT'S USUALLY A GOOD IDEA JUST TO BE YOURSELF.
"BEING MYSELF" IS WHAT GOT ME INTO TROUBLE IN THE FIRST PLACE!
NO, I'VE BEEN LOOKING AT THIS ALL WRONG! MY HEROES DIDN'T LOOK BACKWARDS ALL THE TIME! THEY WERE GREAT BECAUSE THEY WEREN'T AFRAID OF THE NEW... THE BOLD...THE DIFFERENT!
ROWLF...THANK YOU! NOW I KNOW WHAT I HAVE TO DO! I OWE YOU ONE, OLD PAL!
SURE, NO PROBLEM. GLAD IT WORKED OUT!
I SAY THE SAME THING TO EVERYONE. FUNNY HOW IT WORKS EVERY TIME.
HMM—TRICKY
WELL, IT'S TOUGH ALL OVER
BE YOURSELF

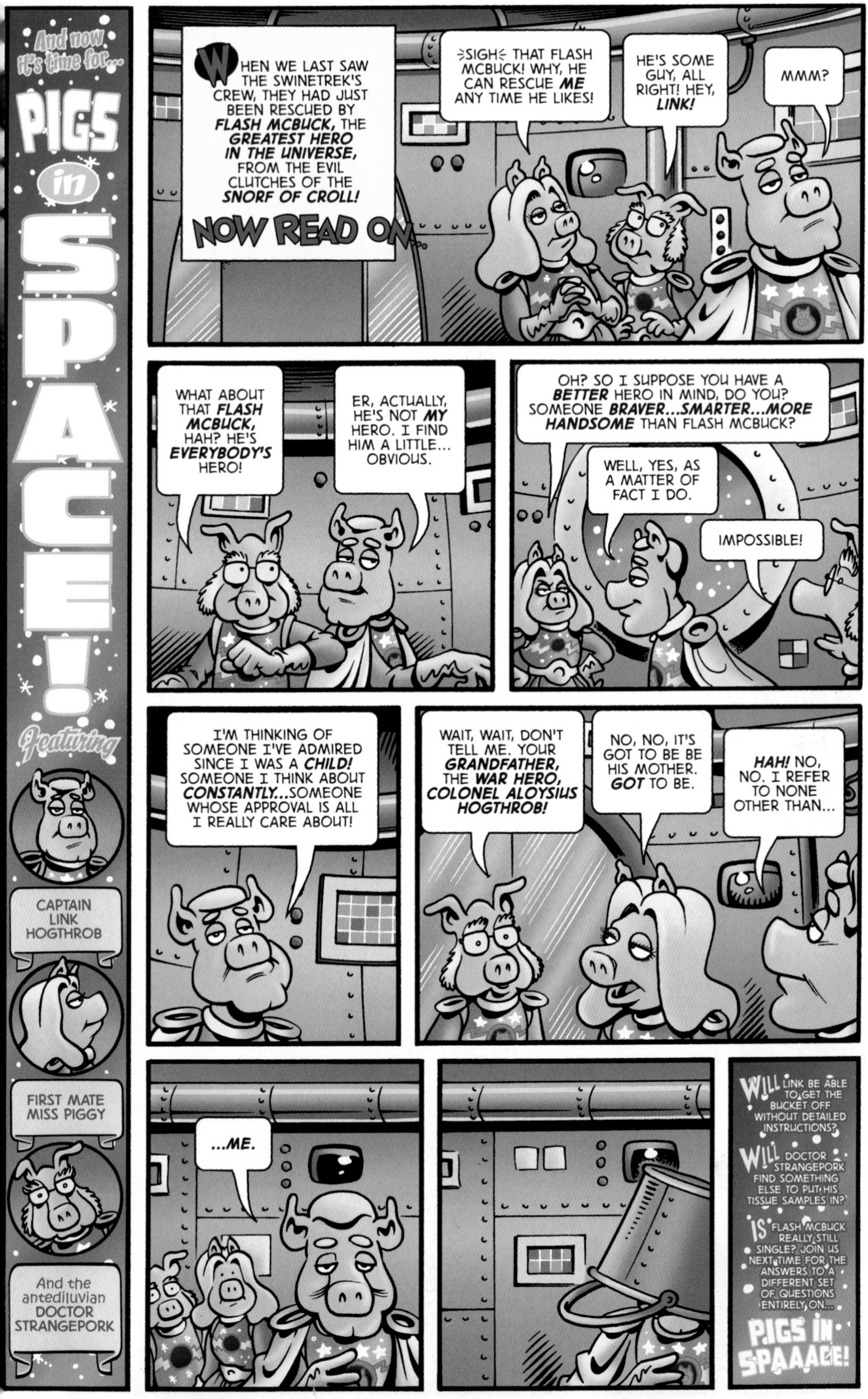
And now it's time for...
PIGS in SPACE!
Featuring
CAPTAIN LINK HOGTHROB
FIRST MATE MISS PIGGY
And the antediluvian DOCTOR STRANGEPORK
WHEN WE LAST SAW THE SWINETREK'S CREW, THEY HAD JUST BEEN RESCUED BY FLASH MCBUCK, THE GREATEST HERO IN THE UNIVERSE, FROM THE EVIL CLUTCHES OF THE SNORF OF CROLL!
NOW READ ON...
SIGH THAT FLASH MCBUCK! WHY, HE CAN RESCUE ME ANY TIME HE LIKES!
HE'S SOME GUY, ALL RIGHT! HEY, LINK!
MMM?
WHAT ABOUT THAT FLASH MCBUCK, HAH? HE'S EVERYBODY'S HERO!
ER, ACTUALLY, HE'S NOT MY HERO. I FIND HIM A LITTLE... OBVIOUS.
OH? SO I SUPPOSE YOU HAVE A BETTER HERO IN MIND, DO YOU? SOMEONE BRAVER...SMARTER...MORE HANDSOME THAN FLASH MCBUCK?
WELL, YES, AS A MATTER OF FACT I DO.
IMPOSSIBLE!
I'M THINKING OF SOMEONE I'VE ADMIRED SINCE I WAS A CHILD! SOMEONE I THINK ABOUT CONSTANTLY...SOMEONE WHOSE APPROVAL IS ALL I REALLY CARE ABOUT!
WAIT, WAIT, DON'T TELL ME. YOUR GRANDFATHER, THE WAR HERO, COLONEL ALOYSIUS HOGTHROB!
NO, NO, IT'S GOT TO BE BE HIS MOTHER. GOT TO BE.
HAH! NO, NO. I REFER TO NONE OTHER THAN...
...ME.
WILL LINK BE ABLE TO GET THE BUCKET OFF WITHOUT DETAILED INSTRUCTIONS?
WILL DOCTOR STRANGEPORK FIND SOMETHING ELSE TO PUT HIS TISSUE SAMPLES IN?
IS FLASH MCBUCK REALLY STILL SINGLE? JOIN US NEXT TIME FOR THE ANSWERS TO A DIFFERENT SET OF QUESTIONS ENTIRELY, ON...
PIGS IN SPAAACE!

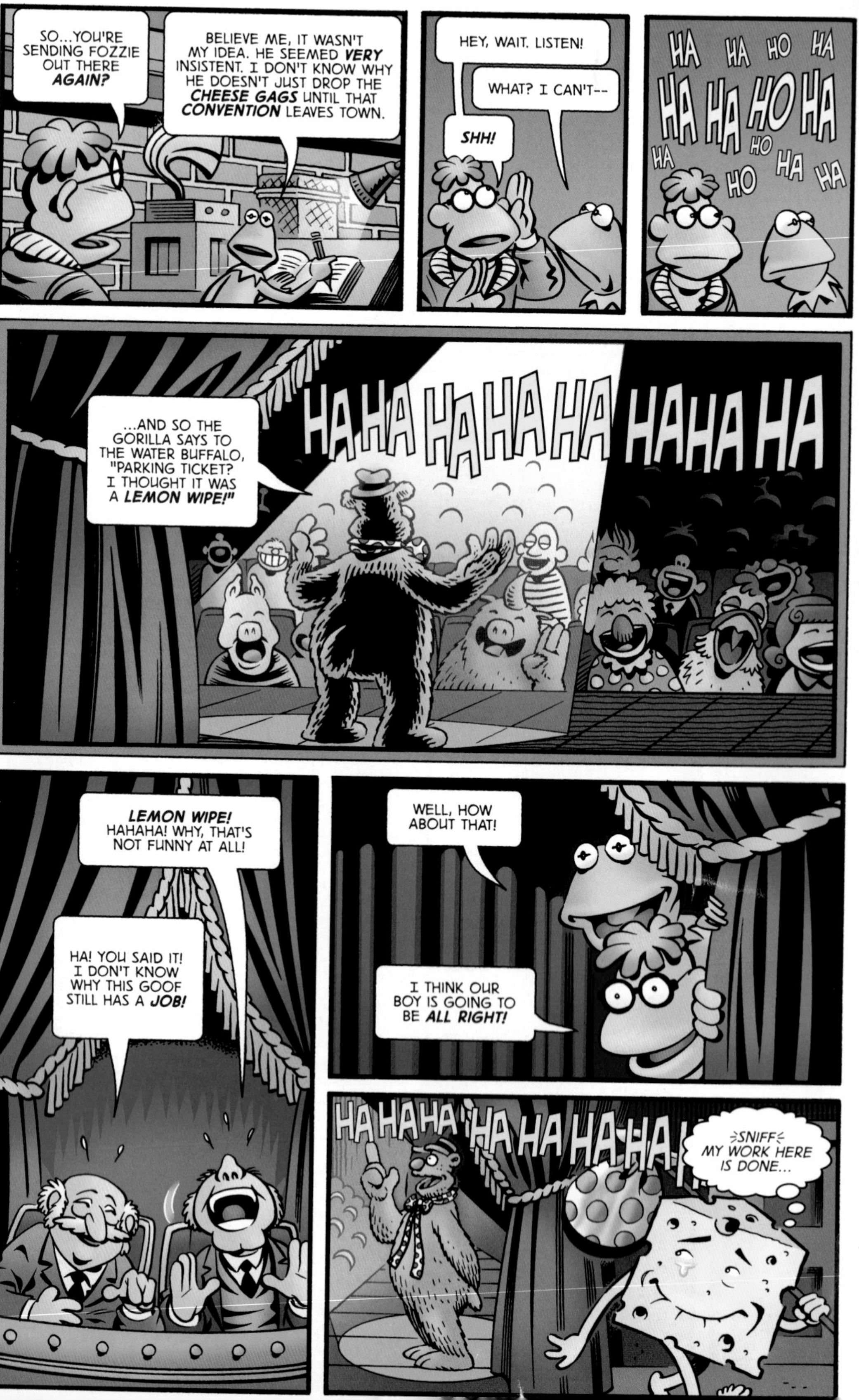
SO...YOU'RE SENDING FOZZIE OUT THERE AGAIN?
BELIEVE ME, IT WASN'T MY IDEA. HE SEEMED VERY INSISTENT. I DON'T KNOW WHY HE DOESN'T JUST DROP THE CHEESE GAGS UNTIL THAT CONVENTION LEAVES TOWN.
HEY, WAIT. LISTEN!
WHAT? I CAN'T--
SHH!
HA HA HO HA
HA HA HO HA
HA HO HA
HO HA HA
...AND SO THE GORILLA SAYS TO THE WATER BUFFALO, "PARKING TICKET? I THOUGHT IT WAS A LEMON WIPE!"
HAHA HAHAHA HAHAHA
LEMON WIPE! HAHAHA! WHY, THAT'S NOT FUNNY AT ALL!
HA! YOU SAID IT! I DON'T KNOW WHY THIS GOOF STILL HAS A JOB!
WELL, HOW ABOUT THAT!
I THINK OUR BOY IS GOING TO BE ALL RIGHT!
HAHAHA HA HA HA HA
SNIFF MY WORK HERE IS DONE...

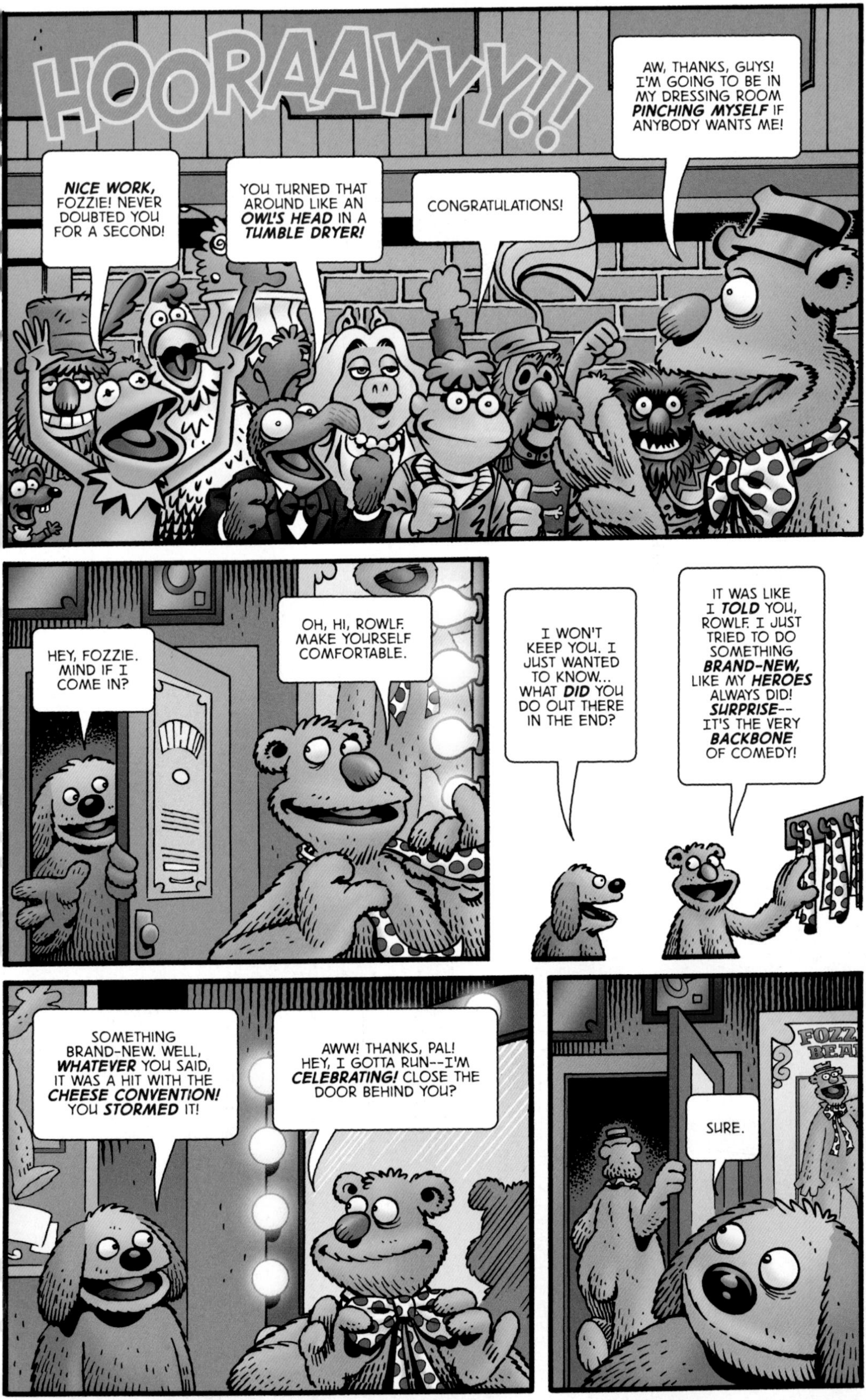
HOORAAYYY!!
NICE WORK, FOZZIE! NEVER DOUBTED YOU FOR A SECOND!
YOU TURNED THAT AROUND LIKE AN OWL'S HEAD IN A TUMBLE DRYER!
CONGRATULATIONS!
AW, THANKS, GUYS! I'M GOING TO BE IN MY DRESSING ROOM PINCHING MYSELF IF ANYBODY WANTS ME!
HEY, FOZZIE. MIND IF I COME IN?
OH, HI, ROWLF. MAKE YOURSELF COMFORTABLE.
I WON'T KEEP YOU. I JUST WANTED TO KNOW... WHAT DID YOU DO OUT THERE IN THE END?
IT WAS LIKE I TOLD YOU, ROWLF. I JUST TRIED TO DO SOMETHING BRAND-NEW, LIKE MY HEROES ALWAYS DID! SURPRISE-- IT'S THE VERY BACKBONE OF COMEDY!
SOMETHING BRAND-NEW. WELL, WHATEVER YOU SAID, IT WAS A HIT WITH THE CHEESE CONVENTION! YOU STORMED IT!
AWW! THANKS, PAL! HEY, I GOTTA RUN--I'M CELEBRATING! CLOSE THE DOOR BEHIND YOU?
SURE.

FOZZIE'S SCRIPT! I'VE JUST *GOT* TO KNOW!

Script

So the dodo says to the zebra, "I'd like some ~~cheese~~ milk please." And the zebra says, "~~Cheese?~~ Milk? I thought it was a sub-cutaneous discharge!" So ~~he~~ goes, "Phew! That's ~~a~~ relief! I'm not ~~only~~ a doctor, ~~I run~~ I'm a milk man from ~~cheese shop in Des~~ ~~ines!~~" But ~~cheese~~ milk funny business...

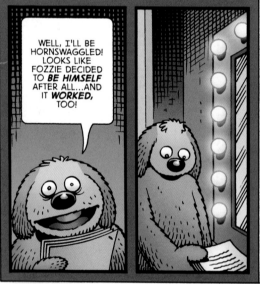

WELL, I'LL BE HORNSWAGGLED! LOOKS LIKE FOZZIE DECIDED TO *BE HIMSELF* AFTER ALL...AND IT *WORKED,* TOO!

FOZZI BEAR

THE FUNNIEST BE IN THE WORL

HMMM...I WONDER IF I SHOULD TELL HIM ABOUT THE DAIRY FARMERS' CONVENTION NEXT WEEK...?

The End

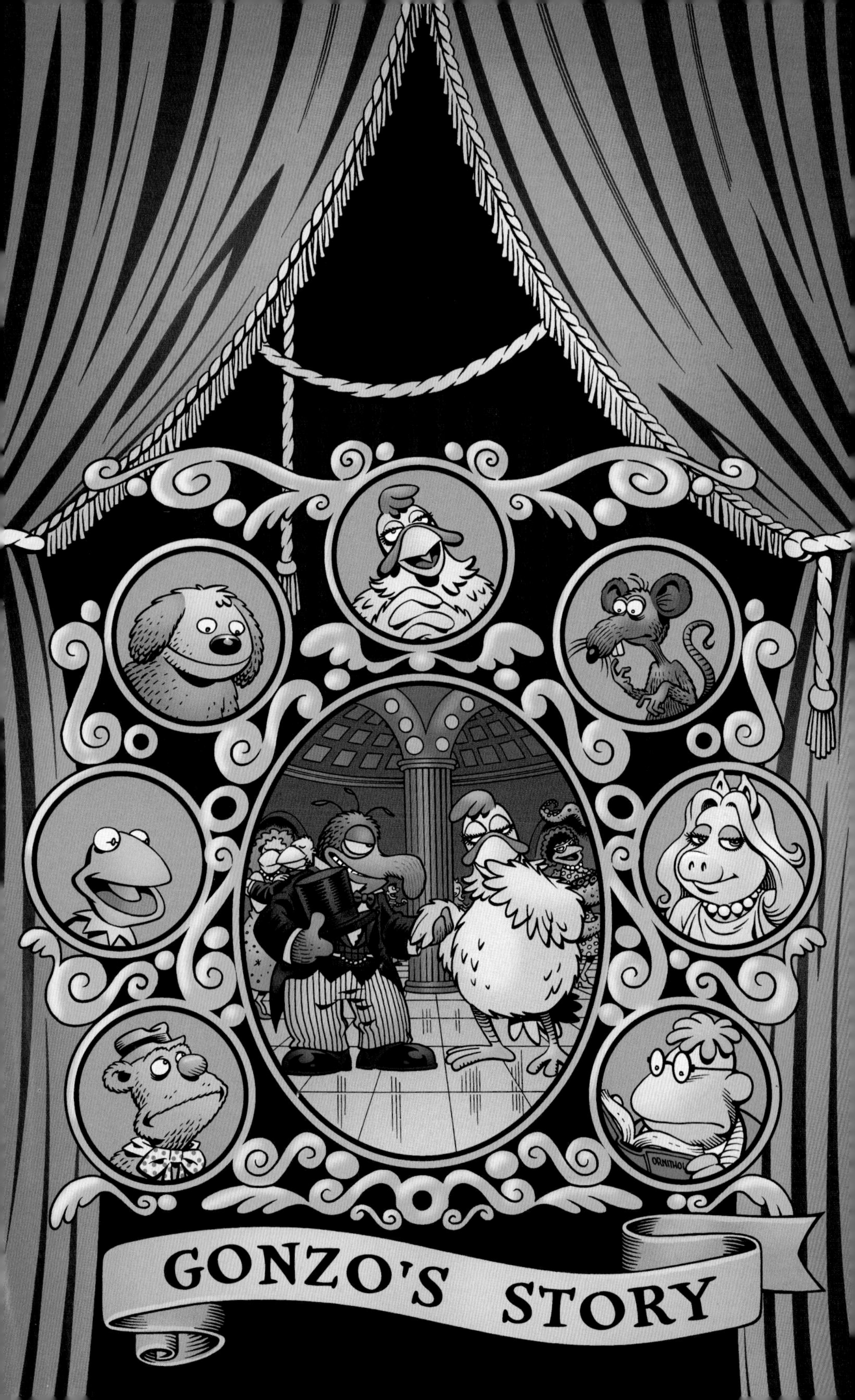
ORNITHOL
GONZO'S STORY

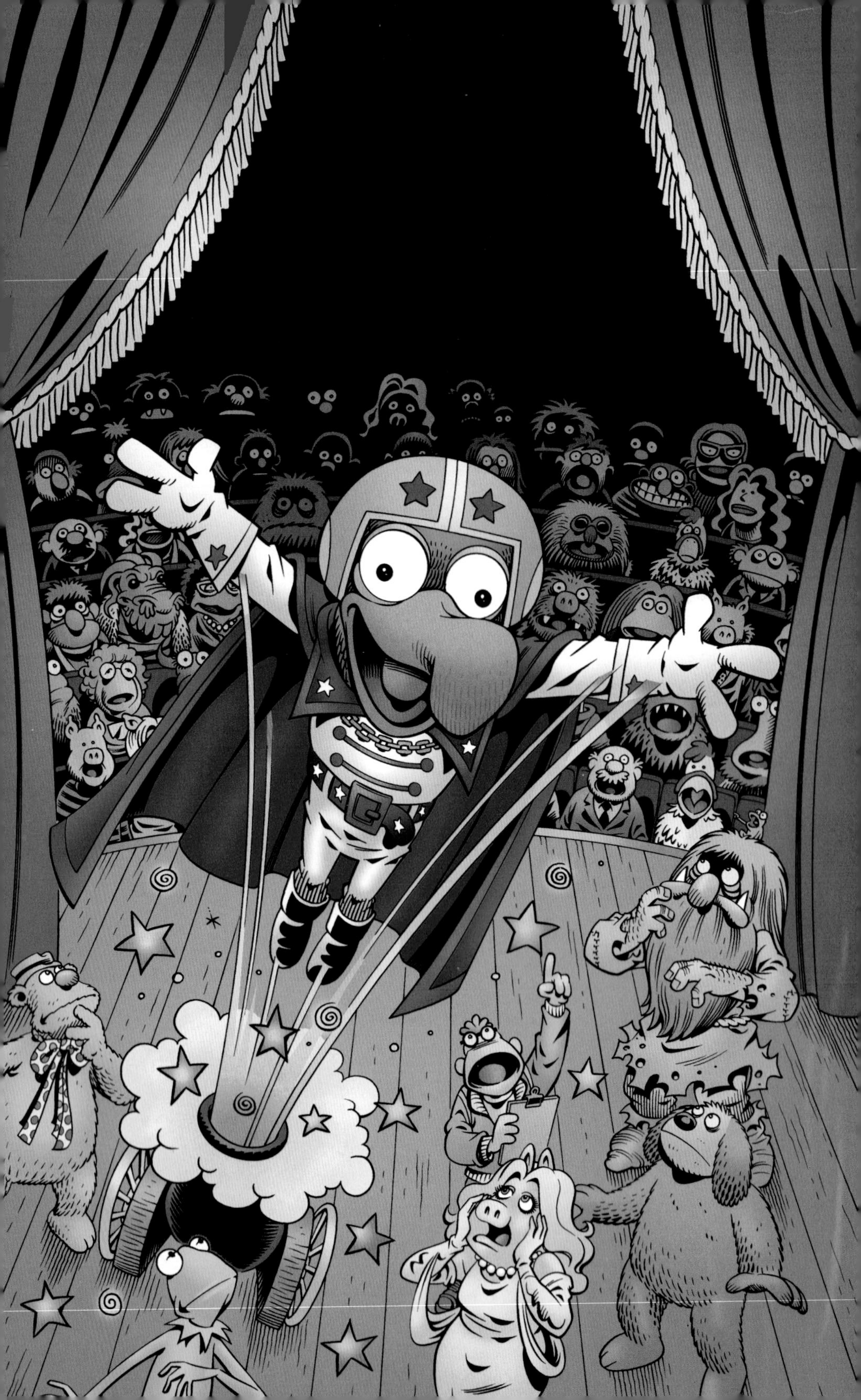

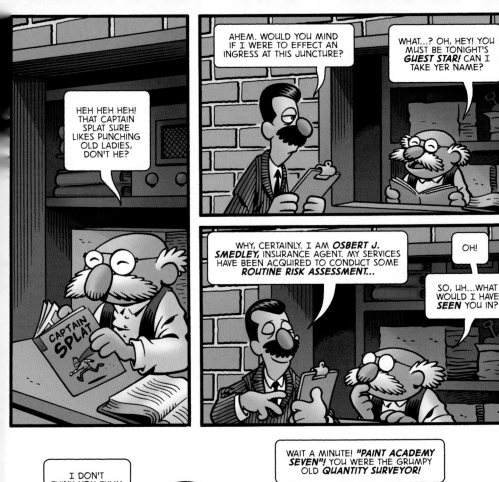

HEH HEH HEH! THAT CAPTAIN SPLAT SURE LIKES PUNCHING OLD LADIES, DON'T HE?

CAPTAIN SPLAT

AHEM. WOULD YOU MIND IF I WERE TO EFFECT AN INGRESS AT THIS JUNCTURE?

WHAT...? OH, HEY! YOU MUST BE TONIGHT'S **GUEST STAR!** CAN I TAKE YER NAME?

WHY, CERTAINLY. I AM **OSBERT J. SMEDLEY,** INSURANCE AGENT. MY SERVICES HAVE BEEN ACQUIRED TO CONDUCT SOME **ROUTINE RISK ASSESSMENT...**

OH!

SO, UH...WHAT WOULD I HAVE **SEEN** YOU IN?

WAIT A MINUTE! **"PAINT ACADEMY SEVEN"!** YOU WERE THE GRUMPY OLD **QUANTITY SURVEYOR!**

I DON'T THINK YOU FULLY APPREHEND THE **NATURE** OF--

HAW! I ALMOST BUST A GUT! YOU WERE **HILARIOUS!**

YOU'RE MISTAKEN, SIR. I--

HEY, WHAT'S SPLAT BAXTER LIKE IN REAL LIFE? I ALWAYS HEARD HE WAS A REAL NICE FELLER, BUT A BIT STAND-OFFISH. IS HE REALLY STEPPIN' OUT WITH **LOLA VAVOOM?** IF SHE AIN'T HAD SOME WORK DONE, I'LL EAT MY **TIE!**

HE'S QUITE RIGHT, YOU KNOW--THE QUANTITY SURVEYOR IN "PAINT ACADEMY SEVEN" **WAS** RATHER DROLL...

AND THAT BIT WITH THE COW! HEY, HOW DID THEY GET IT TO BREAKDANCE WITHOUT FALLING OFF THE STEPLADDER?

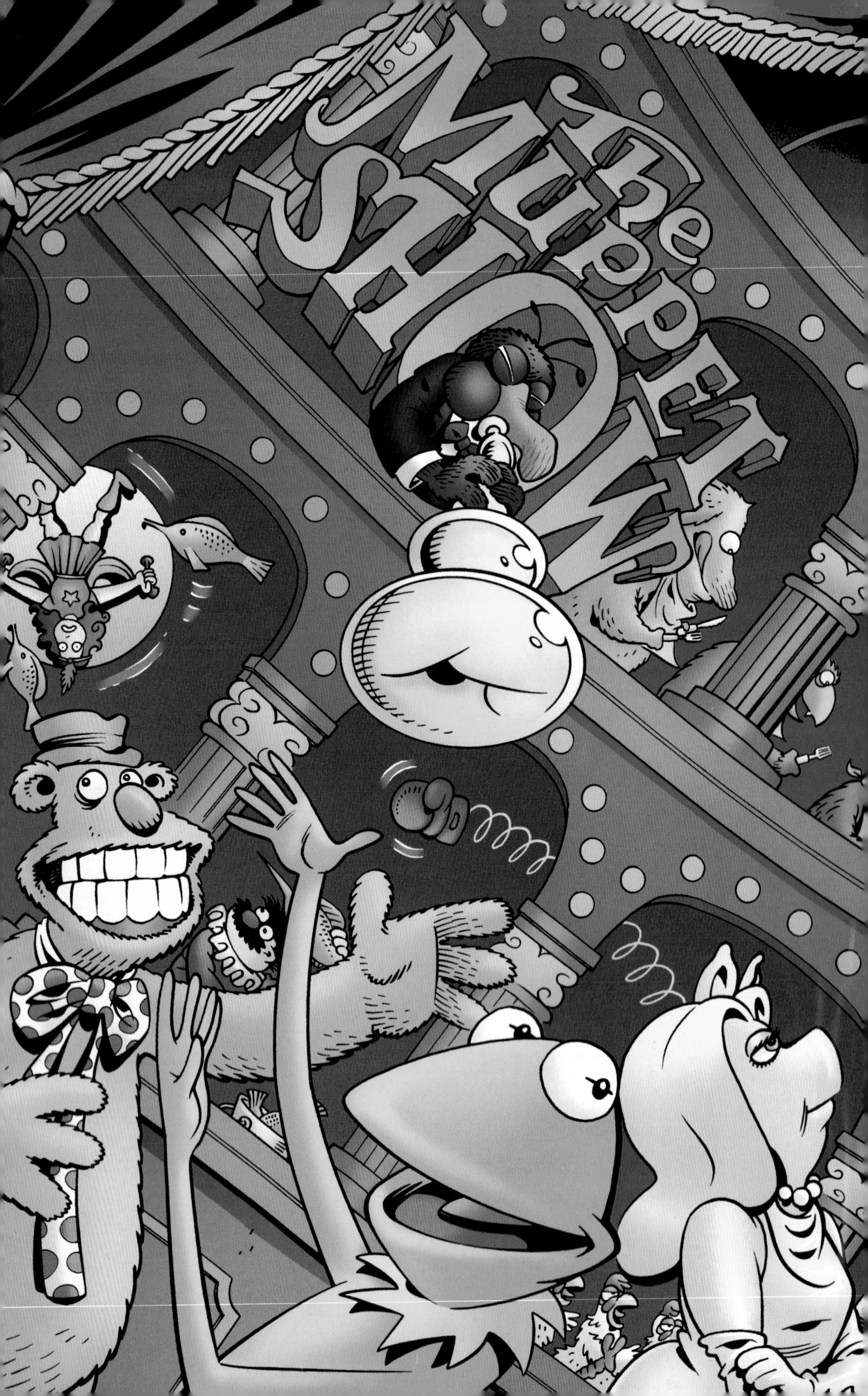
The Muppet Show

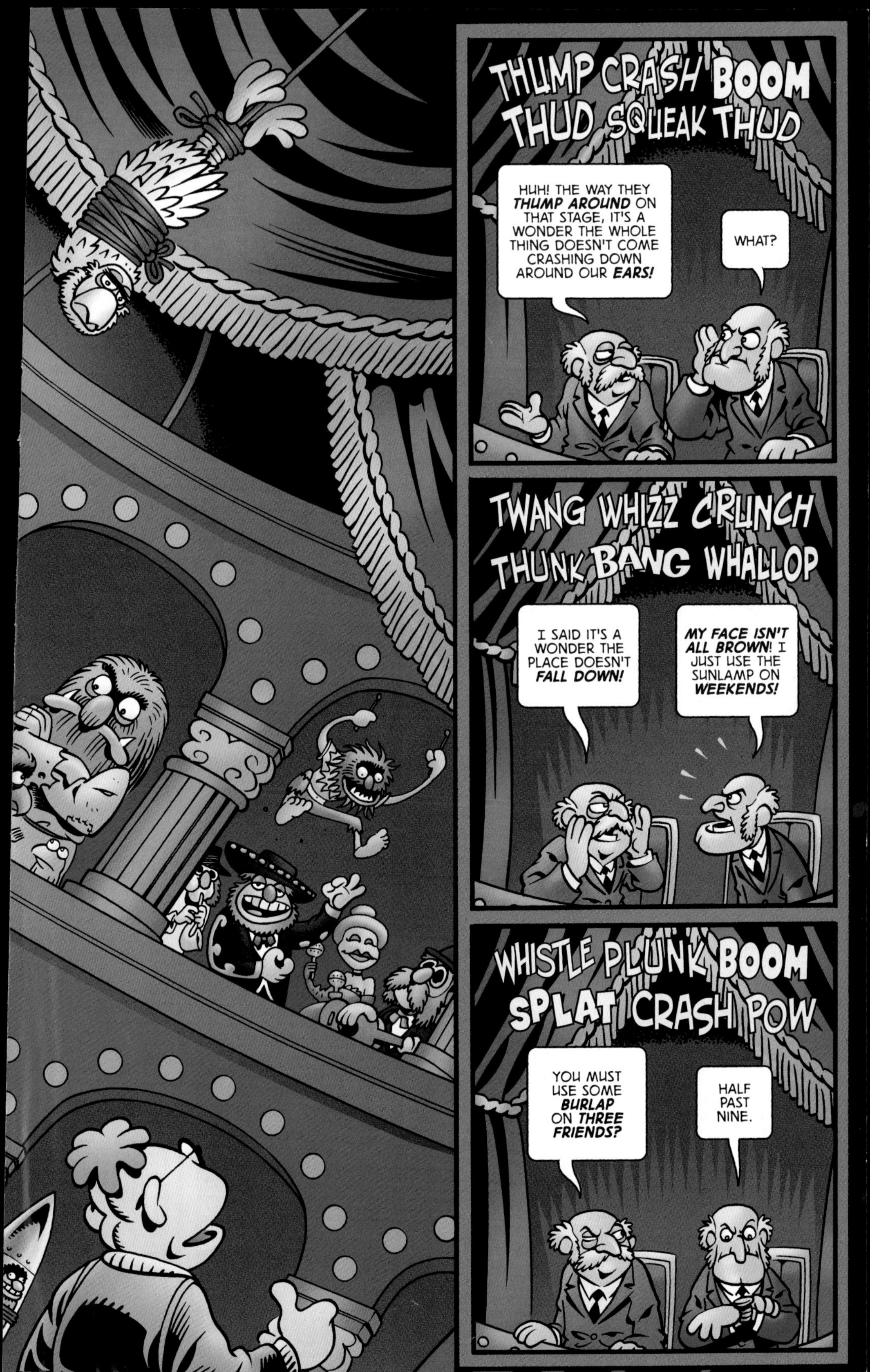

THUMP CRASH BOOM
THUD SQUEAK THUD
HUH! THE WAY THEY *THUMP AROUND* ON THAT STAGE, IT'S A WONDER THE WHOLE THING DOESN'T COME CRASHING DOWN AROUND OUR *EARS!*
WHAT?
TWANG WHIZZ CRUNCH
THUNK BANG WHALLOP
I SAID IT'S A WONDER THE PLACE DOESN'T *FALL DOWN!*
MY FACE ISN'T ALL BROWN! I JUST USE THE SUNLAMP ON *WEEKENDS!*
WHISTLE PLUNK BOOM
SPLAT CRASH POW
YOU MUST USE SOME *BURLAP* ON *THREE FRIENDS?*
HALF PAST NINE.

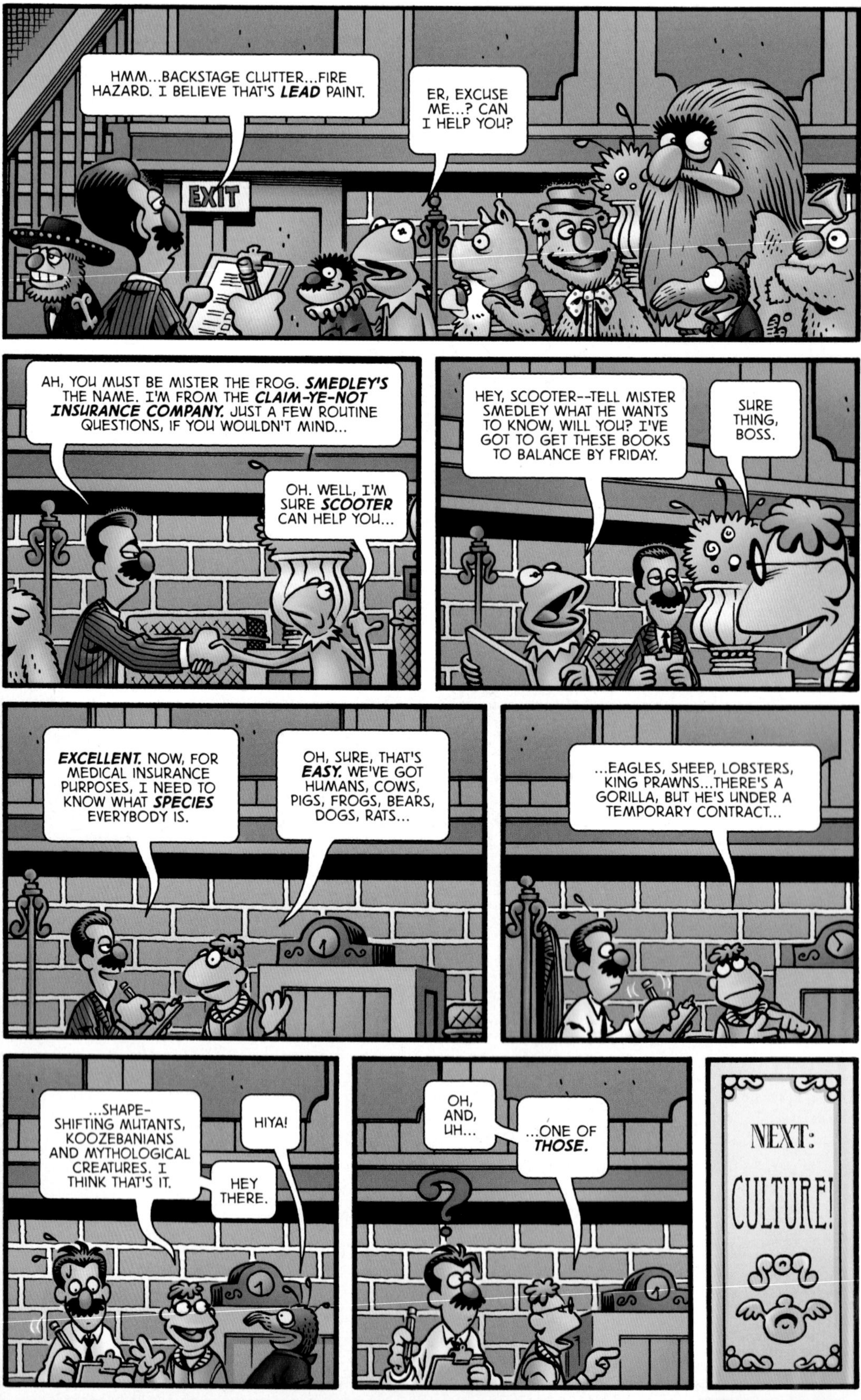
HMM...BACKSTAGE CLUTTER...FIRE HAZARD. I BELIEVE THAT'S **LEAD** PAINT.
EXIT
ER, EXCUSE ME...? CAN I HELP YOU?
AH, YOU MUST BE MISTER THE FROG. **SMEDLEY'S** THE NAME. I'M FROM THE **CLAIM-YE-NOT INSURANCE COMPANY.** JUST A FEW ROUTINE QUESTIONS, IF YOU WOULDN'T MIND...
OH. WELL, I'M SURE **SCOOTER** CAN HELP YOU...
HEY, SCOOTER--TELL MISTER SMEDLEY WHAT HE WANTS TO KNOW, WILL YOU? I'VE GOT TO GET THESE BOOKS TO BALANCE BY FRIDAY.
SURE THING, BOSS.
EXCELLENT. NOW, FOR MEDICAL INSURANCE PURPOSES, I NEED TO KNOW WHAT **SPECIES** EVERYBODY IS.
OH, SURE, THAT'S **EASY.** WE'VE GOT HUMANS, COWS, PIGS, FROGS, BEARS, DOGS, RATS...
...EAGLES, SHEEP, LOBSTERS, KING PRAWNS...THERE'S A GORILLA, BUT HE'S UNDER A TEMPORARY CONTRACT...
...SHAPE-SHIFTING MUTANTS, KOOZEBANIANS AND MYTHOLOGICAL CREATURES. I THINK THAT'S IT.
HIYA!
HEY THERE.
OH, AND, UH...
...ONE OF **THOSE.**
NEXT:
CULTURE!

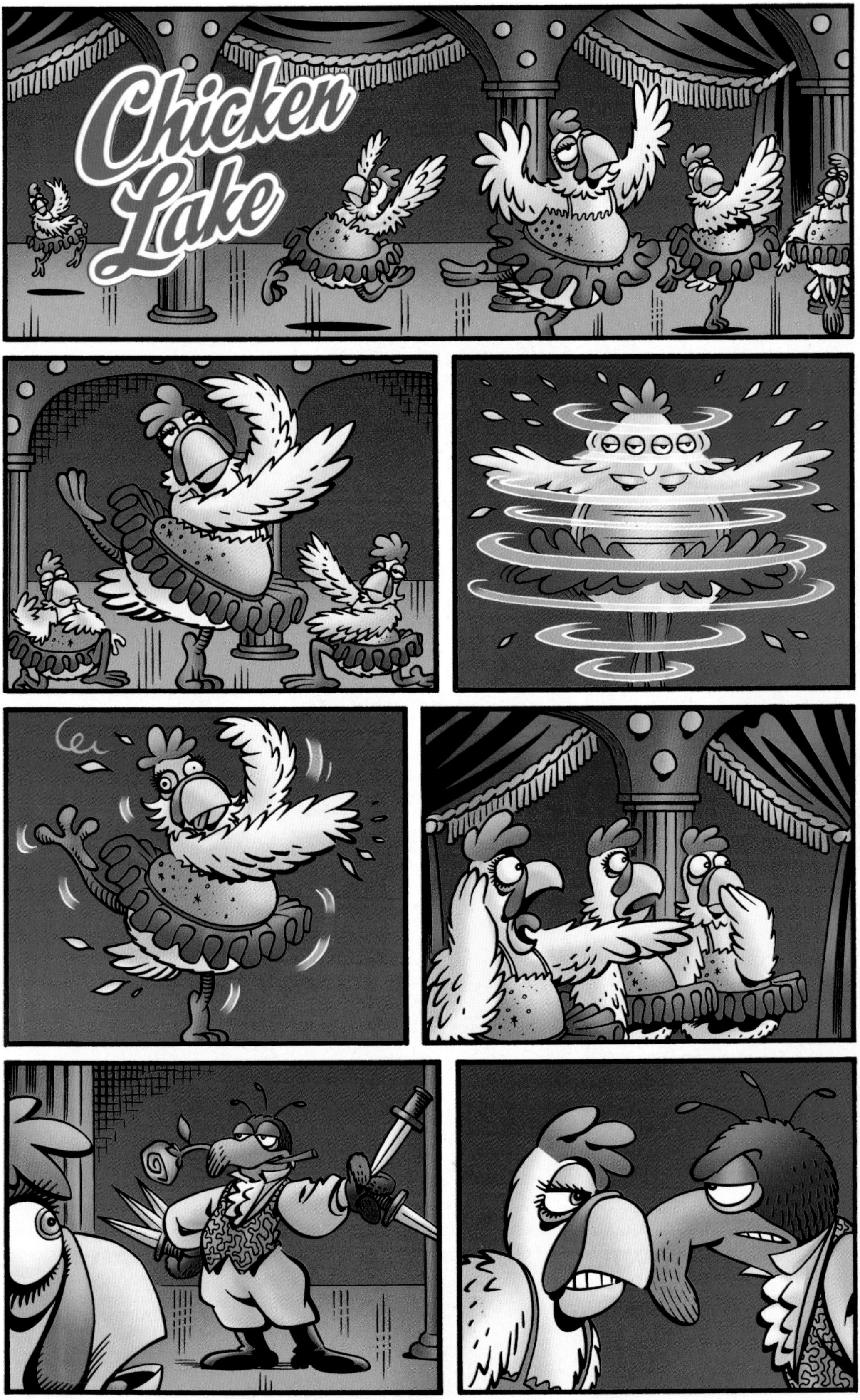
Chicken Lake

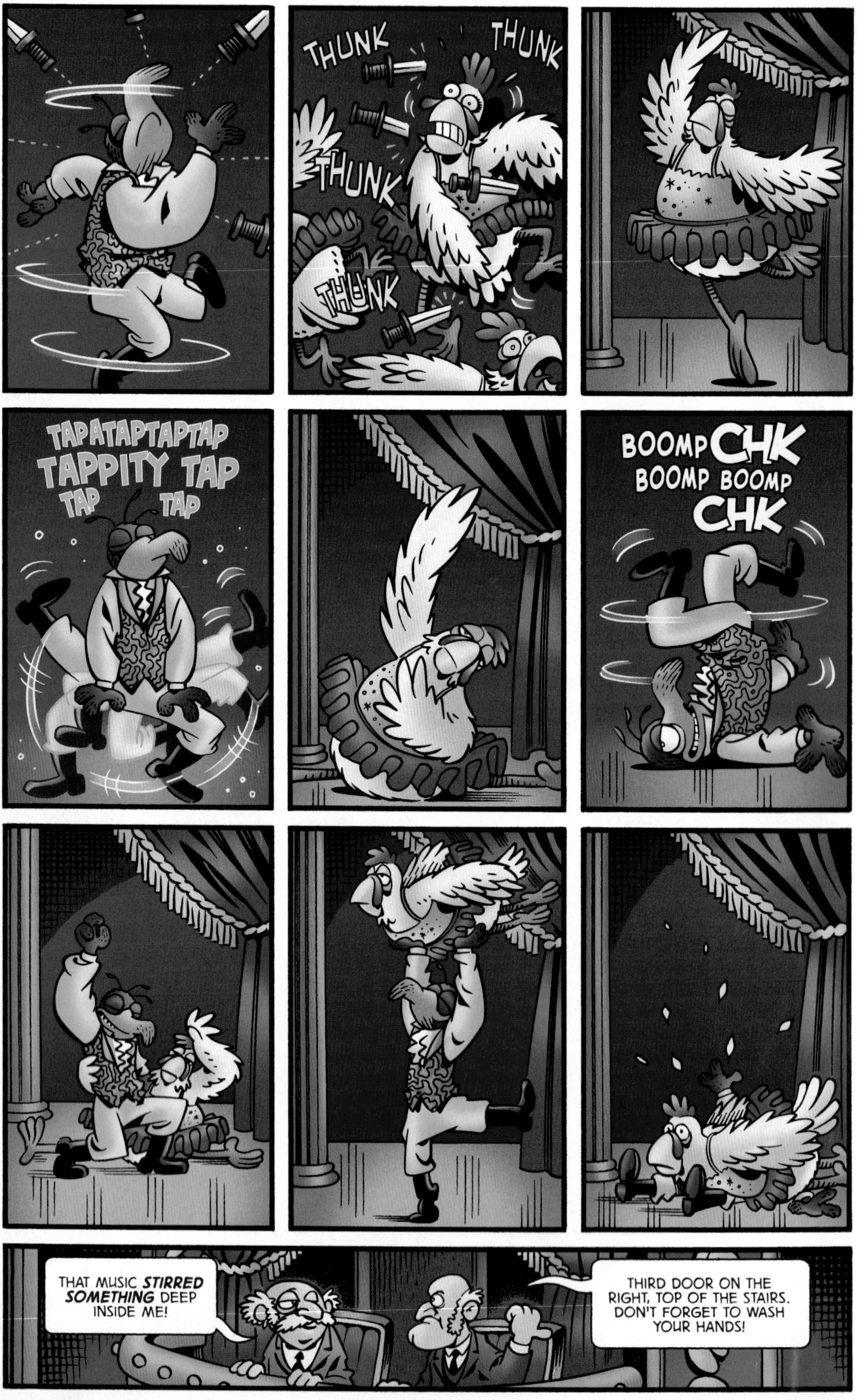
THUNK
THUNK
THUNK
THUNK
TAPATAPTAPTAPTAP
TAPPITY TAP
TAP
TAP
BOOMP CHK
BOOMP BOOMP
CHK
THAT MUSIC STIRRED SOMETHING DEEP INSIDE ME!
THIRD DOOR ON THE RIGHT, TOP OF THE STAIRS. DON'T FORGET TO WASH YOUR HANDS!

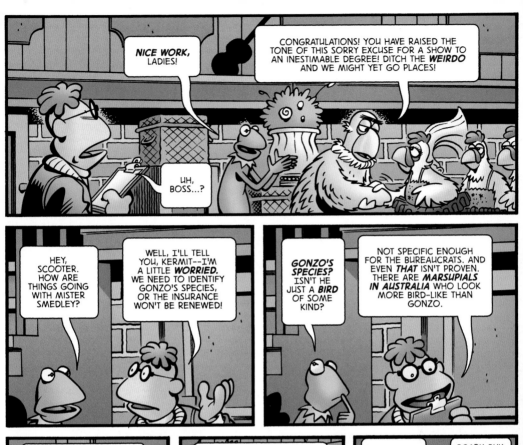

NICE WORK, LADIES!

CONGRATULATIONS! YOU HAVE RAISED THE TONE OF THIS SORRY EXCUSE FOR A SHOW TO AN INESTIMABLE DEGREE! DITCH THE *WEIRDO* AND WE MIGHT YET GO PLACES!

UH, BOSS...?

HEY, SCOOTER. HOW ARE THINGS GOING WITH MISTER SMEDLEY?

WELL, I'LL TELL YOU, KERMIT--I'M A LITTLE *WORRIED.* WE NEED TO IDENTIFY GONZO'S SPECIES, OR THE INSURANCE WON'T BE RENEWED!

GONZO'S SPECIES? ISN'T HE JUST A *BIRD* OF SOME KIND?

NOT SPECIFIC ENOUGH FOR THE BUREAUCRATS. AND EVEN *THAT* ISN'T PROVEN. THERE ARE *MARSUPIALS IN AUSTRALIA* WHO LOOK MORE BIRD-LIKE THAN GONZO.

EXCUSE ME, COBBER! CAN YA TELL US WHERE *LEW ZEALAND* IS?

HE'S USUALLY TENDING HIS FISH TANKS OUT BACK.

EXIT

SWEET AS, MATE.

YOU KNOW, WE COULD ALWAYS JUST *ASK GONZO.*

HEY, GONZO-- WHAT *ARE* YOU, EXACTLY?

GEE, I NEVER REALLY *THOUGHT* ABOUT IT.

WELL, DOES ANYONE *ELSE* KNOW?

CAMILLA? ANY IDEA?

BGARK BUK BUK BUK BGARK

AWWW! THAT'S *SWEET* OF YOU, HONEY!

WHAT DID SHE SAY? *WHAT DID SHE SAY?*

SHE SAID I'LL ALWAYS BE A *CHICKEN* TO HER! ISN'T THAT *ADORABLE?*

YEAH. ADORABLE.

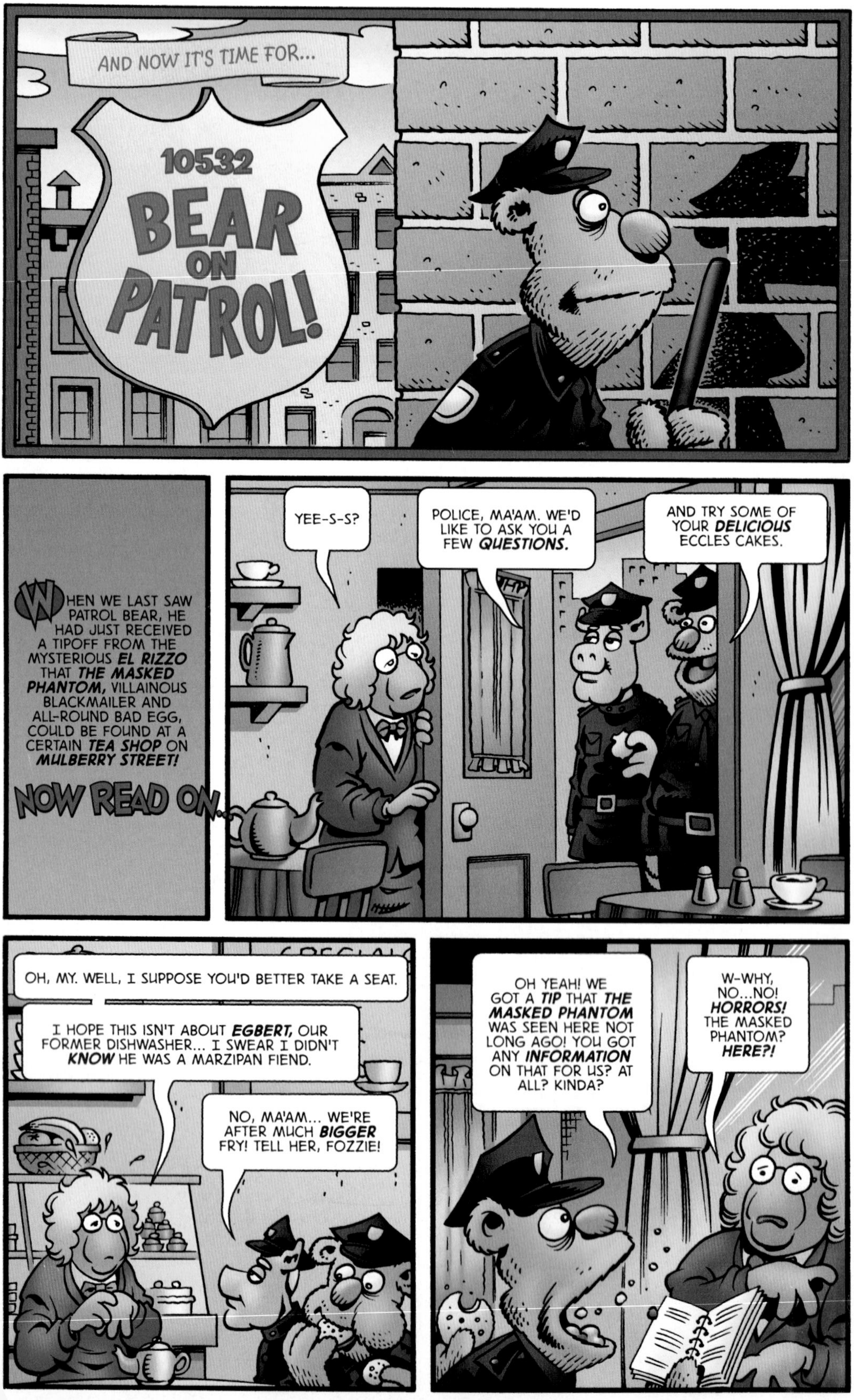
AND NOW IT'S TIME FOR...
10532
BEAR ON PATROL!
WHEN WE LAST SAW PATROL BEAR, HE HAD JUST RECEIVED A TIPOFF FROM THE MYSTERIOUS EL RIZZO THAT THE MASKED PHANTOM, VILLAINOUS BLACKMAILER AND ALL-ROUND BAD EGG, COULD BE FOUND AT A CERTAIN TEA SHOP ON MULBERRY STREET!
NOW READ ON...
YEE-S-S?
POLICE, MA'AM. WE'D LIKE TO ASK YOU A FEW QUESTIONS.
AND TRY SOME OF YOUR DELICIOUS ECCLES CAKES.
OH, MY. WELL, I SUPPOSE YOU'D BETTER TAKE A SEAT.
I HOPE THIS ISN'T ABOUT EGBERT, OUR FORMER DISHWASHER... I SWEAR I DIDN'T KNOW HE WAS A MARZIPAN FIEND.
NO, MA'AM... WE'RE AFTER MUCH BIGGER FRY! TELL HER, FOZZIE!
OH YEAH! WE GOT A TIP THAT THE MASKED PHANTOM WAS SEEN HERE NOT LONG AGO! YOU GOT ANY INFORMATION ON THAT FOR US? AT ALL? KINDA?
W-WHY, NO...NO! HORRORS! THE MASKED PHANTOM? HERE?!

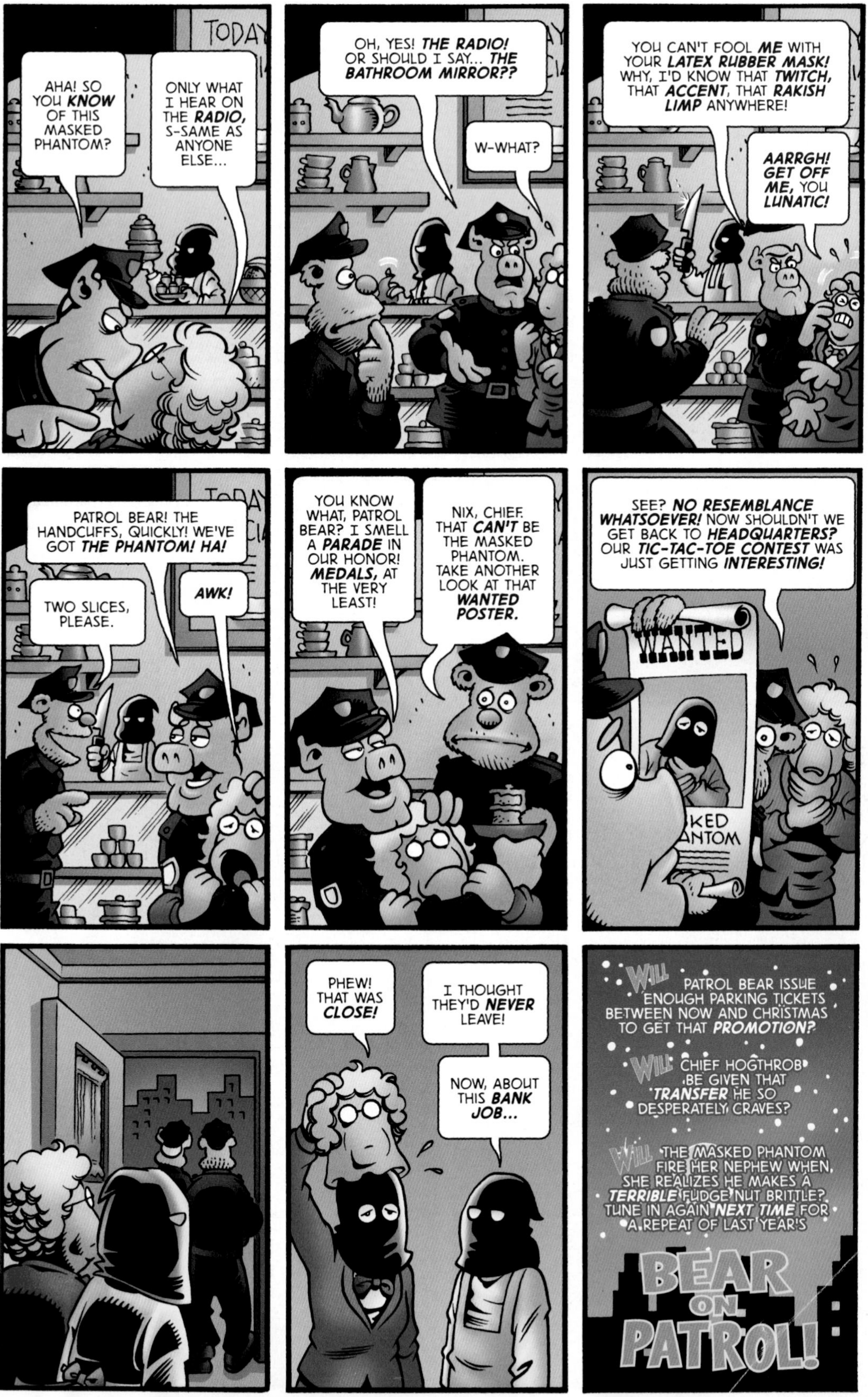

TODAY
AHA! SO YOU KNOW OF THIS MASKED PHANTOM?
ONLY WHAT I HEAR ON THE RADIO, S-SAME AS ANYONE ELSE...
OH, YES! THE RADIO! OR SHOULD I SAY... THE BATHROOM MIRROR??
W-WHAT?
YOU CAN'T FOOL ME WITH YOUR LATEX RUBBER MASK! WHY, I'D KNOW THAT TWITCH, THAT ACCENT, THAT RAKISH LIMP ANYWHERE!
AARRGH! GET OFF ME, YOU LUNATIC!
PATROL BEAR! THE HANDCUFFS, QUICKLY! WE'VE GOT THE PHANTOM! HA!
TWO SLICES, PLEASE.
AWK!
YOU KNOW WHAT, PATROL BEAR? I SMELL A PARADE IN OUR HONOR! MEDALS, AT THE VERY LEAST!
NIX, CHIEF. THAT CAN'T BE THE MASKED PHANTOM. TAKE ANOTHER LOOK AT THAT WANTED POSTER.
SEE? NO RESEMBLANCE WHATSOEVER! NOW SHOULDN'T WE GET BACK TO HEADQUARTERS? OUR TIC-TAC-TOE CONTEST WAS JUST GETTING INTERESTING!
WANTED
KED
ANTOM
PHEW! THAT WAS CLOSE!
I THOUGHT THEY'D NEVER LEAVE!
NOW, ABOUT THIS BANK JOB...
WILL PATROL BEAR ISSUE ENOUGH PARKING TICKETS BETWEEN NOW AND CHRISTMAS TO GET THAT PROMOTION?
WILL CHIEF HOGTHROB BE GIVEN THAT TRANSFER HE SO DESPERATELY CRAVES?
WILL THE MASKED PHANTOM FIRE HER NEPHEW WHEN SHE REALIZES HE MAKES A TERRIBLE FUDGE NUT BRITTLE? TUNE IN AGAIN NEXT TIME FOR A REPEAT OF LAST YEAR'S
BEAR ON PATROL!

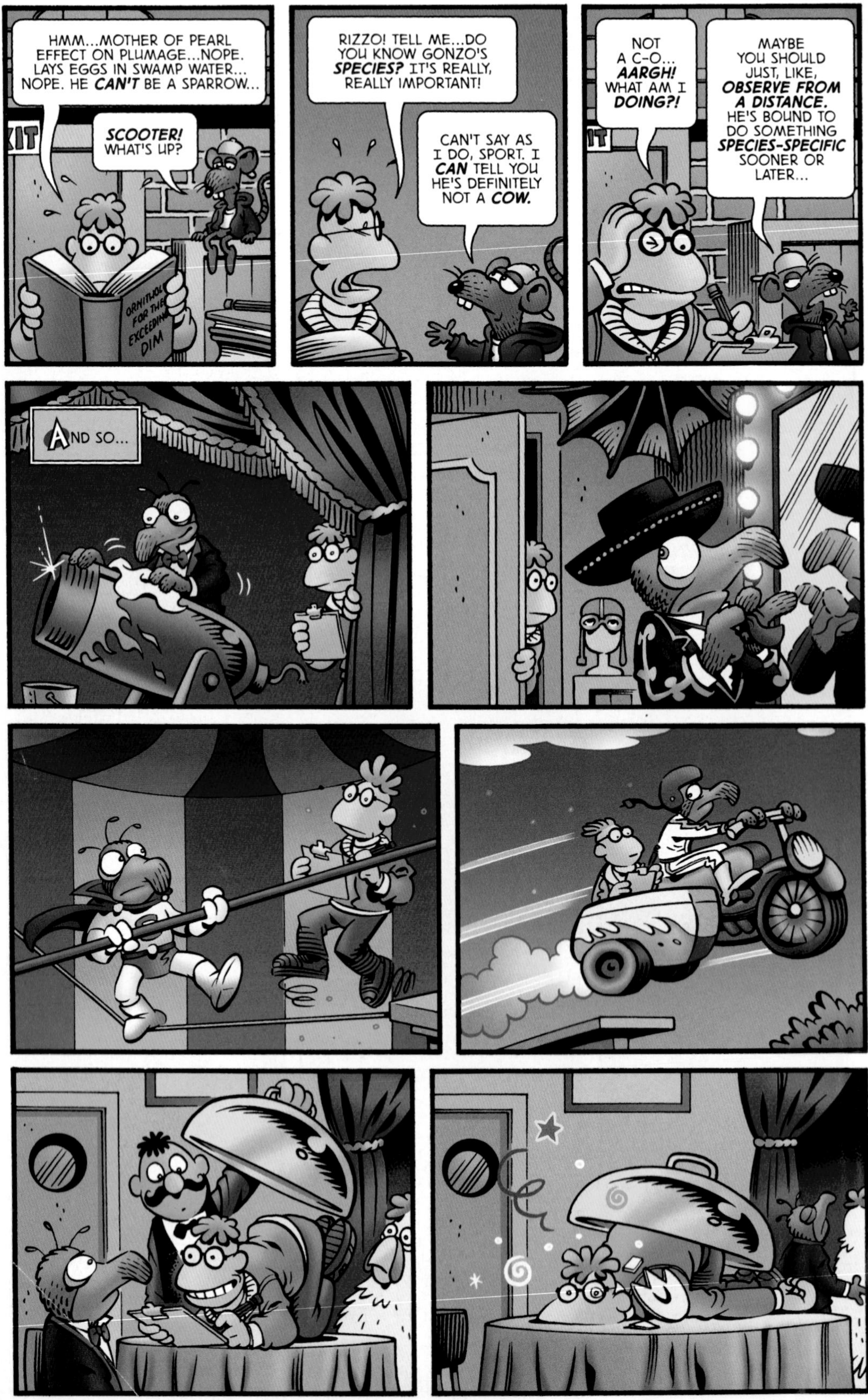
HMM...MOTHER OF PEARL EFFECT ON PLUMAGE...NOPE. LAYS EGGS IN SWAMP WATER... NOPE. HE CAN'T BE A SPARROW...
SCOOTER! WHAT'S UP?
RIZZO! TELL ME...DO YOU KNOW GONZO'S SPECIES? IT'S REALLY, REALLY IMPORTANT!
CAN'T SAY AS I DO, SPORT. I CAN TELL YOU HE'S DEFINITELY NOT A COW.
NOT A C-O... AARGH! WHAT AM I DOING?!
MAYBE YOU SHOULD JUST, LIKE, OBSERVE FROM A DISTANCE. HE'S BOUND TO DO SOMETHING SPECIES-SPECIFIC SOONER OR LATER...
AND SO...

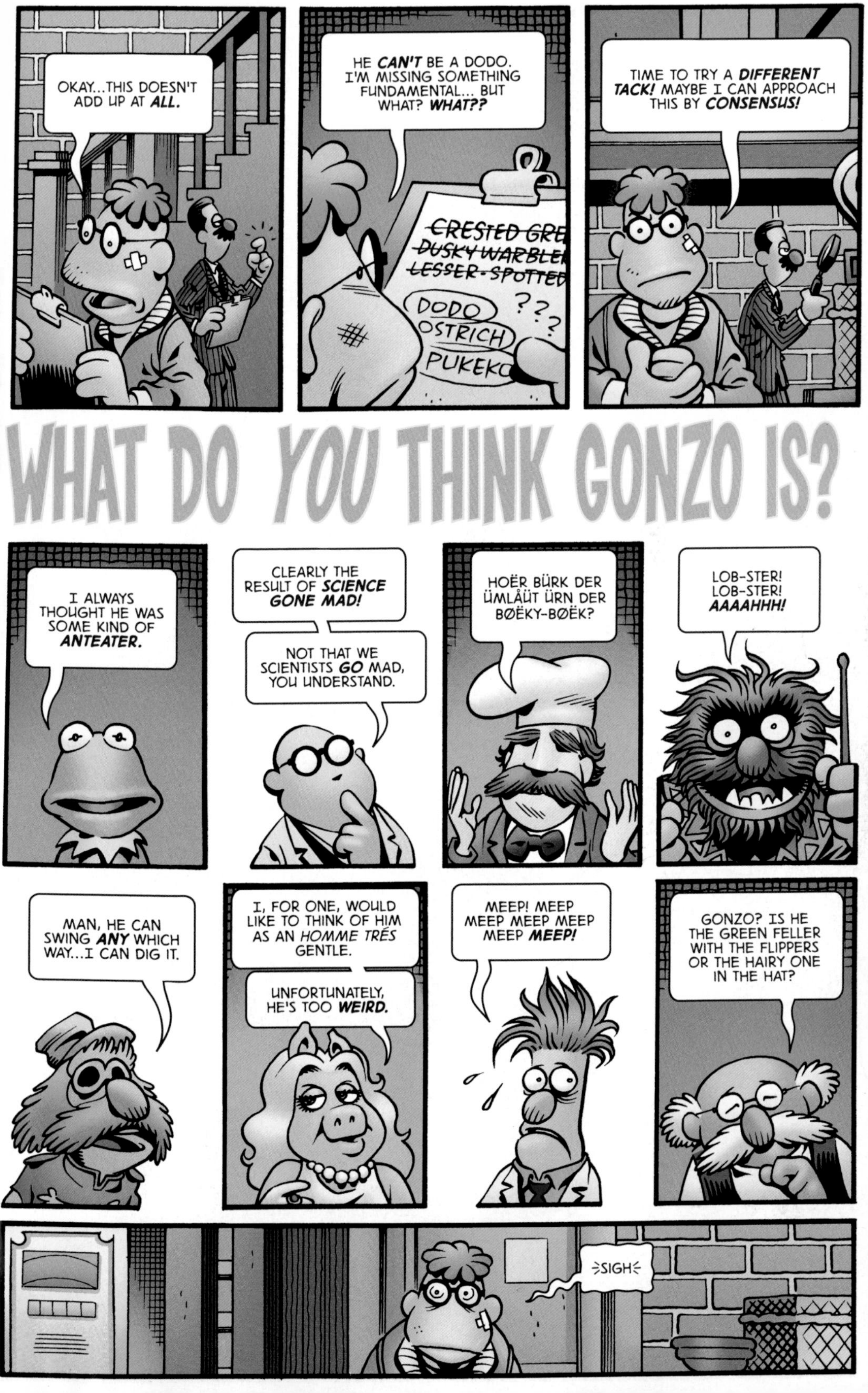
OKAY...THIS DOESN'T ADD UP AT ALL.
HE CAN'T BE A DODO. I'M MISSING SOMETHING FUNDAMENTAL... BUT WHAT? WHAT??
CRESTED GRE
DUSKY WARBLER
LESSER-SPOTTED
DODO
OSTRICH
PUKEKO
???
TIME TO TRY A DIFFERENT TACK! MAYBE I CAN APPROACH THIS BY CONSENSUS!
WHAT DO YOU THINK GONZO IS?
I ALWAYS THOUGHT HE WAS SOME KIND OF ANTEATER.
CLEARLY THE RESULT OF SCIENCE GONE MAD!
NOT THAT WE SCIENTISTS GO MAD, YOU UNDERSTAND.
HOËR BÜRK DER ÜMLÅÜT ÜRN DER BØËKY-BØËK?
LOB-STER! LOB-STER! AAAAHHH!
MAN, HE CAN SWING ANY WHICH WAY...I CAN DIG IT.
I, FOR ONE, WOULD LIKE TO THINK OF HIM AS AN HOMME TRÉS GENTLE.
UNFORTUNATELY, HE'S TOO WEIRD.
MEEP! MEEP MEEP MEEP MEEP MEEP MEEP!
GONZO? IS HE THE GREEN FELLER WITH THE FLIPPERS OR THE HAIRY ONE IN THE HAT?
SIGH

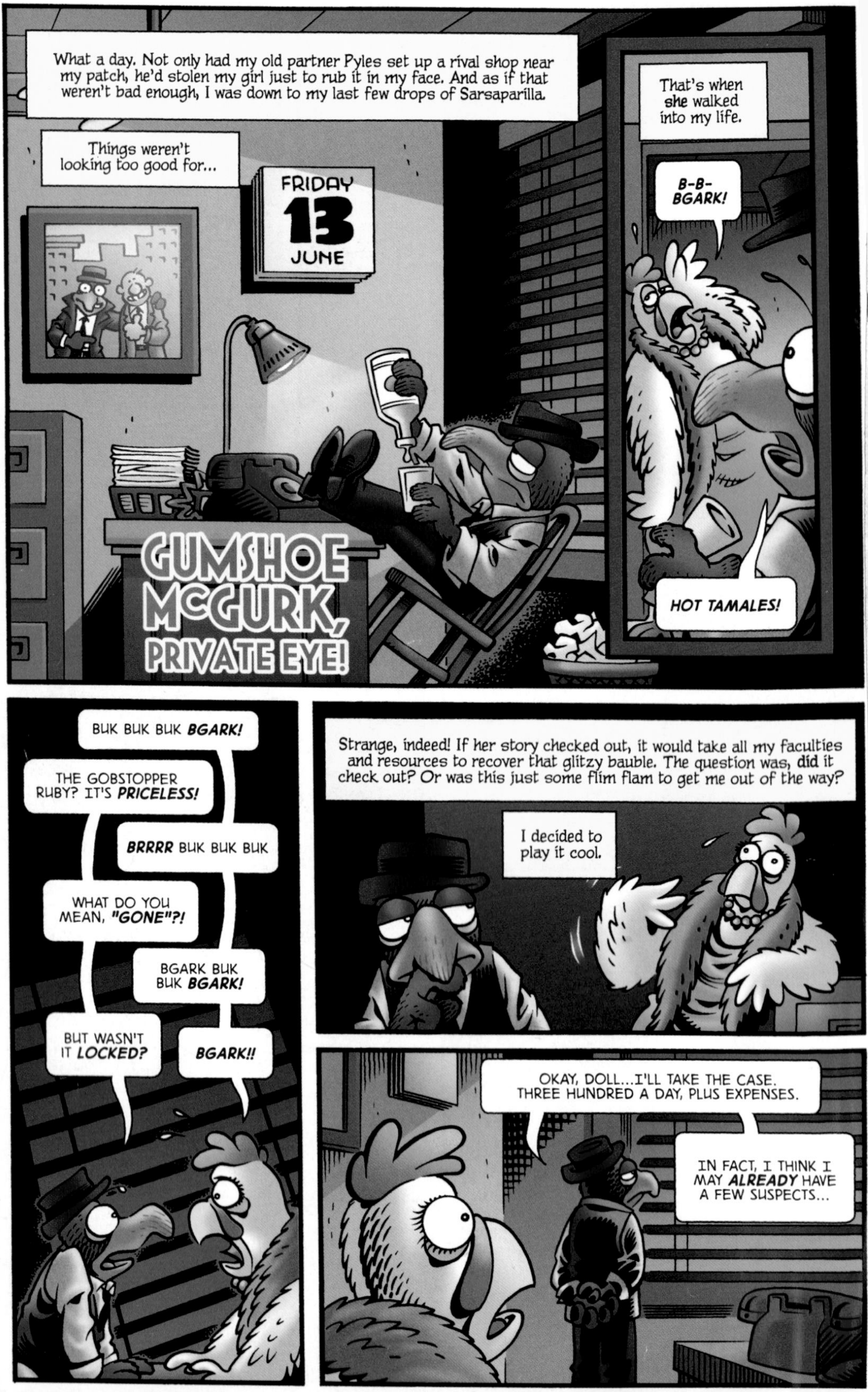
What a day. Not only had my old partner Pyles set up a rival shop near my patch, he'd stolen my girl just to rub it in my face. And as if that weren't bad enough, I was down to my last few drops of Sarsaparilla.
Things weren't looking too good for...
FRIDAY 13 JUNE
GUMSHOE McGURK, PRIVATE EYE!
That's when she walked into my life.
B-B-BGARK!
HOT TAMALES!
BUK BUK BUK BGARK!
THE GOBSTOPPER RUBY? IT'S PRICELESS!
BRRRR BUK BUK BUK
WHAT DO YOU MEAN, "GONE"?!
BGARK BUK BUK BGARK!
BUT WASN'T IT LOCKED?
BGARK!!
Strange, indeed! If her story checked out, it would take all my faculties and resources to recover that glitzy bauble. The question was, did it check out? Or was this just some flim flam to get me out of the way?
I decided to play it cool.
OKAY, DOLL...I'LL TAKE THE CASE. THREE HUNDRED A DAY, PLUS EXPENSES.
IN FACT, I THINK I MAY ALREADY HAVE A FEW SUSPECTS...

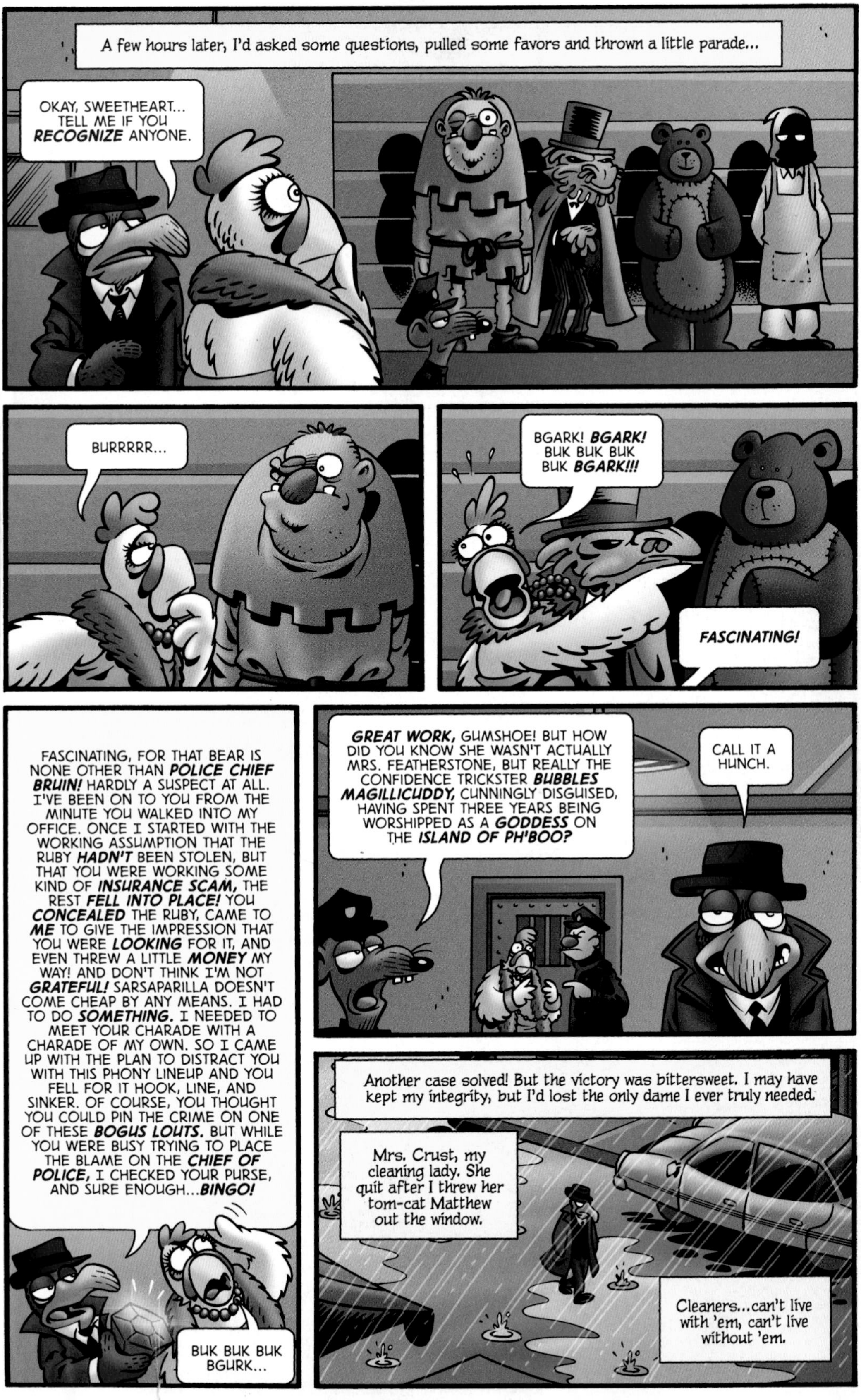
A few hours later, I'd asked some questions, pulled some favors and thrown a little parade...
OKAY, SWEETHEART... TELL ME IF YOU RECOGNIZE ANYONE.
BURRRRR...
BGARK! BGARK! BUK BUK BUK BUK BGARK!!!
FASCINATING!
FASCINATING, FOR THAT BEAR IS NONE OTHER THAN POLICE CHIEF BRUIN! HARDLY A SUSPECT AT ALL. I'VE BEEN ON TO YOU FROM THE MINUTE YOU WALKED INTO MY OFFICE. ONCE I STARTED WITH THE WORKING ASSUMPTION THAT THE RUBY HADN'T BEEN STOLEN, BUT THAT YOU WERE WORKING SOME KIND OF INSURANCE SCAM, THE REST FELL INTO PLACE! YOU CONCEALED THE RUBY, CAME TO ME TO GIVE THE IMPRESSION THAT YOU WERE LOOKING FOR IT, AND EVEN THREW A LITTLE MONEY MY WAY! AND DON'T THINK I'M NOT GRATEFUL! SARSAPARILLA DOESN'T COME CHEAP BY ANY MEANS. I HAD TO DO SOMETHING. I NEEDED TO MEET YOUR CHARADE WITH A CHARADE OF MY OWN. SO I CAME UP WITH THE PLAN TO DISTRACT YOU WITH THIS PHONY LINEUP AND YOU FELL FOR IT HOOK, LINE, AND SINKER. OF COURSE, YOU THOUGHT YOU COULD PIN THE CRIME ON ONE OF THESE BOGUS LOUTS. BUT WHILE YOU WERE BUSY TRYING TO PLACE THE BLAME ON THE CHIEF OF POLICE, I CHECKED YOUR PURSE, AND SURE ENOUGH...BINGO!
BUK BUK BUK BGURK...
GREAT WORK, GUMSHOE! BUT HOW DID YOU KNOW SHE WASN'T ACTUALLY MRS. FEATHERSTONE, BUT REALLY THE CONFIDENCE TRICKSTER BUBBLES MAGILLICUDDY, CUNNINGLY DISGUISED, HAVING SPENT THREE YEARS BEING WORSHIPPED AS A GODDESS ON THE ISLAND OF PH'BOO?
CALL IT A HUNCH.
Another case solved! But the victory was bittersweet. I may have kept my integrity, but I'd lost the only dame I ever truly needed.
Mrs. Crust, my cleaning lady. She quit after I threw her tom-cat Matthew out the window.
Cleaners...can't live with 'em, can't live without 'em.

PIGS in SPACE!

And now it's time for...

Starring *

CAPTAIN
LINK HOGTHROB

FIRST MATE
MISS PIGGY

And the supercilious
DR STRANGEPORK!

WHEN WE LAST SAW THE GOOD SHIP *SWINETREK*, IT HAD BEEN CHARGED WITH BRINGING A *STRANGE, UNIDENTIFIED SHIP* TO THE INTERGALACTIC AUTHORITIES! **NOW READ ON.**

I DON'T KNOW IF IT WAS WISE TO BRING THE PRISONER *ON BOARD,* CAPTAIN!

OH, *PSHAW!* THESE RESTRAINTS ARE *PURE PIG* IRON--WE'RE PERFECTLY SAFE!

AND THE *SCIENTIFIC* OPPORTUNITIES OF STUDYING THIS CREATURE UP CLOSE *FAR* OUTWEIGH THE *RISKS!*

ᕙᗩᒐᕓᕵ ᒪᒐᕓᕵ? ᕽᒎ ᕟᕝᔑᔓ

WAIT, WHAT DID HE JUST SAY? STRANGEPORK, YOU SPEAK WEIRDO, WHAT WAS THAT?

I'M TRYING TO NARROW DOWN HIS SPECIES SO I CAN PROGRAM THE *TRANSLATORS!* WITHOUT KNOWING WHERE HE'S FROM, *YOUR* GUESS IS AS GOOD AS *MINE!*

ᗯᒐᕓᕵ, ᒪᒐᕓᕵ, ᒪᒐᕓᕵ, ᕽᒎ ᕟᕝᕼ ᔑᕵᔓᔓ

WAIT, WAIT, WAIT. HE WAS *DEFINITELY* LOOKING AT *ME* WHEN HE SAID THAT.

OKAY, THAT MAKES HIM AT LEAST *PART MAMMAL,* THAT NARROWS IT DOWN! KEEP GOING!

LET ME TRY... *HEL-LO SPAACE BUUUG THIIIING! WEEE AAARE FROOOM EEEARRRTHHH!*

WHAT ARE YOU DOING?

I DON'T UNDERSTAND... THAT ALWAYS WORKS IN *SPAIN.*

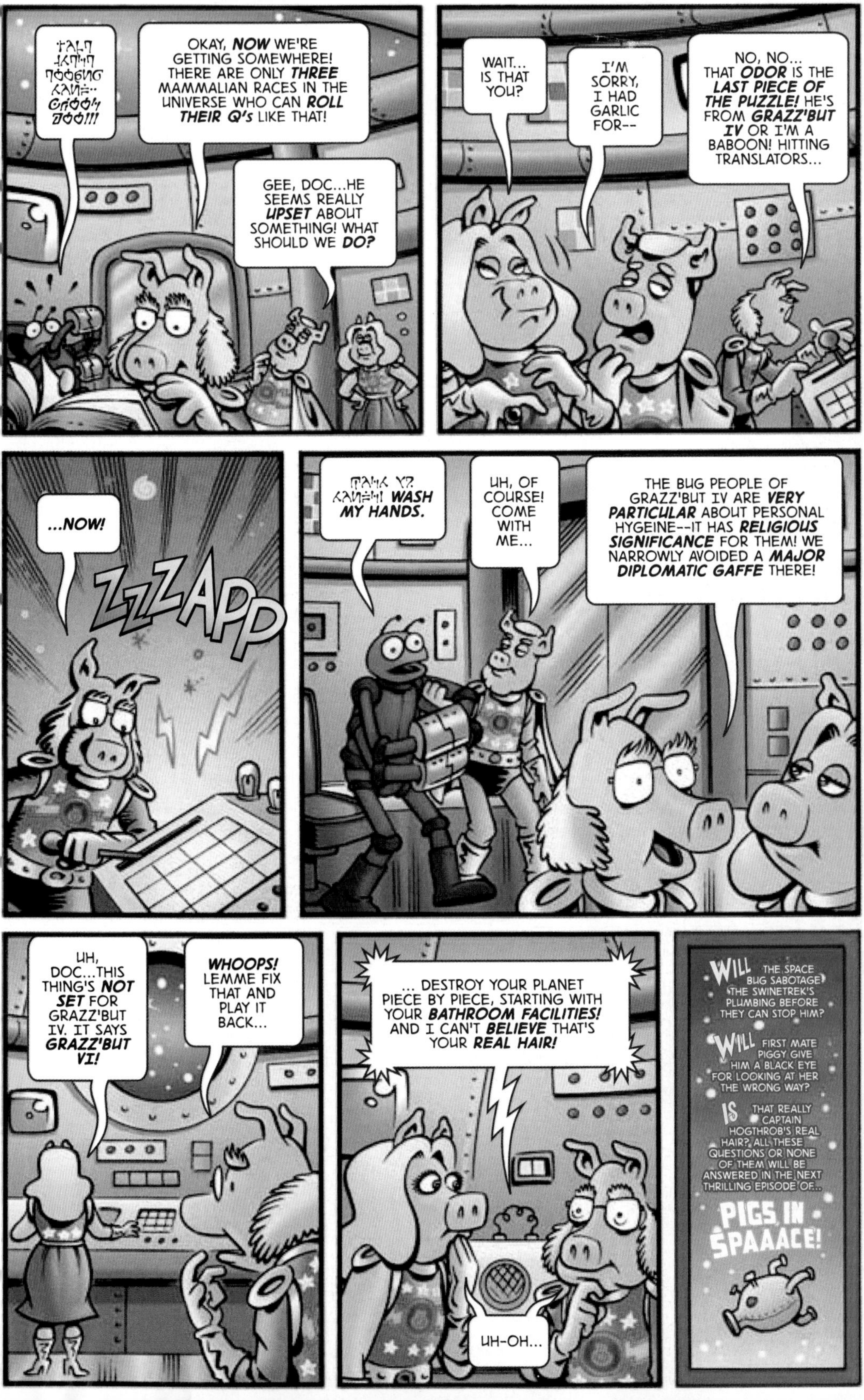
OKAY, NOW WE'RE GETTING SOMEWHERE! THERE ARE ONLY THREE MAMMALIAN RACES IN THE UNIVERSE WHO CAN ROLL THEIR Q's LIKE THAT!
GEE, DOC...HE SEEMS REALLY UPSET ABOUT SOMETHING! WHAT SHOULD WE DO?
WAIT... IS THAT YOU?
I'M SORRY, I HAD GARLIC FOR--
NO, NO... THAT ODOR IS THE LAST PIECE OF THE PUZZLE! HE'S FROM GRAZZ'BUT IV OR I'M A BABOON! HITTING TRANSLATORS...
...NOW!
ZZZAPP
WASH MY HANDS.
UH, OF COURSE! COME WITH ME...
THE BUG PEOPLE OF GRAZZ'BUT IV ARE VERY PARTICULAR ABOUT PERSONAL HYGEINE--IT HAS RELIGIOUS SIGNIFICANCE FOR THEM! WE NARROWLY AVOIDED A MAJOR DIPLOMATIC GAFFE THERE!
UH, DOC...THIS THING'S NOT SET FOR GRAZZ'BUT IV. IT SAYS GRAZZ'BUT VI!
WHOOPS! LEMME FIX THAT AND PLAY IT BACK...
... DESTROY YOUR PLANET PIECE BY PIECE, STARTING WITH YOUR BATHROOM FACILITIES! AND I CAN'T BELIEVE THAT'S YOUR REAL HAIR!
UH-OH...
WILL THE SPACE BUG SABOTAGE THE SWINETREK'S PLUMBING BEFORE THEY CAN STOP HIM?
WILL FIRST MATE PIGGY GIVE HIM A BLACK EYE FOR LOOKING AT HER THE WRONG WAY?
IS THAT REALLY CAPTAIN HOGTHROB'S REAL HAIR? ALL THESE QUESTIONS OR NONE OF THEM WILL BE ANSWERED IN THE NEXT THRILLING EPISODE OF...
PIGS IN SPAAACE!

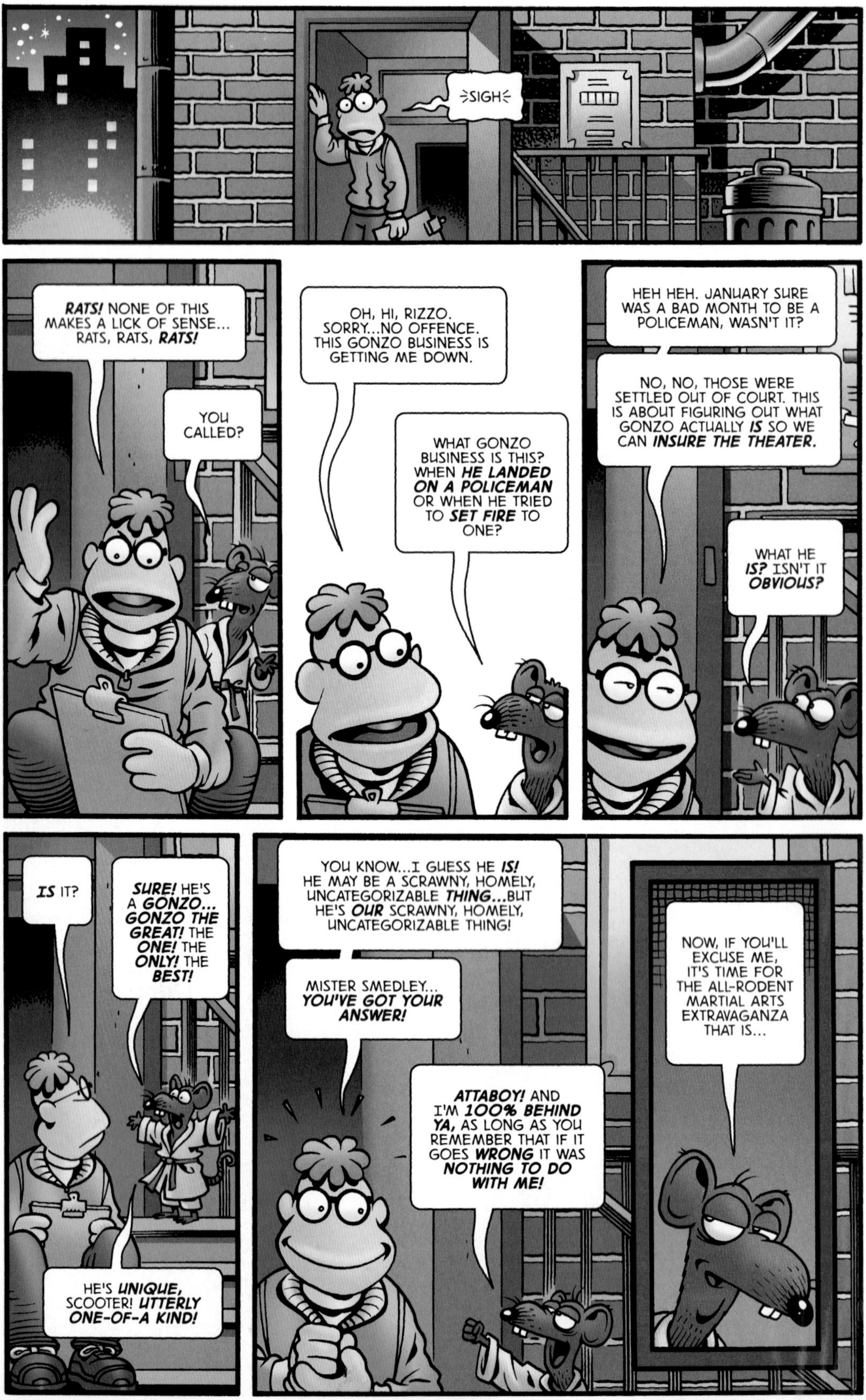

SIGH
RATS! NONE OF THIS MAKES A LICK OF SENSE... RATS, RATS, RATS!
YOU CALLED?
OH, HI, RIZZO. SORRY...NO OFFENCE. THIS GONZO BUSINESS IS GETTING ME DOWN.
WHAT GONZO BUSINESS IS THIS? WHEN HE LANDED ON A POLICEMAN OR WHEN HE TRIED TO SET FIRE TO ONE?
HEH HEH. JANUARY SURE WAS A BAD MONTH TO BE A POLICEMAN, WASN'T IT?
NO, NO, THOSE WERE SETTLED OUT OF COURT. THIS IS ABOUT FIGURING OUT WHAT GONZO ACTUALLY IS SO WE CAN INSURE THE THEATER.
WHAT HE IS? ISN'T IT OBVIOUS?
IS IT?
SURE! HE'S A GONZO... GONZO THE GREAT! THE ONE! THE ONLY! THE BEST!
HE'S UNIQUE, SCOOTER! UTTERLY ONE-OF-A KIND!
YOU KNOW...I GUESS HE IS! HE MAY BE A SCRAWNY, HOMELY, UNCATEGORIZABLE THING...BUT HE'S OUR SCRAWNY, HOMELY, UNCATEGORIZABLE THING!
MISTER SMEDLEY... YOU'VE GOT YOUR ANSWER!
ATTABOY! AND I'M 100% BEHIND YA, AS LONG AS YOU REMEMBER THAT IF IT GOES WRONG IT WAS NOTHING TO DO WITH ME!
NOW, IF YOU'LL EXCUSE ME, IT'S TIME FOR THE ALL-RODENT MARTIAL ARTS EXTRAVAGANZA THAT IS...

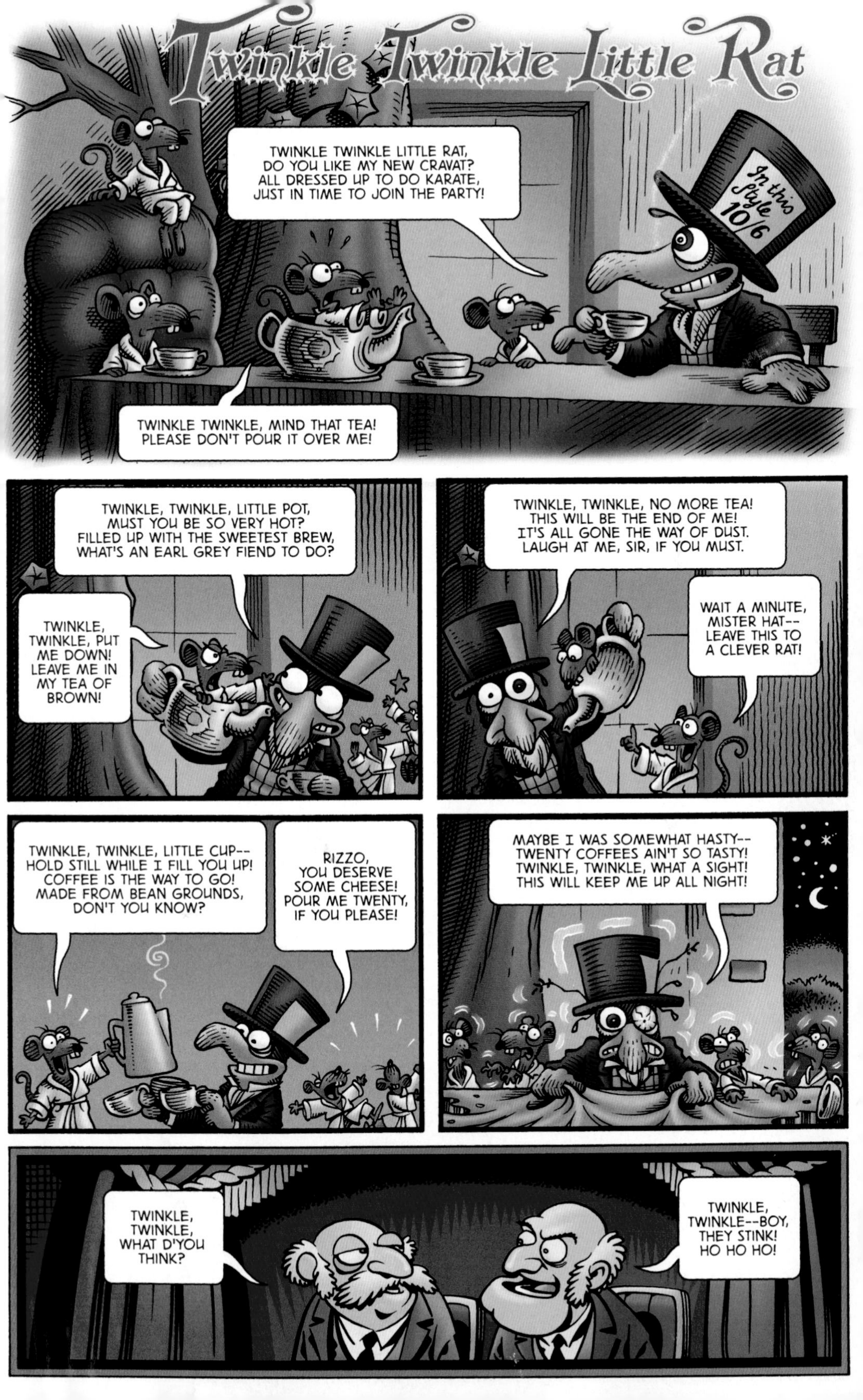
Twinkle Twinkle Little Rat
In this style 10/6
TWINKLE TWINKLE LITTLE RAT, DO YOU LIKE MY NEW CRAVAT? ALL DRESSED UP TO DO KARATE, JUST IN TIME TO JOIN THE PARTY!
TWINKLE TWINKLE, MIND THAT TEA! PLEASE DON'T POUR IT OVER ME!
TWINKLE, TWINKLE, LITTLE POT, MUST YOU BE SO VERY HOT? FILLED UP WITH THE SWEETEST BREW, WHAT'S AN EARL GREY FIEND TO DO?
TWINKLE, TWINKLE, PUT ME DOWN! LEAVE ME IN MY TEA OF BROWN!
TWINKLE, TWINKLE, NO MORE TEA! THIS WILL BE THE END OF ME! IT'S ALL GONE THE WAY OF DUST. LAUGH AT ME, SIR, IF YOU MUST.
WAIT A MINUTE, MISTER HAT-- LEAVE THIS TO A CLEVER RAT!
TWINKLE, TWINKLE, LITTLE CUP-- HOLD STILL WHILE I FILL YOU UP! COFFEE IS THE WAY TO GO! MADE FROM BEAN GROUNDS, DON'T YOU KNOW?
RIZZO, YOU DESERVE SOME CHEESE! POUR ME TWENTY, IF YOU PLEASE!
MAYBE I WAS SOMEWHAT HASTY-- TWENTY COFFEES AIN'T SO TASTY! TWINKLE, TWINKLE, WHAT A SIGHT! THIS WILL KEEP ME UP ALL NIGHT!
TWINKLE, TWINKLE, WHAT D'YOU THINK?
TWINKLE, TWINKLE--BOY, THEY STINK! HO HO HO!

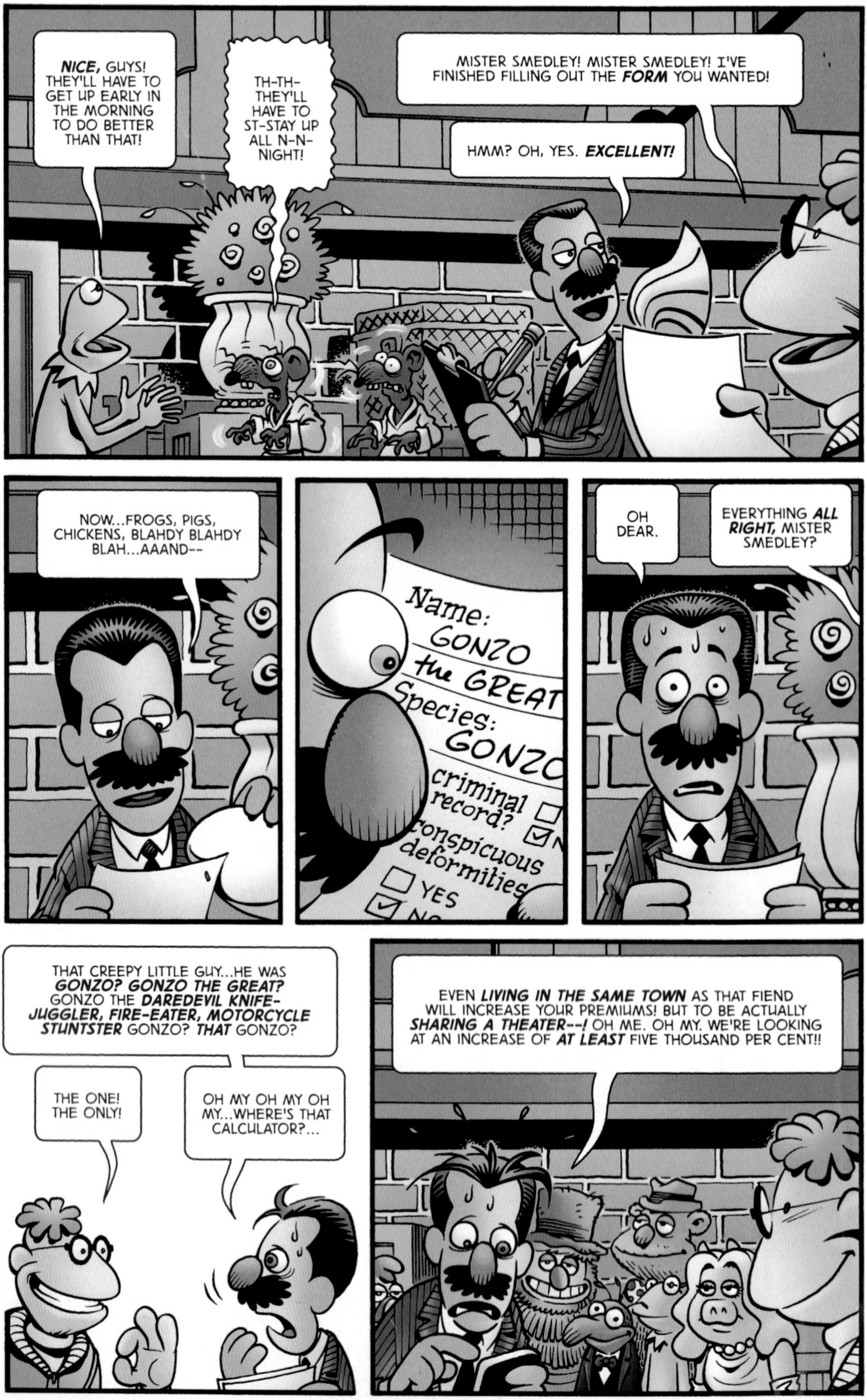
NICE, GUYS! THEY'LL HAVE TO GET UP EARLY IN THE MORNING TO DO BETTER THAN THAT!
TH-TH-THEY'LL HAVE TO ST-STAY UP ALL N-N-NIGHT!
MISTER SMEDLEY! MISTER SMEDLEY! I'VE FINISHED FILLING OUT THE FORM YOU WANTED!
HMM? OH, YES. EXCELLENT!
NOW...FROGS, PIGS, CHICKENS, BLAHDY BLAHDY BLAH...AAAND--
Name: GONZO the GREAT
Species: GONZO
criminal record?
conspicuous deformities
YES
OH DEAR.
EVERYTHING ALL RIGHT, MISTER SMEDLEY?
THAT CREEPY LITTLE GUY...HE WAS GONZO? GONZO THE GREAT? GONZO THE DAREDEVIL KNIFE-JUGGLER, FIRE-EATER, MOTORCYCLE STUNTSTER GONZO? THAT GONZO?
THE ONE! THE ONLY!
OH MY OH MY OH MY...WHERE'S THAT CALCULATOR?...
EVEN LIVING IN THE SAME TOWN AS THAT FIEND WILL INCREASE YOUR PREMIUMS! BUT TO BE ACTUALLY SHARING A THEATER--! OH ME. OH MY. WE'RE LOOKING AT AN INCREASE OF AT LEAST FIVE THOUSAND PER CENT!!

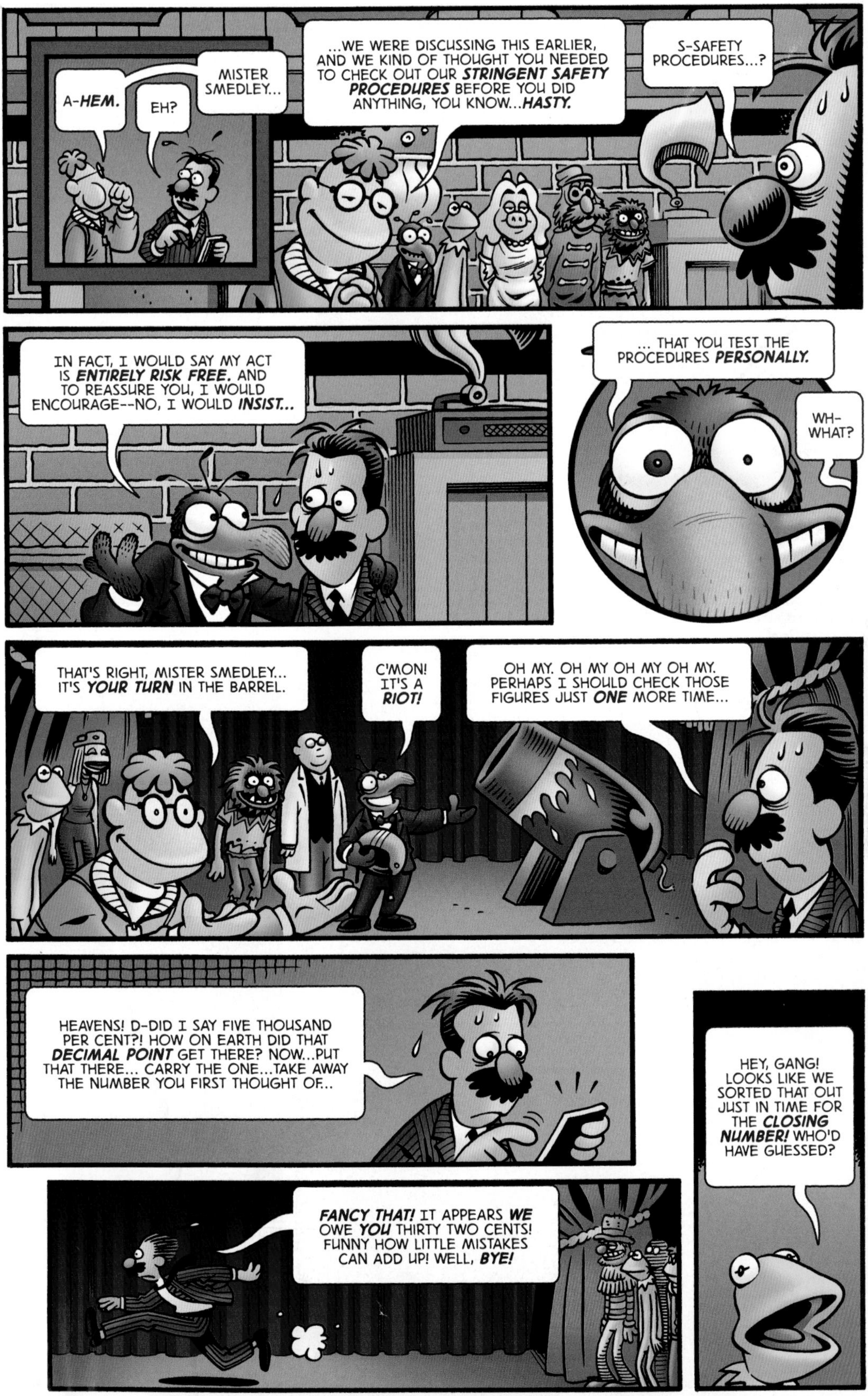

A-HEM.
EH?
MISTER SMEDLEY...
...WE WERE DISCUSSING THIS EARLIER, AND WE KIND OF THOUGHT YOU NEEDED TO CHECK OUT OUR STRINGENT SAFETY PROCEDURES BEFORE YOU DID ANYTHING, YOU KNOW...HASTY.
S-SAFETY PROCEDURES...?
IN FACT, I WOULD SAY MY ACT IS ENTIRELY RISK FREE. AND TO REASSURE YOU, I WOULD ENCOURAGE--NO, I WOULD INSIST...
... THAT YOU TEST THE PROCEDURES PERSONALLY.
WH-WHAT?
THAT'S RIGHT, MISTER SMEDLEY... IT'S YOUR TURN IN THE BARREL.
C'MON! IT'S A RIOT!
OH MY. OH MY OH MY OH MY. PERHAPS I SHOULD CHECK THOSE FIGURES JUST ONE MORE TIME...
HEAVENS! D-DID I SAY FIVE THOUSAND PER CENT?! HOW ON EARTH DID THAT DECIMAL POINT GET THERE? NOW...PUT THAT THERE... CARRY THE ONE...TAKE AWAY THE NUMBER YOU FIRST THOUGHT OF...
FANCY THAT! IT APPEARS WE OWE YOU THIRTY TWO CENTS! FUNNY HOW LITTLE MISTAKES CAN ADD UP! WELL, BYE!
HEY, GANG! LOOKS LIKE WE SORTED THAT OUT JUST IN TIME FOR THE CLOSING NUMBER! WHO'D HAVE GUESSED?

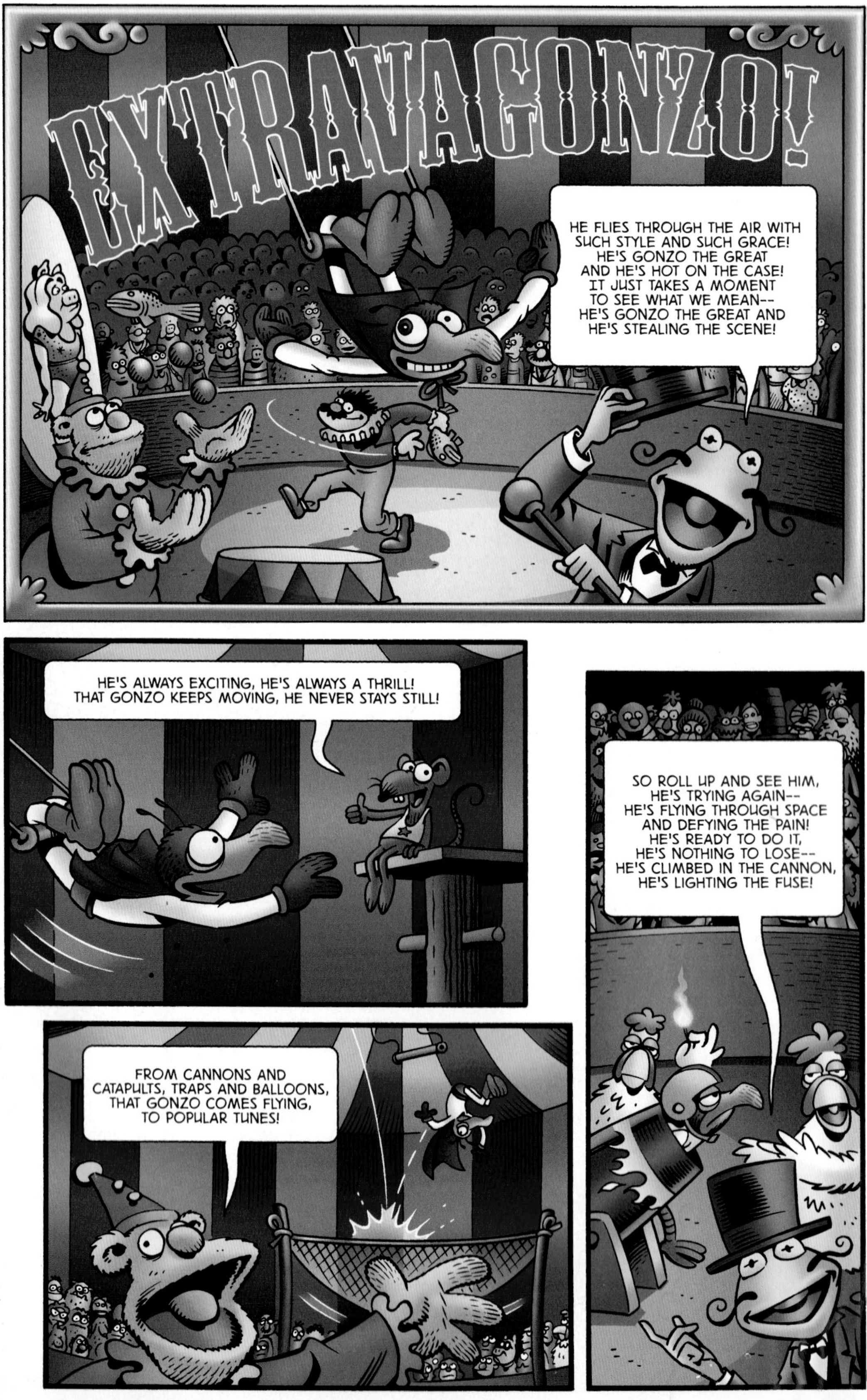
EXTRAVAGONZO!
HE FLIES THROUGH THE AIR WITH SUCH STYLE AND SUCH GRACE! HE'S GONZO THE GREAT AND HE'S HOT ON THE CASE! IT JUST TAKES A MOMENT TO SEE WHAT WE MEAN-- HE'S GONZO THE GREAT AND HE'S STEALING THE SCENE!
HE'S ALWAYS EXCITING, HE'S ALWAYS A THRILL! THAT GONZO KEEPS MOVING, HE NEVER STAYS STILL!
FROM CANNONS AND CATAPULTS, TRAPS AND BALLOONS, THAT GONZO COMES FLYING, TO POPULAR TUNES!
SO ROLL UP AND SEE HIM, HE'S TRYING AGAIN-- HE'S FLYING THROUGH SPACE AND DEFYING THE PAIN! HE'S READY TO DO IT, HE'S NOTHING TO LOSE-- HE'S CLIMBED IN THE CANNON, HE'S LIGHTING THE FUSE!

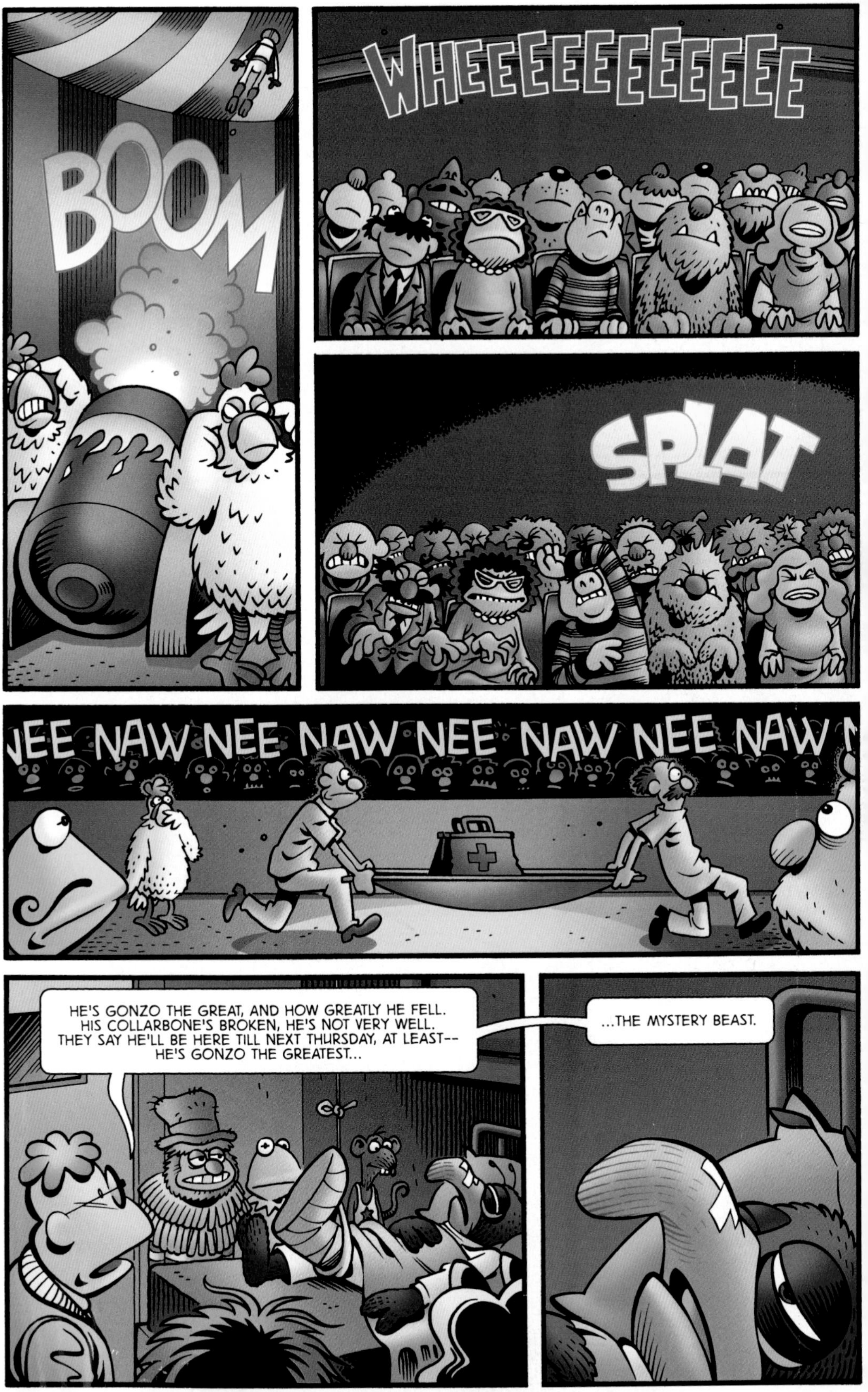
BOOM
WHEEEEEEEEEEEE
SPLAT
NEE NAW NEE NAW NEE NAW NEE NAW
HE'S GONZO THE GREAT, AND HOW GREATLY HE FELL. HIS COLLARBONE'S BROKEN, HE'S NOT VERY WELL. THEY SAY HE'LL BE HERE TILL NEXT THURSDAY, AT LEAST-- HE'S GONZO THE GREATEST...
...THE MYSTERY BEAST.

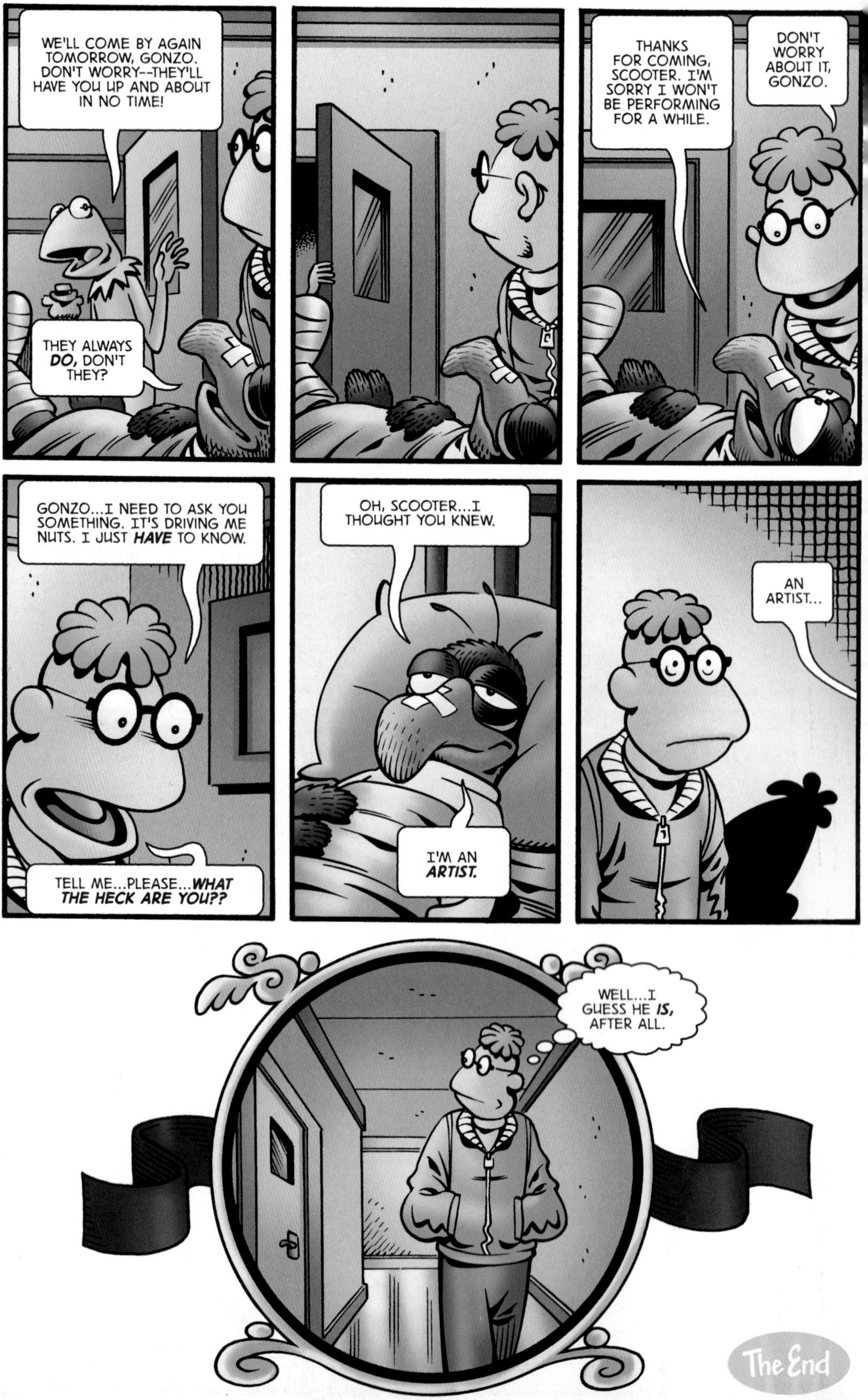
WE'LL COME BY AGAIN TOMORROW, GONZO. DON'T WORRY--THEY'LL HAVE YOU UP AND ABOUT IN NO TIME!
THEY ALWAYS **DO,** DON'T THEY?
THANKS FOR COMING, SCOOTER. I'M SORRY I WON'T BE PERFORMING FOR A WHILE.
DON'T WORRY ABOUT IT, GONZO.
GONZO...I NEED TO ASK YOU SOMETHING. IT'S DRIVING ME NUTS. I JUST **HAVE** TO KNOW.
TELL ME...PLEASE...**WHAT THE HECK ARE YOU??**
OH, SCOOTER...I THOUGHT YOU KNEW.
I'M AN **ARTIST.**
AN ARTIST...
WELL...I GUESS HE **IS,** AFTER ALL.
The End

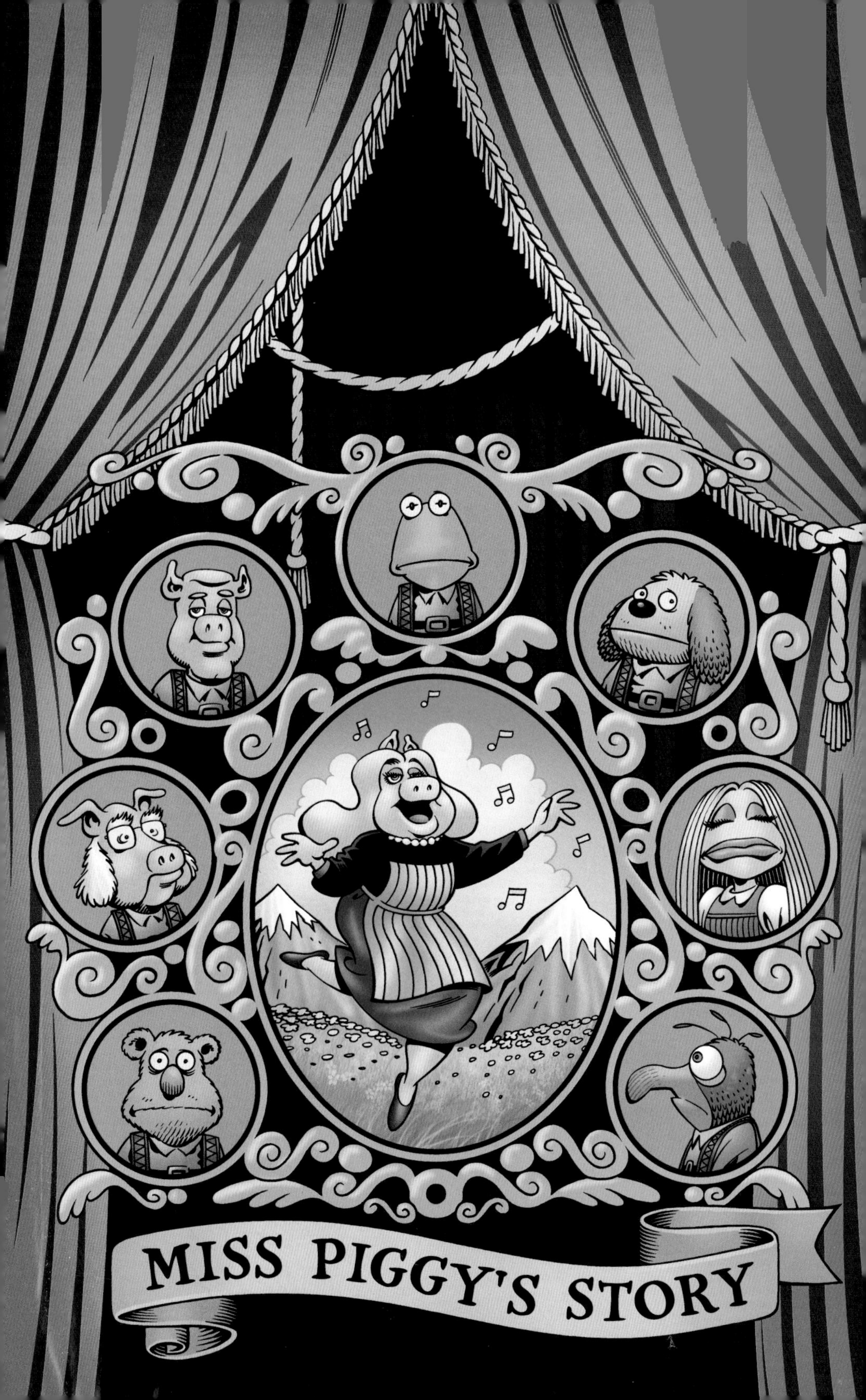
MISS PIGGY'S STORY

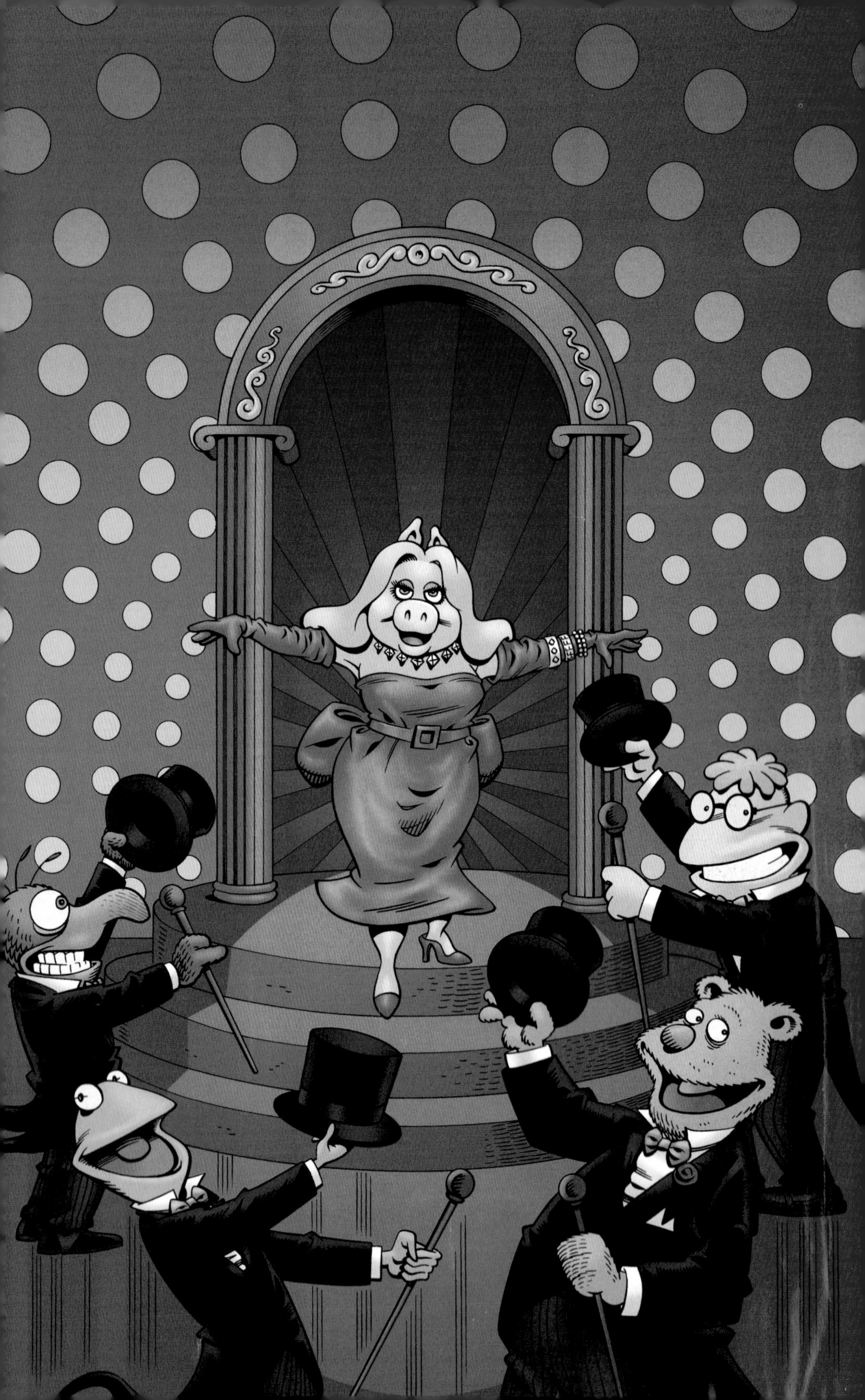

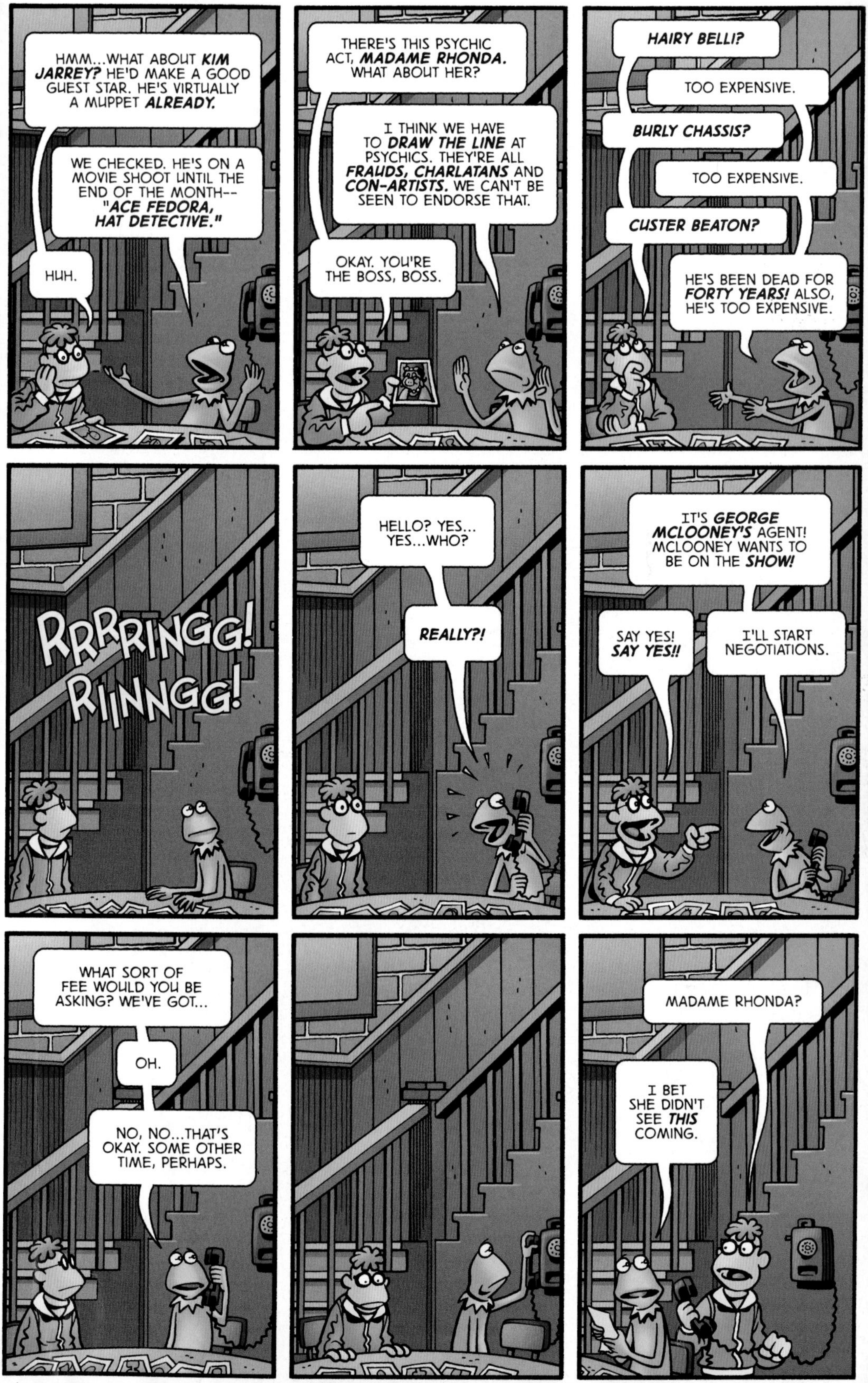
HMM...WHAT ABOUT KIM JARREY? HE'D MAKE A GOOD GUEST STAR. HE'S VIRTUALLY A MUPPET ALREADY.
WE CHECKED. HE'S ON A MOVIE SHOOT UNTIL THE END OF THE MONTH-- "ACE FEDORA, HAT DETECTIVE."
HUH.
THERE'S THIS PSYCHIC ACT, MADAME RHONDA. WHAT ABOUT HER?
I THINK WE HAVE TO DRAW THE LINE AT PSYCHICS. THEY'RE ALL FRAUDS, CHARLATANS AND CON-ARTISTS. WE CAN'T BE SEEN TO ENDORSE THAT.
OKAY. YOU'RE THE BOSS, BOSS.
HAIRY BELLI?
TOO EXPENSIVE.
BURLY CHASSIS?
TOO EXPENSIVE.
CUSTER BEATON?
HE'S BEEN DEAD FOR FORTY YEARS! ALSO, HE'S TOO EXPENSIVE.
RRRRINGG! RIINNGG!
HELLO? YES... YES...WHO?
REALLY?!
IT'S GEORGE MCLOONEY'S AGENT! MCLOONEY WANTS TO BE ON THE SHOW!
SAY YES! SAY YES!!
I'LL START NEGOTIATIONS.
WHAT SORT OF FEE WOULD YOU BE ASKING? WE'VE GOT...
OH.
NO, NO...THAT'S OKAY. SOME OTHER TIME, PERHAPS.
MADAME RHONDA?
I BET SHE DIDN'T SEE THIS COMING.

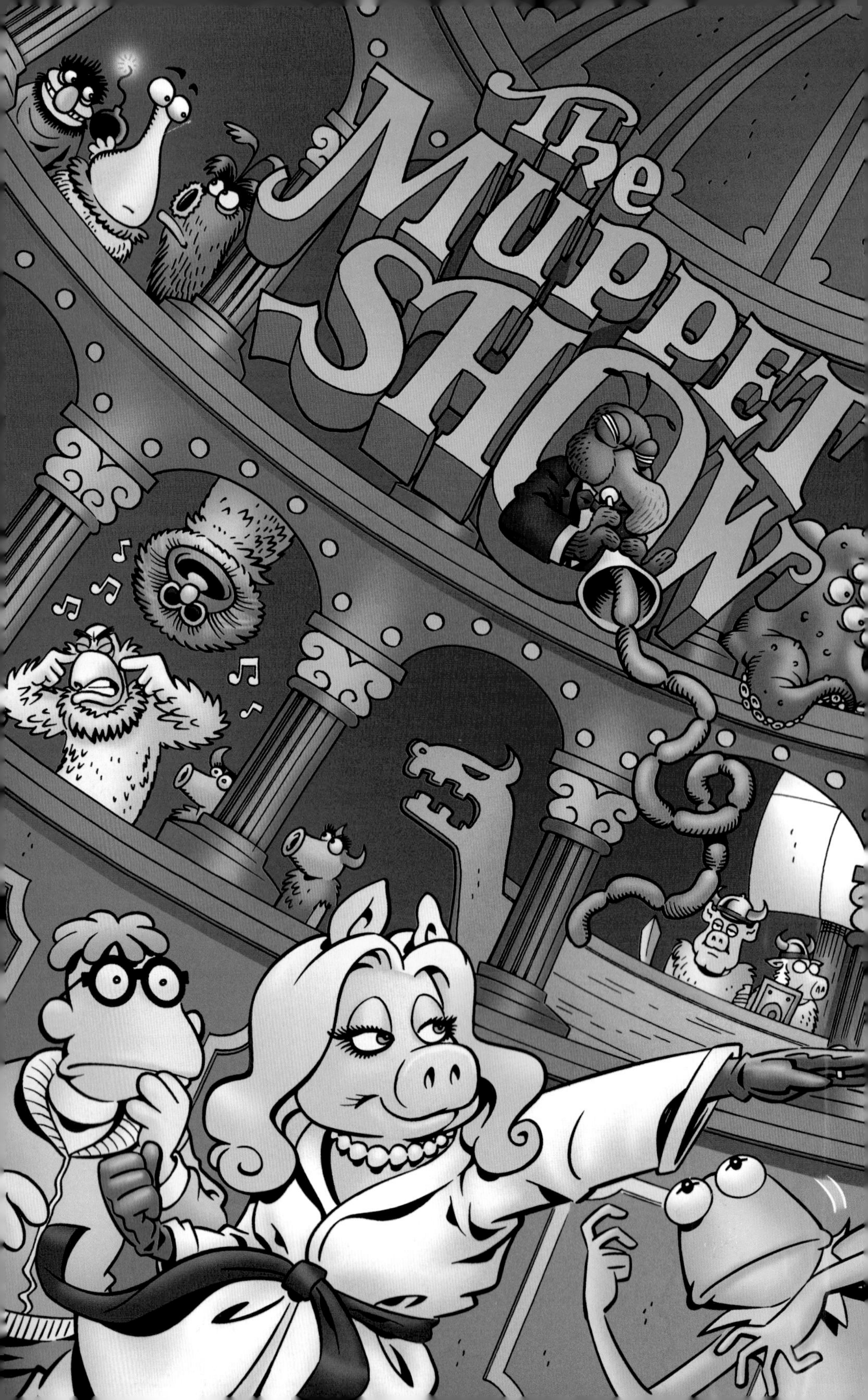
The Muppet Show

MADAME RHONDA? WHO THE HECK IS MADAME RHONDA?

OH, I THINK I'VE HEARD OF HER. SHE'S A MYSTIC.

A MISTAKE?

NO, THAT WAS WHAT WE MADE WHEN WE CAME HERE! HO HO HO!

HERE, GIVE ME YOUR PALM. I USED TO READ THEM MYSELF--IT'S AMAZING WHAT YOU PICK UP IN THE ARMY!

OKAY. CAN YOU SEE ANYTHING?

HMMM...

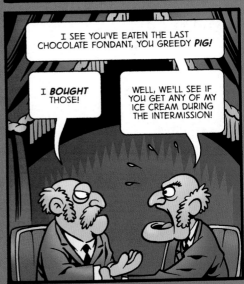

I SEE YOU'VE EATEN THE LAST CHOCOLATE FONDANT, YOU GREEDY PIG!

I BOUGHT THOSE!

WELL, WE'LL SEE IF YOU GET ANY OF MY ICE CREAM DURING THE INTERMISSION!

And now a message from
SAM THE EAGLE

GREETINGS, DEAR READERS. I WISH TO IMPART TO YOU A MATTER OF THE GRAVEST IMPORT.

IT HAS COME TO MY ATTENTION THAT A HITHERTO UNPRECEDENTED DEGREE OF CREDULITY--ONE MIGHT EVEN GO SO FAR AS TO CALL IT *GULLIBILITY*--HAS CREPT INTO OUR WAY OF THINKING IN RECENT TIMES.

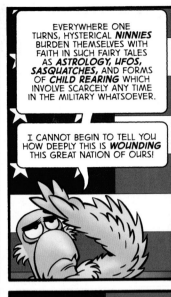

EVERYWHERE ONE TURNS, HYSTERICAL *NINNIES* BURDEN THEMSELVES WITH FAITH IN SUCH FAIRY TALES AS *ASTROLOGY, UFOS, SASQUATCHES,* AND FORMS OF *CHILD REARING* WHICH INVOLVE SCARCELY ANY TIME IN THE MILITARY WHATSOEVER.

I CANNOT BEGIN TO TELL YOU HOW DEEPLY THIS IS *WOUNDING* THIS GREAT NATION OF OURS!

WAS IT NOT *G. K. CHESTERTON* WHO OBSERVED, "WHEN A MAN CEASES TO BELIEVE IN GOD, HE DOESN'T BELIEVE IN *NOTHING,* HE BELIEVES IN *ANYTHING*?" I TRUST THE LESSON IS OBVIOUS ENOUGH NOT TO REQUIRE *FURTHER ILLUMINATION* FROM YOURS TRULY.

SUFFICE IT TO SAY THAT EVERY SO-CALLED "SIGHTING" OF A *SASQUATCH* PUSHES US FURTHER DOWN A SLIPPERY SLOPE TOWARDS *CHAOS AND RUIN!*

I THEREFORE URGE EACH AND EVERY ONE OF YOU, FROM THE BOTTOM OF MY HEART, TO BE *EVER VIGILANT* AGAINST THE FORCES OF *CREDULITY!*

WHEN SOMEBODY WAGGLES THE *BOGEY-MAN OF SUPERSTITION* IN YOUR FACE, SHOW A LITTLE BACKBONE! LOOK AT THE *EVIDENCE!*

AND GIVE THAT *MUMBO-JUMBO* THE KARATE CHOP OF LOGIC IT SO *RICHLY* DESERVES!

WISHING YOU ALL A BRIGHTER TOMORROW, I REMAIN, EVER TRULY YOURS, SAM THE EAGLE.

I THANK YOU.

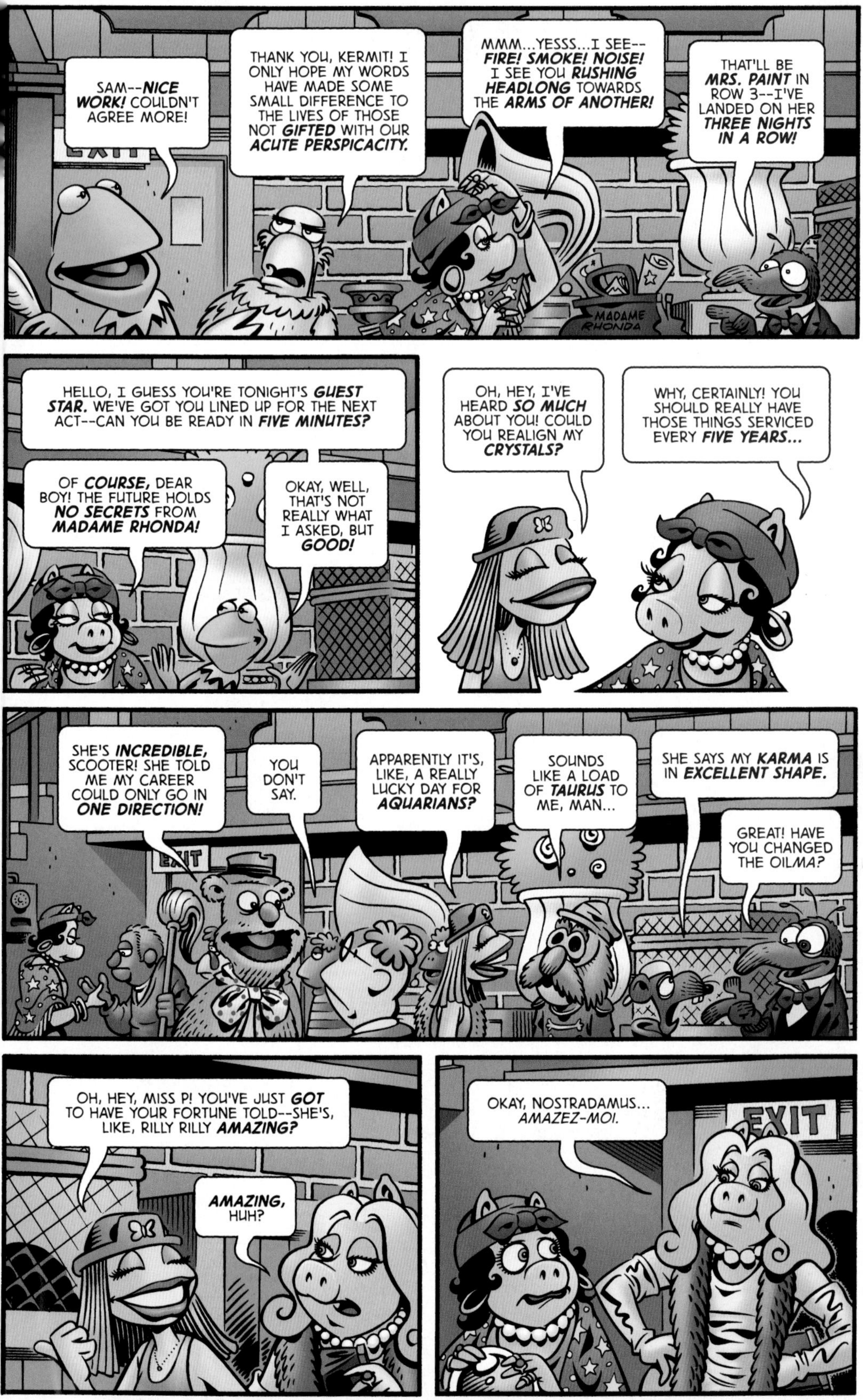
SAM--**NICE WORK!** COULDN'T AGREE MORE!
THANK YOU, KERMIT! I ONLY HOPE MY WORDS HAVE MADE SOME SMALL DIFFERENCE TO THE LIVES OF THOSE NOT **GIFTED** WITH OUR **ACUTE PERSPICACITY.**
MMM...YESSS...I SEE-- **FIRE! SMOKE! NOISE!** I SEE YOU **RUSHING HEADLONG** TOWARDS THE **ARMS OF ANOTHER!**
THAT'LL BE **MRS. PAINT** IN ROW 3--I'VE LANDED ON HER **THREE NIGHTS IN A ROW!**
MADAME RHONDA
HELLO, I GUESS YOU'RE TONIGHT'S **GUEST STAR.** WE'VE GOT YOU LINED UP FOR THE NEXT ACT--CAN YOU BE READY IN **FIVE MINUTES?**
OF **COURSE,** DEAR BOY! THE FUTURE HOLDS **NO SECRETS** FROM **MADAME RHONDA!**
OKAY, WELL, THAT'S NOT REALLY WHAT I ASKED, BUT **GOOD!**
OH, HEY, I'VE HEARD **SO MUCH** ABOUT YOU! COULD YOU REALIGN MY **CRYSTALS?**
WHY, CERTAINLY! YOU SHOULD REALLY HAVE THOSE THINGS SERVICED EVERY **FIVE YEARS...**
SHE'S **INCREDIBLE,** SCOOTER! SHE TOLD ME MY CAREER COULD ONLY GO IN **ONE DIRECTION!**
YOU DON'T SAY.
APPARENTLY IT'S, LIKE, A REALLY LUCKY DAY FOR **AQUARIANS?**
SOUNDS LIKE A LOAD OF **TAURUS** TO ME, MAN...
SHE SAYS MY **KARMA** IS IN **EXCELLENT SHAPE.**
GREAT! HAVE YOU CHANGED THE OIL*MA?*
EXIT
OH, HEY, MISS P! YOU'VE JUST **GOT** TO HAVE YOUR FORTUNE TOLD--SHE'S, LIKE, RILLY RILLY **AMAZING?**
AMAZING, HUH?
OKAY, NOSTRADAMUS... *AMAZEZ-MOI.*
EXIT

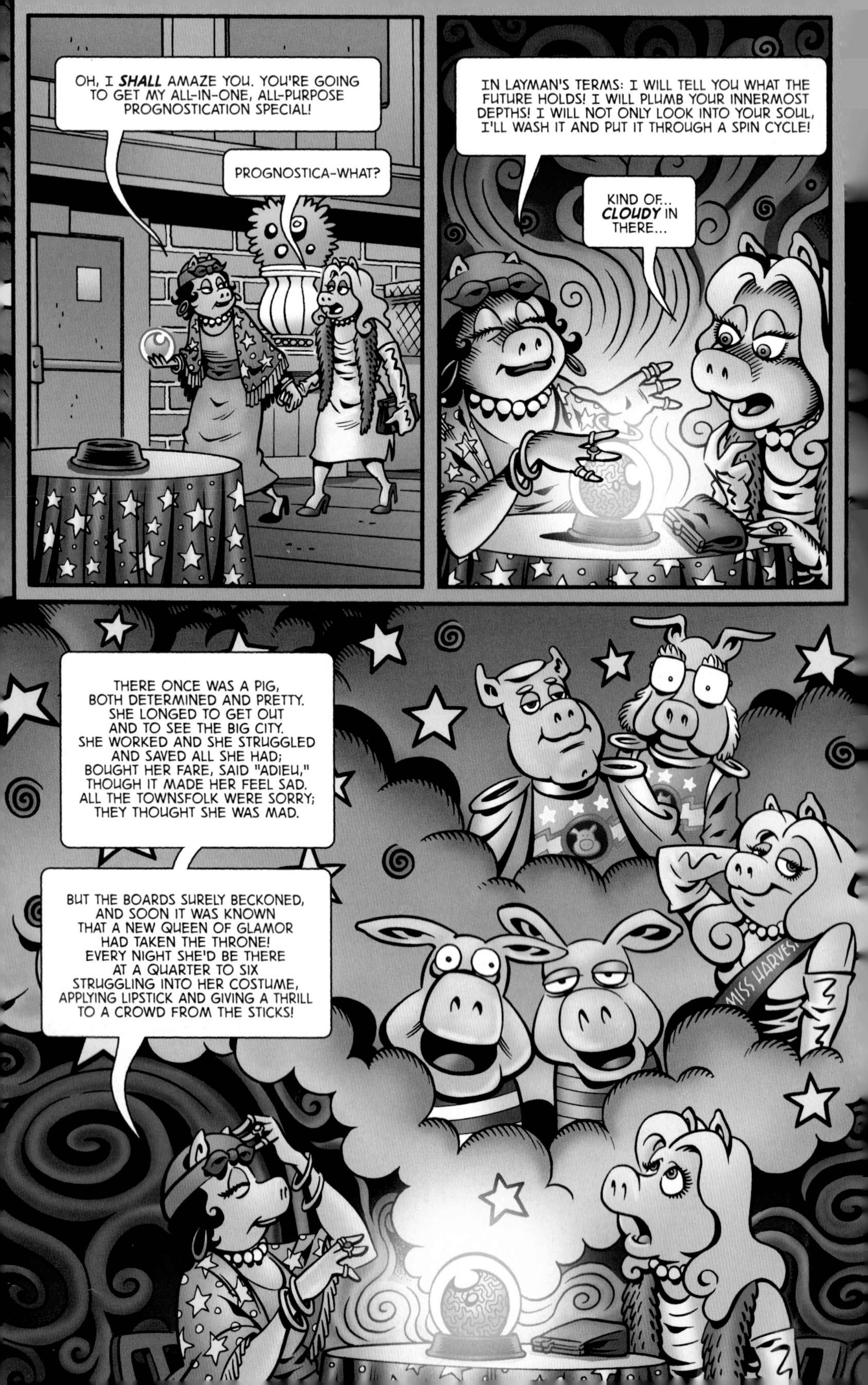
OH, I SHALL AMAZE YOU. YOU'RE GOING TO GET MY ALL-IN-ONE, ALL-PURPOSE PROGNOSTICATION SPECIAL!
PROGNOSTICA-WHAT?
IN LAYMAN'S TERMS: I WILL TELL YOU WHAT THE FUTURE HOLDS! I WILL PLUMB YOUR INNERMOST DEPTHS! I WILL NOT ONLY LOOK INTO YOUR SOUL, I'LL WASH IT AND PUT IT THROUGH A SPIN CYCLE!
KIND OF... CLOUDY IN THERE...
THERE ONCE WAS A PIG, BOTH DETERMINED AND PRETTY. SHE LONGED TO GET OUT AND TO SEE THE BIG CITY. SHE WORKED AND SHE STRUGGLED AND SAVED ALL SHE HAD; BOUGHT HER FARE, SAID "ADIEU," THOUGH IT MADE HER FEEL SAD. ALL THE TOWNSFOLK WERE SORRY; THEY THOUGHT SHE WAS MAD.
BUT THE BOARDS SURELY BECKONED, AND SOON IT WAS KNOWN THAT A NEW QUEEN OF GLAMOR HAD TAKEN THE THRONE! EVERY NIGHT SHE'D BE THERE AT A QUARTER TO SIX STRUGGLING INTO HER COSTUME, APPLYING LIPSTICK AND GIVING A THRILL TO A CROWD FROM THE STICKS!
MISS HARVEST

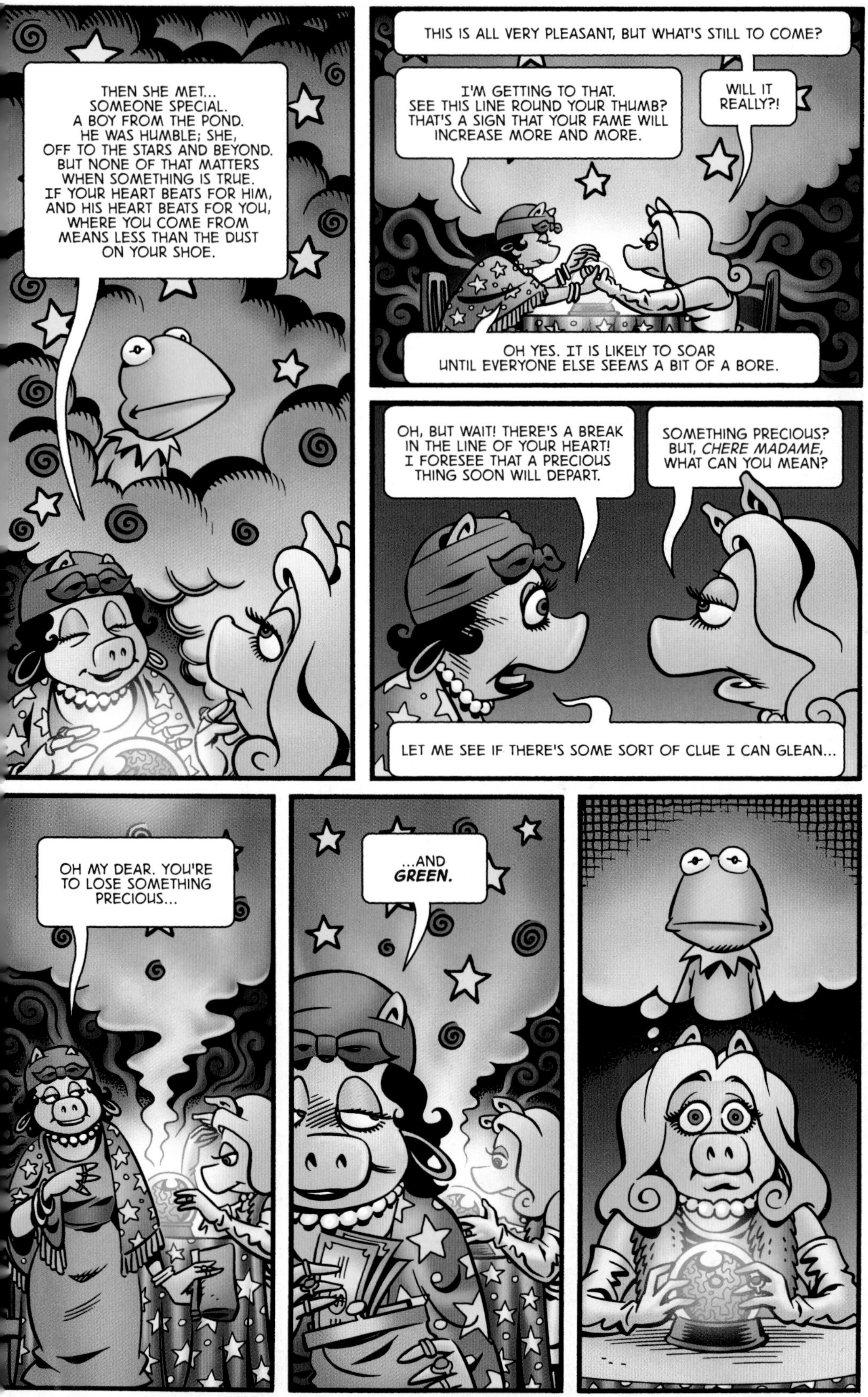
THEN SHE MET... SOMEONE SPECIAL. A BOY FROM THE POND. HE WAS HUMBLE; SHE, OFF TO THE STARS AND BEYOND. BUT NONE OF THAT MATTERS WHEN SOMETHING IS TRUE. IF YOUR HEART BEATS FOR HIM, AND HIS HEART BEATS FOR YOU, WHERE YOU COME FROM MEANS LESS THAN THE DUST ON YOUR SHOE.
THIS IS ALL VERY PLEASANT, BUT WHAT'S STILL TO COME?
I'M GETTING TO THAT. SEE THIS LINE ROUND YOUR THUMB? THAT'S A SIGN THAT YOUR FAME WILL INCREASE MORE AND MORE.
WILL IT REALLY?!
OH YES. IT IS LIKELY TO SOAR UNTIL EVERYONE ELSE SEEMS A BIT OF A BORE.
OH, BUT WAIT! THERE'S A BREAK IN THE LINE OF YOUR HEART! I FORESEE THAT A PRECIOUS THING SOON WILL DEPART.
SOMETHING PRECIOUS? BUT, *CHERE MADAME,* WHAT CAN YOU MEAN?
LET ME SEE IF THERE'S SOME SORT OF CLUE I CAN GLEAN...
OH MY DEAR. YOU'RE TO LOSE SOMETHING PRECIOUS...
...AND ***GREEN.***

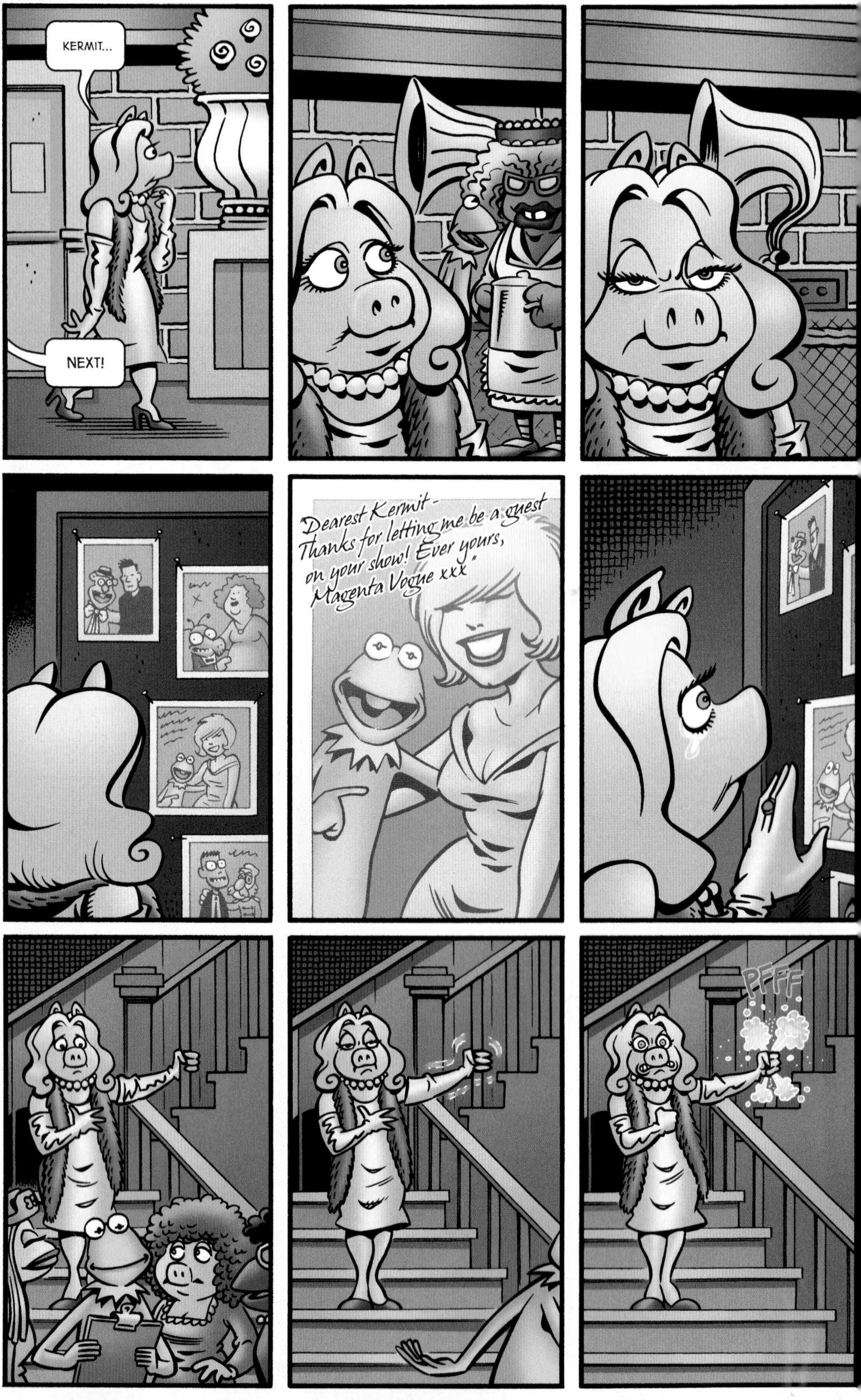
KERMIT...
NEXT!
"Dearest Kermit -
Thanks for letting me be a guest
on your show! Ever yours,
Magenta Vogue xxx"
PFFF

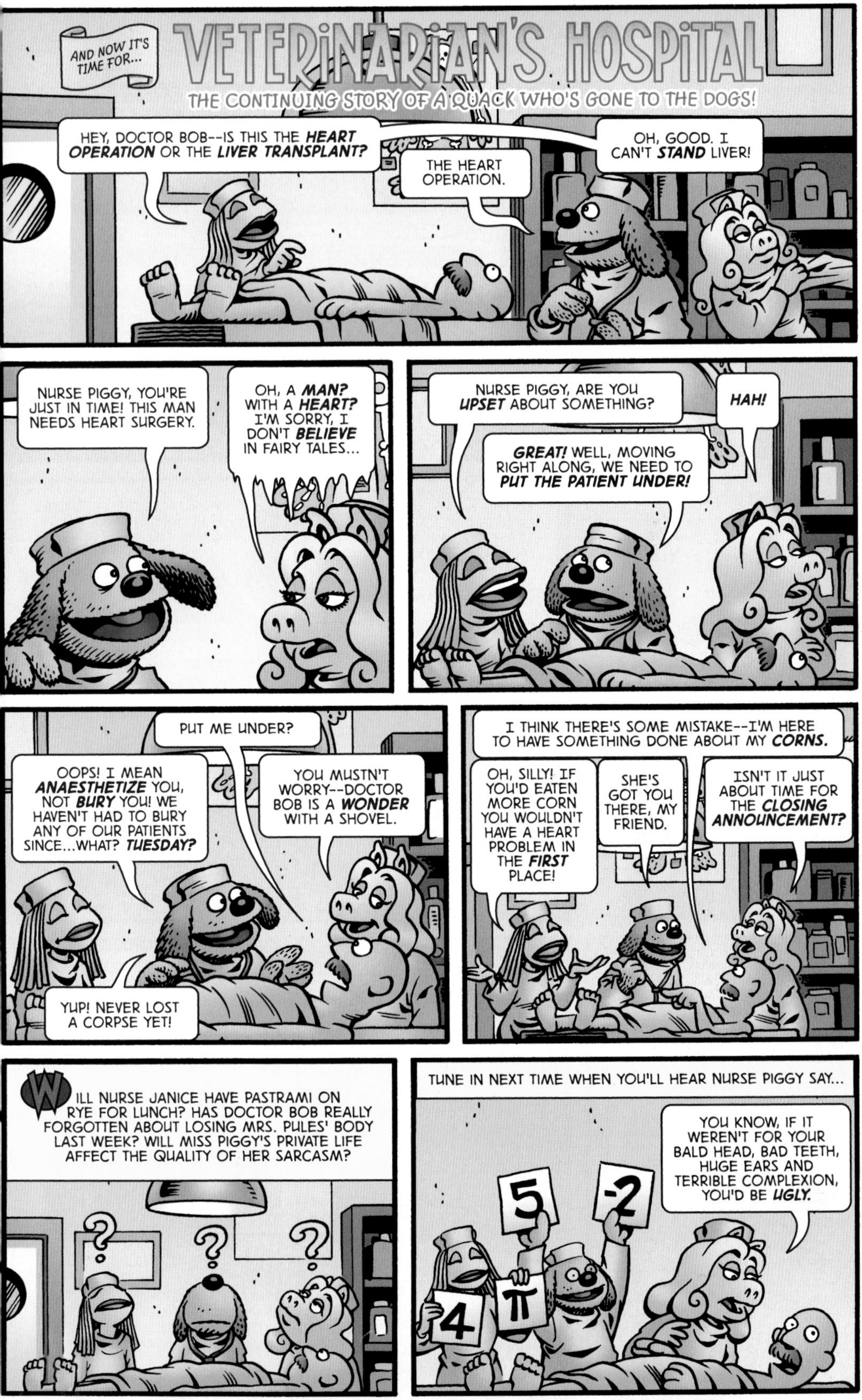
AND NOW IT'S TIME FOR...
VETERINARIAN'S HOSPITAL
THE CONTINUING STORY OF A QUACK WHO'S GONE TO THE DOGS!
HEY, DOCTOR BOB--IS THIS THE HEART OPERATION OR THE LIVER TRANSPLANT?
THE HEART OPERATION.
OH, GOOD. I CAN'T STAND LIVER!
NURSE PIGGY, YOU'RE JUST IN TIME! THIS MAN NEEDS HEART SURGERY.
OH, A MAN? WITH A HEART? I'M SORRY, I DON'T BELIEVE IN FAIRY TALES...
NURSE PIGGY, ARE YOU UPSET ABOUT SOMETHING?
HAH!
GREAT! WELL, MOVING RIGHT ALONG, WE NEED TO PUT THE PATIENT UNDER!
PUT ME UNDER?
OOPS! I MEAN ANAESTHETIZE YOU, NOT BURY YOU! WE HAVEN'T HAD TO BURY ANY OF OUR PATIENTS SINCE...WHAT? TUESDAY?
YOU MUSTN'T WORRY--DOCTOR BOB IS A WONDER WITH A SHOVEL.
YUP! NEVER LOST A CORPSE YET!
I THINK THERE'S SOME MISTAKE--I'M HERE TO HAVE SOMETHING DONE ABOUT MY CORNS.
OH, SILLY! IF YOU'D EATEN MORE CORN YOU WOULDN'T HAVE A HEART PROBLEM IN THE FIRST PLACE!
SHE'S GOT YOU THERE, MY FRIEND.
ISN'T IT JUST ABOUT TIME FOR THE CLOSING ANNOUNCEMENT?
WILL NURSE JANICE HAVE PASTRAMI ON RYE FOR LUNCH? HAS DOCTOR BOB REALLY FORGOTTEN ABOUT LOSING MRS. PULES' BODY LAST WEEK? WILL MISS PIGGY'S PRIVATE LIFE AFFECT THE QUALITY OF HER SARCASM?
TUNE IN NEXT TIME WHEN YOU'LL HEAR NURSE PIGGY SAY...
YOU KNOW, IF IT WEREN'T FOR YOUR BALD HEAD, BAD TEETH, HUGE EARS AND TERRIBLE COMPLEXION, YOU'D BE UGLY.
5
-2
4
π

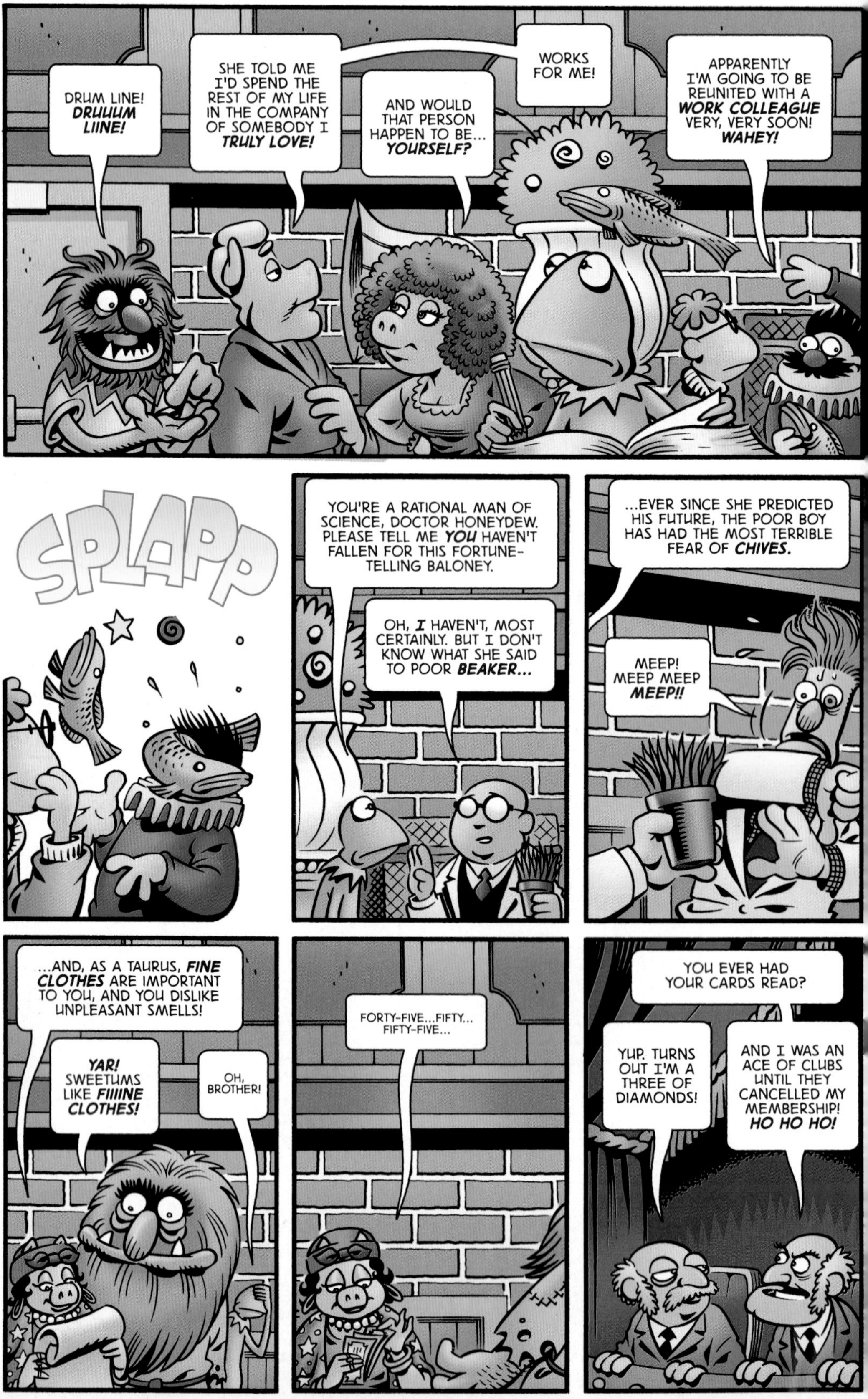
DRUM LINE! DRUUUM LIINE!
SHE TOLD ME I'D SPEND THE REST OF MY LIFE IN THE COMPANY OF SOMEBODY I TRULY LOVE!
AND WOULD THAT PERSON HAPPEN TO BE... YOURSELF?
WORKS FOR ME!
APPARENTLY I'M GOING TO BE REUNITED WITH A WORK COLLEAGUE VERY, VERY SOON! WAHEY!
SPLAPP
YOU'RE A RATIONAL MAN OF SCIENCE, DOCTOR HONEYDEW. PLEASE TELL ME YOU HAVEN'T FALLEN FOR THIS FORTUNE-TELLING BALONEY.
OH, I HAVEN'T, MOST CERTAINLY. BUT I DON'T KNOW WHAT SHE SAID TO POOR BEAKER...
...EVER SINCE SHE PREDICTED HIS FUTURE, THE POOR BOY HAS HAD THE MOST TERRIBLE FEAR OF CHIVES.
MEEP! MEEP MEEP MEEP!!
...AND, AS A TAURUS, FINE CLOTHES ARE IMPORTANT TO YOU, AND YOU DISLIKE UNPLEASANT SMELLS!
YAR! SWEETUMS LIKE FIIIINE CLOTHES!
OH, BROTHER!
FORTY-FIVE...FIFTY... FIFTY-FIVE...
YOU EVER HAD YOUR CARDS READ?
YUP. TURNS OUT I'M A THREE OF DIAMONDS!
AND I WAS AN ACE OF CLUBS UNTIL THEY CANCELLED MY MEMBERSHIP! HO HO HO!

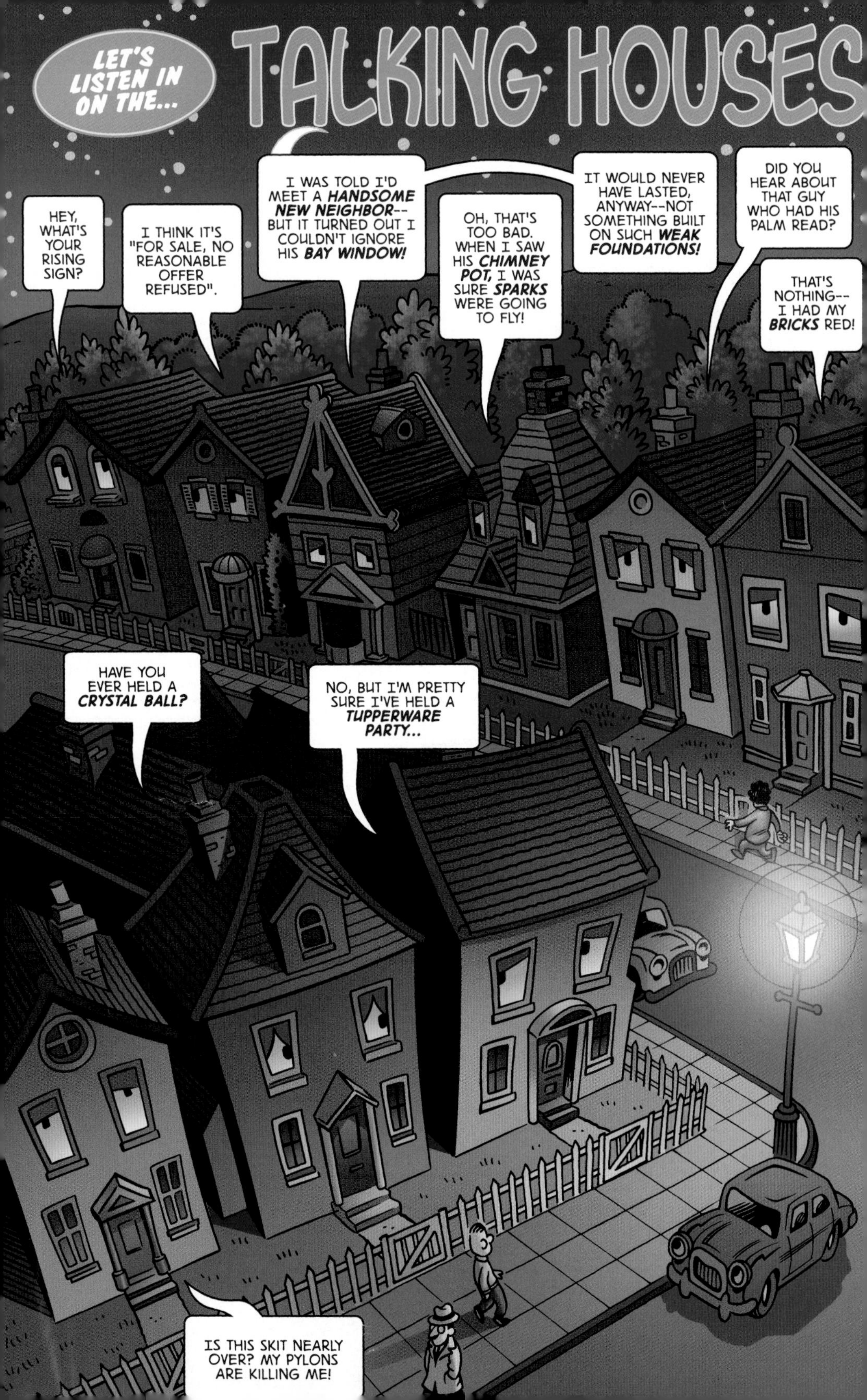
LET'S LISTEN IN ON THE...
TALKING HOUSES
HEY, WHAT'S YOUR RISING SIGN?
I THINK IT'S "FOR SALE, NO REASONABLE OFFER REFUSED".
I WAS TOLD I'D MEET A HANDSOME NEW NEIGHBOR-- BUT IT TURNED OUT I COULDN'T IGNORE HIS BAY WINDOW!
OH, THAT'S TOO BAD. WHEN I SAW HIS CHIMNEY POT, I WAS SURE SPARKS WERE GOING TO FLY!
IT WOULD NEVER HAVE LASTED, ANYWAY--NOT SOMETHING BUILT ON SUCH WEAK FOUNDATIONS!
DID YOU HEAR ABOUT THAT GUY WHO HAD HIS PALM READ?
THAT'S NOTHING-- I HAD MY BRICKS RED!
HAVE YOU EVER HELD A CRYSTAL BALL?
NO, BUT I'M PRETTY SURE I'VE HELD A TUPPERWARE PARTY...
IS THIS SKIT NEARLY OVER? MY PYLONS ARE KILLING ME!

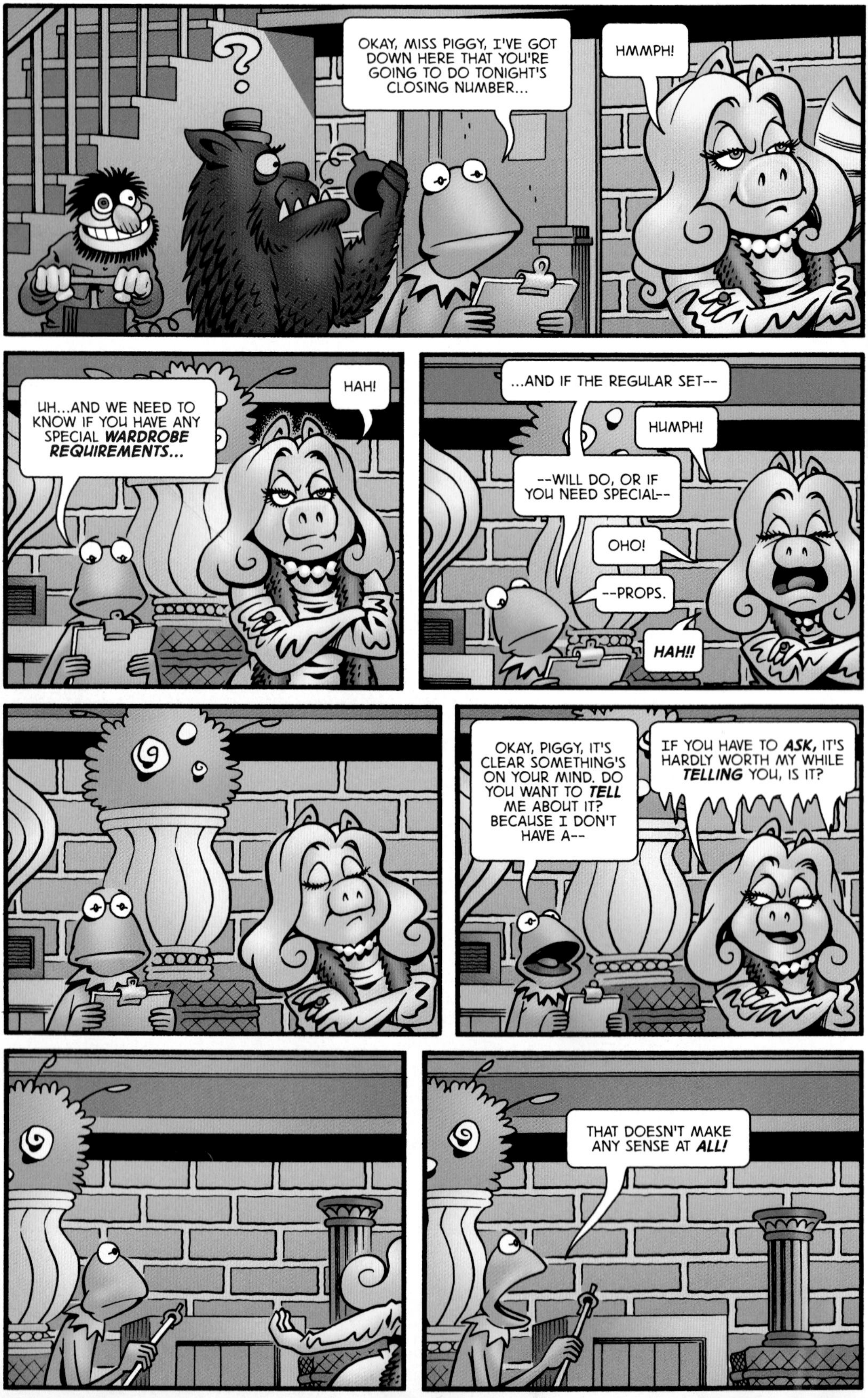

?
OKAY, MISS PIGGY, I'VE GOT DOWN HERE THAT YOU'RE GOING TO DO TONIGHT'S CLOSING NUMBER...
HMMPH!
UH...AND WE NEED TO KNOW IF YOU HAVE ANY SPECIAL **WARDROBE REQUIREMENTS...**
HAH!
...AND IF THE REGULAR SET--
HUMPH!
--WILL DO, OR IF YOU NEED SPECIAL--
OHO!
--PROPS.
HAH!!
OKAY, PIGGY, IT'S CLEAR SOMETHING'S ON YOUR MIND. DO YOU WANT TO **TELL** ME ABOUT IT? BECAUSE I DON'T HAVE A--
IF YOU HAVE TO **ASK,** IT'S HARDLY WORTH MY WHILE **TELLING** YOU, IS IT?
THAT DOESN'T MAKE ANY SENSE AT **ALL!**

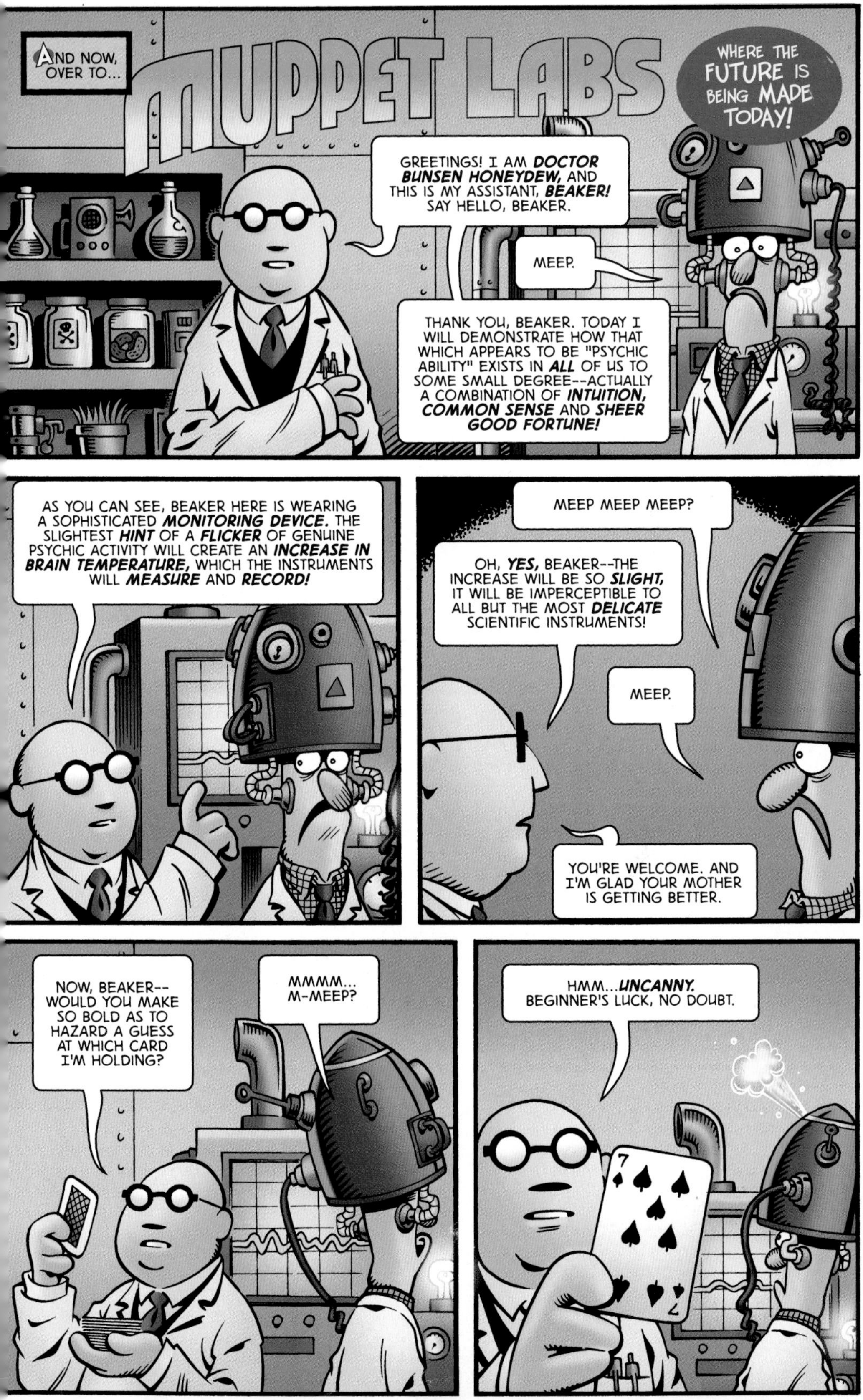
AND NOW, OVER TO...
MUPPET LABS
WHERE THE FUTURE IS BEING MADE TODAY!
GREETINGS! I AM DOCTOR BUNSEN HONEYDEW, AND THIS IS MY ASSISTANT, BEAKER! SAY HELLO, BEAKER.
MEEP.
THANK YOU, BEAKER. TODAY I WILL DEMONSTRATE HOW THAT WHICH APPEARS TO BE "PSYCHIC ABILITY" EXISTS IN ALL OF US TO SOME SMALL DEGREE--ACTUALLY A COMBINATION OF INTUITION, COMMON SENSE AND SHEER GOOD FORTUNE!
AS YOU CAN SEE, BEAKER HERE IS WEARING A SOPHISTICATED MONITORING DEVICE. THE SLIGHTEST HINT OF A FLICKER OF GENUINE PSYCHIC ACTIVITY WILL CREATE AN INCREASE IN BRAIN TEMPERATURE, WHICH THE INSTRUMENTS WILL MEASURE AND RECORD!
MEEP MEEP MEEP?
OH, YES, BEAKER--THE INCREASE WILL BE SO SLIGHT, IT WILL BE IMPERCEPTIBLE TO ALL BUT THE MOST DELICATE SCIENTIFIC INSTRUMENTS!
MEEP.
YOU'RE WELCOME. AND I'M GLAD YOUR MOTHER IS GETTING BETTER.
NOW, BEAKER-- WOULD YOU MAKE SO BOLD AS TO HAZARD A GUESS AT WHICH CARD I'M HOLDING?
MMMM... M-MEEP?
HMM...UNCANNY. BEGINNER'S LUCK, NO DOUBT.

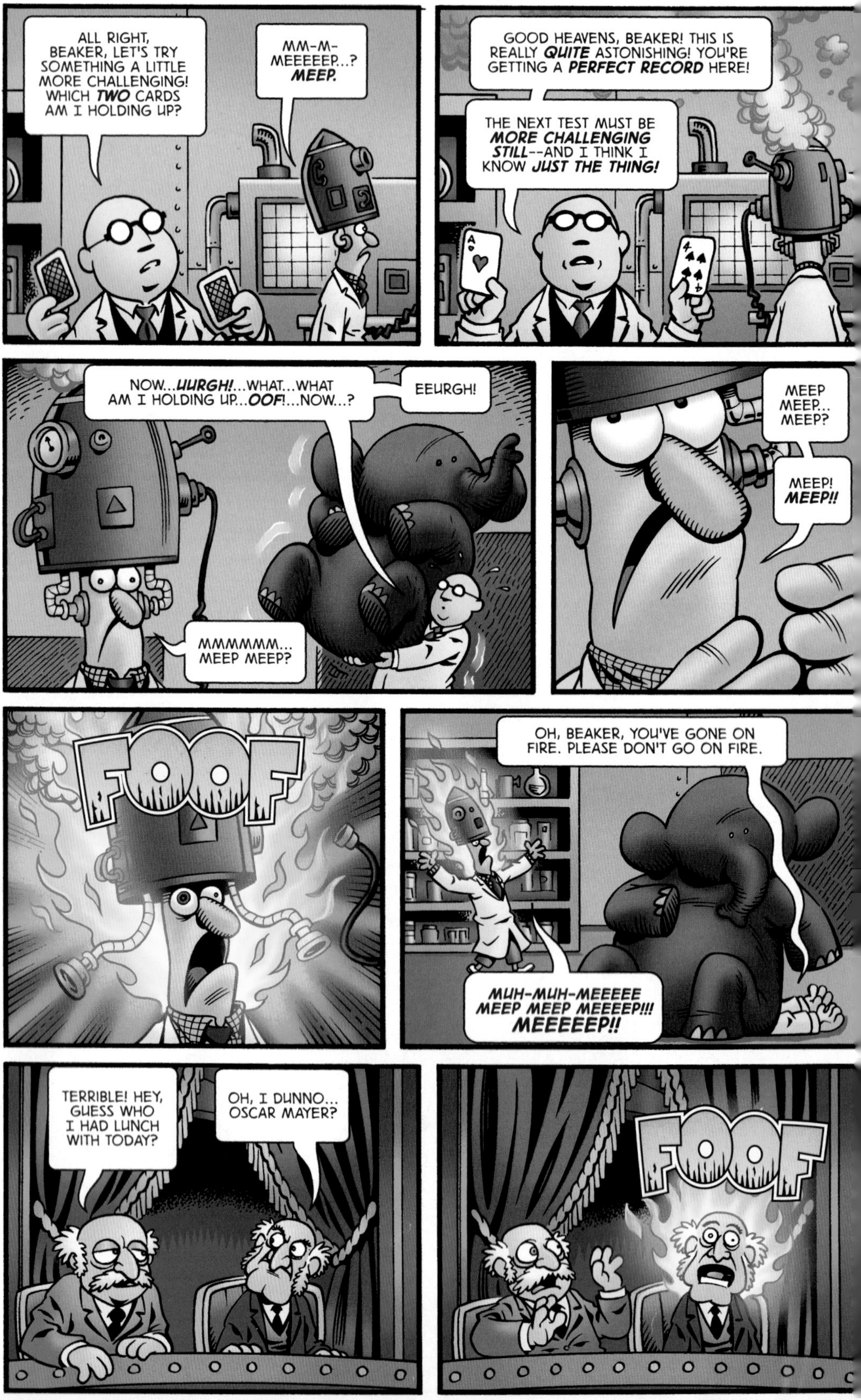
ALL RIGHT, BEAKER, LET'S TRY SOMETHING A LITTLE MORE CHALLENGING! WHICH TWO CARDS AM I HOLDING UP?
MM-M-MEEEEEP...? MEEP.
GOOD HEAVENS, BEAKER! THIS IS REALLY QUITE ASTONISHING! YOU'RE GETTING A PERFECT RECORD HERE!
THE NEXT TEST MUST BE MORE CHALLENGING STILL--AND I THINK I KNOW JUST THE THING!
NOW...UURGH!...WHAT...WHAT AM I HOLDING UP...OOF!...NOW...?
EEURGH!
MMMMMM... MEEP MEEP?
MEEP MEEP... MEEP?
MEEP! MEEP!!
FOOF
OH, BEAKER, YOU'VE GONE ON FIRE. PLEASE DON'T GO ON FIRE.
MUH-MUH-MEEEEE MEEP MEEP MEEEEP!!! MEEEEEP!!
TERRIBLE! HEY, GUESS WHO I HAD LUNCH WITH TODAY?
OH, I DUNNO... OSCAR MAYER?
FOOF

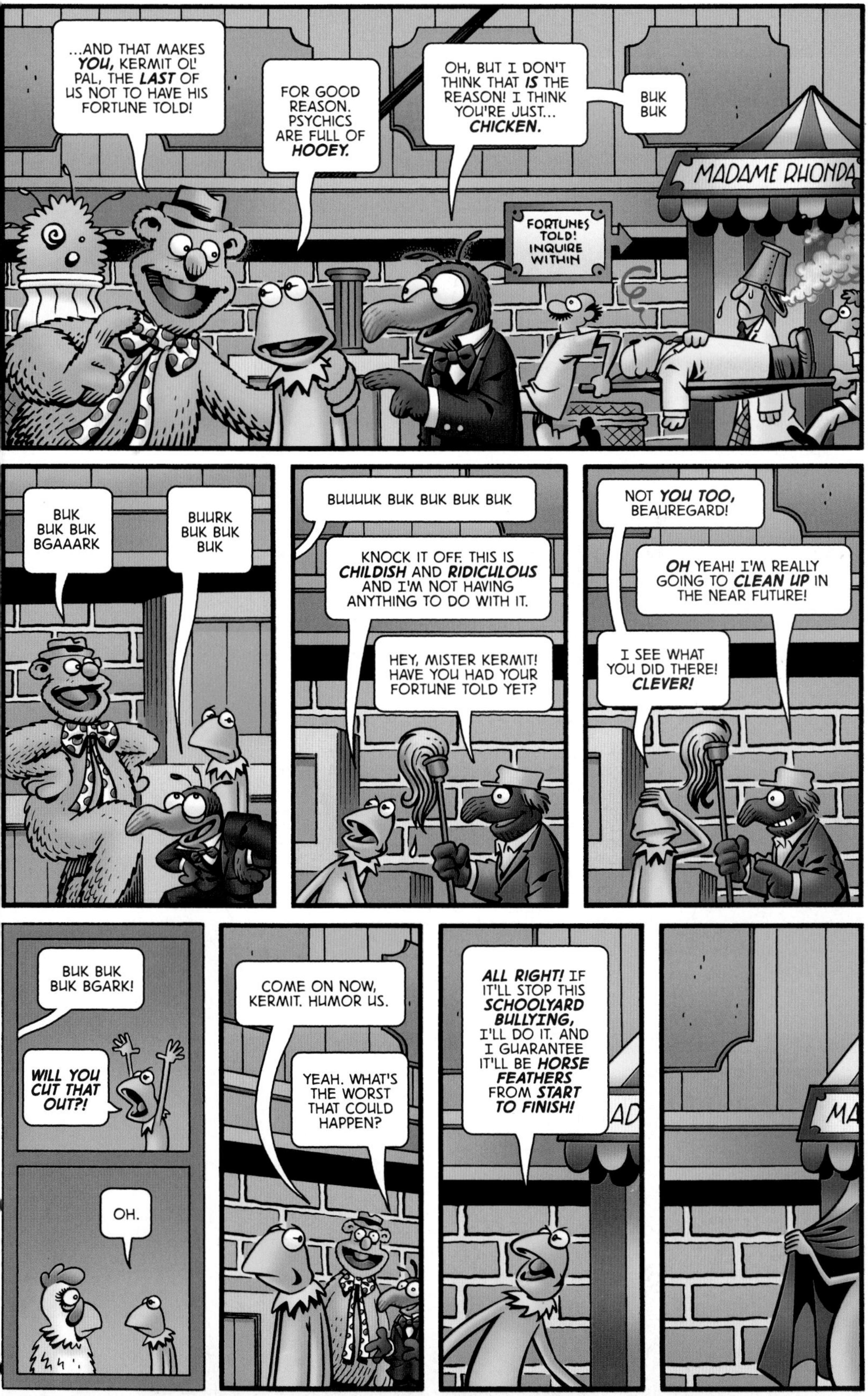

...AND THAT MAKES *YOU,* KERMIT OL' PAL, THE *LAST* OF US NOT TO HAVE HIS FORTUNE TOLD!
FOR GOOD REASON. PSYCHICS ARE FULL OF *HOOEY.*
OH, BUT I DON'T THINK THAT *IS* THE REASON! I THINK YOU'RE JUST... *CHICKEN.*
BUK BUK
MADAME RHONDA
FORTUNES TOLD! INQUIRE WITHIN
BUK BUK BUK BGAAARK
BUURK BUK BUK BUK
BUUUUK BUK BUK BUK BUK
KNOCK IT OFF. THIS IS *CHILDISH* AND *RIDICULOUS* AND I'M NOT HAVING ANYTHING TO DO WITH IT.
HEY, MISTER KERMIT! HAVE YOU HAD YOUR FORTUNE TOLD YET?
NOT *YOU TOO,* BEAUREGARD!
OH YEAH! I'M REALLY GOING TO *CLEAN UP* IN THE NEAR FUTURE!
I SEE WHAT YOU DID THERE! *CLEVER!*
BUK BUK BUK BGARK!
WILL YOU CUT THAT OUT?!
OH.
COME ON NOW, KERMIT. HUMOR US.
YEAH. WHAT'S THE WORST THAT COULD HAPPEN?
ALL RIGHT! IF IT'LL STOP THIS *SCHOOLYARD BULLYING,* I'LL DO IT. AND I GUARANTEE IT'LL BE *HORSE FEATHERS* FROM *START TO FINISH!*

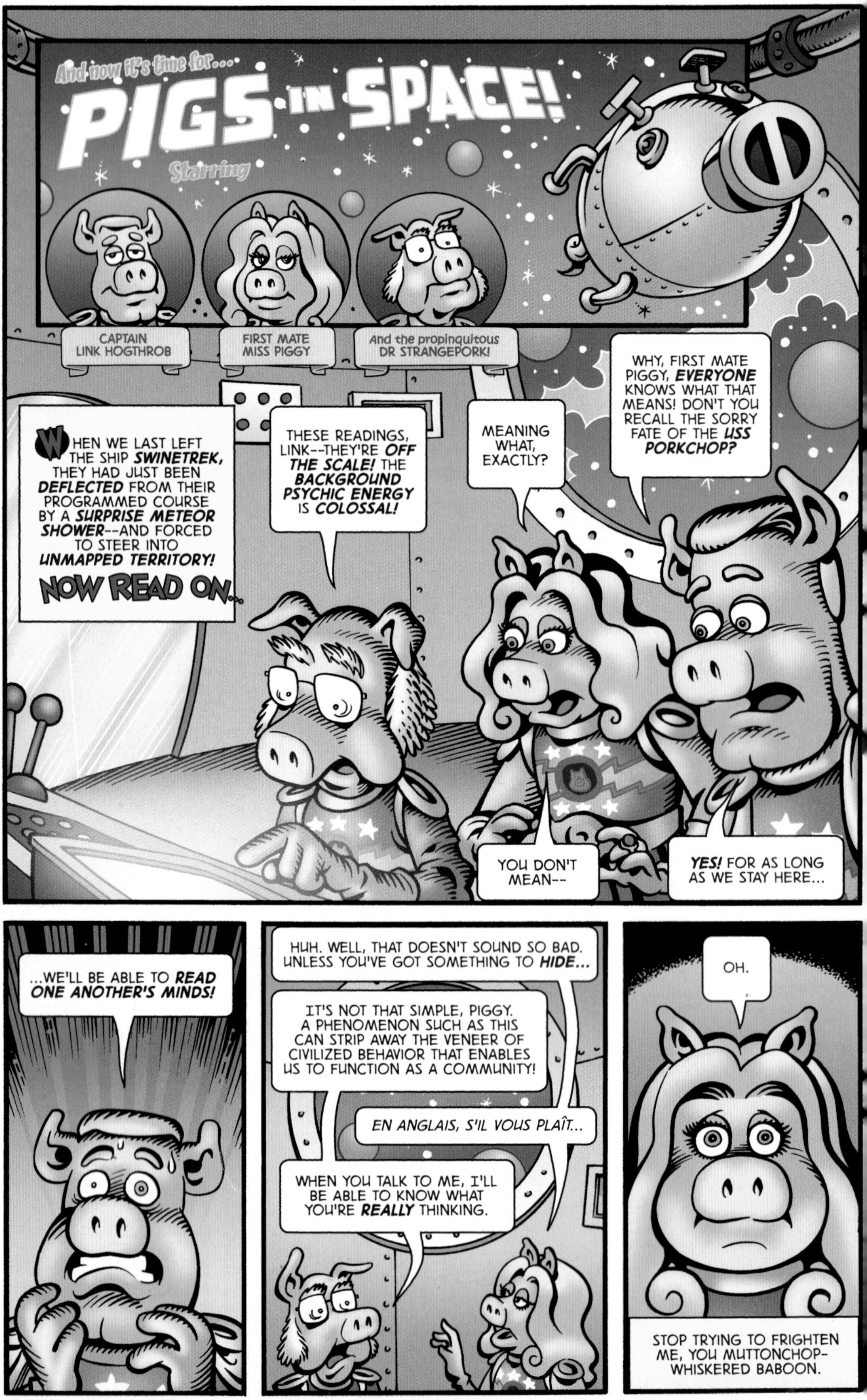
And now it's time for...
PIGS IN SPACE!
Starring
CAPTAIN LINK HOGTHROB
FIRST MATE MISS PIGGY
And the propinquitous DR STRANGEPORK!
WHEN WE LAST LEFT THE SHIP SWINETREK, THEY HAD JUST BEEN DEFLECTED FROM THEIR PROGRAMMED COURSE BY A SURPRISE METEOR SHOWER--AND FORCED TO STEER INTO UNMAPPED TERRITORY!
NOW READ ON...
THESE READINGS, LINK--THEY'RE OFF THE SCALE! THE BACKGROUND PSYCHIC ENERGY IS COLOSSAL!
MEANING WHAT, EXACTLY?
WHY, FIRST MATE PIGGY, EVERYONE KNOWS WHAT THAT MEANS! DON'T YOU RECALL THE SORRY FATE OF THE USS PORKCHOP?
YOU DON'T MEAN--
YES! FOR AS LONG AS WE STAY HERE...
...WE'LL BE ABLE TO READ ONE ANOTHER'S MINDS!
HUH. WELL, THAT DOESN'T SOUND SO BAD. UNLESS YOU'VE GOT SOMETHING TO HIDE...
IT'S NOT THAT SIMPLE, PIGGY. A PHENOMENON SUCH AS THIS CAN STRIP AWAY THE VENEER OF CIVILIZED BEHAVIOR THAT ENABLES US TO FUNCTION AS A COMMUNITY!
EN ANGLAIS, S'IL VOUS PLAÎT...
WHEN YOU TALK TO ME, I'LL BE ABLE TO KNOW WHAT YOU'RE REALLY THINKING.
OH.
STOP TRYING TO FRIGHTEN ME, YOU MUTTONCHOP-WHISKERED BABOON.

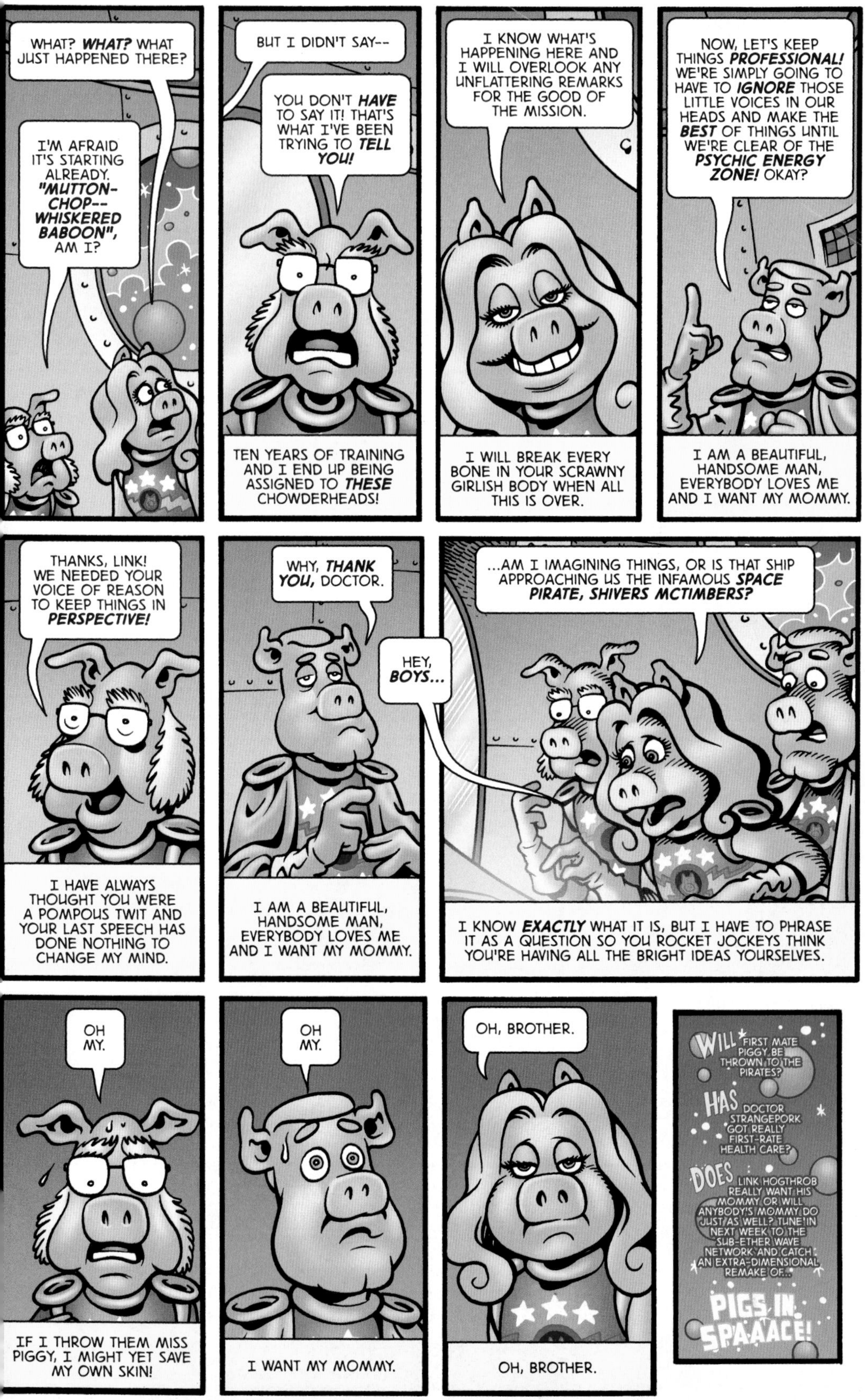
WHAT? *WHAT?* WHAT JUST HAPPENED THERE?
I'M AFRAID IT'S STARTING ALREADY. *"MUTTON-CHOP-- WHISKERED BABOON"*, AM I?
BUT I DIDN'T SAY--
YOU DON'T *HAVE* TO SAY IT! THAT'S WHAT I'VE BEEN TRYING TO *TELL YOU!*
TEN YEARS OF TRAINING AND I END UP BEING ASSIGNED TO *THESE* CHOWDERHEADS!
I KNOW WHAT'S HAPPENING HERE AND I WILL OVERLOOK ANY UNFLATTERING REMARKS FOR THE GOOD OF THE MISSION.
I WILL BREAK EVERY BONE IN YOUR SCRAWNY GIRLISH BODY WHEN ALL THIS IS OVER.
NOW, LET'S KEEP THINGS *PROFESSIONAL!* WE'RE SIMPLY GOING TO HAVE TO *IGNORE* THOSE LITTLE VOICES IN OUR HEADS AND MAKE THE *BEST* OF THINGS UNTIL WE'RE CLEAR OF THE *PSYCHIC ENERGY ZONE!* OKAY?
I AM A BEAUTIFUL, HANDSOME MAN, EVERYBODY LOVES ME AND I WANT MY MOMMY.
THANKS, LINK! WE NEEDED YOUR VOICE OF REASON TO KEEP THINGS IN *PERSPECTIVE!*
I HAVE ALWAYS THOUGHT YOU WERE A POMPOUS TWIT AND YOUR LAST SPEECH HAS DONE NOTHING TO CHANGE MY MIND.
WHY, *THANK YOU,* DOCTOR.
I AM A BEAUTIFUL, HANDSOME MAN, EVERYBODY LOVES ME AND I WANT MY MOMMY.
...AM I IMAGINING THINGS, OR IS THAT SHIP APPROACHING US THE INFAMOUS *SPACE PIRATE, SHIVERS MCTIMBERS?*
HEY, *BOYS...*
I KNOW *EXACTLY* WHAT IT IS, BUT I HAVE TO PHRASE IT AS A QUESTION SO YOU ROCKET JOCKEYS THINK YOU'RE HAVING ALL THE BRIGHT IDEAS YOURSELVES.
OH MY.
IF I THROW THEM MISS PIGGY, I MIGHT YET SAVE MY OWN SKIN!
OH MY.
I WANT MY MOMMY.
OH, BROTHER.
OH, BROTHER.
WILL FIRST MATE PIGGY BE THROWN TO THE PIRATES?
HAS DOCTOR STRANGEPORK GOT REALLY FIRST-RATE HEALTH CARE?
DOES LINK HOGTHROB REALLY WANT HIS MOMMY OR WILL ANYBODY'S MOMMY DO JUST AS WELL? TUNE IN NEXT WEEK TO THE SUB-ETHER WAVE NETWORK AND CATCH AN EXTRA-DIMENSIONAL REMAKE OF...
PIGS IN SPAAACE!

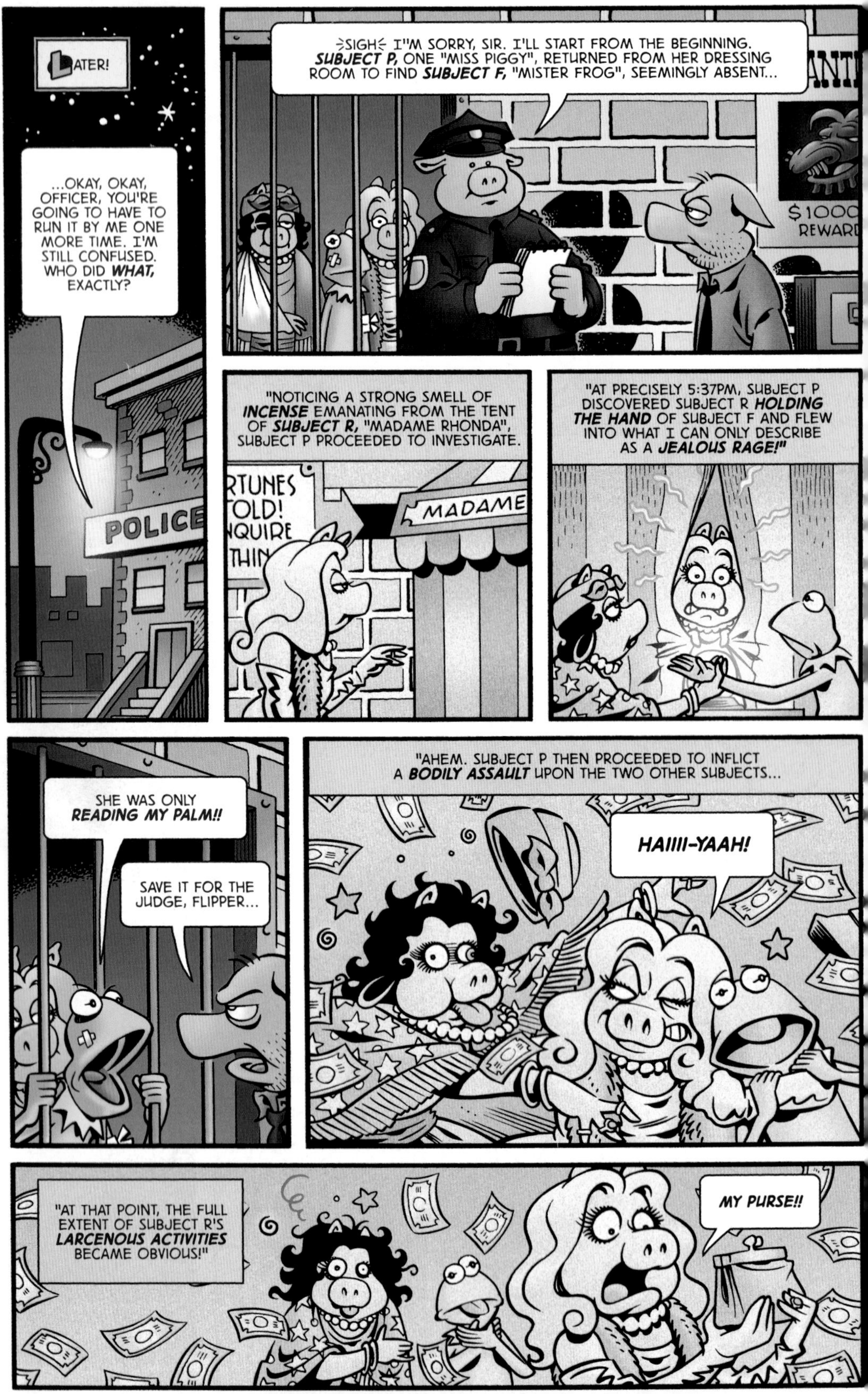
LATER!
...OKAY, OKAY, OFFICER, YOU'RE GOING TO HAVE TO RUN IT BY ME ONE MORE TIME. I'M STILL CONFUSED. WHO DID WHAT, EXACTLY?
POLICE
SIGH I'M SORRY, SIR. I'LL START FROM THE BEGINNING. SUBJECT P, ONE "MISS PIGGY", RETURNED FROM HER DRESSING ROOM TO FIND SUBJECT F, "MISTER FROG", SEEMINGLY ABSENT...
$1000
REWARD
"NOTICING A STRONG SMELL OF INCENSE EMANATING FROM THE TENT OF SUBJECT R, "MADAME RHONDA", SUBJECT P PROCEEDED TO INVESTIGATE.
RTUNES TOLD! NQUIRE THIN
MADAME
"AT PRECISELY 5:37PM, SUBJECT P DISCOVERED SUBJECT R HOLDING THE HAND OF SUBJECT F AND FLEW INTO WHAT I CAN ONLY DESCRIBE AS A JEALOUS RAGE!"
SHE WAS ONLY READING MY PALM!!
SAVE IT FOR THE JUDGE, FLIPPER...
"AHEM. SUBJECT P THEN PROCEEDED TO INFLICT A BODILY ASSAULT UPON THE TWO OTHER SUBJECTS...
HAIIII-YAAH!
"AT THAT POINT, THE FULL EXTENT OF SUBJECT R'S LARCENOUS ACTIVITIES BECAME OBVIOUS!"
MY PURSE!!

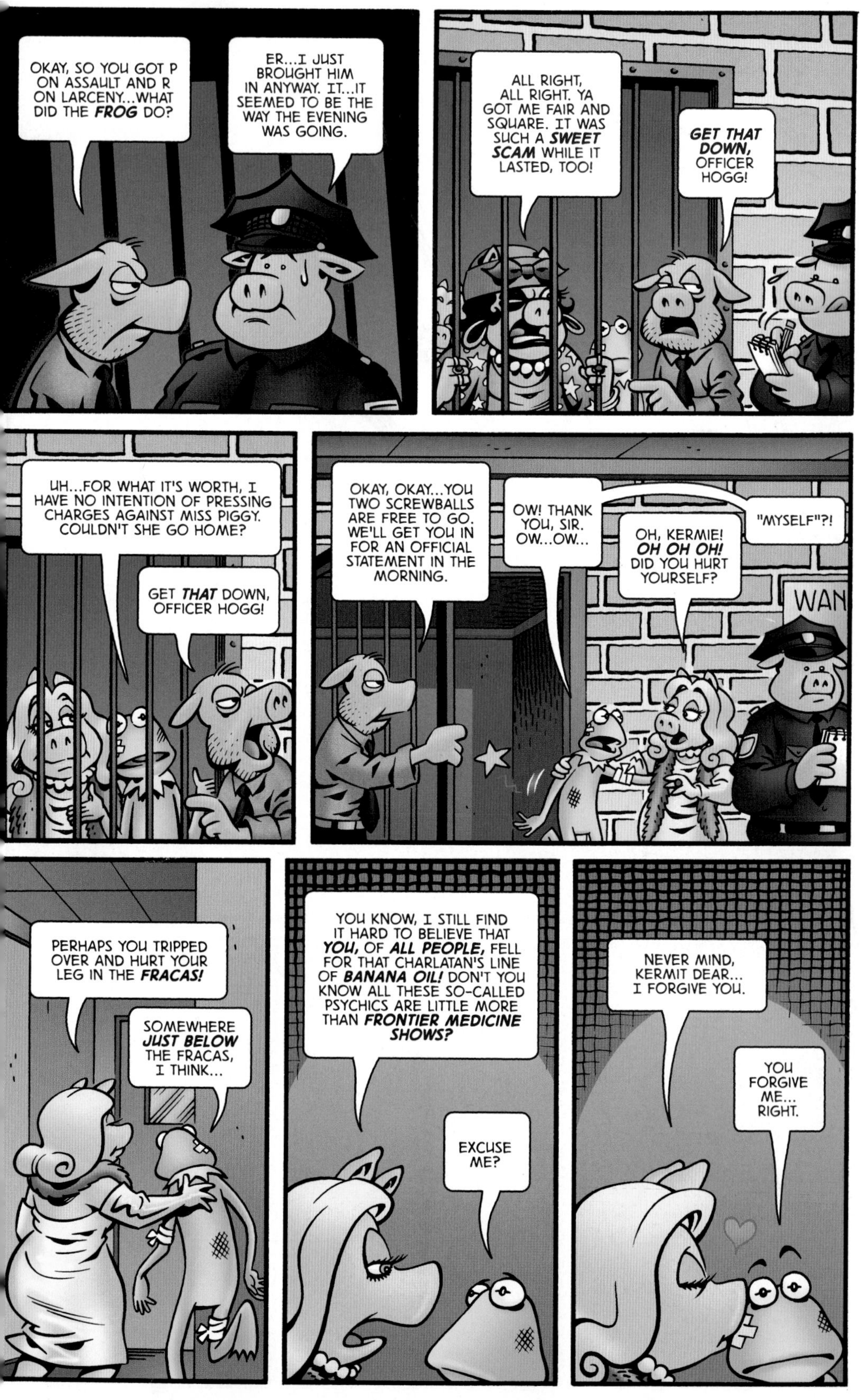
OKAY, SO YOU GOT P ON ASSAULT AND R ON LARCENY...WHAT DID THE *FROG* DO?
ER...I JUST BROUGHT HIM IN ANYWAY. IT...IT SEEMED TO BE THE WAY THE EVENING WAS GOING.
ALL RIGHT, ALL RIGHT. YA GOT ME FAIR AND SQUARE. IT WAS SUCH A *SWEET SCAM* WHILE IT LASTED, TOO!
GET THAT DOWN, OFFICER HOGG!
UH...FOR WHAT IT'S WORTH, I HAVE NO INTENTION OF PRESSING CHARGES AGAINST MISS PIGGY. COULDN'T SHE GO HOME?
GET *THAT* DOWN, OFFICER HOGG!
OKAY, OKAY...YOU TWO SCREWBALLS ARE FREE TO GO. WE'LL GET YOU IN FOR AN OFFICIAL STATEMENT IN THE MORNING.
OW! THANK YOU, SIR. OW...OW...
OH, KERMIE! *OH OH OH!* DID YOU HURT YOURSELF?
"MYSELF"?!
WAN
PERHAPS YOU TRIPPED OVER AND HURT YOUR LEG IN THE *FRACAS!*
SOMEWHERE *JUST BELOW* THE FRACAS, I THINK...
YOU KNOW, I STILL FIND IT HARD TO BELIEVE THAT *YOU,* OF *ALL PEOPLE,* FELL FOR THAT CHARLATAN'S LINE OF *BANANA OIL!* DON'T YOU KNOW ALL THESE SO-CALLED PSYCHICS ARE LITTLE MORE THAN *FRONTIER MEDICINE SHOWS?*
EXCUSE ME?
NEVER MIND, KERMIT DEAR... I FORGIVE YOU.
YOU FORGIVE ME... RIGHT.

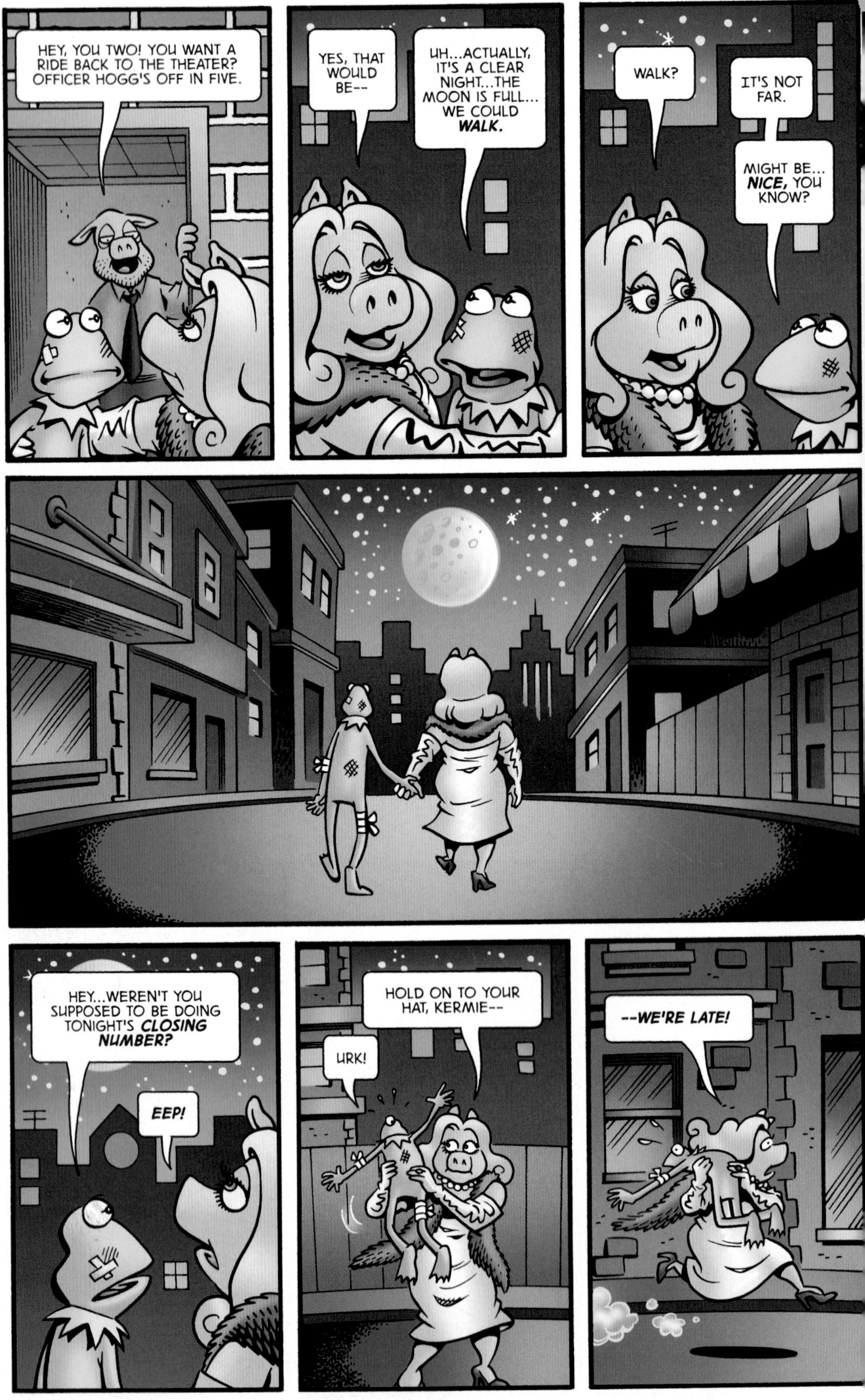
HEY, YOU TWO! YOU WANT A RIDE BACK TO THE THEATER? OFFICER HOGG'S OFF IN FIVE.
YES, THAT WOULD BE--
UH...ACTUALLY, IT'S A CLEAR NIGHT...THE MOON IS FULL... WE COULD WALK.
WALK?
IT'S NOT FAR.
MIGHT BE... NICE, YOU KNOW?
HEY...WEREN'T YOU SUPPOSED TO BE DOING TONIGHT'S CLOSING NUMBER?
EEP!
HOLD ON TO YOUR HAT, KERMIE--
URK!
--WE'RE LATE!

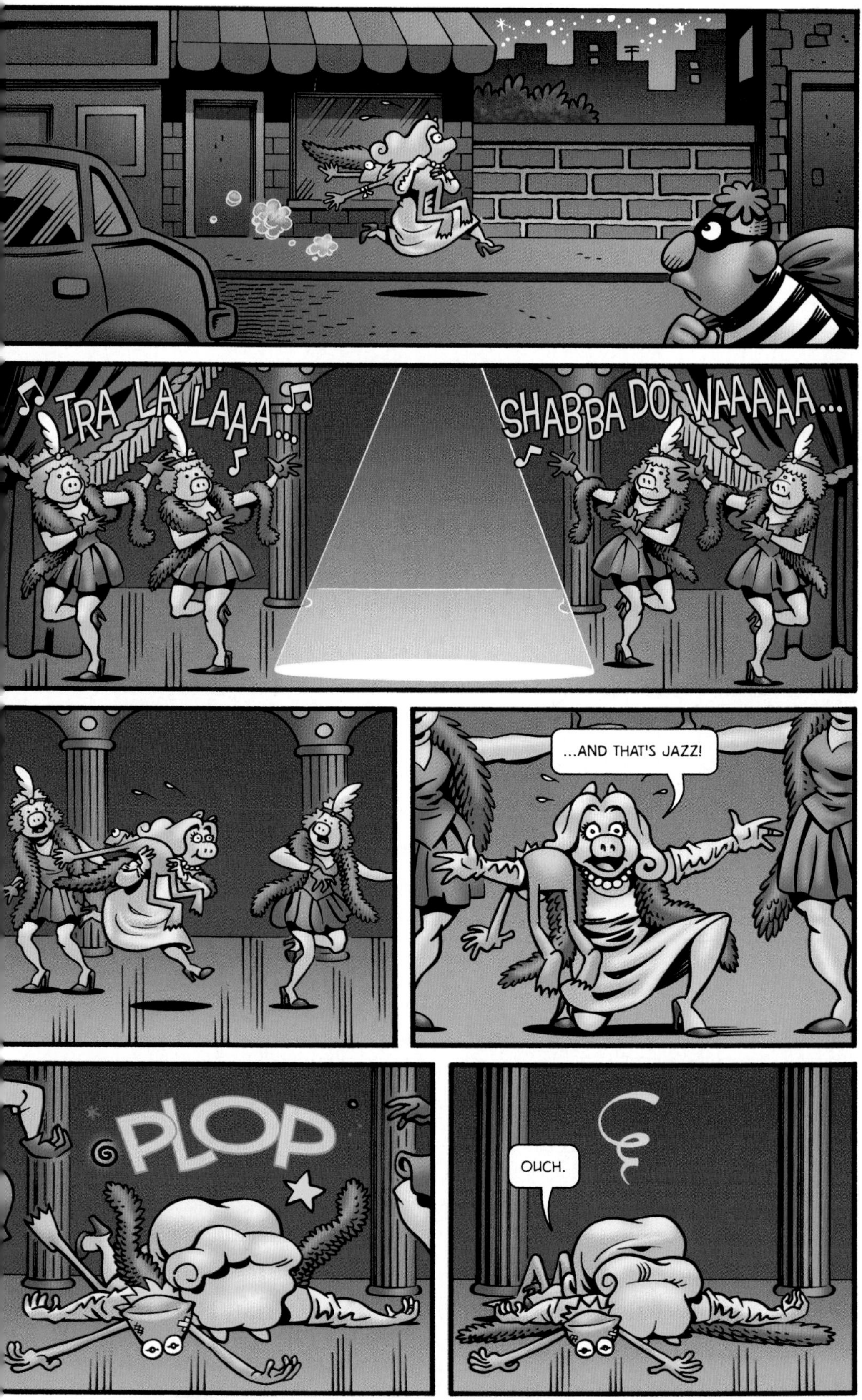
TRA LA LAAA...
SHABBA DO WAAAAA...
...AND THAT'S JAZZ!
PLOP
OUCH.

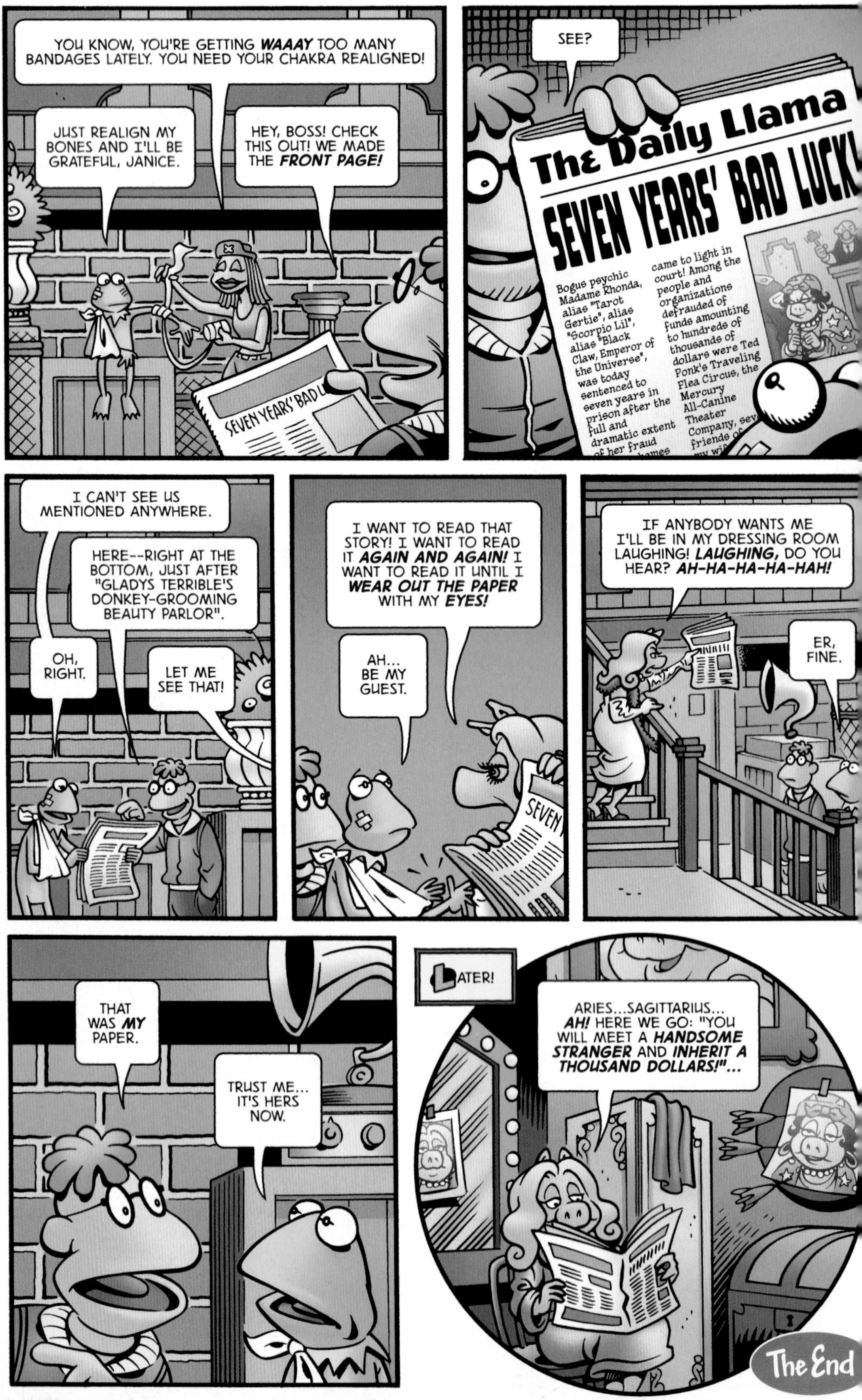
YOU KNOW, YOU'RE GETTING **WAAAY** TOO MANY BANDAGES LATELY. YOU NEED YOUR CHAKRA REALIGNED!
JUST REALIGN MY BONES AND I'LL BE GRATEFUL, JANICE.
HEY, BOSS! CHECK THIS OUT! WE MADE THE ***FRONT PAGE!***
SEVEN YEARS' BAD
SEE?
The Daily Llama
SEVEN YEARS' BAD LUCK
Bogus psychic Madame Rhonda, alias "Tarot Gertie", alias "Scorpio Lil", alias "Black Claw, Emperor of the Universe", was today sentenced to seven years in prison after the full and dramatic extent of her fraud
came to light in court! Among the people and organizations defrauded of funds amounting to hundreds of thousands of dollars were Ted Ponk's Traveling Flea Circus, the Mercury All-Canine Theater Company,
I CAN'T SEE US MENTIONED ANYWHERE.
HERE--RIGHT AT THE BOTTOM, JUST AFTER "GLADYS TERRIBLE'S DONKEY-GROOMING BEAUTY PARLOR".
OH, RIGHT.
LET ME SEE THAT!
I WANT TO READ THAT STORY! I WANT TO READ IT ***AGAIN AND AGAIN!*** I WANT TO READ IT UNTIL I ***WEAR OUT THE PAPER*** WITH MY ***EYES!***
AH... BE MY GUEST.
SEVEN
IF ANYBODY WANTS ME I'LL BE IN MY DRESSING ROOM LAUGHING! ***LAUGHING,*** DO YOU HEAR? ***AH-HA-HA-HA-HAH!***
ER, FINE.
THAT WAS ***MY*** PAPER.
TRUST ME... IT'S HERS NOW.
LATER!
ARIES...SAGITTARIUS... ***AH!*** HERE WE GO: "YOU WILL MEET A ***HANDSOME STRANGER*** AND ***INHERIT A THOUSAND DOLLARS!"...***
The End

Before BOOM! Studios approached me to draw *The Muppet Show* comics, I'd already taken a stab at the characters a couple of years earlier for the magazine *Disney Adventures*. They'd been running some distinctly off-model Mickey Mouse strips by Glenn McCoy, drawn in a scratchy, underground-comix sort of style, which had proven popular enough that they were looking to apply a similar treatment to some other Disney property. I'd been doing a bit of freelance illustration for the magazine, and the editors at *Disney Adventures* were familiar with my other comics work and thought I'd be a good fit for the experiment.

I ended up producing a mere 15 pages of material before I got word that *Disney Adventures Magazine* had been canceled. Only one page of that initial run saw print in the pages of *DA*, a Fozzie Bear strip. The rest were consigned to the dark recesses of some hard drive somewhere, never to see the light of day... I thought.

The thing is, I was inordinately proud of those pages. For the next year, I was aggressively showing them around to anybody who would look at them, and quite a few people who probably had no interest in them whatsoever; not with the hopes of finding a publisher or anything, but simply because I desperately wanted them to be read, by whatever means. And presumably they were circulating behind the scenes at Disney, too, because BOOM! Studios eventually approached me on the strength of those pages and invited me to do a full-length, slightly more on-model comic book version of the show.

Let me be honest here. The primary impulse for me taking the job on, at least in the first instance, was to get the *Disney Adventures* pages into print somehow. It seemed to me that there would be a much greater chance of them finally being published if I were to associate myself with the Muppets for a few months longer and get enough material together for a book. Put the *Disney Adventures* in the back as a bonus feature and voilà! Mission accomplished! And the Muppets and I would be done with one another.

It hasn't quite worked out that way. The BOOM! Studios *Muppet Show* comic has picked up a terrible momentum of its own and I hope to be associated with it for a while yet. It's been one of the most satisfying projects of my professional life, fitting my own interests and sensibilities like some crazy three-fingered glove. But I'm still thrilled to have my original Muppet Show material presented to the world in its entirety, in full colour and without me having to buy anybody a drink, for the very first time. This is the tiny, ugly baby that would eventually grow up to be the eight foot gorilla you hold in your hands today. Enjoy.

Roger Langridge
London, July 2009

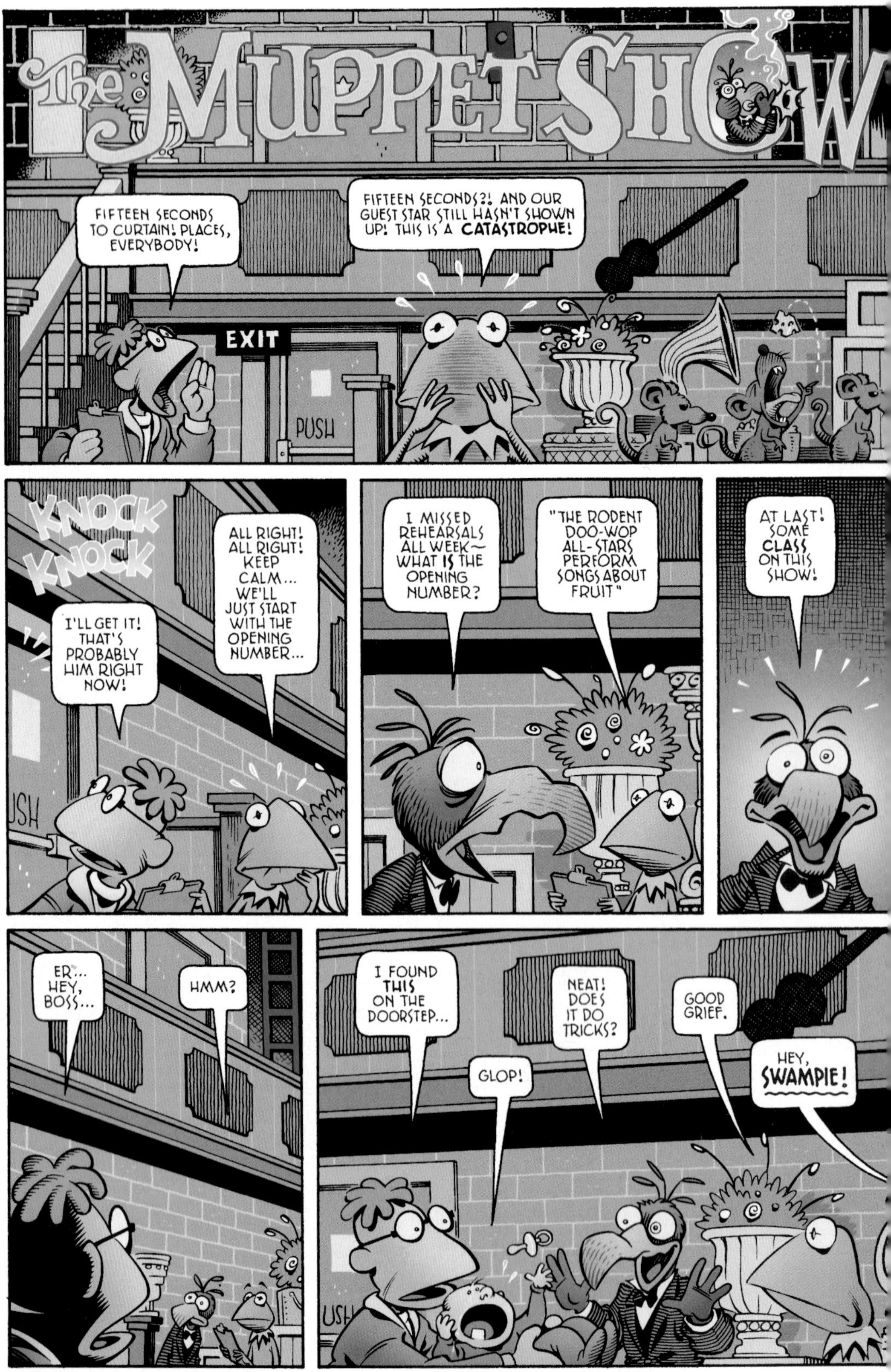

The Muppet Show
FIFTEEN SECONDS TO CURTAIN! PLACES, EVERYBODY!
FIFTEEN SECONDS?! AND OUR GUEST STAR STILL HASN'T SHOWN UP! THIS IS A **CATASTROPHE!**
EXIT
PUSH
KNOCK KNOCK
I'LL GET IT! THAT'S PROBABLY HIM RIGHT NOW!
ALL RIGHT! ALL RIGHT! KEEP CALM... WE'LL JUST START WITH THE OPENING NUMBER...
I MISSED REHEARSALS ALL WEEK~ WHAT **IS** THE OPENING NUMBER?
"THE RODENT DOO-WOP ALL-STARS PERFORM SONGS ABOUT FRUIT"
AT LAST! SOME **CLASS** ON THIS SHOW!
ER... HEY, BOSS...
HMM?
I FOUND **THIS** ON THE DOORSTEP...
GLOP!
NEAT! DOES IT DO TRICKS?
GOOD GRIEF.
HEY, **SWAMPIE!**

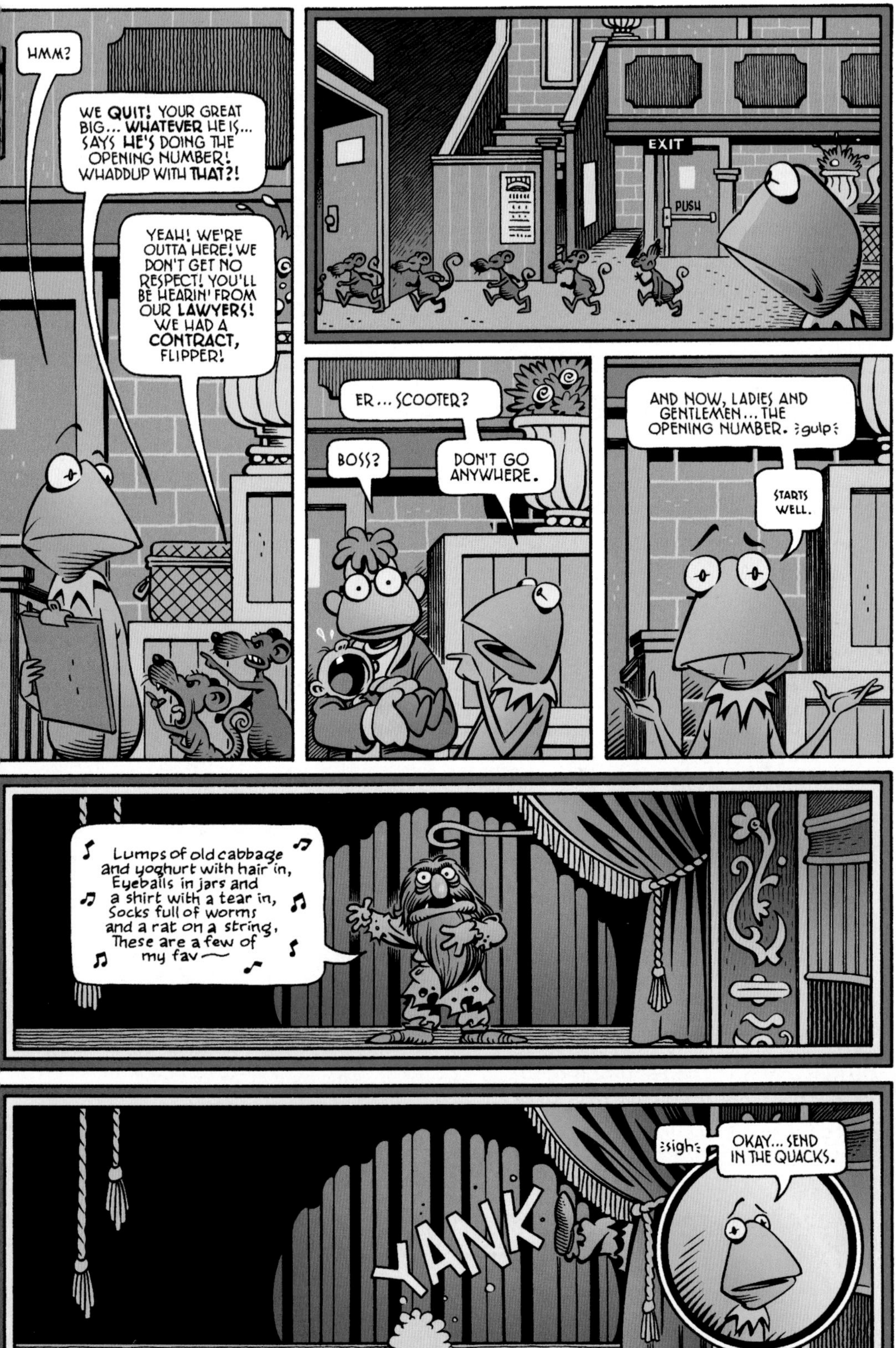

HMM?
WE QUIT! YOUR GREAT BIG... WHATEVER HE IS... SAYS HE'S DOING THE OPENING NUMBER! WHADDUP WITH THAT?!
YEAH! WE'RE OUTTA HERE! WE DON'T GET NO RESPECT! YOU'LL BE HEARIN' FROM OUR LAWYERS! WE HAD A CONTRACT, FLIPPER!
EXIT
PUSH
ER... SCOOTER?
BOSS?
DON'T GO ANYWHERE.
AND NOW, LADIES AND GENTLEMEN... THE OPENING NUMBER. gulp
STARTS WELL.
Lumps of old cabbage and yoghurt with hair in, Eyeballs in jars and a shirt with a tear in, Socks full of worms and a rat on a string, These are a few of my fav—
YANK
sigh
OKAY... SEND IN THE QUACKS.

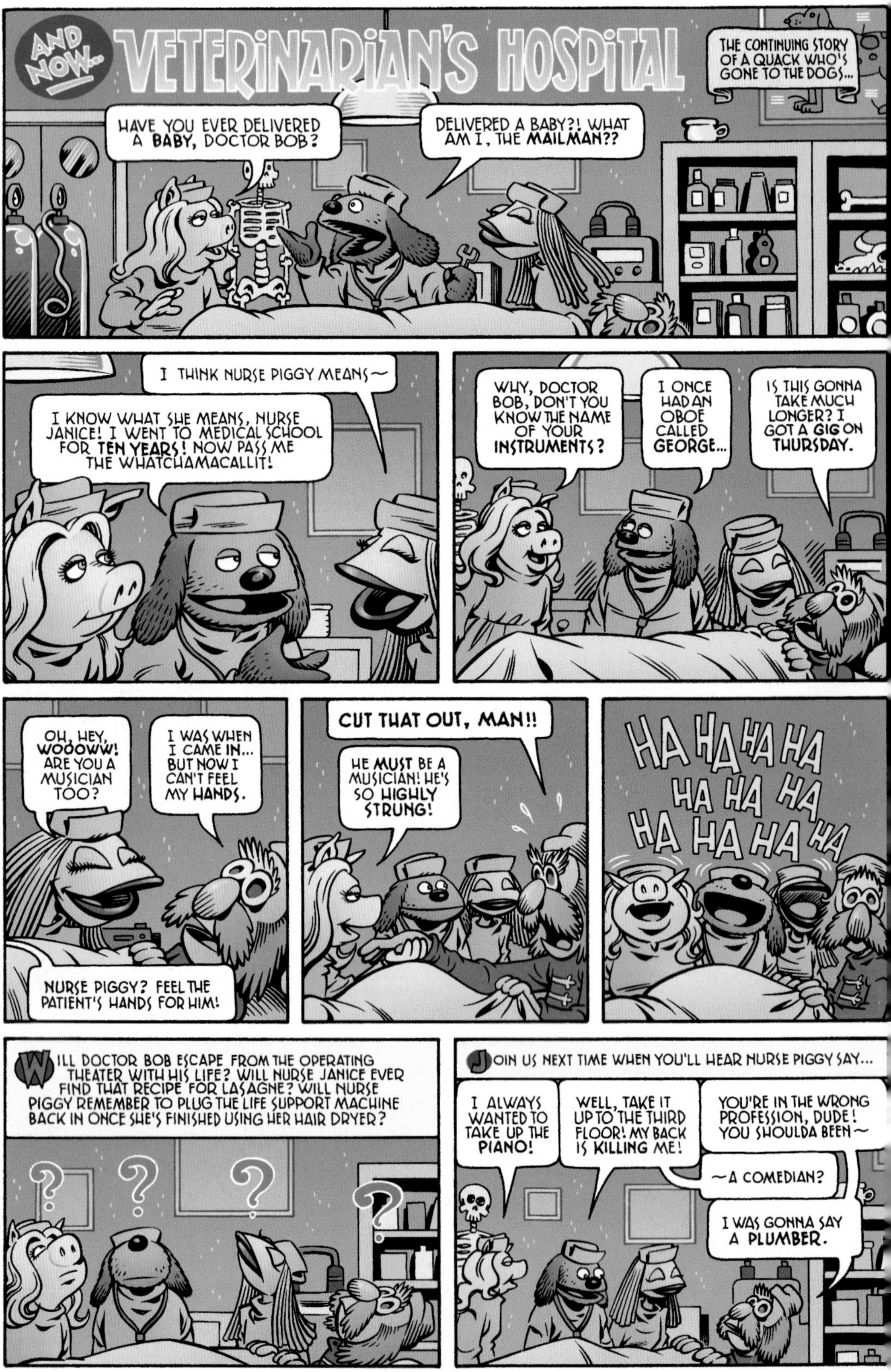
AND NOW...
VETERINARIAN'S HOSPITAL
THE CONTINUING STORY OF A QUACK WHO'S GONE TO THE DOGS...
HAVE YOU EVER DELIVERED A BABY, DOCTOR BOB?
DELIVERED A BABY?! WHAT AM I, THE MAILMAN??
I THINK NURSE PIGGY MEANS~
I KNOW WHAT SHE MEANS, NURSE JANICE! I WENT TO MEDICAL SCHOOL FOR TEN YEARS! NOW PASS ME THE WHATCHAMACALLIT!
WHY, DOCTOR BOB, DON'T YOU KNOW THE NAME OF YOUR INSTRUMENTS?
I ONCE HAD AN OBOE CALLED GEORGE...
IS THIS GONNA TAKE MUCH LONGER? I GOT A GIG ON THURSDAY.
OH, HEY, WOOOWW! ARE YOU A MUSICIAN TOO?
I WAS WHEN I CAME IN... BUT NOW I CAN'T FEEL MY HANDS.
NURSE PIGGY? FEEL THE PATIENT'S HANDS FOR HIM!
CUT THAT OUT, MAN!!
HE MUST BE A MUSICIAN! HE'S SO HIGHLY STRUNG!
HA HA HA HA HA HA HA HA HA HA HA HA HA
WILL DOCTOR BOB ESCAPE FROM THE OPERATING THEATER WITH HIS LIFE? WILL NURSE JANICE EVER FIND THAT RECIPE FOR LASAGNE? WILL NURSE PIGGY REMEMBER TO PLUG THE LIFE SUPPORT MACHINE BACK IN ONCE SHE'S FINISHED USING HER HAIR DRYER?
JOIN US NEXT TIME WHEN YOU'LL HEAR NURSE PIGGY SAY...
I ALWAYS WANTED TO TAKE UP THE PIANO!
WELL, TAKE IT UP TO THE THIRD FLOOR! MY BACK IS KILLING ME!
YOU'RE IN THE WRONG PROFESSION, DUDE! YOU SHOULDA BEEN~
~A COMEDIAN?
I WAS GONNA SAY A PLUMBER.

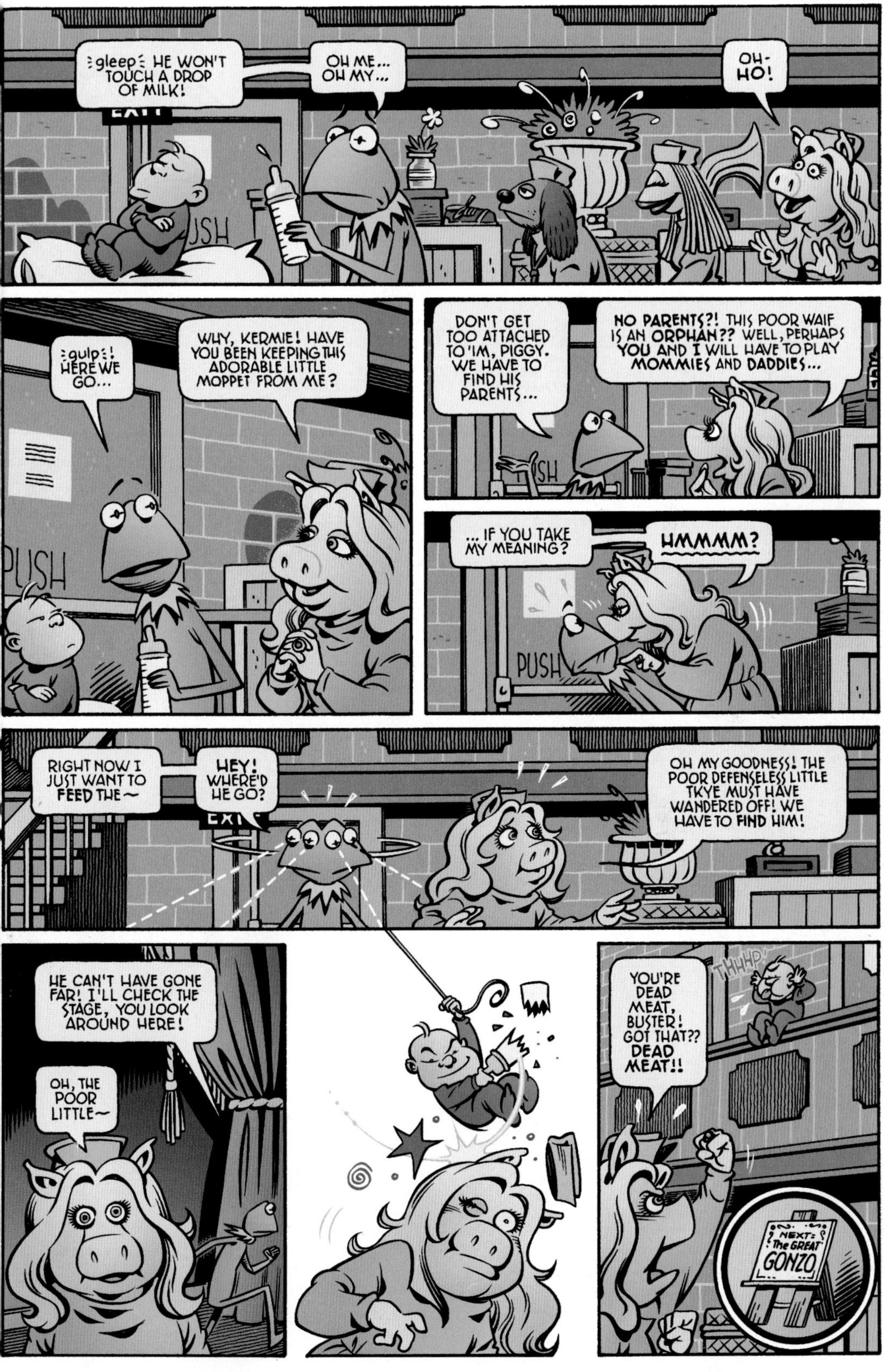

⁝gleep⁝ HE WON'T TOUCH A DROP OF MILK!
OH ME... OH MY...
OH-HO!
⁝gulp⁝! HERE WE GO...
WHY, KERMIE! HAVE YOU BEEN KEEPING THIS ADORABLE LITTLE MOPPET FROM ME?
PUSH
DON'T GET TOO ATTACHED TO 'IM, PIGGY. WE HAVE TO FIND HIS PARENTS...
NO PARENTS?! THIS POOR WAIF IS AN ORPHAN?? WELL, PERHAPS YOU AND I WILL HAVE TO PLAY MOMMIES AND DADDIES...
... IF YOU TAKE MY MEANING?
HMMMM?
PUSH
RIGHT NOW I JUST WANT TO FEED THE~
HEY! WHERE'D HE GO?
OH MY GOODNESS! THE POOR DEFENSELESS LITTLE TKYE MUST HAVE WANDERED OFF! WE HAVE TO FIND HIM!
HE CAN'T HAVE GONE FAR! I'LL CHECK THE STAGE, YOU LOOK AROUND HERE!
OH, THE POOR LITTLE~
THHHP!
YOU'RE DEAD MEAT, BUSTER! GOT THAT?? DEAD MEAT!!
NEXT: The GREAT GONZO

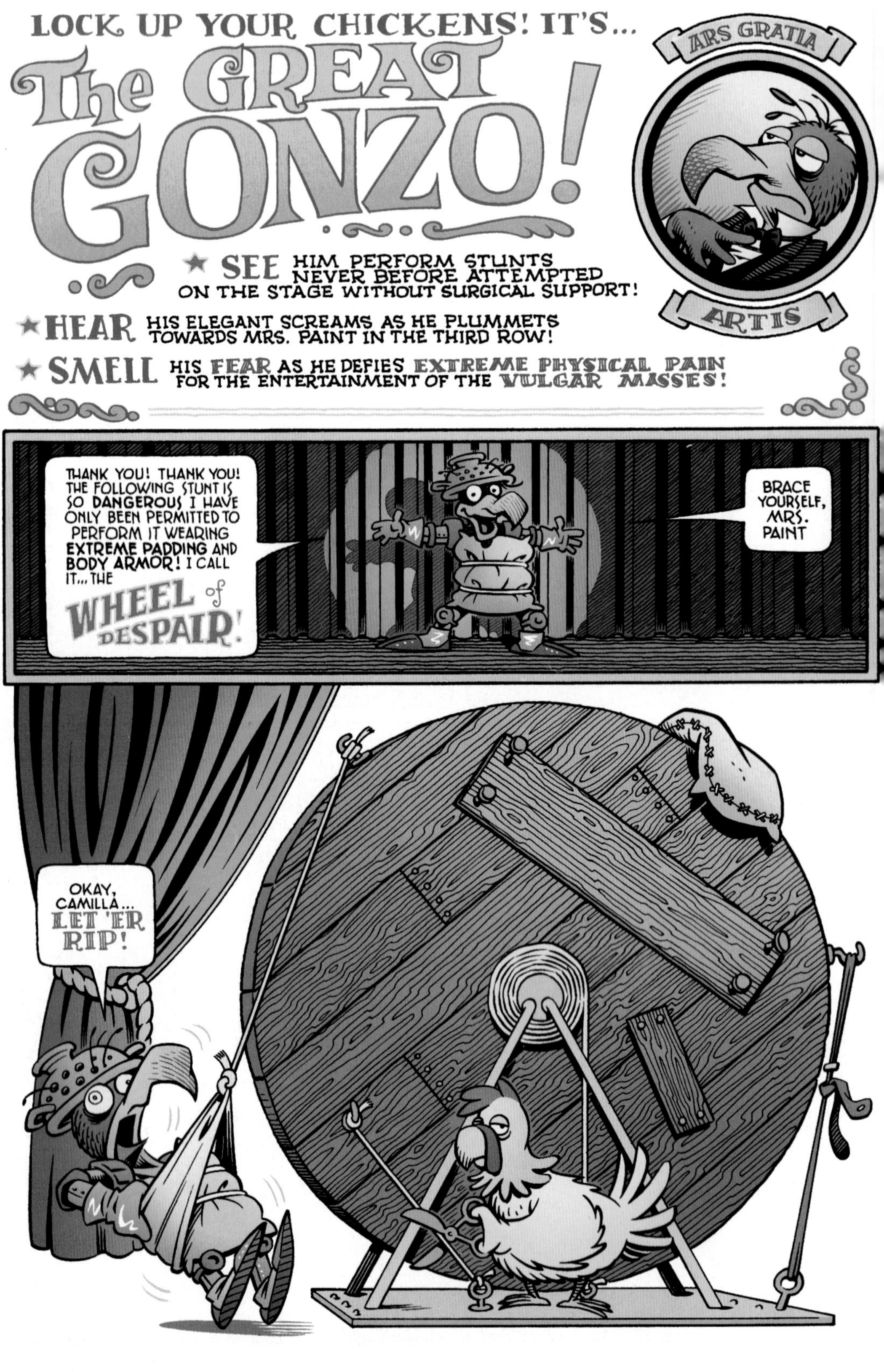

LOCK UP YOUR CHICKENS! IT'S...
The GREAT GONZO!
ARS GRATIA ARTIS
★ SEE HIM PERFORM STUNTS NEVER BEFORE ATTEMPTED ON THE STAGE WITHOUT SURGICAL SUPPORT!
★ HEAR HIS ELEGANT SCREAMS AS HE PLUMMETS TOWARDS MRS. PAINT IN THE THIRD ROW!
★ SMELL HIS FEAR AS HE DEFIES EXTREME PHYSICAL PAIN FOR THE ENTERTAINMENT OF THE VULGAR MASSES!
THANK YOU! THANK YOU! THE FOLLOWING STUNT IS SO DANGEROUS I HAVE ONLY BEEN PERMITTED TO PERFORM IT WEARING EXTREME PADDING AND BODY ARMOR! I CALL IT... THE WHEEL of DESPAIR!
BRACE YOURSELF, MRS. PAINT
OKAY, CAMILLA... LET 'ER RIP!

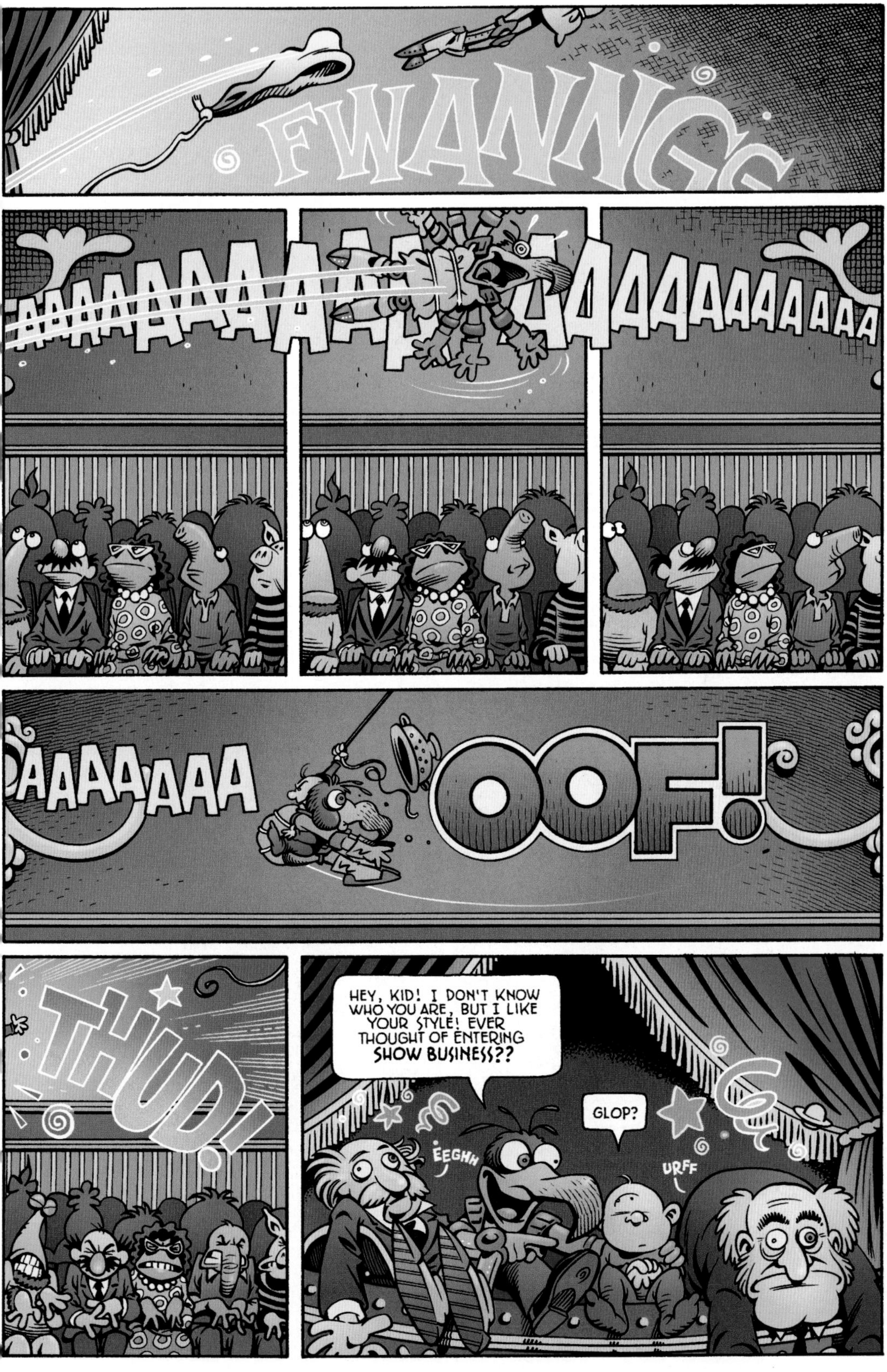
FWANNG
AAAAAAAAAAAAAAAAAAAAAAAAAAA
AAAAAAA
OOF!
THUD!
HEY, KID! I DON'T KNOW WHO YOU ARE, BUT I LIKE YOUR STYLE! EVER THOUGHT OF ENTERING SHOW BUSINESS??
GLOP?
EEGHH
URFF

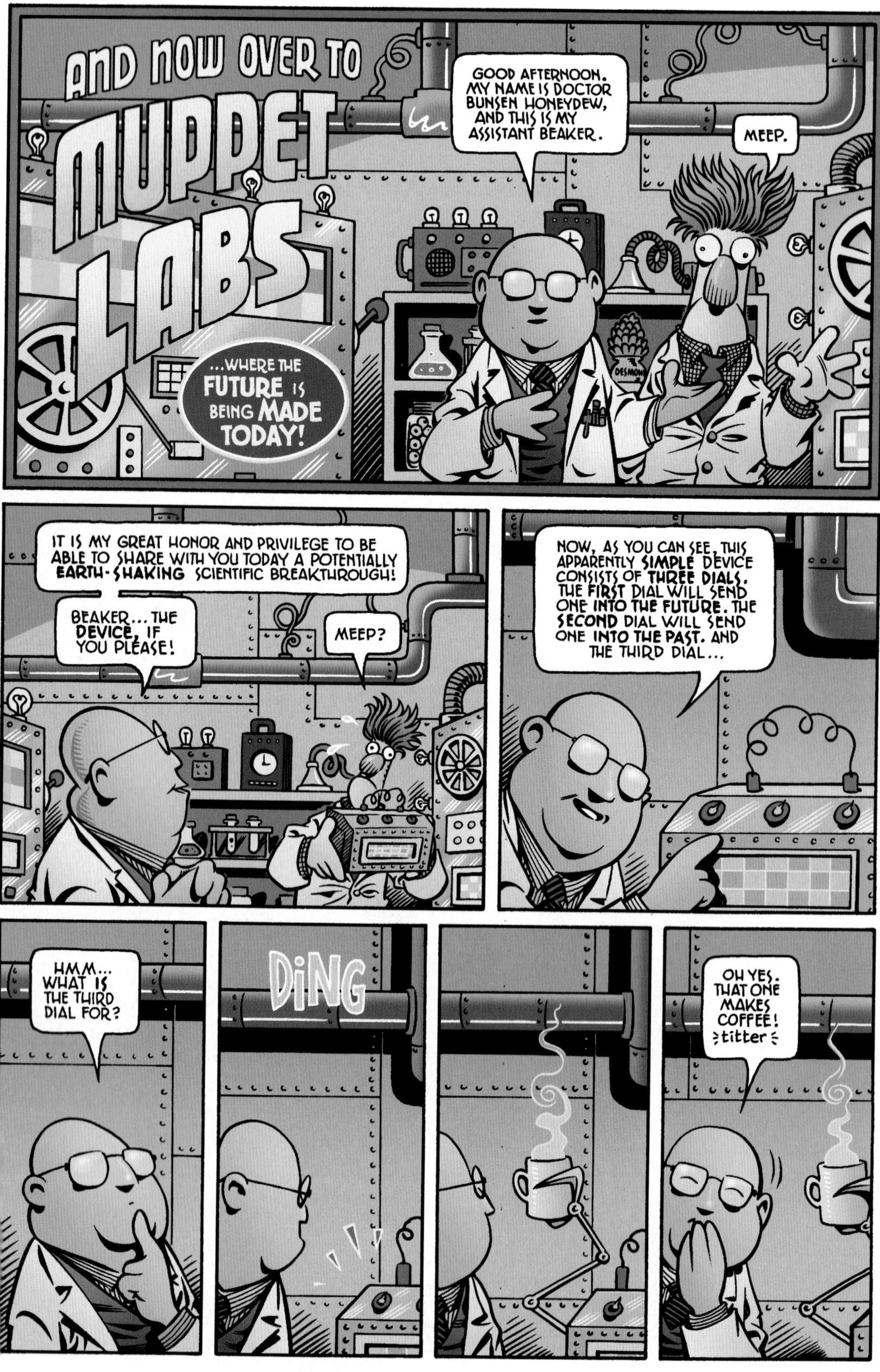
AND NOW OVER TO
MUPPET LABS
...WHERE THE FUTURE IS BEING MADE TODAY!
GOOD AFTERNOON. MY NAME IS DOCTOR BUNSEN HONEYDEW, AND THIS IS MY ASSISTANT BEAKER.
MEEP.
DESMOND
IT IS MY GREAT HONOR AND PRIVILEGE TO BE ABLE TO SHARE WITH YOU TODAY A POTENTIALLY EARTH-SHAKING SCIENTIFIC BREAKTHROUGH!
BEAKER... THE DEVICE, IF YOU PLEASE!
MEEP?
NOW, AS YOU CAN SEE, THIS APPARENTLY SIMPLE DEVICE CONSISTS OF THREE DIALS. THE FIRST DIAL WILL SEND ONE INTO THE FUTURE. THE SECOND DIAL WILL SEND ONE INTO THE PAST. AND THE THIRD DIAL...
HMM... WHAT IS THE THIRD DIAL FOR?
DING
OH YES. THAT ONE MAKES COFFEE! titter

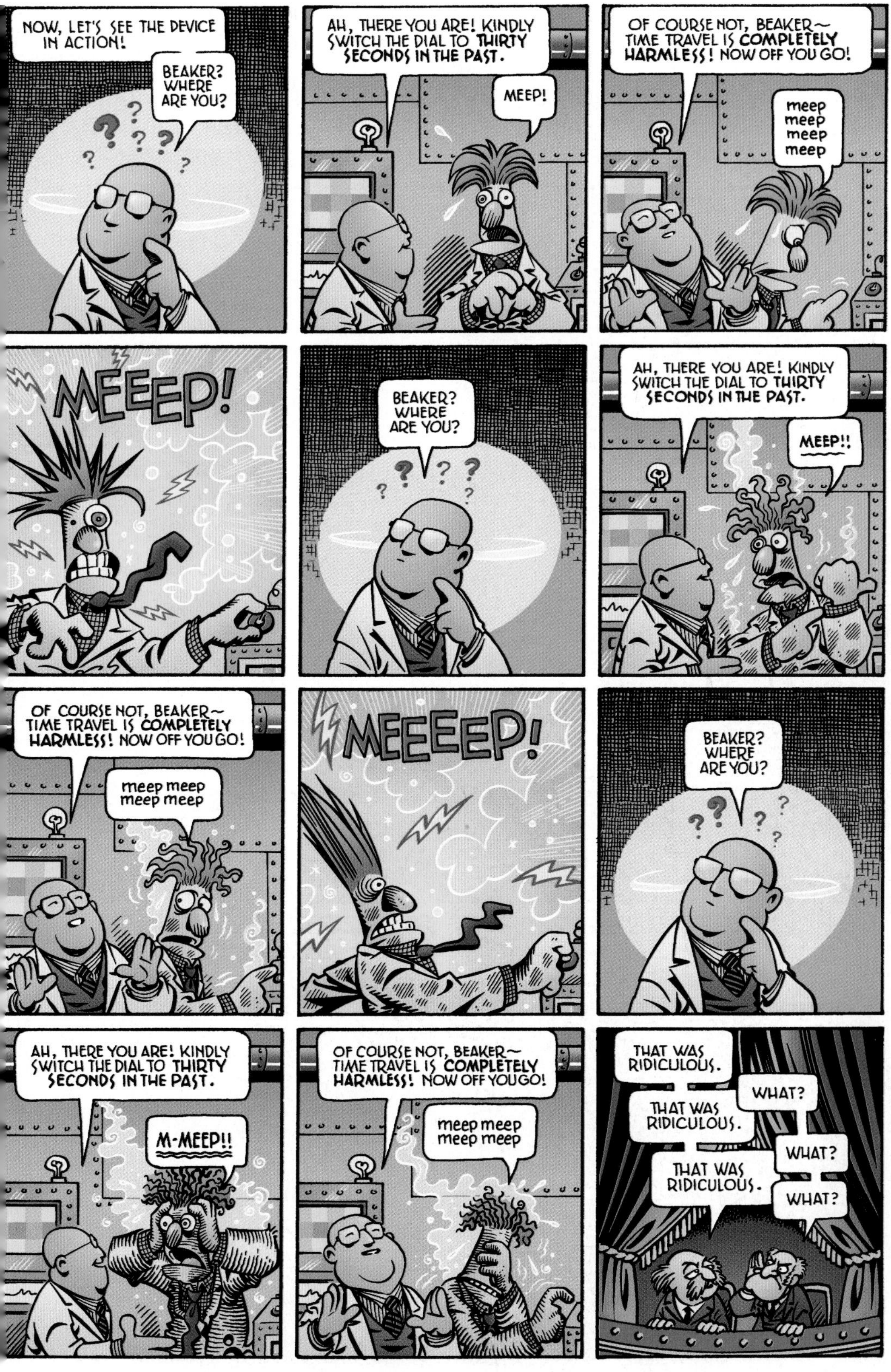
NOW, LET'S SEE THE DEVICE IN ACTION!
BEAKER? WHERE ARE YOU?
AH, THERE YOU ARE! KINDLY SWITCH THE DIAL TO THIRTY SECONDS IN THE PAST.
MEEP!
OF COURSE NOT, BEAKER~ TIME TRAVEL IS COMPLETELY HARMLESS! NOW OFF YOU GO!
meep meep meep meep
MEEEP!
BEAKER? WHERE ARE YOU?
AH, THERE YOU ARE! KINDLY SWITCH THE DIAL TO THIRTY SECONDS IN THE PAST.
MEEP!!
OF COURSE NOT, BEAKER~ TIME TRAVEL IS COMPLETELY HARMLESS! NOW OFF YOU GO!
meep meep meep meep
MEEEEP!
BEAKER? WHERE ARE YOU?
AH, THERE YOU ARE! KINDLY SWITCH THE DIAL TO THIRTY SECONDS IN THE PAST.
M-MEEP!!
OF COURSE NOT, BEAKER~ TIME TRAVEL IS COMPLETELY HARMLESS! NOW OFF YOU GO!
meep meep meep meep
THAT WAS RIDICULOUS.
WHAT?
THAT WAS RIDICULOUS.
WHAT?
THAT WAS RIDICULOUS.
WHAT?

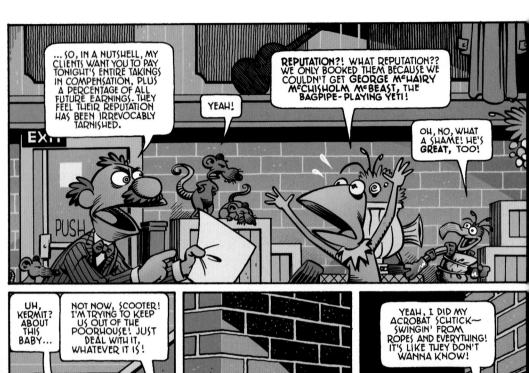

...SO, IN A NUTSHELL, MY CLIENTS WANT YOU TO PAY TONIGHT'S ENTIRE TAKINGS IN COMPENSATION, PLUS A PERCENTAGE OF ALL FUTURE EARNINGS. THEY FEEL THEIR REPUTATION HAS BEEN IRREVOCABLY TARNISHED.

YEAH!

REPUTATION?! WHAT REPUTATION?? WE ONLY BOOKED THEM BECAUSE WE COULDN'T GET GEORGE McHAIRY McCHISHOLM McBEAST, THE BAGPIPE-PLAYING YETI!

OH, NO, WHAT A SHAME! HE'S GREAT, TOO!

EXIT

PUSH

UH, KERMIT? ABOUT THIS BABY...

NOT NOW, SCOOTER! I'M TRYING TO KEEP US OUT OF THE POORHOUSE! JUST DEAL WITH IT, WHATEVER IT IS!

OKAY, YOU'RE THE BOSS, BOSS...

YEAH, I DID MY ACROBAT SCHTICK~ SWINGIN' FROM ROPES AND EVERYTHING! IT'S LIKE THEY DON'T WANNA KNOW!

I SWEAR, IF YOU EVER BOOK ME INTO A DIVE LIKE THIS ONE AGAIN, I'LL FIND MYSELF SOME OTHER AGENT TO~

UH, MISTER MAGEE?

WHAT IS IT, KID?

I'VE BEEN THINKING, AND... WELL, I THINK IT MIGHT BE BETTER COMING FROM YOU.

MUPPET BALLROOM ... YOU'RE UP NEXT!

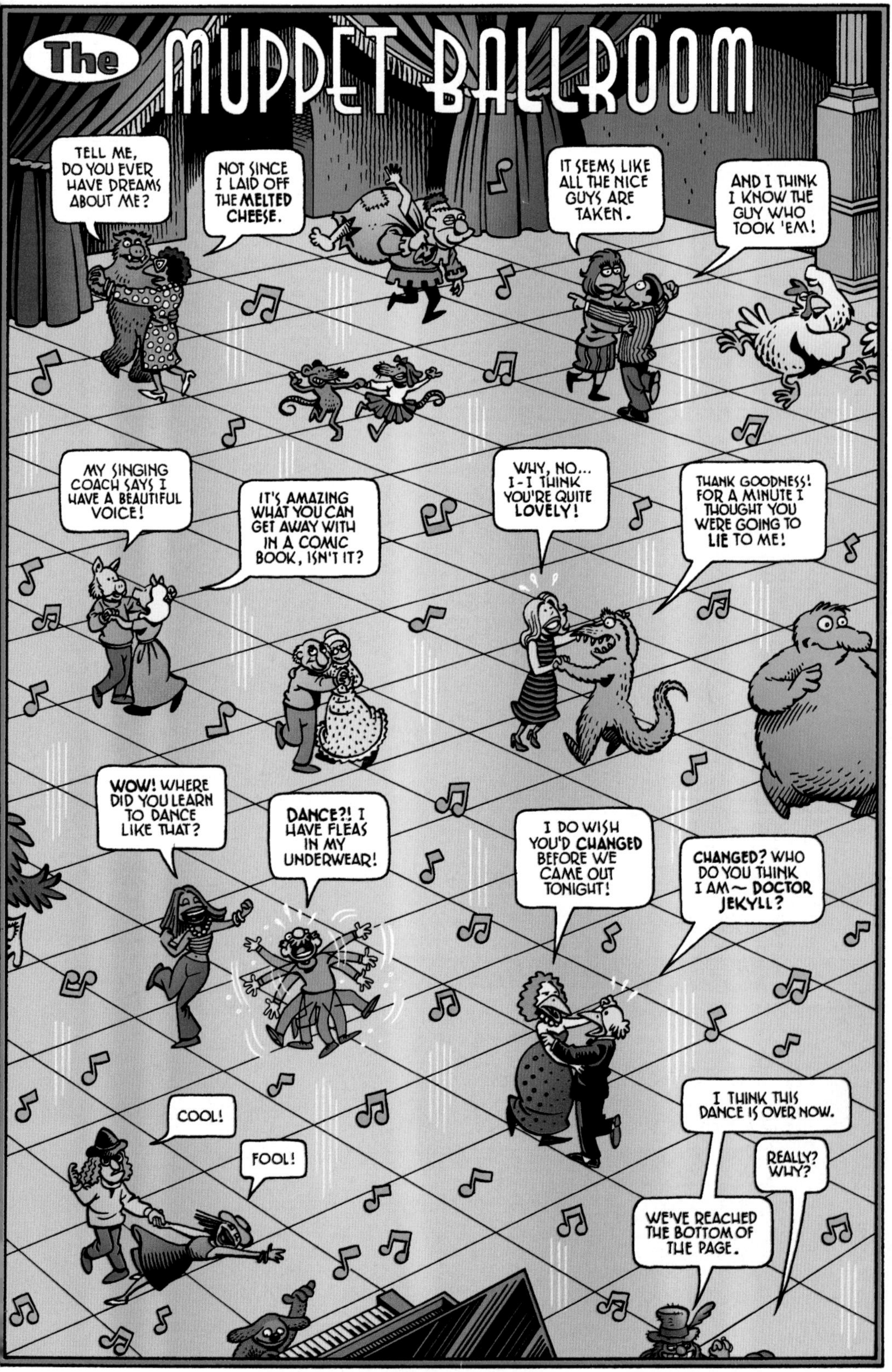
The MUPPET BALLROOM
TELL ME, DO YOU EVER HAVE DREAMS ABOUT ME?
NOT SINCE I LAID OFF THE MELTED CHEESE.
IT SEEMS LIKE ALL THE NICE GUYS ARE TAKEN.
AND I THINK I KNOW THE GUY WHO TOOK 'EM!
MY SINGING COACH SAYS I HAVE A BEAUTIFUL VOICE!
IT'S AMAZING WHAT YOU CAN GET AWAY WITH IN A COMIC BOOK, ISN'T IT?
WHY, NO... I-I THINK YOU'RE QUITE LOVELY!
THANK GOODNESS! FOR A MINUTE I THOUGHT YOU WERE GOING TO LIE TO ME!
WOW! WHERE DID YOU LEARN TO DANCE LIKE THAT?
DANCE?! I HAVE FLEAS IN MY UNDERWEAR!
I DO WISH YOU'D CHANGED BEFORE WE CAME OUT TONIGHT!
CHANGED? WHO DO YOU THINK I AM ~ DOCTOR JEKYLL?
COOL!
FOOL!
I THINK THIS DANCE IS OVER NOW.
REALLY? WHY?
WE'VE REACHED THE BOTTOM OF THE PAGE.

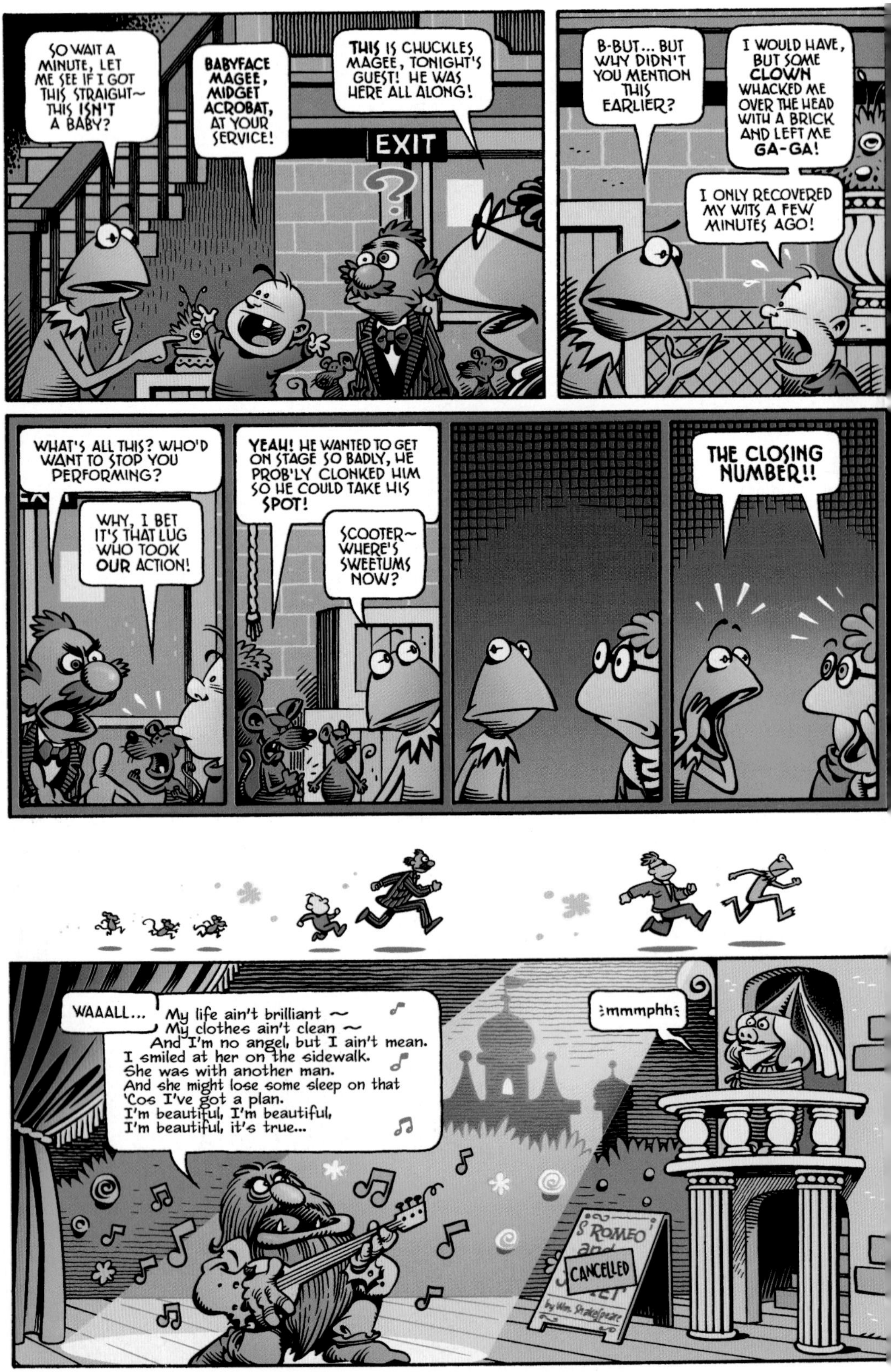

SO WAIT A MINUTE, LET ME SEE IF I GOT THIS STRAIGHT~ THIS ISN'T A BABY?
BABYFACE MAGEE, MIDGET ACROBAT, AT YOUR SERVICE!
THIS IS CHUCKLES MAGEE, TONIGHT'S GUEST! HE WAS HERE ALL ALONG!
EXIT
B-BUT... BUT WHY DIDN'T YOU MENTION THIS EARLIER?
I WOULD HAVE, BUT SOME CLOWN WHACKED ME OVER THE HEAD WITH A BRICK AND LEFT ME GA-GA!
I ONLY RECOVERED MY WITS A FEW MINUTES AGO!
WHAT'S ALL THIS? WHO'D WANT TO STOP YOU PERFORMING?
WHY, I BET IT'S THAT LUG WHO TOOK OUR ACTION!
YEAH! HE WANTED TO GET ON STAGE SO BADLY, HE PROB'LY CLONKED HIM SO HE COULD TAKE HIS SPOT!
SCOOTER~ WHERE'S SWEETUMS NOW?
THE CLOSING NUMBER!!
WAAALL...
My life ain't brilliant ~
My clothes ain't clean ~
And I'm no angel, but I ain't mean.
I smiled at her on the sidewalk.
She was with another man.
And she might lose some sleep on that
'Cos I've got a plan.
I'm beautiful, I'm beautiful,
I'm beautiful, it's true...
mmmphh
ROMEO
CANCELLED
by Wm. Shakespeare

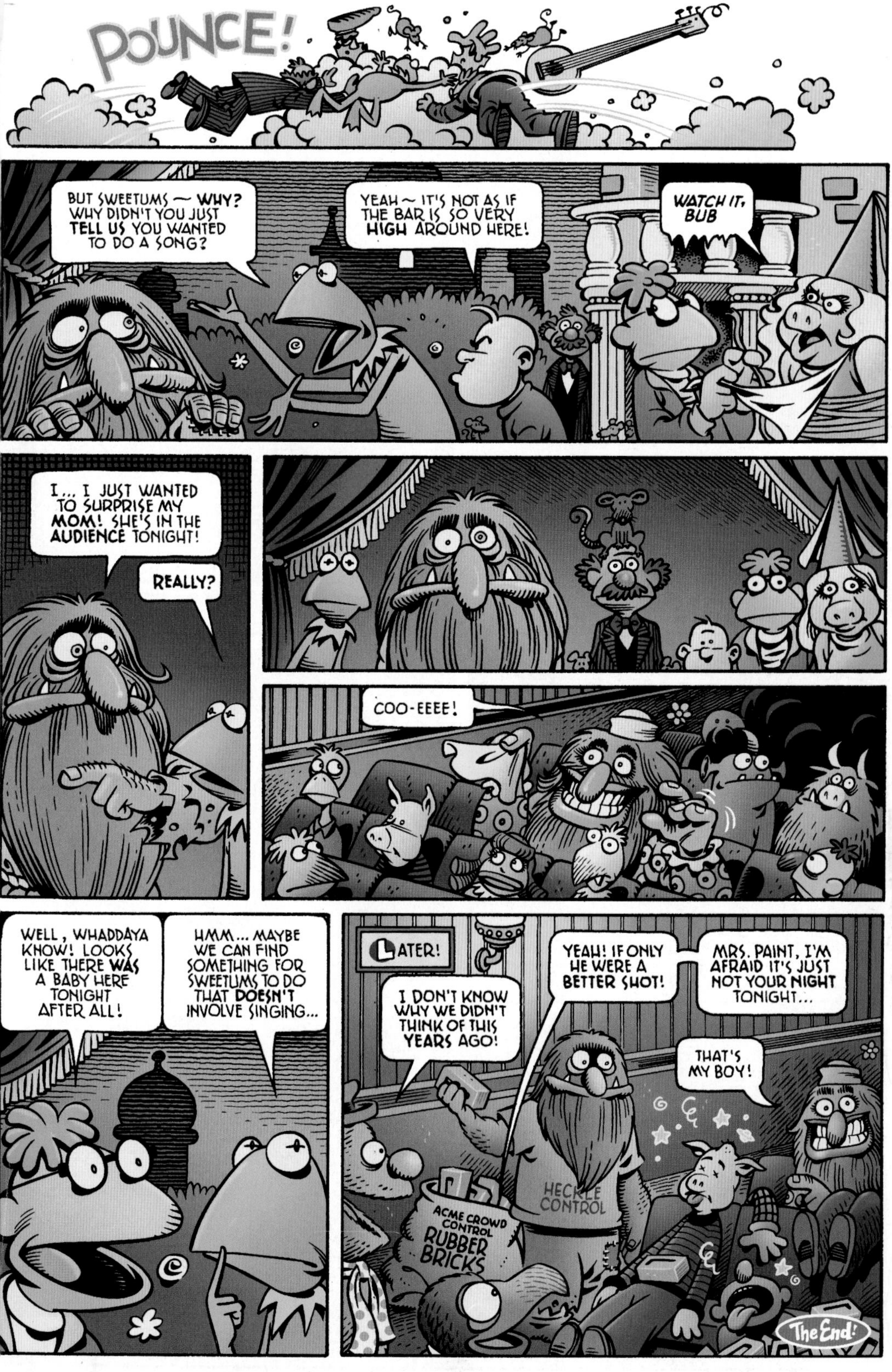
POUNCE!
BUT SWEETUMS — WHY? WHY DIDN'T YOU JUST TELL US YOU WANTED TO DO A SONG?
YEAH — IT'S NOT AS IF THE BAR IS SO VERY HIGH AROUND HERE!
WATCH IT, BUB
I... I JUST WANTED TO SURPRISE MY MOM! SHE'S IN THE AUDIENCE TONIGHT!
REALLY?
COO-EEEE!
WELL, WHADDAYA KNOW! LOOKS LIKE THERE WAS A BABY HERE TONIGHT AFTER ALL!
HMM... MAYBE WE CAN FIND SOMETHING FOR SWEETUMS TO DO THAT DOESN'T INVOLVE SINGING...
LATER!
I DON'T KNOW WHY WE DIDN'T THINK OF THIS YEARS AGO!
YEAH! IF ONLY HE WERE A BETTER SHOT!
MRS. PAINT, I'M AFRAID IT'S JUST NOT YOUR NIGHT TONIGHT...
THAT'S MY BOY!
HECKLE CONTROL
ACME CROWD CONTROL RUBBER BRICKS
The End!

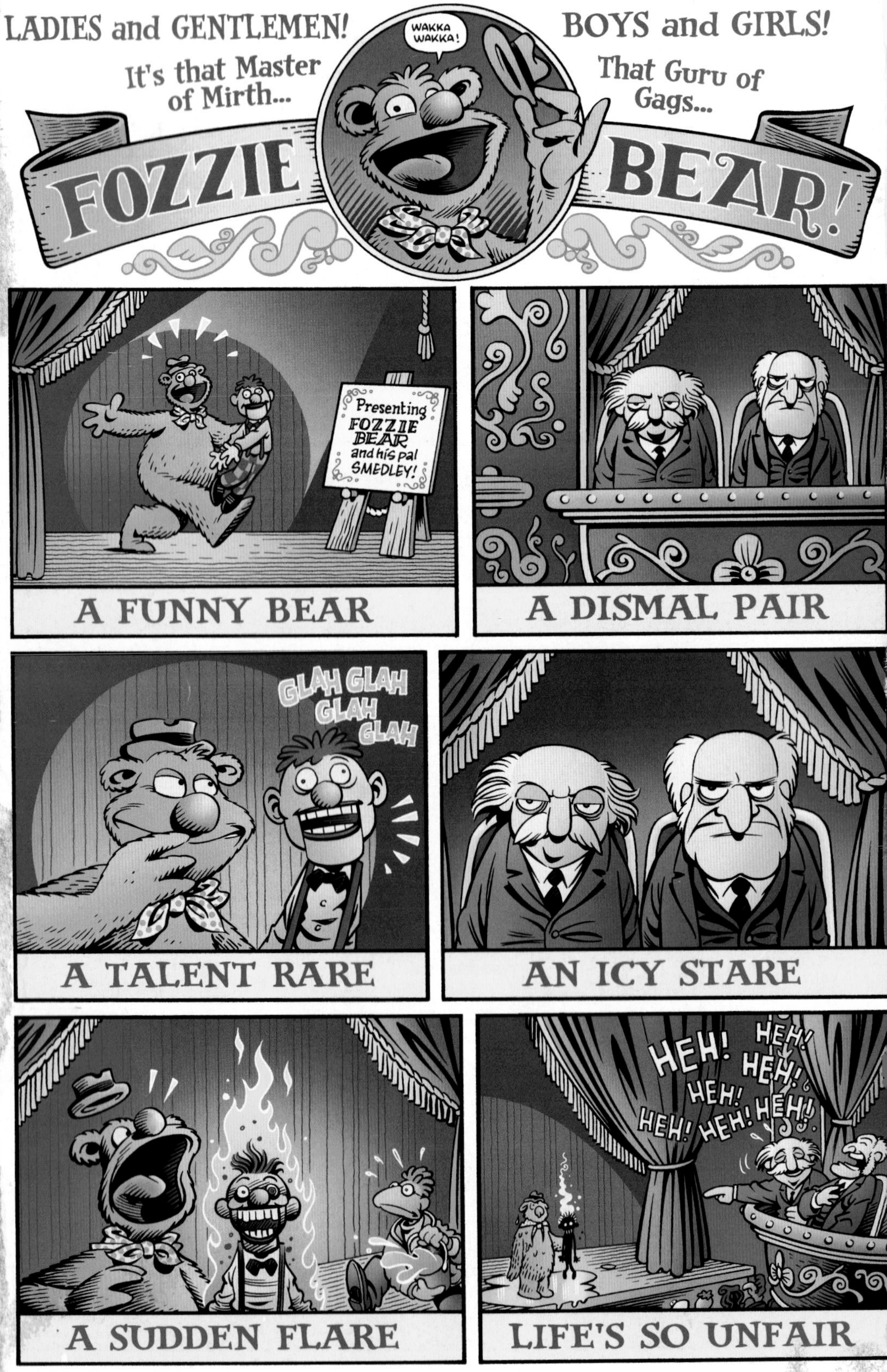
LADIES and GENTLEMEN!
It's that Master of Mirth...
WAKKA WAKKA!
BOYS and GIRLS!
That Guru of Gags...
FOZZIE BEAR!
Presenting FOZZIE BEAR and his pal SMEDLEY!
A FUNNY BEAR
A DISMAL PAIR
GLAH GLAH GLAH GLAH
A TALENT RARE
AN ICY STARE
A SUDDEN FLARE
HEH! HEH! HEH! HEH! HEH! HEH! HEH!
LIFE'S SO UNFAIR

LOOSE BINDING
4/19

SEPT. 2010